The Last Days of Summer

The Last Days of Summer

VANESSA RONAN

PENGUIN

IRELAND

PENGUIN IRELAND

UK | USA | Canada | Ireland | Australia
India | New Zealand | South Africa

Penguin Ireland is part of the Penguin Random House group of companies
whose addresses can be found at global.penguinrandomhouse.com.

First published 2016

001

Copyright © Vanessa Ronan, 2016

The moral right of the author has been asserted

Set in 13.75/16.5 pt Garamond MT Std
Typeset by Jouve (UK), Milton Keynes
Printed in Great Britain by Clays Ltd, St Ives plc

A CIP catalogue record for this book is available from the British Library

ISBN : 978–1–844–88366–0

www.greenpenguin.co.uk

For my family, who taught me the magic of books, and for my husband, eternal love

July

July flies call in the humid evening, song thick as heat, rolling in uneven waves across the lawn to wash up tuneless on the front porch. The tide of summer. When they were children, they would lie beneath those heavens and marvel at how big God must be to paint the sky that way. Heat would drip sweat down their cheeks, necks, the backs of their knees. Grass would cling to their moist bodies, their scabby legs. Sometimes she itched all over lying there like that, but still she lay on the crisp summer grass burned brown by July sunshine; still she marvelled at the great big sky, too awed, too lazy to move. And sometimes he would tell her the constellations – the Big Dipper, Orion's Belt, Cassiopeia – his fingers tracing their outlines in the sky, connecting dot to dot. Once he had run an ice cube down her side while they lay there, evening muggy with traces of day, ice exciting, chilling, scary on her skin. Up her bare leg to where her shorts began. Along her tiny arm up to the shoulder. Neck. Collarbone. She didn't know how to stop it. Stop him. The ice cube felt good in all that heat. Wrong, somehow, but good melting against bare skin. Sometimes when he traced the summer stars he would take her hand and use her finger for the mapping.

He will be here soon. He will be here tomorrow.

Lizzie leans back in Mama's old rocker and wonders

what welcome Mama might have had for him. Tomorrow. Imagines it before, if things had never happened. Imagines it now, after all that has. She feels sweat gather around her, feels it draw her T-shirt to her. Tries to imagine him and her sitting on this porch, side by side, talking. Or lying in the grass, like all those years ago. Can't.

The evening primroses have unfurled, their blossoms worshipping what little sunset remains, yellow and pink and deeper dark purple stretched across the endless sky. It will be hours still till they will shut, twisting back into tight closed lips, waiting for tomorrow's dusk to breathe again, and when they do the moths will come to dance against the porch light, beating their fragile hairy bodies against the bulb with primal dedication while the stars above shine from horizon to horizon over the open prairie.

'I don't got nothin' to say to you.'

No one there to answer.

Fireflies flick on and off across the lawn. The cicadas are still singing. The primroses have begun their retreat, but she waits, watching darkness fall till each last flower has shut tight. The girls will be home soon. She rises, stands a moment at the top of the steps looking out into the blackness that stretches across the prairie before her, the porch light illuminating her silhouette but no one there to witness. Her ponytail lightly brushes her shoulders, sticky with sweat. Had anyone been watching they might have thought Lizzie was waiting for someone. For him perhaps. Or the girls to come home. Or perhaps she was looking out beyond that darkness to another time when things seemed simpler, the stars more than

4

children's wishes trapped. But no one is there. Just memories and the ghosts of memories and whatever new memories tomorrow will bring. In time Lizzie turns and goes inside, screen door slamming.

He's been staring at the wall for hours. All day, maybe. He hasn't taken time to notice it passing. Just stares. And what's confusing him is that he's never noticed it before. Ten years and somehow he's never seen it – a crack. Thin black line there in the whitewash. Bottom corner. Runs like a tiny river waist-high to floor. *How could he never have noticed it?* So he sits, staring. But it does not go away. It does not grow or shrink or move. It's like it's been there all along but just now is showing itself. Disguised. Undisguised. Mocking him. The walls cracking around him. Too perfect, like he's seeing things. And it bothers him. It's not the image he wants to leave with.

When he first came here it was the ceiling he used to stare at. Lie on his cot all day, if he could, just looking up. Naked women pencilled there, a gift left from whatever sad fucker had lain there before. Some were like 1940s pin-ups, classy and curvy, hair wavy, curls, big breasts and butts, sexy in what's not shown. Others were more graphic, long legs opened wide, asses, nipples offered for the sucking. *God, if that weren't whitewash, too, how nice to be there sucking.* Big pouty lips looking down at him. He memorized those constellations lying on the cot, tracing them with an outstretched finger, one eye closed to make believe he actually touched them, breasts, nipples and the dark canyons between the women's legs. In the darkness he'd wish on those stars to come quickly. Sometimes he even thought he could feel them, and the bitches always moaned, always whimpered and begged for more when his finger found them. He still liked the girls. Still fell asleep admiring their beauty, wishing on them again and again, but their thrill had faded with the years. He'd tried to draw his own gal once, but he was no artist, and her uneven proportions marred the perfect ceiling sky. That, he did regret.

But this crack is something different altogether. No artist's rendering, just time. Just a mark of how very long he must have been here, the walls decaying around him as he's felt himself decay within them. He isn't a young man any more.

'Jasper Curtis, rise!'

The warden is calling him, standing at the bars with a guard on either side. Sad fat bastard stuck in here with all these killers and madmen and thieves. 'Which one of us do you think is really the lunatic, Warden,' he'd asked the man once, years ago. 'I may be locked in here, but you chose this prison.' His answer had been solitary confinement for a week. It'd been worth the price.

Reluctantly Jasper tears his eyes from the crack. He wishes he'd been there when it first formed, had been able to see the cheap wall split. He rises and walks to the bars, wrists through them, handcuffs clicking on for the last time. Down the hall a button's pressed and the heavy bars slide open. Creak and clink and slam as they do. He meets the warden's eyes. Not defiant. Not aggressive or remorseful or even curious. Just meets them to meet them. *Goodbye, girls*, he thinks, stepping for the last time from the cell that has been home. The warden looks at him. Cold, dark little eyes, thin and narrowed. He spits a wad of tobacco onto the concrete. In the summer heat the moisture starts to evaporate the moment it lands.

'Should have fried you while we had the chance.'

Jasper smiles slightly. Nods. 'Well, Warden, I suppose I'll miss you, too.'

Katie cuts the engine and sits staring at the house, key still in the ignition and the radio still on. Floyd Tillman crooning some country song, words sad enough to break the heart, but tune upbeat. *All the sunshine and sweet things in life, Are all just a memory* . . . Sun has set and the lawn lies dark, all traces of pink gone from the sky, porch light glowing dimly, flickering from time to time. There's a light on in the kitchen. It glows yellow gold through the lace curtains. Granny curtains. White two-storey wooden granny house. But it's hard to get Mom to change anything about the house. 'It's not how Mama would have liked it,' Mom always says. Like Mom's still caught somehow in those walls in childhood. Like in Mom's mind she still ain't the woman of the house. Katie hates this house. The old style of it. The paint peeling outside, the wallpaper yellowed within. She would rather live somewhere modern, in one of the houses closer to town or the stylish places she's seen on TV. It's never truly felt like home to her. Still feels like Grandma's house most times, and like they are only visitors. Even though it's been years now. Still feels like Grandma's just in the next room somewhere, rocking, rubbing her arthritic knees, watching her afternoon soaps. When Katie was little, back before they'd moved up from town, she used to love visiting

Grandma. Used to love the quiet of the old farmhouse, the vast open yawn of the prairie. It will be hers, though. One day. This house. Or half hers, at least. Like how it stands now, she muses. Half Mom's, half Uncle Jasper's.

I'll never find another sweetheart, I know it can never be . . . Joanne is asleep in the passenger seat. Dark blonde hair falls loose around her face. Perfect July tan. Dirt under unpolished nails. Her eyelids flicker with passing dreams, hands resting in her lap. A speck of glitter from her eye-shadow has fallen on her cheek, catching and reflecting what little light there is, the eye-shadow cheap, poorly applied, unnatural on Joanne's still-child face. It's Katie's eye-shadow, one she never used that she'd given her sister at the start of summer. Shimmery blue glittery stuff that clumps up too easy. A mistake, she thinks now. It makes the kid look cheap. Katie sees more of herself mirrored in her sister than she would like. Not just in the face, the hair, the skinny body not yet filled out: she sees her own insecurities remade, her own stubborn rebellions recycled, and it makes her angry. She's not ready to pass them on just yet. But tonight Joanne is not foremost on Katie's mind. Not even Josh. Or cheering. Or her upcoming shift waiting tables at the diner. The graveyard shift. Tonight all she can think about is him. The strangeness of him. His approaching arrival.

She remembers him vaguely. Tall, dark figure of childhood. Swinging her up into strong arms. Giving her sweets. She confuses memories of him with her father, as though somehow, oddly, the two for her are one before they both gone off. Daddy run off and Uncle Jasper . . . well. She knows the stories about what he did more than

8

she remembers him. Hard not to, working in the diner nights with headlines screaming at her above cooling coffee cups and key lime pies. Hard not to with everyone always whispering. It'll just get worse from here on out, school only a month away, and cheer camp starting in two weeks. She envies Joanne her lack of memories.

The backs of Katie's legs stick to the seat. Uncomfortable yet familiar. Mama will be waiting. She tears her eyes from Joanne back to the kitchen window. So peaceful, this house. This view. This night. Now, at least. *They took the stars out of Heaven the day they took her from me* . . . Katie clicks the radio off, pulling the key out of the ignition. Can't help but think how tomorrow all will be changed. This house. This garden. This familiar feeling. Coming home.

Joanne stirs when the music shuts off, sleepy eyes glassed over as lids struggle open. Katie nudges her, forcing a smile. 'Come on, Lady, beauty sleep some other time. Mama'll be waitin'.'

He was bitten by a cicada once. Lizzie's not sure what made her remember that, but it was the image she woke with: his face unnaturally white as he cried out in pain, the July fly holding on to him tight as though he were a tree branch where it had just settled. Alien exoskeleton shed as it perched there on his arm. She had screamed louder than he had, seeing the creature emerge, its old self left attached to his skin. Mama'd screamed. She can't remember how Mama finally got the bug off or what happened to the skeleton – they were so young then – but that's the face Lizzie keeps seeing now, Jasper's child face all those years back screaming and screaming, distorted with fear.

That boy isn't the man who's coming home today.

Reverend Gordon pulls up in his sleek red Ford pickup. Paint still shiny and new. She can see him from the kitchen window driving up the lane towards the house. She puts the breakfast plates back into the luke-warm soapy water and hangs the dish rag on its hook. She's glad Joanne's gone off doing chores already. Wonders where Katie is.

By the time the reverend's pulled up the driveway, parked the pickup and eased himself out of the driver's seat, she is waiting for him, hands on hips, standing on the front porch, leaning on its supports. Top of the steps. He hesitates a moment as he strolls towards her. 'Morning, Elizabeth.'

'Reverend.'

'Mighty fine day, isn't it? Why, I don't think I seen a cloud in the sky.'

She looks up at the stretch of blue above them. Says nothing.

'Shame 'bout the heat, though, isn't it?' He forces a smile. 'I heard it on the news last night we ain't seen rain for nearin' thirty days. My, your roses are beautiful this summer! Lord himself musta blessed your garden to keep them flowers bloomin' so nicely.' He wipes sweat from his brow. A mockingbird calls out from a shrub somewhere nearby. Not even nine and the heat bakes.

'Yes, Reverend,' Lizzie says slowly, picking her words with care. 'I reckon I'm just 'bout as blessed as can be.'

His smile drops. A pause, the type when most men

would shuffle the dirt with their boots or might spit tobacco. A throat-clearing pause, but he just stands there, silent, staring at her.

'I suppose you want to come in.'

'I'd be mighty obliged.'

Silence for a moment while she gets the coffee and the mugs and sets them out on the table. 'Milk?'

'Don't mind if I do.' He pours till the cup almost spills over.

'Sugar?'

'Just a spoonful, hon.' That smile again. Forced. Four heaping teaspoons. He stirs. Lizzie watches. She drinks her coffee. Black.

He places the spoon carefully on the table. Takes the time to take a sip. Places the mug back down. Little splashes of milky coffee pool around the spoon. 'Now, Elizabeth, hon, we ain't seen so much of you on Sunday since your mother passed.' He watches her. She struggles to keep her face neutral. 'And, see, we're all worried 'bout y'all, you and the girls that is. I know things mustn't be easy out here on your own, two young girls and all.' He forces a laugh, smiles. 'I was thinking maybe you should come round more often. Bring the girls down. We'd all like to see y'all more down there. You know, your mother was a *fine* woman, Elizabeth. A fine, God-fearin' woman.'

'You've come 'bout him, ain't you?'

'I heard you're fixin' to take him in.'

'That's right.'

'We're worried 'bout y'all, Elizabeth. We're worried 'bout the girls. Quite frankly, I ain't sure that it's a good idea them bein' round a man like that.'

'He ain't just some man, Reverend. This is Jasper we're talkin' 'bout.'

'Is it, Elizabeth? When was the last time you seen him? You been down to Huntsville holding his hand? Christ almighty, his own mother didn't dare go down there!'

Cold eyes meet his. Lizzie is not smiling. 'When was the last time *you* went down to Huntsville, Reverend? When did *you* ever go there to see if Jasper was all right? I may not be no perfect sister after all he's done, I may have been no perfect sister before, but don't you go preachin' to me when you done gone 'n' turned your back, too.'

His mouth opens to object.

'No, you hear me out, Reverend – this house here is as much his as mine. By law it's half his. We both done grown up in these rooms, and damned if I'm gonna turn him from the only home he ever known.'

'Elizabeth . . .'

Quiet enough to hear the clock tick. That mocking-bird still calling from out in the prairie somewhere. Clock just there tick-tocking.

'When does he arrive?'

'Round noon.'

'You pickin' him up from the bus stop?'

'Reckon someone's got to.'

He nods. Sips his coffee. 'You sure you know who you're lettin' into your home?'

She thinks about Jasper's child face all them years back, distorted in that cicada scream. She thinks of mapping constellations and ice cubes in summer darkness. Remembers that cicada shell. 'Reckon I don't know at all.'

He nods again. 'Any chance to change your mind?'

12

'I'll walk you to the door.'

She watches from the top of the porch steps as he crosses the lawn back towards his pickup. So red in all the burned-brown grass, so red against the gravel and the pavement. He's put on weight since last she seen him, his jeans and belt cutting the gut into a forced hour-glass. His hair, maybe, is greyer, too. She hadn't noticed before just how brown the prairie had grown. They could really use rain soon. *Maybe the flowers are blessed.*

'Reverend.'

He turns, hand just reaching for the pickup's door handle.

Pleading in her voice, her eyes: 'Where else he gonna go?'

As the Greyhound pulls off of I-10 up the exit ramp, Jasper feels his first moment of panic. It's hard to breathe. Then it passes, and he's left with the flutters in his gut, heavier than butterflies, more like caterpillars crawling back into their cocoons. He thinks about the feel of prairie grass burned by the sun. Imagines his hands against it, running through it, like combing out a woman's dry, tangled hair. The sting of the grass against him. This calms him a little.

When they first let him out and he walked from Huntsville's high electric gates onto the waiting bus, his pulse was even, steady. He didn't turn to look back at the penitentiary one last time. Just stared out of the window, waiting for whatever was left of life to take him away. He didn't feel panicky on I-45 either, looking out at all that forest and rolling hills. It was around Houston when the trees turned to prairie, far as the eye could see, tumbleweed drifting, that traffic on I-10 seemed to blur round him. He didn't remember buses going so fast.

He is wearing the same clothes as the day they locked him up. Jeans. Grey T-shirt with the Coca-Cola slogan on it. Nikes. He never wore boots much. There was a ten-dollar bill in his pocket. A packet of chewing-gum that he tossed away, spearmint. This is all he has with him now – the clothes on his back. He's surprised at how well they still fit him. 'Got to keep your wits 'n' fists about you in prison.' That's what he told himself those first days that turned to months that turned to years. And the letter. He has the letter too, folded and refolded in his jeans pocket. The only letter she wrote in all those years.

Heard you're getting out. Reckon you should come on home. There's a bed for you if you need it.

Not even her name at the end, but he knows her hand. Reckons the letter is more than she could have done. Might be more than he deserves.

The Greyhound slows as it pulls into the station, brakes squeaking. He is the only one to exit, though the bus is far from full, few folks in Houston having boarded, and even fewer still now heading further west. Stepping past the driver, Jasper nods to the other man. 'Thank you,' he says, and even to himself his voice sounds out of practice. He steps down onto the pavement and watches the bus pull away, easing itself back into the rushing flow. He watches it go till it becomes a tiny silver speck.

He had fretted for a time over the welcome party that might be waiting for him. Had wondered how many hostile faces might come to see him home, but fear had never dictated Jasper's life and he does not intend to let it now. Many restless nights in the penitentiary he had pondered if his first free steps back home might be his last, but Jasper has promised himself he will step off the bus fighting, if that's what freedom requires, and he feels no different now. He scans the near-empty service station. The only welcome he had not imagined was the one with no one there to greet him at all.

He'd written her back the date, time, place. Never doubted that Lizzie would come. A tiny part of him now almost wishes she won't. Maybe it's enough just to stand here feeling the warm sun on his face, humid air thick around him. At the same time, if he's honest with himself, Jasper knows he's well past ready to go home.

It's an old gas station, not one of the fancy well-lit new ones, like closer to Huntsville, Houston or Dallas. Out here folks don't care so much about what's shiny and new. Or else the world just don't care so much about making out here seem shiny and new 'cause who really comes all the way out here anyway? This station's been here long as Jasper can remember. Looks just like he remembers too – old-style rusted pumps, diesel and unleaded the only options. Just two pumps. Texaco sign hangs off its post a bit crooked. No cover over the pumps. No credit cards accepted. Rust everywhere rust can rust. Just a tiny shop down the back with windows that look like they always need washing even right after they've been washed, a couple old pickups parked in front of it.

The bell rings as the door opens. Two loud chimes and then a softer one as the bell settles again, gently rocking on the handle. A red string ties it there. That sound, so familiar, and Jasper pauses in the doorway, savouring the comfort of it, as his eyes adjust to the dark interior of the shop. Momentarily blind from all that sunshine. Blinks to clear the eyes. Lets the door slam softly with another jingle behind him. They've got air-conditioning. That's new.

The boy behind the counter looks up when Jasper enters. Boy. That's all he is, really. Some high-school kid. Blond and tanned and clean. Skin still soft, like a baby's. Bit of baby fat still clinging to chubby, almost feminine cheeks, baby-boy face swallowed by his ten-gallon hat. The effect borders on comical – a child playing dress-up, not a hero of the west. *That boy wouldn't last five hours in Huntsville.* Jasper doesn't recognize him, but he nods to him anyhow, wondering who the boy's folks might be, thinking back on the blurry children's faces of Sunday mornings ten years back, but no face comes into focus and Jasper reckons he must never have troubled himself back then with noting what wasn't of concern to him.

Jasper passes the shelves of candies, potato chips, beef jerky hung up in long red plastic packets, passes the household essentials – toilet paper, paper towels, soap, shampoo. The car essentials – oil, air pump, windshield-wiper fluid, air fresheners shaped like leaves with names like 'Maple', 'Forest', 'Garden', 'Pine'. He picks up 'Garden'. Thinks of the roses by Mama's front porch. The primroses unfurling come dusk. Bluebonnets in early spring, and Indian paintbrushes blood-red. Breathes deep. His memories don't smell a thing like 'Garden'.

He puts it back and walks on. Pauses a moment by the

magazine rack. Can feel the boy's eyes on him, drilling into his back. *People. US Weekly.* Last month's *Cosmopolitan.* Last month's *Playboy*, the slut's boobs concealed by the magazine's plastic wrapper. All you see is hungry eyes begging for cock, lips moist and parted. Whore. A redhead. Different. He likes that. Just those eyes peeking at him is almost enough. Almost. Another nudie mag, all bound up in plastic, too. *Time* magazine, but who wants to pick that up? One copy of the *Reader's Digest* that looks like it's been sitting there a while, pages all crinkly and browned as though soda got spilled on them and then the magazine dried out. The *National Enquirer* claims to have found the world's fattest baby, and something about the model's smile on the cover of *Southern Living* reminds him of his mama back when he was small. He doesn't look at the newspaper headlines. Doesn't want to see what might be there.

Eyes back to that hungry redhead, and he thirsts for her, and she thirsts for him, and he thinks about buying the magazine just to pass the time, to see what constellations might lie within, but he can feel the boy's eyes still on him, judging him, so he doesn't even pick it up. Grabs a Coke from the fridge instead.

'Fifty-nine cents.'

Jasper hands over the ten-dollar bill. He doesn't like being in the shop. It's stuffy. Too small. Dark. Reminds him of rooms just left never again to be entered. And yet it's familiar. It's nice to feel that familiarity. He looks out at the sunshine still baking the pavement, cooking the rust, then back to the boy and tries out a smile. 'You know,' he says, 'I used to work here when I was 'bout your age.'

'That so?'

'Yep.' He glances out of the window again. So *much* sunshine. Eyes back to the boy. He hesitates. *Cold cans of beer snuck out the back. Long days spent over magazines and staring down I-10 imagining the distant life he'd lead.* 'Mo still running the place?'

'I reckon.' Something hostile in the boy's eyes. He places the change on the counter.

Jasper hesitates another moment before scooping it up. 'Don't suppose Mo's here?'

'Don't suppose he is.'

Jasper nods. Hands deep in his front pockets, he glances out at all that sunshine and back into the darkness of the shop. 'Any work going at the minute?'

The boy leans against the cigarette counter behind him. Arms crossed over his still skinny chest. Hasn't filled out in the shoulders yet, and his red Texaco T-shirt hangs off his frame. Desperately needs to lose that baby fat before he'll be anything remotely like a man. The boy looks Jasper up and down with cold eyes. Blue as ice under all that blond hair, under that ridiculous ten-gallon hat. Jasper seldom wore hats. The boy's eyes flick from the newspaper rack to below the register and back again. Unless it's moved in the last twenty years, Jasper knows Mo's old Remington bolt action's kept there. Shot plenty of beer cans and a few squirrels with it back in the day. The boy's eyes meet Jasper's. 'I reckon there ain't much of any work round these parts.'

He's sitting on the kerb when she pulls up. Right out in the sunlight where the heat is roasting. Empty Coke bottle beside him. A slight flush in his cheeks. Lizzie didn't intend to be late. Or maybe the bus was early. No traffic and all that. But she couldn't have tolerated the thought of being early and waiting for him either. For a moment, pulling up, Lizzie wants to turn around. Back the pickup right out of the station. He might not have seen her yet. Drive till she's right back home in her own driveway, no Jasper to think about or worry about or be a sister to. For a moment she imagines growing up without him. Running alone through drying clothesline sheets. Lying alone under the stars, taking her own finger to map them out. Sitting alone with Mama and Daddy at the supper table. He used to make faces at her when they weren't looking and she had to swallow her giggles to keep them from being found out. Once she couldn't and Daddy's belt had come out fast, and that welt on her legs took weeks to heal. But that's how it always was, her laughing and getting in trouble for it, and Jasper's eyes clouding over as Daddy hit her. Sometimes it was worth it. The laughter. Those funny faces breaking the solemn silence of the dinner table.

She pulls the pickup close. Cuts the engine. Bits of grey in his mousy hair. Lines on his face she doesn't remember. But it's Jasper. Or some aged form of Jasper, a shadow of himself that is no shadow, stranger, darker, her brother and not her brother, and Jasper all the same. *You sure you know who you're lettin' into your home?* The reverend's voice on repeat all morning.

She doesn't get out of the truck. He walks over slow. Taking his time with each step. Not like he's scared. Not like he doesn't want to reach her. Just carefully, as though each step changes his life, and it does in a way, she reckons. And, anyway, Jasper was never one to rush. He stops beside the pickup, gazes at her through the rolled-down window.

She leans across to open his door even though he could have reached right in the window himself. The hum of insects from the tall grasses beside the ditch vibrates the summer heat. And I-10 has its own wave sounds as cars speed below. He looks at her a long time through that rolled-down window, both of them saying nothing, sun reddening his neck and ears, heat moistening their skin. At length he nods, the most thanks she's likely to get from him, she reckons, and he reaches for the handle.

The floorboards creak under his footsteps. Rocking the same way the wood of the house rocks in bad storms, except now it's just the floorboards, each step rocking each board – a childhood sound. He closes his eyes. Stands still a moment, listening to the house sounds that create home. Pots and pans and a faucet down in the kitchen. A door that opens to close again, a young girl's voice calling, 'I'm home.' Curtains rustle as July heat blows warm breezes through the muggy rooms. Humid even inside. He used to tiptoe across these same boards, tiny socked feet sliding if he wasn't careful. And then, when he was a bit older, he used to slide on purpose, gliding over the creaks, skidding down the hall till Mama'd catch him and make him still. End of the hall. He's not a man to tiptoe, and it's been a long time now since he chose to slide. He pushes open the door to his boyhood room.

No trace of him inside.

No football trophies. Baseball trophies. No school photographs. No old concert tickets. A whole childhood so long preserved now erased. Just a lone twin bed, chair, desk with a lamp. Not one poster or picture on the walls. Just a clock that never was his and it's ticking rather loudly. The hall was empty of him, too, the whole length of the stairs. He noticed that coming in. Baby photos of Lizzie in her stroller, smiling. On a blanket, smiling. Cake all over her face, smiling, pictures of Mama and Daddy growing up, and married, and getting old, pictures of Lizzie and her girls, but not one of him. And, oddly, not a one of Bobby, neither. He wonders if it was her that done it or Mama before she passed. Wonders what Bobby must've done to earn that same treatment. He crosses the room and sits on the bed and thinks about his cell in Huntsville. Then he starts to think back further to before, to dark curls and tan lines and big dark eyes. Stops himself. He doesn't allow himself to think about that. His face hardens, then twists. *How dare those bitches erase me?* He rises and smashes his fist into the wall. The impact shakes it but he doesn't notice. A low moan escapes him, something more beast than man, and he holds his now throbbing fist to his chest, rocking back and forth, back and forth, feeling his bones like creaking floorboards. *This isn't what home should feel like. This isn't what home should feel like . . .*

A sound makes him turn. A girl in the doorway. Barefoot and brown. Still more child than woman, though the woman's creeping in. Eyes like a doe's widening. But the girl doesn't run. Doesn't turn like a doe would. Just stares, frozen in the doorway. *God, she looks like Lizzie.*

He pushes that rage back down. Suffocates it in his gut, like he long ago learned was sometimes best in prison. Tries to smile at the child. Face twisting human again, twisting, he hopes, kind.

She looks at him as though sizing him up. Head to toe, not quite trusting. Not quite not. He finds the directness of her gaze unsettling.

'You're my uncle Jasper.'

More statement than question but he answers anyway, aware of his pulse throbbing. 'That's right.'

She seems to hesitate. He doesn't know what to say. When was the last time he saw a little girl? Shared a cell with Melvin Douglas for a while. Melvin was *real* fond of little girls.

'I'm Joanne.'

He nods.

'Mom says supper's ready.'

He nods again. The girl still lingers in the door frame. Doesn't seem right to leave her standing there so he invites her in. But what does he have to say to a little girl? Melvin told him he used to give them candy. Little sweets shaped like hearts that said things like 'Cutie Pie' and 'Sweetheart' on them. Tiny pastel shades of spring, colours, Melvin said, little girls like. And Melvin used to touch their hair. Comb it with his fingers. And he said after, always after, he'd lay them on the front porch like they were sleeping, bag of 'Be Mine' candy hearts clutched to their chest like a bouquet of flowers, so that when their mommy and daddy realized they were missing they'd find them laid out all pretty, returned home intact. Or, well, almost intact. Jasper doesn't have any candy, and there's nothing pastel or cute in this whitewashed room. And, anyway, this little girl's creeping into woman.

'This was mine.' She inches forward, stepping through the door frame. He can feel the closeness of her. She smells like cut grass.

'Well, it was mine once, too.'

'She made me move my stuff out.'

'Seems she moved mine, too.' Silence between them. 'Where you sleepin' now?'

'Mom says they shouldn't have let you out.' One bare toe is scratching the other bare ankle. Her legs burned brown as prairie grass. No, browner. The colour his legs once were, back when he used to tiptoe. Tiny hairs bleached blonde-white catch what little lamplight there is. She looks at him with big blue eyes, and he notices traces of Bobby in her, too. Lizzie mostly, but Bobby round the eyes.

'She might be right.'

'When you leave, can I have my room back?'

He laughs then. Can't help but laugh. Throws his head back to let the sound out better. When was the last time he laughed? And Doe Eyes is still standing there, watching. Like it's her business. More of Bobby in her than he first guessed. 'Where's your daddy at?' His voice rougher than intended, but the child doesn't start, just keeps on staring with her big eyes, now widened even more with slight surprise.

'Didn't Mom tell you?'

He looks around the stark room. The bare desk. The pictureless walls. He thinks about funny faces that used to make Lizzie laugh, about her stubborn silence in the truck earlier that afternoon, which chilled him despite the baking sun and thick humidity. Whole drive home and not one word between them till they were up the porch steps, Jasper's hand reaching out to open the screen door. She caught it then, by the wrist, and Lizzie's grip was stronger than he would have guessed. 'You listen here,' she had said, her voice weathered in ways he did not remember, face lined by hardships he did not truly wish to learn of. 'You listen good. This here is my house now. And my family. My girls. And you so much as set one toe out of line, Jasper Curtis, 'n' I'll make them years in Huntsville look close enough to Heaven.'

Pots and pans down in the kitchen. 'Joanne! Jasper!' Lizzie's voice, strained. He meets the girl's quizzical gaze, the echo of their names still fading. Looks into those blue doe eyes. 'I suspect there's a lot your mama don't tell me.'

Downstairs, right now, Lizzie regrets having sent her up to get him. 'Fetch your uncle down to supper,' she'd said. Matter-of-fact, like it was the most natural thing in the world. *Fetch your uncle down to supper.* Moment the words left her lips, Lizzie felt uneasy. Wanted to suck them back in but it was too late. What the hell was she doing, acting like they were just a normal family fixing to have a normal supper?

Hearing her mother's command, Joanne's eyes had widened. 'He's *here*?'

'Told you he was comin', didn't I?'

'Yeah, but . . .'

Never you mind, hon, I'll fetch him myself. The words rose

24

within her but remained unspoken. Lizzie had made up her mind when she wrote Jasper that letter months back. She wouldn't have them all living under the same roof in fear. No matter what. *What kind of life would that be?* Too late to take words back now. She'd cut her daughter short instead. 'You set that table for four, you hear? Then fetch your uncle.'

But now Joanne is gone, and every bone in Lizzie's body wants to call the child back. Almost does but holds it in. Bites her tongue. The taste of blood fills her mouth, and when she swallows, it's blood not saliva that goes down. Outside, streaks of pink and gold mar the day's clear blue. Evening breezes struggle to cool. *It's just Jasper*, she tells herself. *Jasper come on home.* But still the painful heart-lock, gut-lock, like Joanne's first day of school, or Katie's first night off at a slumber party. And worse somehow. Still the lingering taste of blood oozing from Lizzie's tongue.

The cutlery's stopped clinking in the dining room, and Lizzie's ears strain for footsteps on the stairs. A loud thud from above. Footsteps creaking, pausing, resuming, then stopping, and the stop is even worse. Voices loud enough to hear the murmur but too soft to make out words.

'She'll be fine,' she tells the mash, ears straining as she stirs in the milk, butter, sour cream. The potatoes are fluffy, smooth as icing, but for once Lizzie isn't even aware of her wrist tiring from the mashing. She releases a breath she did not realize was held. Reaches for the salt. Doesn't notice the top's not on right. Swears under her breath as a small white mountain pours down. 'The mash's near ruined,' she hisses, and the sound of her own voice in the quiet kitchen surprises her.

Then Jasper's laugh erupts. At least, it *must* be him, but it's no sound Lizzie remembers. Jasper always had a deep laugh. Throaty. Even when he was a boy. The kind of laugh that catches you off guard and tickles you and warms you up and makes you chuckle, too. Infectious. But that is not this sound.

That is not this sound.

It hits her chest hard, like the breath is knocked out of her, and she stands, dazed. The brisket needs to come out of the oven. There's still bread to butter. But Lizzie stands paralysed, listening to her brother's laugh that is not her brother's, spoon held before her like some useless shield against whatever unknowns may come to pass. The reverend's words haunt her. Half a day with Jasper and her inner response is still the same: *I reckon I don't know at all.* Except he's here now. His strange laughter tearing through the thin walls. An inhuman sound that peels the yellowed wallpaper right off till there's only bare wood left, every room a skeleton, the whole house a skeleton, and inside it Lizzie feels stripped raw too, like there is no hiding or place to hide even if she wanted to.

'Joanne!' she manages to gasp then shout. 'Jasper! Supper!' but now her voice, too, rasps: unnatural. Harsh yet quivering. And had she been in another room listening in, Lizzie would not have claimed that sound as hers. She sets the sweet tea on the table. Hurriedly slaps butter on the bread. Doesn't breathe natural till two sets of footsteps are coming down the stairs.

It's been years since a man sat at the head of the table. Used to be Daddy's spot when they were children. He would sit still and powerful and silent, glaring down if ever they were heard instead of merely seen. Not that Mama got freedom of speech exactly either, but she could talk about church and gardening and the weather, little bits of town gossip. She could talk about some things, woman things, but not about others. And before Bobby run off, he sat there awhile. Sunday dinners. Christmas. Easter. Thanksgiving. For the important meals, that was his spot. But after he left, Lizzie took over that chair. It felt strange at first. But Katie and Joanne had set the table up that day, and they'd put a plate at the head, small as the girls were back then, not knowing maybe it weren't right with there being no man in the house. Not knowing yet that their daddy was gone for good. So when she saw that plate there, Lizzie had sat down. For the girls. That's why she'd done it.

She had imagined being her father. There, sitting for the first time in his chair, she had seen a fleeting glimpse of the world through his eyes. It was not a kind or pretty one. Mama was staring at her from across the table. Like she'd never set eyes on Lizzie before. The girls were too little to notice, squirming and restless and hungry in their chairs. Mama had looked long and hard at Lizzie and there had been something like pride in her eyes. And something else a bit like shame.

So when Lizzie comes into the dining room it stops her short to see Jasper sitting there at the head of the table. That seat has never been his.

'Something smells good.' Jasper leans back in the chair so that the two front legs hang off the ground. Arms crossed behind his head. Mama would have slapped the back of his skull if he'd ever sat there like that. He's still wearing the grey Coca-Cola T-shirt, and from him the slight smell of sweat sweetens the already sticky room. He's smiling. That cold, mischievous smile that is her brother and isn't her brother, and for a moment Lizzie wonders who this man is, sitting in her chair, smelling of sweat, about to eat her supper. But the twinkle in the corner of his brown eyes, that *is* Jasper. That's the spark that pulled the faces that made her laugh at all those childhood suppers. It's the spark that now relaxes her enough to step forward and set the brisket down.

'Glad to see you're comfortable.'

'That there grub looks mighty fine.'

She takes the seat at the foot of the table. Feels wrong somehow to be sitting in Mama's old seat. She turns to Joanne. 'Where's your sister?'

Joanne shrugs.

Jasper goes on as if there's been no pause: 'Reckon they fed us all right in there but this here smells a whole lot finer.'

Lizzie glances at the grandfather clock. Quarter past seven. Told Katie be home by half. *So she isn't late yet. It's the brisket that's early* . . . Lizzie sighs. 'We might as well start.' She rises to carve the meat.

Jasper rises too. 'Let me. As I recall it's the man that usually does the carving.'

Above the table their eyes meet. Like how many countless times before. Stealing glances round the room while Mama said grace. Sneaking bits of food. Making those funny faces. The twinkle is still in Jasper's eyes. He's smiling at her.

There's nothing sinister in that smile. Nothing bad.

He's older, tireder, greyer, but it's Jasper. For the first time all day it's really Jasper. Her brother, home. Lizzie hands him the carving knife handle first. He takes it. 'Yep,' he murmurs, as the first cut slices, blood and juices dripping from the pink meat onto the serving plate, 'this here sure is a lot nicer than what we was bein' fed.'

He dishes out four platefuls. Sits back down. The mash is passed round. And the corn. The bread. Half past now. *Where is that girl?* Lizzie takes a big bite of mash. Jasper's eyes across the table stop her. 'Don't we say grace no more?'

Joanne looks up from her plate. Head turns from her uncle to her mother and her gaze sticks. Lizzie can feel the girl's eyes on her, but she holds Jasper's cool gaze. Brakes squeak in the driveway and a car door slams. Crickets and July flies have started to come out to greet the evening, and their songs mix with the falling night, blown in through the open window and its screen. The front door opens and slams, and Katie's clear young voice calls, 'Sorry! I'm home!' Footsteps fast approaching in the hall.

Lizzie meets Jasper's eyes, feeling her own go cold. 'Whatever prayers you got to say, I reckon you can say in private.'

Jasper comes out on the front porch and sits in the other rocker beside his sister. They are silent for a while as sunset fades to darkness. The evening primroses bloom, releasing their subtle scent, and the fragrance of the flowers mixes with that of the fresh-cut grass and the sunburned prairie, and Jasper breathes deep. At length he says, 'I remember that smell.' Lizzie turns to him, not asking, just nodding. Laughter drifts out from the kitchen window round the back where the girls are washing up. Jasper lights a cigarette. Drags on it long and deep. In the darkness the tiny butt moving from hand to lips looks like a caught firefly trapped and now forced in repeated migration. The porch light is off. And the stars can just about be seen.

'Do you remember that time when you was a boy 'n' that July fly shed its skin on you?'

He searches for her face in the dark. It is not turned towards him. He cannot read whatever shadowed secrets might have offered themselves there. He looks back out across the garden and breathes in again the familiar smell. Garden. Closes his eyes and opens them and it's still there. Garden. 'Haven't thought 'bout that in a long time.'

Silence between them, but not the uncomfortable kind. 'What did it feel like?' Lizzie says at last.

'What?'

'That July fly.'

'Stung like crazy.'

She laughs a little, but not for long, and when she's stopped and fallen silent he says softly, so that she can barely hear him, 'Must be nice to hold on to someone and shed your skin like that.'

Together, they watch darkness fall. She hums under her breath, but he does not recognize the tune, and when she falls silent, he does not ask. He wonders if she is even aware that she was humming. He tips his rocker back far as it goes, digging his heels into the porch, enjoying the slight strain on his legs as he watches the last streaks of golden light disappear. At length he releases his heels, letting the rocker rock itself still, soothed by the changing pace of the motion. He looks out across the lawn and tries to find the horizon, but can't make out where prairie turns to sky. Too dark now. He breathes deep, holding Garden in his lungs. Thinks about the family photographs that line the stairs. All the pictures, once hung, now missing. He'd thought, maybe earlier, when he'd sat at the head of the table, Lizzie might have said something. Might have mentioned not to sit there, that was Bobby's seat. He thinks again of Doe Eyes' surprise when he asked where her father was. Out loud, Jasper says, 'I could use a change of clothes. Reckon I could borrow some of Bobby's things?'

Her rocker stops rocking. Crickets call out and answer. Lizzie rises slowly, looking out over the garden to the prairie and up to the night sky. 'He don't got no things to borrow.' Voice just above a whisper but hard. Too hard. She turns and walks to the door. Pauses as she opens it, inside light spilling out. She looks back at him but her face is shadowed. 'There's a box of Daddy's old things up in the attic. Reckon that can tide you over. I'll take you into town in a couple days. Get you them things you need. But I won't have you growin' lazy in this house neither. You'll have to see to that, too.' The door closes quietly behind her. A little girl's laughter drifts out into the falling night, constellations brightening.

'I'm obliged.'

Only darkness there to hear his answer.

'Katie?'

'Yeah.'

'You sleepin'?'

'Yeah.'

Joanne rolls to face her sister, mattress springs squeaking as she turns. In the darkness she can just make out Katie's shadowed silhouette, back to her. She can feel the heat radiating off her sister's body. The sticky cling of the sheets is uncomfortable against Joanne's clammy skin. She is thinking of her own small bed down the hall. Of the man who's sleeping in it. How cosy and comfy that bed always was, how she could kick the covers right off her if she wanted to, but Katie likes the sheet tucked up around them, and she smells of the perfume that Joshua Ryan gave her last Easter. Like one of those pink gumballs left out in the sun too long that's melted into its own sticky sweet paste. Joanne did that once. By accident. Melted a gumball. It rolled out of her pocket and melted in Mom's pickup, right there on the seat, baked into the torn leather by the heat of the sun. Mom made her clean it up, and the gum got under her nails, stuck her fingers together, even got in her hair somehow, and Mom had to snip the tangle right out. Whole truck smelt like bubble gum for about a week. That's how Katie smells, like warm, sticky, melted bubble gum. Joanne wishes she smelt like that.

'Katie . . .'

'Ummmmm.'

The curtain blows and a warm breeze finds its way into the room, bits of moonlight creeping with it through the open window, catching and reflecting on the tiny flowers embroidered in the curtain lace. Too late for crickets now. Night dark and silent outside that screen. Even darker inside in the muggy room.

'How long you think he'll stay?'

Katie is still, breath steady. For a second Joanne wonders if maybe she is asleep after all, but at length her sister answers. 'I dunno.'

'You scared of him?'

Katie tosses onto her back. Her shadowed face turns to search for her sister's eyes. 'Are you?'

'A little.' Joanne's voice barely a whisper. 'I feel sorry for him, too.'

'Why?'

A lone coyote somewhere far off on the prairie calls, then falls silent to call again. Joanne wishes she could see Katie's face. It feels strange lying here with her sister talking to the darkness like this. Feels strange that Katie's listening to her, actually *listening*, and asking questions when it seems like lately all Katie tells her is to 'piss off 'n' shut it'.

Eventually Joanne whispers, 'He reminds me of that dog we found. The one by the road that'd been hit. You remember, Katie, how he was howling when Mom picked him up?' Silence for a moment. Then, to the darkness, Joanne adds, 'Maybe if he hadn't died we coulda kept him.'

Katie does not reply.

When Mom first told them Uncle Jasper was coming home, she'd sat the girls down in the living room all formal, same way she did when Grandma finally passed. The mood in the room felt the same too. Except someone was coming home, and that felt even stranger. There'd never been anyone *to* come home before – people were always leaving. All summer she had heard folks in town

33

whispering about him and about him getting out, but when they noticed Joanne near they always fell silent. She had no real notion of what he'd done. Just bits and pieces to string together. When they'd been really small, Katie used to play detective with Joanne as they gathered Uncle Jasper clues. How the Saunders wouldn't talk to Mama when they saw her in town. A photo of him when he was only young, his head thrown back, laughing, his arm around the shoulders of a smaller skinny boy. A letter they found up in the attic with only a court date on it, written from some attorney, folded and refolded as though read a thousand times. But Uncle Jasper had never been real before. Just a shadowy storybook figure from Mom's childhood. A name forbidden to be spoken. A game they used to play. But when Mom sat them down and told them about how he was gonna come live with them, Uncle Jasper began to solidify. Joanne had felt cold all over, unsettled and itchy inside. 'You girls is gonna have to be here for each other,' Mom had said. 'It won't be easy havin' him around, 'n' I reckon it won't be so easy for him comin' back. I'm gonna need you girls, too. I'm gonna need you to be strong for me.' And then Mom had held them both too long and too tight and real close.

But still no one would tell Joanne what Uncle Jasper'd done, and Mom cancelled their newspaper subscription soon after she told the girls that he was coming home. It didn't seem real. None of it seemed real. Even after cleaning out her room so he could have it. It wasn't until earlier that night, when he'd been sitting on her old bed in her old room, looking at her with dark eyes, that Uncle Jasper had become real. He didn't *look* like the gaunt man of her imaginings. He just looked sad. And tired, maybe. And like his eyes had seen great troubles.

Joanne had never imagined that all this might change things with Katie, though. That Katie might actually listen to her now, might become her friend again instead of just her sister. She wonders if Katie might let her tag along more. Downstairs the grandfather clock strikes the hour and the two girls listen as the chimes drift through the sleeping house to fall silent, letting the house grow quiet again. A floorboard squeaks as though someone walks the hall, and Joanne catches her breath, wondering if it's him, but only silence greets her straining ears.

'I talked to him.' Joanne can feel her older sister's eyes on her even in the dark. 'I think he punched the wall. I fetched him down to supper. He asked where Daddy was.'

'Oh.' Silence between them. 'Why'd he punch it?'

'Dunno.'

Joanne kicks one foot out from the sheets. Knee down, her left leg is free and the skin feels like it can breathe again. She wishes she could kick the sheet all off. Wonders if maybe Katie will let her.

'What'd you tell him?'

''Bout what?'

''Bout Daddy.'

'That he's gone.' She hesitates. 'Katie . . .'

'Yeah?'

'What'd he do?'

'Go to sleep, Jo.'

'You know, don't you?'

The thick silence her only answer. No breeze blows in

now. Again Joanne misses her bed in her room where she could look through the curtains and count stars till she fell asleep. Counting stars works better than counting sheep. Mom taught her that. 'Tell me 'bout Daddy again.' Then softer, barely a whisper, 'Please.'

Repeated and repeated as lullabies on sleepless nights, Joanne knows Katie's memories of their father as if they were her own. How he used to hold a cold beer can to Katie's cheek and dare her not to smile. How he'd toss Katie in the air till she felt like she was flying. The roughness of the calluses on his palms. How he always called Katie 'Lady', and could wiggle his ears. Joanne was three when he left. Her only memory of him is being carried back to bed one night after she'd woken from a bad dream, his arms around her, breath stale, shirt smelling of tobacco.

Into the darkness, 'Katie?'

'Yeah?'

'Do you think maybe Daddy might come home like Uncle Jasper did?'

Silence thick as humidity in the air between them. Wind blows through the open window, pulling the curtain out long. Katie reaches across the bed and lightly touches Joanne's cheek. 'Daddy ain't coming back, Lady.' The curtain hangs limp again before the window. Breeze spent. Joanne smiles. She likes it when it's just the two of them and Katie calls her that. Even if the nickname's a hand-me-down.

'Jo . . .'

'Yeah?'

'Don't feel too sorry for Uncle Jasper, OK? He ain't here to be our friend.'

Sleep does not come quickly. On the cell block there was the metallic creak and groan of locking bars to scream, 'Lights out.' There were the rough voices of prison guards and the convicts' rougher sneered replies. And then the click of every lamp falling dark. And sometimes the moans of men overpowered. And sometimes low groans in the darkness. And sometimes crude jokes and laughter called from cell to cell before the guards would knock the bars again and demand, 'All quiet.' And then later sometimes the sounds of haunted men crying out in dreams.

Here there is just silence.

Silence of the prairie stretching out beyond, the huge openness of which, after so long enclosed in concrete, unsettles him. Silence of the house all dark and sleeping. Silence suffocating him in this room, wrapped around his ears, his head deafening in all its lack of sound. Then a lone coyote calls somewhere far off and he thinks perhaps there is hope, perhaps there is life beneath, beyond, this stillness.

His door locks from the inside. He can't resist the sweet temptation. Rises to cross the room to open the door, just to shut it, just to open it once more. And he can walk the hall. No bars. No guards. He pauses by each door listening. Not to be nosy. Just because he *can*. Just because each pause spells freedom.

Back in bed. Feet hanging off the edge, he is surprised to discover it does not bother him. Something nice about his heels suspended like that, floating above the floor. He stares out of the window. Part of Capricorn is visible. A couple of its stars missing. Not perfect, but it's there. He thinks about those other constellations above his prison bunk. The curves of them. And he misses them, the strange comfort of the fuck-me eyes looking down on him.

Her dark hair smelt like coconut. The real fruit, not store-bought oils. And there was a shimmer in her chestnut eyes that always reminded him of candlelight. Pearly whites with one tooth slightly chipped. And her laughter, like porch chimes blown gently by a passing breeze. Soft like that. And sweetly musical. On the pillow he shakes his head slightly to clear it. Thinks instead of the stars outside. Must keep his mind focused, but in a dream that night he looks down to see blood under his fingernails, and when he wakes his sweat feels cold.

Lizzie rises early. Sun not yet quite up, but already day's weight in the thickness of the air. The endless sky lightens above the still dark prairie. Not yet quite light enough to cast sunrise's short shadows across the lawn, but already the birds are stirring. She didn't sleep well. Heard his footsteps once in the hall, creaking the floorboards with each careful step. Start and stop. One room to the next, pausing. Then the quiet click of his door closing. Then silence. She didn't sleep much after that. Didn't dream. Woke before the sun. And now, standing in the kitchen, something feels wrong, like she's woken up in a stranger's home, in a stranger's life that is not her own, nor will it ever be, nor does she want it.

Christmas mornings when they were little neither was allowed to go downstairs before the other. It was their own rule, for once, not one of the many inflicted upon them. And that made it all the more sacred. They had to see the Christmas tree together. One morning Lizzie snuck down before Jasper. Crept down the stairs on tippy-toe, careful as she could. Didn't even dare to breathe as she slid past Jasper's door. Mama and Daddy were still sleeping too, and Lizzie felt like an outlaw as she tiptoed through the darkness, sky already turned a blue grey dawn that in its silence screamed of winter. The tree looked like something on a Christmas card come to life, covered with strands of tiny silver tinsel that captured the pre-dawn light, Santa's presents a small sea spilling into the room. She sucked in her breath: it looked so pretty. And straight away she wished Jasper was there to see it with her. Later on, she pretended to be surprised as they came down the stairs. She had to. But the moment was ruined. And she felt so guilty that she 'fessed up. And Jasper just laughed at her and said, 'You think I ain't done that every Christmas morning?' And her cheeks had burned hot with anger, bright with shame.

Somehow, entering the kitchen this morning, Lizzie feels like that girl again, snuck down in the dark. Not that it's a special day. Not that it's a holiday. Not that she's sure she even really wants Jasper there beside her. In fact, she's fairly sure she doesn't. Just somehow in this early hour, before the girls are stirring, it feels as though she is the one now sneaking through the house, pausing to look and listen where she shouldn't. As if it's still Mama's house and not her own.

She makes a cup of coffee. Black. Sits down at the small table and stares into the dark depths of that cup. Too scalding to drink yet. Bobby and she used to wake up this hour Sunday mornings. While she'd lie in bed, eyes adjusting to the lightening room, he'd go down and fetch them coffee and bring the cups back up to bed. Both piping hot and black but his had sugar in it. And they would drink those coffees in silence side by side, burning their tongues to get the liquid down faster. And then in silence, as the sun rose, they would make love. In church later on those mornings, so close to her husband in the pew, Lizzie would remember the feel of him inside her, the taste of the coffee still thick in his mouth, and she would forget sometimes to call out, 'Amen!' after the reverend had spoken, would rise delayed to sing the hymns, her mind still tangled in bed sheets not yet remade. And then there was that last Sunday, the day he left. Eyes like stone. Coffee placed on the bedside table, not a word between them. He didn't crawl into bed. She knew from the cold in his eyes he was leaving. Felt the knowledge deep in her gut. He picked up a bag, already packed. No kiss goodbye. That morning she did not at first drink her coffee. Sat and watched it cool till steam stopped circling the cup. When the sun finally rose, her voice found her again. 'Stay.' Silence enough of an answer. Bobby was never the same after Jasper went away.

'Mom?'

She looks up. Streaks of pink across a golden sky. 'You're up early, hon.'

Katie slides into the chair beside her. Yawns. 'So are you.'

A sad smile. Tired smile. 'Can't you sleep?'

Loose T-shirt and shorts, tangled hair everywhere, no makeup, but Katie still glows beautiful. Sunshine in the still dark room. She shakes her head. 'Not really.'

'Coffee?'

She sets out milk and sugar for her daughter. But at least the brew's still hot and she doesn't have to make a fresh pot. 'Where's Joanne?'

'Sleeping.'

Lizzie nods. They drink in silence, letting the room grow light around them.

At length Katie turns to look at her mother square on. A ray of sunlight has fallen through the kitchen window and across her brow. Same transparent colour as a buttercup held under a chin. 'She's been askin' what he done.'

Lizzie takes a long, slow sip. Holds the coffee in her mouth and lets it cool there before she swallows. Sets the mug back down. A tiny ring of moisture where the mug rested before. Without thinking, she matches the mug into its former spot. 'You know?'

'Yeah.'

'You tell her?'

'No.'

Grosbeaks and orioles call from the shrubs praising the risen sun, jays and flycatchers and wrens soon waking to join their symphony before all is drowned in the harsh cackle of a crow. Lizzie rises from the table and takes their mugs to the sink, rinsing both before setting them upside down on the rack to dry.

'She'll find out,' Katie whispers.

Lizzie grips the edge of the sink with both hands and

lets her head fall down between her shoulders, neck stretched long. Stays unmoving there for a spell. The rim of the sink feels damp and cool beneath her palms. Smooth and foreign even though she must have touched it one thousand times. She imagines crumpling down onto the linoleum. Worn-out body concave. She imagines the linoleum cool against her face, imagines pressing her face down into that cool. She straightens. 'Not if I can help it.'

'He gives me the creeps.'

She lets out a deep sigh. *He does me too, hon.* But she can't say that, can never say that. Aloud. 'It's what we don't know that eats at me,' Lizzie says at last.

'What's there not to know, Mom? He's guilty of what he done.' Katie looks down at her nails, brow furrowed, fingers fidgeting, entwined. Picks a piece of dirt from under one nail and flicks it to the floor. A strand of blonde hair falls across her face.

Lizzie watches, saying nothing. The grosbeaks outside have fallen silent but from somewhere a wren still sings.

At length Katie's eyes rise to find her mother's, and as her chin lifts, her hair brushes from her face. A tangled halo in the growing morning light. 'I saw the photos,' she says quietly. 'Of the others. In the paper a few weeks back. They all looked so nice. So happy.' And then her eyes fall again to hide behind long shadowed lashes.

Lizzie draws herself up tall, arms crossed. Remembered newspaper faces flash in her eyes. Faces that don't know trouble's coming. 'Don't believe everything you read. That jury was far from unbiased, 'n' there's as many lies printed as truths.'

42

'What 'bout Eddie Saunders?'

Lizzie stiffens, surprised. 'What about him?'

'Word is he ain't too happy 'bout Jasper comin' home.'

She opens her mouth to speak. The faint smell of cigarettes and sweat stops her. The creak of a floorboard in the doorway. 'Thought I smelt coffee.' That same Coca-Cola T-shirt. Jeans unbuttoned. Mousy hair in all directions, sunlight catching on the patches of grey. He crosses to the kettle, grabs himself a mug and pours himself a cup.

Lizzie unfolds her arms, leans her hip now against the sink and can feel the coolness even through the fabric of her nightshirt, heartbeat quickened. 'You standin' there long?'

He drinks down to the dregs, then pours another cup. Smacks his lips as he finishes the second and lets out a sigh. And as silently as he appeared, Jasper pads barefoot out of the room and into the quiet of the still sleeping house. The smell of cigarettes lingers.

The a/c in the diner doesn't make much difference. Every time the door opens what little cool air there is seeps right out. Old fans still spin up on the ceiling, gathering dust as they try to aid the a/c in circulating the stagnant air, but the a/c just makes the room stuffy and traps in the stench of greasy food and the fans merely circulate the sour odour of customers' sweat. Mostly truckers stop out this way, exiting I-10 as they drive cargos from New Mexico and El Paso back east, or sometimes the drivers are heading out the other way, across the prairie and into desert country. A man tells Katie he is heading all the way out to California. Truck full of Hoovers from a factory in Detroit. 'I've seen most of the country in that eighteen-wheeler. Yep, that's right,' he says, 'I don't think there's a road I ain't driven.' Grease stains on his hands. Beard stubble grown past two days. He looks Katie up and down real slow as she refills his coffee. Places his toast, well buttered, back on his plate. 'You ever seen the ocean?'

'Me? No.' She blushes. Laughs slightly. 'I ain't seen anywhere, Mister.' And she turns to walk back behind the counter, coffee-pot heavy in her hands. She would like to see the ocean. Would like to head out on those open highways going beyond the known. And there've been plenty of truckers that summer who have offered to drive Katie somewhere. Anywhere. Even up the road. But she knows better than to trust them. She may not have been to a city. She may not have seen the ocean. But working nights in Penny's Diner, Katie has come to recognize the hunger that clouds a man's eyes. No food can fill that craving. She takes their orders. Refills their coffee cups. Listens to their stories on the slow nights. But there's a line between hospitable and friendly, and Katie's always careful not to cross it. And, anyway, for the most part, she's happy here.

'Miss.'

She turns.

'A slice of key lime pie when you're ready.' He's got the non-food hunger in his eyes. A bit of ketchup smudges his lips.

'Comin' right up.' She nods and places the coffee-pot back on its burner.

Katie's shift starts after the dinner rush when things are slow, and she's usually the only girl working. Most nights it's just her, and Tom in the kitchen. She sits, for hours sometimes, refilling the bottles of Heinz, topping up the salt and pepper shakers. Only a handful of truckers stops in at that late hour. Not fun work. But there's something about the monotony of it that Katie secretly likes. She likes the way when the diner's quiet and the floors are freshly mopped that the black and white tiles seem to shine. She likes the quiet stretch of the prairie that surrounds them. It comforts her. The vast emptiness reassures. And, anyway, Mom needs her to help make ends meet.

It was on those quiet nights that Katie first started reading the papers. Was on a headline that she first heard Uncle Jasper was getting out. The caption next to his photograph had read 'A MONSTER RELEASED: Jasper Curtis, Convict, Shows No Remorse'. In the photo, he was not smiling. She had stared into his eyes for a long time, bottle of Heinz half empty in one hand, screwed-off lid in the other. She had stared at him, and he'd stared back, but she couldn't tell nothing by looking at him – he just looked pixellated, mass-produced, papery thin. The ink under his name had smudged.

Tonight Katie's grateful for the familiar quiet of the diner, though she wishes Key Lime Pie's eyes wandered less. Patsy Cline sings a sad love song on the radio. Feels good to be out of the house, away from all that's different. Feels good to be somewhere where it's possible to imagine things remain unchanged. She brings the man his pie and sets it on the counter. Takes his dirty plate.

Catches a glimpse of his eighteen-wheeler parked outside. 'Thanks, baby,' he says, his voice low and gravelly, and she doesn't like him calling her that, but she smiles all the same, nodding towards his pie.

'Everything all right now?'

He grunts in response and she can feel his eyes on her as she walks away. She leans against the glass of the pie display just to feel the cool. Greasy heat from the kitchen still slides down her back even though right now Tom isn't cooking. Chances are he's outside having a cigarette.

The door opens. A gush of heat sweeps in with it. A tiny bell chimes. She turns to see who's there. *Another table, good, maybe tips will be decent.* Then stops short and smiles. 'Josh!' Two steps and he's from the door over to her already, arms around her waist. They kiss. And the taste of him makes her dizzy, clouds her head and sends her floating. The trucker looks up from his pie and grunts. Then looks down again.

'Slow night, huh?' Joshua's eyes quickly take in the empty diner, linger on the lone trucker. His half-eaten pie. 'What time you off?'

'One.' She makes a pouty face, a face she knows he likes.

He lets out his breath. 'You serious? I was hoping maybe you could get off early. Go on a drive for a while.'

She makes that sad face again. Hopes she looks cute. 'It's just me 'n' Tom. You know I'm stuck.'

He sits down on one of the stools. Shakes his head slightly. Light brown hair that curls when it starts to grow long. He could use a haircut soon. 'I don't much like you working here.'

46

Head still spinning from that kiss, she stiffens. An old argument. 'You know as good as I there ain't many jobs in this town 'n' Penny only needs me nights.' She pops the top off a bottle of Coke and hands it to him. He reaches across the counter and takes a straw. His daddy's an oil man so he doesn't have to work summers. And come this time next year he'll be packing off to go to college some-where, no doubt on some football scholarship, Mr All-American. And she? Well, Katie reckons she'll still be here. Left well and true behind. She shudders, shakes her head to clear such thoughts. *Don't be stupid. Josh loves me.* He says something, but she doesn't hear it. Watches his lips move, just doesn't hear it. She tries to bring herself back to now. *Josh came to see me, that's all that matters.* Head still light and spinning.

'Did you miss me?'

'Course I missed you.' His smile falters. 'But I came round to see you for another reason too.'

Here, now, focus. Big blue eyes meet his. 'Yeah?' *Keep your breath steady.*

'I don't like him in your house.'

Her breath's calm, the nearness of him less intoxicat-ing as he frowns. 'I don't have much choice in the matter.'

'There's always a choice.'

She looks away from him, then back. 'He's family, Josh.'

His fist slams down hard on the counter and the Coke bottle rattles, almost falls, but at the last second rights itself. Key Lime Pie looks over and this time does not look away, nosy eyes prying into them. 'Goddamn it,

Katie, you know what he done! Do you hear what folks round here are sayin'? They reckon your mother's clear lost her mind takin' him back in.'

She struggles to meet his angry eyes. Isn't even sure she believes the words as she speaks them. 'He's done his time.'

'He ain't done enough.'

'That's the law's decision.'

'You serious?' He laughs. No humour in the sound. 'Jesus Christ! Do you hear yourself? Do you hear how stupid you sound?'

Katie bristles.

'He's a ticking bomb waiting to be set off. It's just a matter of time. I swear to God, Katie, someone ought to take it into their own hands and set him straight before any more people start turnin' up missin'.'

'Don't talk like that!'

'Like what? I ain't gonna pussyfoot around and pretend he's some saint just 'cause you and your lot's been blinded by y'all's shared blood.'

'He weren't convicted of all that, Josh. There weren't ever any proof.'

'That man ain't right in the head, Katie. We don't need no proof of that.'

'You don't know what you're talking about!'

'Do you?' Hurt in Josh's eyes she doesn't expect, isn't quite sure she understands. Then softly, his voice almost a whisper, 'What if he hurts you, Katie? I don't think I could bear it.'

She reaches out, uncertain, and lays her hand to rest on

his shoulder. 'He ain't gonna hurt me, Josh. He don't seem so dangerous.'

The strain in his eyes frightens her. 'How do you know?'

The trucker clears his throat. 'Miss.'

'Yes?'

'More coffee, please, 'n' the bill.'

Lizzie watches as the hens gather round Joanne's feet in a swarm of brown feathers. Joanne tries to scatter the feed as far from her feet as possible, but the action makes no difference – seeds still fall down close enough that, standing barefoot out the back, chickens nibble her toes. She dances and prances in place, shrieking as chicken feed scatters around her. Lizzie smiles. It was the same for her when she was young. The occasional hen bite doesn't sting so bad; it's more the apprehension of unexpected nibbles that cause the shrieking. Jasper used to laugh at her when she did the feed. Told her she was 'chicken dancing'.

Lizzie tears her eyes from her daughter and looks away from the clothesline, pins in mouth, to see Jasper standing in the shadows of the house. It's hard to see his face clearly, but he seems to be smiling. She follows his gaze. He's watching Joanne too. She takes a pin from her mouth and fastens a sock to the line. Starts to secure a shirt. One of Katie's. Jasper turns, as though feeling Lizzie's eyes on him. Stands still a moment facing her. They are close enough that he could easily call out to her, but he stands in silence. Lizzie can't help but wonder what he's thinking.

He looks like a stranger, standing there in the shade, their daddy's old clothes hanging loose off his slender frame. She almost calls to him, but something stops her. Maybe it's the deep shadows crossing his face. Maybe it's his silence. Jasper raises a hand and waves. A smile lights his face, and Lizzie finds her hand automatically raised in response. Clothespins still in mouth, she does not smile back.

Mid-morning. But already the sun sits high, sky marked with scattered dots of cloud. Joanne shrieks again as a hen pecks at her toes, then giggles. Jasper turns back to watch her. That funny smile once again stretches his lips. The house shadow lies cast short across the browning lawn. Him right in its shade. *Must be the only shade for miles.* His pale figure fits there, Lizzie thinks. Summer too brown and blooming for his sallow skin. Too healthy. She wonders how often he saw the sun in there. Wonders now, left unguarded, how quickly his skin might burn.

Lizzie finishes hanging the last bits of the wash. Joanne's socks – one pair pink, one blue, one green. A skirt of Katie's. Brown. Her own floral nightshift. Two towels. Both white. She dumps the clothespins back into the now empty laundry basket, bends and lifts it to rest on her hip, momentarily letting her eyes slip from Jasper's frame. Spray from wet sheets blows against her skin. Evaporates.

His eyes never leave Joanne. Not even as Lizzie comes to stand beside him, though she is sure he heard her approach, is sure he feels her standing there. The closeness of their bodies intensifies the sticky cling of morning heat. But his head does not turn. He does not acknowledge she exists. At length, as though to no one, he murmurs, 'I can't remember the last time I heard a child laughing.'

Joanne's chasing the chickens now. Jumping over them. Teasing them with bits of feed. Laughing. 'She reminds me of you,' he says. Voice soft, but not a whisper. Not quite.

Lizzie follows his gaze. Makes no reply. Watches her daughter. Sees herself. Sees bits of Bobby that she both cherishes and shies away from. Looks back to Jasper's stern profile. Says nothing.

'It ain't just her looks neither.' Eyes still on the girl. 'You had that same spark in you.'

A deep breath to steady. 'I reckon that was a long time ago.'

He looks at her then, his movement drawing her face to his. Eye to eye. Close enough for their breath to touch. Warm, sticky, stale. Dark eyes drilling into her. Searching. A rawness in them that alarms, makes her want to back away. But she doesn't. She hadn't realized how very close she stood to him. When he speaks again, his voice sounds husky, as if it has become part of the deeper shade in which they stand.

'Has it really been so long?' Husky, husky, shadowed voice.

His gaze contradicts the softness of his tone, his eyes like two spotlights forced and focused upon her. Relentless in their drilling. Their searching. She turns away. Has to. Shifts the basket from her hip to hold it long and low before her stomach. Presses it against her just to feel the reassurance of the pressure. Even the shade feels too hot. No breeze so close to the house. 'A lot's changed, Jasper.'

He laughs then. A soft, rumbling chuckle. Her brother's laugh. The one that she remembers. The one that maybe means he's really home. 'You're telling me?' That softening twinkle in his eyes.

She smiles then. Just a little. Can't help it. A sad smile, playing with the corners of her mouth, teasing them up. An unfamiliar feeling of late. But it doesn't stick. She answers, 'Am I really so changed?'

The laughter drains from his face, leaving it sallower, tenser than before. He looks at her. The same unflinching gaze. The pause between them grows, suspended, uncomfortable. A breath too long held. He looks down. Away across the lawn. Out over the prairie. Beyond. 'Sometimes,' he says, 'I think maybe I'm dreamin'. I think I'm gonna wake up 'n' find things ain't so changed. Then I realize I'm awake. And it's like I've always been awake, and truth is, now I forget how good it used to feel to dream.'

Lizzie makes no reply.

A cloud nearly covers the sun, but fails, beams of light and heat burning right through it. A crow lands on the porch railing with its harsh cackle.

One of the hens pecks Joanne's ankle, and she hollers. Pain and laughter mixed together. Lizzie pulls her eyes away from Jasper. Regrets having come to stand beside him. Buries that regret. *No time for such luxuries.* 'Joanne!' she snaps. 'You stop messin' now 'n' hurry up 'n' get 'em chickens fed, you hear?' She does not look at her brother again. Turns before even her own voice has faded, walks up the three back steps and opens the screen door, basket still balanced on her hip. She pauses in the doorway. Jasper has not moved. She cannot see his face or eyes. She opens her mouth to say something. Closes it. Lets the screen door slam shut behind her. Joanne's laughter fades.

Walking along the country road that leads from the house back towards town, Jasper's not fully sure he likes how Lizzie has divided up Daddy's land. The Turners rent and farm the north cornfields now. The Grays rent out the south acres to graze their longhorns. That's how Lizzie scrapes by – those rents and the odd bits of mending she picks up. Not a good living but enough to scrape by. He can see that. Can see the stress of a hard life worn into her weathered skin. She's not the sister he remembers. He respects her for that.

Around the house stretches unused prairie that was there even when Jasper was a boy. He likes that. Likes that she kept it, kept the wildness of it. Wishes all the land had grown wild like that, had never been farmed again.

When Daddy died, Jasper never went back out to work the fields. Didn't feel right out there without him. Worked with Bobby for a couple years instead. A small garage in town. Grease on his hands all day instead of dirt. The hum of motors sparked to life. A part of him wonders if that's why he watched his father die.

Jasper had looked on helpless as the heart attack shook all life from the big man's frame. Daddy's eyes had rolled back in his head till just the whites showed. Mouth moved and twisted as dried lips gasped for breath. Jasper had wondered if perhaps Daddy were praying under all that pain. Jasper himself said no prayers. Just watched in silence till the tremors no longer spasmed through Daddy's body. He's thought back on that many times. Has often wondered why he didn't pray. Has wondered, if he had, might Daddy have survived?

They were forty-five acres from the house when it happened. Ploughing season. Daddy fell right off the tractor, left arm clutched, face pale. Jasper could have run for help. He's thought over that many times, too. Has asked himself what it means that he didn't. If it means anything at all. Deep inside, Jasper knows nothing could have saved his daddy. When your time is up, it's up. Nothing can save you. A simple fact. Praying, running, screams for help – all useless and he knows it. Jasper watched his father die. Simple as that.

It took only two minutes. Kneeling there, watching his father's lips dry as they gasped for final breaths, Jasper did not shed one single tear. Not then. Not later. Not at the open casket or even back at the house during the after-funeral spread the church ladies had laid out. Mama cried, frail and white and lost in a sea of well-wished condolences. And Lizzie, eyes red with newly dried tears. At the funeral, behind his pulpit, Reverend Gordon had described Daddy as an 'outstanding citizen', a 'man of morals'. Stretched truths at best. But Jasper had never been a man to cry. Had never been a man to hold grudges against kin. And he'd never been a man to run for help neither.

He asked that therapist once, the one in Huntsville sent that first year to evaluate his mental health. He asked him what it meant that he watched his father die. That he didn't run for help. But the therapist had just sat there in his pinstripe suit, peering down through bug-eyed glasses, marking things on a pad Jasper could not read. Eventually Bug Eyes had looked up at him, chewing on his pencil's eraser, and had asked Jasper if his daddy had ever touched him 'inappropriately', and Jasper had laughed right in his fat face at the stupidity of such a question. His father never touched him. No slap. Or pat. Or hug goodnight. Even when he was young and acted up and Daddy had to put manners in him, it was always Daddy's belt that touched Jasper, never Daddy's hand. They shook hands once that Jasper could remember. High-school graduation. And their eyes had met. And Daddy had said, 'I guess you're a man now. Reckon you'd best start actin' like one.' Releasing Jasper's hand before the words even faded. It was a firm handshake. A calloused hand.

How dare that asshole therapist insult his daddy's memory? Jasper had answered, 'How many times did *your* daddy jerk *you* off, Doc? How many times? Did you like it?' and Bug Eyes had sweat real bad and squirmed and sunk down in his chair a little, and that was the last time Bug Eyes tried to assess Jasper's mental health.

Until they'd let him out, that is.

They didn't talk about his daddy that time.

The clock on the whitewashed office wall sounded like a ticking bomb. Though ticking down his doom or freedom, Jasper could not decide. Bug Eyes' pencil rasped and wheezed, like strangled breaths, as it scraped against his notepad. And this time all Bug Eyes wanted to talk about was her.

Jasper could have told him how her cum smelt.

Coconut oil and sweat and saliva and canned salmon all musky and divine tangled in one sour scent. He could have mapped out and drawn the lines that marked her palms. Heart. Head. Life. He could have told him how in the mornings her breath smelt like coffee beans. Dry-roasted. But he didn't. He sat there in silence, steering his mind from her, padlocking the doors that guarded his memories, listening to the clock tick, the pencil rasp. He sat there, not defiant, not insolent. Just there.

A tiny bead of sweat ran down Bug Eyes' brow. He wiped it. A new bead formed. He cleared his throat. 'Mr Curtis, do you understand that you are due to be released at six a.m. on this upcoming Tuesday, the tenth of July?'

'Yessir.'

'You understand that the board of directors of this here institution has granted you release due to good behaviour during time served?'

A small smirk he did not attempt to hide. 'Yessir.'

'Is something funny?' The pencil stopped. Lifted off the page. Bug Eyes' bulging eyes bored into him as if they knew him, wanted to know him, to understand. *Typical therapist psycho bullshit.*

'We both know why I'm being let out, Doc.' His voice even. Steady.

A raised eyebrow arched way up high on that shiny bald head. Looked out of place so high with no hair above it. A fuzzy caterpillar climbing with no real place to go. No cocoon. Bug Eyes leaned back in his chair. Another bead of sweat dripped. 'Oh? And why is that?'

The whir of a ceiling fan replaced the scratch of the pencil. Jasper wondered why he hadn't noticed the fan before. The shaky sound of its whir. He smiled. 'Over-crowding. Y'all want my bunk for some new sinner.' He laughed. 'And I've served my time, Doc. Fact is, no matter how you sugar-coat it, y'all can't keep me here no longer. I reckon this here interview is just 'bout pointless.'

Bug Eyes smiled. A tight, tiny smile that did not reach his eyes or stretch beyond his lips. Pencil back to page. Scratch. Rasp. Wheeze. 'Is that so, Mr Curtis? I assume, then, that you know *why* you are meeting with me today.'

'I reckon I do.'

'And that would be?'

'To evaluate my mental health.'

An identical tight-lipped smile. 'That is correct, Mr Curtis, very good indeed.' Pencil scratch, scratch, scratched on the page.

Jasper was surprised to realize he didn't care what was written there. He knew the words were about him, but he also knew what lay inside far better than anyone else. He had never cared much what others thought. Time served did not alter that. And now, soon, he would be free. *She* cared. She always cared a bit too much what other folks thought. He could have told Bug Eyes that, but he didn't. Held his tongue. Didn't want to think about the way she used to be.

'To be frank with you, Mr Curtis, I have been assigned to deem whether or not you remain a menace to society.' The pencil stopped scratching. Bulging eyes met his. 'Tell me about Miss Saunders.'

Dark hair. And dark eyes. And a smile just for him. A smile no other man could have. Jasper paused. A door creaked open, just a crack. He lowered his eyes. Thought about prairie grass running through open fingers. Her lying down in it, bluebonnets and daisies crushed beneath her hair. Carefully he shut down the memory. Met the therapist's gaze. 'Do you meet with all the men coming in 'n' out of this place?'

'Yes.'

Jasper nods. ''N' you evaluate 'em?'

'That's right, yes.'

'All of 'em?'

'Most of them, yes. It's a standard procedure, Mr Curtis. We need to be sure that the convicts released pose no threat to themselves or others.'

Jasper nodded slowly, as though thinking. He shifted his weight in his chair. Met the therapist's gaze with cold, hard eyes. 'Who evaluates you?'

'Excuse me?'

'Who's to say there ain't a bit of a "menace to society" inside you too, Doc?' Jasper laughed then, low and deep and long. 'You know, I think I see it, that menace, lurkin' deep in there. It's in your eyes, you see. The way you squint. You can tell a lot from a man's eyes, Doc, and fact is you don't seem so different to me than the folks I shared cells with.'

Bug Eyes shifted in his chair. Swallowed. 'We are here to talk about you, Mr Curtis, not me.'

'And what do you decide exactly?'

'I'm not sure I follow you.'

'I mean, what difference does this make? I'm already due release. Board's granted that. Time's nearly up now. I've served. So I guess what I'm askin', Doc, is how does what I say here matter?'

'Everything we say matters, Mr Curtis, don't you agree?'

'No, that's not what I mean, Doc, 'n' you know it. Don't sidestep the question now, you hear?' Defiant eyes met defiant eyes, all trace of laughter drained from Jasper's voice. 'What I want to know is: can anything I say here keep me locked up?'

The doctor shifted his weight from left to right. Back again. Looked uncomfortable squished in that tiny chair behind the massive desk. Sweat still beaded on his brow before rolling down his forehead to be wiped away only to form again. Clock a ticking bomb. Bug Eyes cleared his throat. Fidgeted with his pencil. Put it down. Picked it up. Chewed on the eraser.

'No.'

'So I'm a free man?'

'Do you want to be free?' Pencil calmed, raised, ready to be back in action, busy on the page.

Jasper smiled. 'Every man seeks freedom, Doc.'

'You've been avoiding my question, Mr Curtis. About Miss Saunders. Does it bother you to talk about her?'

'What do you want to know?'

'Do you regret your actions?'

'You mean my crime?' A smile played on Jasper's lips but did not settle there.

'Yes. I mean your crime.'

Jasper shifted in his chair, his hands clasped and folded in his lap before him. His cuticles, grown long, covered the half-moons on his nails. He stretched his legs out long, feet flexed before him. Thought about sunlight and open fields and showers not shared. Thought about long dark lashes. And tan lines. And remembered the taste of Mama's peach cobbler hot on his tongue. At length he lifted his gaze. 'That bitch got what she deserved.'

The pencil stopped scratching. 'No regrets?'

'Plenty.'

The road to town feels longer than Jasper remembers. Can't quite guess how many miles still to go, though there was a time, not really so very long ago, when, without thinking, he would already have known. He had left Lizzie in Mama's old chair in the parlour, bent over someone's lace tablecloth, mending. Open window beside her, but scarcely a breeze blowing in. Doe Eyes at her feet, lying on her belly, flipping the pages of a fashion magazine. Feet kicked up behind her. Blonde hair slipped loose from her ponytail falling down onto her face. Lizzie didn't look up as Jasper slipped out of the door, but Doe Eyes did. He paused for a moment, caught by her bright blue gaze. She stared back. Gaze too unflinching for a child. A woman's gaze. Almost. He didn't bother saying goodbye. Just slipped out of the door. It's been years since he could leave a room without permission. A long time since he could simply rise, and walk, and go. Unlocked doors amaze. He almost said something to Doe Eyes when her look caught him like that. But he halted the words on his tongue before they were spoken. Thank God. Little bitch in the making. More of Bobby in her than he'd like. Eyes he's not sure he trusts. And yet a softness to her that somehow makes him think perhaps there's still a chance to feel at home.

A mirage on the open road ahead rises up on the

concrete, like a pool of water, only to distort back into pavement as Jasper approaches. The afternoon sunshine feels healthy on his face, his neck, his arms. He can feel himself tanning, browning. He wonders how quickly he might burn. Doesn't care. Step by step, he feels his heart pumping, blood flowing. He can't remember the last time he felt that. Healthy.

Wind rustles burned prairie grasses together, a sound like crickets dying. No coolness in the breeze. June bugs buzz through the tall grasses. Too early still for cricket song. Far off the whir of a truck engine makes itself known and can be heard speeding closer. A sound low and lost as a brewing storm.

He stands on the shoulder and watches the Ford get closer. Blue. Bright, shiny, new-paint blue. He can see even from a distance not many miles have been put on that pickup yet. More toy car than true truck. The kind that folks in the cities and suburbs buy in an attempt to look country. *That truck has probably never driven a proper haul.* He watches it all the same, though. A speck at first far off on the prairie road, barrelling closer and bigger, approaching with almost alarming speed.

It's been a great while since he saw something move so fast, and he stands still, watching its rapid approach as though transfixed.

The wind hits him as the pickup passes him, and he closes his eyes better to enjoy the cooling blast of air. Over in a second, but still that second makes him smile. It feels like freedom on his face.

Brakes and tyres screech their halt. Jasper opens his eyes. Turns to look behind him. The pickup has stopped about fifty yards up the road. Dark skid marks from the brakes darken the concrete. He can't see who is inside. Just the shadowed silhouette of the driver turned round in his seat to look behind him. A Stetson. Wide shoulders. For a second, Jasper thinks the pickup will back up to him. When it doesn't, he wonders if he should walk up to it. Wonders if he knows the driver. Wonders if perhaps he should wave or call out. Instead he stands in silence, hands in pockets, squinting into the reflected light from the shiny pickup's truck bed. A mirage on the road far beyond reflects and sparkles like water. Wind rustles dry grass. Earth parched for rain.

Jasper takes a step forward towards the truck, and as he does, it dawns on him. Dread rises in his gut. There is only one frame he can think of that matches that broad silhouette. And it's the one frame he had hoped not to see. Not yet. The engine revs once. Jasper pauses. Confusion creases his brow. He knows in his gut who this must be, though he'd imagined their paths crossing differently, had hoped maybe time could bandage up at least some wounds. He has done his term, served society's penance. But Jasper knows all too well how vengeance feeds. He cannot imagine a reality where her brother will not want blood. He draws a deep breath and walks forward. His knuckles crack as his hands fist. Ahead, the shadow abruptly turns, twisting to face the steering-wheel again, and the truck speeds on, tyres screeching. Jasper stops mid-stride. Watches for a moment, wondering. Eventually he can no longer find the Ford on the flat, open road. Eddie Saunders had never shied away from a fight. Jasper stands motionless, feeling an uneasiness creep up inside him. When he finds his stride again, his footsteps lead back up the road he's walked already. Back the way the truck just sped, back towards home.

Hands in and out of the warm soapy water. Brought in and out of the faucet's steady drip in steady bursts of hot and cold. The heat feels soothing on Lizzie's aching knuckles as she massages them back to life. Too long sewing, but at least the lace is done. Nearly good as new. Mama had arthritis. In her hands. Her thumbs. Her knees. Used to sit out on her rocker on the front porch, rubbing her knees with the palms of her hands as she rocked back and forth, back and forth. For hours. Used to say the movement eased the pain, but when she stood up her walk was as stiff as ever. Lizzie wonders if she'll be like that one day. If pain runs in her blood. Shakes her head. *Don't be ridiculous.* Hopes not.

She hears the truck before she sees it. Looks up out of the kitchen window beyond the tall prairie grasses and low-lying shrubs to the road beyond. Rumbling sound of the engine low as thunder and as distant, but uninterrupted and now quickly coming closer, growing louder, faster than any storm. Cobalt blue. Bright, shiny, new. Puts her rusted Chevy parked out front to shame. Lizzie turns the faucet off. Dries her hands on a dish towel. Places it, crumpled, on the counter beside her. Her hand fists around the cool fabric, gripping, squeezing, as it knots inside her palm. To her surprise, she is not shaking.

She knows that truck.

Whole town knows that truck. And it's the one truck

she hoped never to see. Or at least not yet. *It's too soon. He's only just home . . .*

Lizzie knows that Jasper left the house. She didn't try to stop him. Didn't tell him, 'Stay.' Or ask him if he wanted company or even a lift somewhere. He is not a prisoner in this house. And yet Lizzie couldn't help but feel uneasy as Jasper quietly walked to the door, as he paused there, hand already outstretched for the screen-door handle. For a moment, not looking up but still fully aware of where he stood, she wondered if he might not come back. It would be easier to leave with no good-bye. A part of her hoped he might never again enter through that door. A part of her worried to let him out of her sight.

When the door shut behind him, she looked up. Watched the empty doorframe for some time, staring through the screen into the nothingness beyond. Mid-afternoon, the sun golden above the golden grass.

But now there is that blue pickup speeding down the road, dust rising in a small brown cloud around it, and all Lizzie can wonder is, *Where is Jasper? He's been gone – what? An hour? Two?* Her fear sticks like a lump in her chest. Like the panic that gripped her when Jasper had called all those years ago from the prison cell when Sheriff Adams had first dragged him in for questioning. His one phone call. And he'd called her.

'I couldn't bear it.' That was all he'd said.

And her heart had stopped. Had never beaten the same since. 'Bear what?' But on the other side of the tele-phone were only shallow breaths and hiccuped sobs and then, at length, strange, hollow laughter that was not her brother's, and was her brother's, and then she'd cried until the opposite receiver clicked its silence, only the hollow drone of the dial tone there to question or to comfort.

Lizzie'd known that Jasper come back home might bring its share of trouble. She'd known, but still she'd hoped the past might stay gone.

Now, dish towel crumpled in her fist's tightening grip, she watches as the truck draws closer. Breath shallow and short. But, to her surprise, it does not slow. And then she knows. *No. Not yet. Not now.* A warning. And the warning chills her, freezes her insides and her heart with dread even as the afternoon heat eases in from the window before her to slide warm and sticky, honey-thick down her skin in dripping lines of perspiration.

Long after the pickup has sped away, Lizzie still grips the dish towel, her knuckles white from the pressure. 'Oh, Jasper,' she finally gasps. Then mouths his name over and over softer and softer till the word itself crumbles into a dry rasp that cannot be heard. Dry lips rub together and chap to form his silent name.

Somewhere a blue jay calls, then an oriole, till both fall mute mid-song.

Katie's hair glows golden where the lamplight hits it. She's counting under her breath, '. . . forty-one, forty-two, forty-three, forty-four . . .' with every brushstroke. She looks like a princess. Like a picture from a story book Joanne remembers seeing. She can't remember what fairy tale it was – Rapunzel maybe, or maybe it was Goldilocks, or that princess from Rumpelstiltskin. But, no, that princess was spinning golden thread, not hair. Joanne wishes she had hair like that. Like Katie's. Soft and shiny like the models in the magazines. Like golden thread. But all her hair does is tangle. That's why she ties it up. Wears it in the ponytail. And, anyway, she doesn't have the patience to brush her hair like that. It takes too long to reach one hundred. Hurts when she hits the tangles.

For supper they'd had leftover brisket and mash and peas straight from the garden. It was Joanne's job to shell the peas. Slow, monotonous work, but she likes peeling open the husks and finding the tiny green balls cradled inside. She likes how every pod holds a different number of peas. Grandma used to do it with her. Back when Grandma was alive. She'd sit in her rocker on the front porch, Joanne in a little heap on the floor beside her, the pea pot placed between them, Grandma rocking back and forth, creaking the floorboards of the porch with every rock. Joanne liked that sound. Misses it. Grandma used to give the pea pods names. Said every one was a family they knew. Peeling one open, four peas inside, she'd say, 'Look here, hon, you see this? This must be the Philips.' And then she'd dump the peas and shuck the pod away and move on to the next, six peas, the Adams, or five, the Clarks. She knew it was silly, but Joanne still liked the game. It always made her giggle. She still plays it as she shucks the peas herself, even though there's no one there to tell the names to. Says them softly to herself instead, whispers without sound. *Three peas, the Teagues. Five, Gordons. Four, Walters. Seven . . . a hard one . . . Grandma would have known.*

Dinner had been long and boring. Uncle Jasper didn't

say much, his face a hard mask that scared Joanne a little. And Mom had that stressed look she'd had when Grandma died, and when Joanne had tried to ask if they might go swimming real soon, Mom had snapped at her, 'You just be silent now 'n' eat your supper.' And Joanne hadn't tried to say much after that. Katie didn't even try to talk. And when she'd cleared her plate Joanne was grateful to be excused.

It's late now. Joanne doesn't know the time, doesn't care about the time, but it's late enough the crickets have stopped calling, and she can see a sliver of the moon high in the sky through Katie's parted curtains. Katie's murmured counting is the only sound beside the creaks and groans of the house. The light woke Joanne, even though Katie only switched on the small lamp by her vanity and not the brighter overhead. Tangled in bed sheets, in silence Joanne watched her sister change from her diner uniform into shorts and a cami. As she watched, she wondered when her body might start to curve like that.

'. . . forty-seven, forty-eight, forty-nine, fifty.' Katie sets down the brush and moves her long hair from one shoulder to the other. She picks up the brush again, eyes never leaving the mirror. 'Fifty-one, fifty-two, fifty-three . . .' Brush gliding smoothly through the hair, not one single tangle. Voice steady and slow as a lullaby. As hushed.

'Katie . . .' Sleep thick in her voice.

The brush stops. Katie turns. Blonde strands lifting from her shoulder with the sudden movement. 'Shit! Sorry, Lady, I didn't mean to wake you.'

'It's OK.' A yawn she can't control.

Katie turns back to the mirror. Brush back to hair, steady once again. She watches her younger sister's reflection. 'Go back to sleep. I'll only be another minute.'

Joanne rolls onto her side, facing her sister. Fluffs the pillow up more under her head. Kicks one leg free from the tangled sheets. Shadows from the lamp cross and overlap each other on the wooden floor. Joanne can make out what some shadows are – Katie's perfume bottle, a teddy bear, the roses hung up and dried that Josh had given Katie when he first asked her out – but other shadows are lost in darkness, and all shape is lost to Joanne's sleep-filled eyes. 'It's OK. I'm not tired.'

Katie laughs. 'Yeah, right, kiddo. *OK.*' And she winks at her sister in the mirror. Playful. Teasing.

Joanne smiles. Tries to hide another yawn. Fails.

'Seventy-one, seventy-two, seventy-three . . .' The brushstrokes almost hypnotic on the gently glowing golden hair. It's like Katie's hair lights up the room. Joanne wants to touch it. Wants to comb through it with her fingers, wants to hold that light, but she knows Katie won't let her. She never lets her play with her hair.

'Katie?'

'Ummmmm?'

'Why do you think Mom was so cross?'

'When?'

'At dinner.'

'Was she?'

'You didn't notice?'

The brush pauses. Resumes. 'Yeah, OK, I guess I did.'

'Do you think she'll take me swimming next week? I don't understand why askin' made her so angry.'

'It wasn't you, hon. Mom's just going through a lot.'

Silence stretches through the room, broken only by the distant ticking of a clock. Joanne bites a hangnail. Pulls the skin loose with her teeth and swallows it. She tastes blood from where the skin broke and sucks her finger to stop the blood spreading around the base of the nail. She likes the rubbery feel of the skin in her mouth. Works it between her teeth. A bad habit. One she's only half trying to break.

'That's gross.' Katie's seen her in the mirror. Nose wrinkled in distaste. 'That is *so* disgusting.'

Joanne giggles, embarrassed. 'No, it's not!' Still giggling, she pulls the sheets up higher to her chin. Kicks her other foot free.

Nose still wrinkled, Katie shakes her head. 'Ewww.' Brush glides smoothly.

Joanne watches, silent. Downstairs, the grandfather clock strikes the hour and its chime echoes softly through the sleeping house.

'The Saunders' new truck drove by earlier.'

Katie's hand freezes mid-air, brush suspended. Cautiously, she lowers it back to her hair. Resumes. Voice forced passive, steady. 'What happened?'

'Nothing. It just drove by.'

'You're sure it was that truck?'

Joanne tosses onto her back. Suspends a leg up long into the air and looks at her foot. Indian brown with dirt under the nails. She wonders if maybe she should start painting her nails. Like Katie does. Wonders if maybe Katie might let her borrow her polish. 'I think so.'

'You have to be sure, Joanne. This is important.' Strain in the hoarseness of the whisper.

Surprised, Joanne looks back to Katie. She's turned around on her stool and is facing Joanne, leaning forward slightly, a line of worry etched into her brow. Same line Mom has, but not as deep. Joanne lowers her leg, feels the coolness of the sheet meet the arch of her foot. Likes the feeling. Curls her toes around it.

'Why don't we talk to the Saunders, Katie?'

Her sister looks at her long and hard. A sizing-up look, and Joanne knows it. Can feel it. She wonders what it is that Katie is trying to see in her. Prays to God she finds it. Whispers, softly, 'Please tell me.'

Katie turns slowly back to the mirror. Picks up the brush, discarded on the vanity. Turns it over in her hand, regarding it before raising it to her head. Starts again to brush her hair, slow and steady, as though each stroke holds weight. 'Eighty-five, eighty-six, eighty-seven . . . If Mom won't take you swimming next week, I will. How's that sound, Lady?' In the mirror, Katie smiles.

Joanne sits up so fast she's dizzy. 'You *know*, don't you? I just know you *know*! Why won't you tell me? This is *so* unfair!' The last words a high-pitched whine.

'Ssssh!' Katie hisses. 'Shut up or you'll wake Mom.'

Joanne bites her pouting lip. Glares at her sister's reflection. 'It's 'cause of *him*, isn't it?' She can't keep the excitement from her voice. 'It's 'cause of Uncle Jasper.'

Through the mirror, eyes lock and hold. At length, Katie nods.

Joanne pulls her knees to her chest and wraps her arms around them. Even across the room she can smell grease from the diner still thick on Katie's skin, cigarette smoke still cloudy in her sister's golden hair. Most nights Joanne would hate sleeping next to her sister when she smells like that. But not tonight. Not now that she can feel Katie softening. Excitement rises like butterflies in Joanne's chest.

'He hurt someone, didn't he?'

In the mirror, Katie nods.

Joanne can feel her heart racing, slamming against her ribs, trying to break free as she tries to pull her still sleep-clouded thoughts together. 'He hurt one of the Saunders? That's why they won't talk to Mom?'

A hesitation. In the mirror, Katie nods.

'What'd he do?' She crosses her legs and leans forward on the bed, whisper strained with excitement.

'You ask too many questions.' A snapped reply. Then, softer, 'Just be careful, OK? Don't talk to the Saunders.'

'They don't talk to us anyway.'

Katie's reflection is drawn and serious. A cloudiness across her eyes Joanne does not recognize. It clears, and Katie smiles. 'Just don't talk to no strangers, OK? Saunders or no Saunders.' She winks. Forced wink. Forced smile. Brush back to hair. Slow and steady with each stroke. Under her breath, 'Ninety-four, ninety-five, ninety-six . . .'

Mind racing, Joanne listens to the whispers fade. There's a million questions she wants to ask, but she

71

knows Katie won't answer them. Not now. She's got to be careful. She likes that her sister is trusting her more. Doesn't want to push and spoil it. Joanne wonders if maybe one day they will tell each other secrets again, like they did when they were little. She picks one floating question. One of the millions spinning round her head. One she thinks Katie might actually answer. 'Was it like that when Daddy was around?'

Brush strokes pause mid ninety-nine. 'Was what?'

'Dinner. Was it always silent like that? Is that what it's like to be a family?'

Second half of ninety-nine somehow tangles, catches in the hair, and Katie pulls it free. 'We've always been a family.' Eyes search for hers, reflected in the mirror.

One hundred does not catch, and Katie places the hairbrush down.

'Morning, Elizabeth.'

The truck door slams behind him, the sound foreign among the softer tones of morning.

'Reverend.'

He smiles. 'Mighty fine day, isn't it?'

She regards him coolly. Takes in his gut, the sweat on his brow, the sweat marks already forming on the crisp white of his newly pressed shirt, small circles round his armpits quickly forming, spreading. Now that he has emerged from the comfort of his fancy new pickup's a/c, the reverend struggles in the heat, large form moving awkwardly in the thick humidity. She says nothing. Waits for him to speak.

Around them the prairie stretches brown and dry as

72

ever, parched earth screaming for rain, the sky unmerciful blue and cloudless. He pauses at the foot of the porch steps. Smiles. 'I know I said it last time, but your roses truly are divine, Elizabeth. My wife would be mighty jealous if she saw them.'

'Come on in, Reverend.' No welcome in her tone.

They sit across from each other at the kitchen table. Coffee's already been poured and now sits before them cooling. At length, the reverend breaks the silence. 'How are you, Elizabeth? And the girls. Y'all doing OK out here?' She watches him survey the room, glance out to the hallway. She can guess what he's looking for.

'We're just fine, Reverend. Good as ever.'

'I'm glad to hear that. I truly am. I know you've kept yourself scarce from church since your mother died – no, don't argue, Elizabeth, you know it's true, and that's not for me to question. I reckon that's between you and God. I ain't here to lecture you today.' He chuckles. 'I just want you to know that we haven't forgotten about y'all. We still remember your mother in our prayers each Sunday.'

'That's mighty kind of you.' Voice hard, unrelenting.

'Well . . .' He regards her a moment and shifts his weight. 'It ain't really a matter of kindness, Elizabeth, it's just the Christian thing to do. And, as I said, we worry about you and the girls all alone out here.'

'Reverend, I don't hold much on ceremony so I'll cut straight to the point. As I see it, small-talk wastes breath. Mama's been gone a long time now, and it's only the last few days that y'all found it in your hearts to remember my girls 'n' me. We both know why you're really here.'

He doesn't try to deny her statement. Sips his coffee

instead. Looks at her long and hard over his cup as he chooses his words with care, thinking each over in his head. At length, he says only, 'Is he here?'

'Yes.'

The reverend smiles. Nervous. A quick smile that does not reach his eyes. 'Is he . . . well?'

'Depends what you mean by that, Reverend. Something makes me guess you aren't enquiring about his health.'

A nervous laugh. In the silence that follows, a drop from the faucet can be heard falling. A stair creaks under the pressure of a footstep. Laughter drifts in from outside where Joanne is chasing chickens as she does their feed. A bobwhite calls its name, falls silent and calls again. A fly buzzes in the window and rests and is still.

'Morning, Reverend.' His voice still husky with sleep, hair a tangled mess, one of their daddy's old flannel shirts unbuttoned halfway down his chest. He fills the door-frame and leans just inside it. Not overpowering. Not aggressive. And yet there is a menace to his presence that makes Lizzie miss a breath and wonder once again whom she has let into her home. The reverend tenses. He places his coffee cup down quickly, too quickly, and coffee sloshes over, spilling onto the table. Milky white in the brown as it pools.

'Morning, Jasper.' He struggles to regain his composure. 'I – I – I was just, ah, asking about you there.' His smile twitches where the lip turns up. Freezes there and sticks.

Jasper moves with ease into the room. As though he belongs there. As though he has always belonged there.

74

He crosses it in four easy strides, takes a mug from the press and pours himself some coffee. The kettle is still hot. Carefully he adds milk. Stirs in sugar. Then he smiles at the reverend. An easy Sunday-morning smile like he's no care in the world. 'I've been meaning to call in to you, Reverend. Was thinking I might stop by on Sunday morning. It's been far too long since I heard a proper sermon.'

The reverend pales. He opens his mouth to speak, but words fail him and he sits, mouth gaping wide, as though his jaw, long overworked, has finally broken down. Jasper's eyes sparkle as he watches the other man's discomfort. He pulls a chair out from the table, letting its legs screech as they scrape across the floor, and seats himself beside the reverend. Sips his coffee, smiles, blows once on the brew, then places the mug on the table to cool. To her surprise, Lizzie finds words have left her, too. She rises quickly, and a burst of blood shoots up into her head, dizzying her. She blinks to steady herself. To regain vision. Crosses the room and reaches across the counter and grabs the dish towel and comes back to the table and wipes up the coffee the reverend spilled. Coffee stains right through the fabric as it soaks it up.

Jasper pushes his chair back from the table so he can stretch his legs out long. Leans his weight back so that the chair's two front legs rise up off the floor. Just a little bit. He crosses his arms behind his head, the fabric of his flannel shirt pulling up a bit to partially expose his stomach. Dark hairs twist and curl out of the gap between it and his jeans. Mama would have been ashamed seeing him sit in front of the reverend like that. And, for Mama's sake, Lizzie feels her own blood begin to simmer, even as another part of her can't help but share in Jasper's amusement at the reverend's open trout-mouthed stare. As she walks back to the sink and wrings out the towel, Lizzie imagines smacking Jasper, like Mama would have. Imagines the sound the chair would make as the wooden legs hit the linoleum. Wordlessly, she rinses, then twists the towel dry. Shakes it.

'Yessir,' Jasper says cheerfully, at the table behind her. 'Sure has been an awful long time since I heard a proper sermon. Can't exactly say the services inside were inspired.' And he chuckles softly, almost to himself. 'What's Sunday's topic, Reverend?'

The reverend's mouth closes sharply. Reopens. He looks down at the table where the coffee had spilled. Blinks as though expecting it still to be there. Glances around quickly, uncertainly, as he struggles to regain his composure. No joy in the false cheer of his voice when he answers, but then again, Lizzie thinks, for once no falseness either.

'Forgiveness.'

A fly brushes past Lizzie's cheek, buzzing loudly in her ear, and she fumbles and almost drops the dish towel mid-fold. She lays it down flat on the counter and irons it with her hands till the wrinkles spread and dissolve smooth. Shakes it once and hangs it back up on the rack, then turns, walks back to the table and sits down. Back straight.

'Forgiveness.' Jasper rolls the word off his tongue slowly, as though trying it, tasting it, for the first time. 'Forgiveness.' He nods slowly, looking down towards his

76

feet. Unhooks his hands from behind his head and leans forward in his chair, elbows on knees, head down, hands entwined before him in a single clasped fist. Almost like praying. Almost.

Lizzie takes a sip of her coffee. Holds the mug to feel the heat of the brew relax into her palms. Glances at the reverend. His face still unnaturally pale. Tries to force her own voice sweet. 'More coffee, Reverend?'

He looks at her as if he'd forgotten she was there. 'Oh . . .' Looks back down into his mug. Still half full. 'Uh, no, Elizabeth, uh, thank you, no . . .' and his words fade as his eyes drift back to focus on the man beside him.

'Forgiveness,' Jasper says again. And then he nods. A solid, definitive nod. He sits up straight and meets the reverend's eyes. 'That's a mighty fine topic for a sermon, Reverend.'

'Why . . . uh . . . thank you, Jasper.' The reverend looks awkward there in the kitchen sitting in that chair. Too stiff. Straight-backed when his frame seems more accustomed to slouching. Oversized. Uncomfortable. Somehow it never seemed so strange to see him sitting there back when Mama was alive. But that was a long time ago now, over cups of coffee long since rinsed and dried.

''N' what was your sermon on last week, Reverend?'

Lizzie can guess how much it costs him, can see the stress slowly etching into the reverend's sweaty brow, but he meets Jasper's stare, his own gaze steady, firm. Despite herself, Lizzie respects him for that. Just a little.

'Being kind unto one's neighbour.' His voice does not

crack. Does not falter. It's the voice from the pulpit on Sunday mornings. The voice she used to tune out when Bobby would brush her fingertips in the pew.

Jasper smiles. ''N' next week, Reverend?'

'Well . . . I haven't yet decided. One week at a time, son, one week at a time.'

The two men regard each other in silence for a moment. Jasper's eyes do not leave the reverend's face. 'I reckon that's an important lesson to learn. Forgiveness.'

'Well, yes, Jasper. Forgiveness is a fine thing. A powerful thing. Something earned.' His eyes shift, sizing Jasper up. Taking him in. 'Though all Jesus's lessons were important.' He smiles. 'I would hope you've remembered that.' He forces a chuckle, the sound a hollow echo in the otherwise quiet kitchen.

From outside another burst of Joanne's laughter drifts in, only to fade as quickly as it came, leaving the kitchen once more still. A chill creeps down Lizzie's spine and makes her shudder, though the room itself cooks oven hot. Not much of a breeze blows in the open window and, though early, the day's already a scorcher. Lizzie wonders at the chill. *Maybe it's just me.* A fly buzzes and settles on the press and Lizzie watches it a moment. Its front legs rise and rub together, then touch its face. She waits to hear its buzz, but even the fly seems silent.

The reverend clears his throat. Shifts his large frame in his chair. Lizzie's eyes move from fly to reverend to brother and back again. And again. Gaze unable to settle. To rest.

At length, Jasper reaches forward and grabs hold of his mug and takes a long, slow sip. 'Oh, I remember,

Reverend, I remember.' Words soft as a breeze. As gentle. He smiles. 'Jesus said to turn the other cheek, didn't he?'

'Yes . . .'

''N' he said repent, 'n' he'd forgive. Ain't that right?'

The reverend's cheeks pinken, though whether from discomfort or heat, Lizzie cannot be certain. He pauses a moment, weighing his words. His options. 'That's right.'

Jasper nods. Smiles slightly. 'And what do you think, Reverend? Do you think God forgives?'

'If you forgive men when they sin against you, your heavenly Father will also forgive you. But if you do not forgive men their sins, your Father will not forgive your sins. Matthew six: fourteen.' Spoken in that pulpit voice. Unwavering.

Lizzie looks at her brother. His face is soft. The softest she's seen it since . . . well, since long before.

As she watches, Jasper nods again. No rush to his action, as though his movements operate suspended in some sort of uncertainty. He says, 'Now I don't mean no disrespect, Reverend, but I was hoping for your thoughts on this, not words straight from the Bible.'

'The Bible is God's word, son. I was under the impression it was His forgiveness you were enquiring about.' Cold words despite the plastered-on smile. Cold eyes above it.

'It was your sermon I asked after.'

The reverend picks up his coffee, then sets the mug down without taking a sip. He opens his mouth to speak again, that same trout-mouthed pause. Says nothing.

To Lizzie's amazement, Jasper smiles. No malice in his eyes, no anger hidden in his lips. It's the warmest smile

Lizzie's seen cross his face these last few days. The warmest she's seen since long before the trouble started. She wonders why he hasn't smiled like that at her. At her girls.

'You know,' Jasper says, 'I always liked that thought – turning the other cheek. That's forgiveness, ain't it? Reckon that always made sense to me somehow.'

She puts her mug down too hard on the table and it rattles against the wood as it spins for balance. Loud. Too loud in the quiet of the kitchen. Both men turn to her, startled, as though they had forgotten she was there. She gets up from the table fast, cheeks burning, anger rising, though she's not sure exactly why. *It's that smile. That goddamn smile.* That smile that is not hers. The scrape of her chair against the linoleum as she rises from the table startles her. She snaps, 'Doesn't work no more once you've turned both cheeks.' Then she turns and walks to the sink, empties and rinses out her mug.

'Elizabeth . . .' Confusion in the reverend's tone.

She cuts him off. Turns back to face the men. Can't hold back. Doesn't try to. Feels herself crumble, dissolve, melt before them, and even as the words slip off her tongue, she already regrets them, regrets being so raw. Being seen so raw. 'Reverend, I appreciate your faith. I appreciate your new-found, overbearing Christian concern for myself and my daughters. I can appreciate that you've come here with all your best Christian intentions. But God turned His back on this family long ago. 'N' it don't matter none how many cheeks are turned. The slaps just keep on comin'. So I'd kindly appreciate it if you 'n' all your moral concerns regarding myself 'n' my brother 'n' my family would kindly leave us the fuck alone. Sure as heck we need help. We need healin'. I ain't too proud to admit that. I ain't sayin' we's OK 'n' things out here is perfect. But God ain't gonna patch us up, Reverend. He ain't been out here listenin' to none of our prayers. 'N' I won't have neither of you puttin' such ideas in my girls' heads. What we got out here is each other. 'N' God got nothin' to do with that. Not any more. Far as I see it, not ever.'

Silence thick in the kitchen as her words fade out. Not even a drip from the faucet. Not even the buzz of a fly.

Then Jasper's voice, cotton soft. Softer. Goosedown soft. Feathers flying. She feels the fire leave her eyes as she meets his. Her brother's eyes. Sad and lonely and understanding. 'God still listens.'

Silence between them.

Silence around them.

She turns back to the sink.

Behind her the reverend clears his throat. Voice forced cheery. In this moment, she hates him. For his happiness. His selfishness in their hard times, his self-righteousness. The judgements. For all the gossip she can guess he's spread around the town. Years and years of hurtful gossip. *Mama trusted you.* She can feel the falseness of his smile in his words. Doesn't turn.

'Well, thank you for the coffee, Elizabeth.'

Jasper stands beside his sister in silence as they watch the reverend's shiny red pickup reverse down the drive. At the gate the reverend pauses and tips his hat to them before pulling out onto the road and easing back towards town. Jasper raises his hand to the other man in farewell, though does not wave. Lizzie stands in silence, arms crossed, unsmiling. They watch the pickup till it reaches the horizon, becomes a dot and disappears. Fluffy white clouds slowly drift south-east, no sign of rain inside them. The scent of roses drifts up from the garden only to fade as the breeze drops and dies down. Heat sticky on their skin. Far off, across the prairie, burned grasses meet the blue of the sky, like golden sand stretching into a wave-less sea.

Lizzie saw the ocean once. Eighteen years ago. With Bobby on their honeymoon. It frightened her. The crash of the waves. Their froth and foam. And the crabs that nibbled at her toes underwater. They drove to Galveston in darkness. Windows rolled down in the pickup the whole way, and when they neared the coast, she could taste salt in the breeze. They stayed in a motel right on the beach. Three nights, four days. All they could afford. A dream come true. She heard the ocean before she ever saw it, on that dark, windy drive. A roar she could feel inside her that was like nothing on the prairie. Not even the hollow, desperate roar of winter winds that some-times shook the house. Bobby carried her from the pickup that night right into the motel room and laid her on the bed, and that was all that mattered that first night. All that ever mattered.

Sometimes, oddly, the prairie takes her back to those sandy days. Sometimes sea and sky seem kin, and Lizzie can imagine sand between her toes again and Bobby's lips on hers. Back then, though, gazing out at different shades of blue met on the horizon, she had felt lost and small, and had craved the comfort of the prairie around them again. She didn't tell Bobby that. She never told Bobby that. When he turned to her and said, 'I could stay out here for ever,' she had smiled and taken his hand, and said, 'Me, too.' But those words were lies.

Today is one of those days. One of those sea-and-sky days that bring her back. But she doesn't want to go there. Not now. Not today. She doesn't want to see the ocean again. Not without Bobby by her side.

Jasper's words bring her crashing back. To the heat. To the reverend's truck just now out of sight far off across the prairie. To her shame and pride, all tangled up and mixed together. And tangled up some more.

'Did you mean all that in there?'

She leans against the railing of the porch, considering his question. Stares down at the rail before her. Picks a fleck of paint off it with her nails. *House could use a new coat soon.* 'Yeah, I meant it.'

Jasper nods. Silent.

She smooths a peeling fleck of paint down with her fingers, pressing it into the wood, but it does not reattach. Pops right back up the instant her finger leaves it. Softly, 'Do you really intend to go to church on Sunday?'

He turns to her, eyes trying to read her face, but the hard, masked profile that will not meet his gaze offers up no secrets. 'I do.'

Silence between them as they both look out over the prairie. Standing on the shaded porch, the heat is not so bad. Sticky still, but less burning than in the direct sun. *Too dry for mosquitoes, though, and that's at least somethin'.*

At length, he asks, 'Will you drive me?'

83

'To church?' She turns to him, and they regard one another in silence, her body braced, his at ease.

He nods.

She studies him for a long time before answering, her eyes searching his more deeply than his search hers. 'What are you lookin' for, Jasper? What on earth are you hopin' for there?'

He smiles then. His big-brother smile. The one he gave her when she was crying after Daddy's belt had smacked her. Or that time when she'd been climbing up behind him on the apple tree out back and had fallen off the branch, tumbling down onto the lawn, arms and legs all over the place. He had smiled down at her from the branches. So kind. So understanding. But him up there. And her below. And he had only called down, 'You OK?' and when she'd whimpered, 'Yes,' he had not come down to comfort her. She'd scraped her knee. Skin peeled right off and underneath all bloody. But somehow his smile had warmed her. Made her feel brave enough not to cry. It's that smile he gives her now. That same big-brother smile that always gave her strength.

Softly, he says, 'I ain't lookin' for God, Lizzie.'

'What then?'

He stares out across the prairie. Burned grasses rustle in the breeze, composing their own symphony as dry stalks rub together. The roses around the house are shockingly red in contrast to the dried-out land. The sky above so vast. So ocean blue. There is anger in his eyes, and sadness too, and she's sorry for that.

'I just aim to live again.' He turns from her then and walks down the porch steps out onto the lawn. Turns back to her halfway across the garden. 'I'll weed out the flowerbeds, if you like. Saw some dandelions startin' up near the primroses. You let 'em flower 'n' next you know whole garden'll be weeds.'

Once, she used to pick dandelions. Used to wish on them and blow their seeds out across the prairie. But that was long ago. She meets his eyes, and he nods once, then turns to walk round the back.

The dirt feels good against his hands. Cool. Like the sun hasn't had a chance to cook it and toast it and burn it, as it seems to have everything else, which he supposes it hasn't. Untouched. That's how it feels. Yes, he likes that. The earth feels 'untouched'. Except he's touching it now, and he likes that too. He's feeling it roll cool over his hands. Get stuck, cool and sticky under his nails. Like mortar. He's the first one ever to touch it, this particular earth, in this particular way, and he likes that, too. He smiles at the thought. And he likes the way the smile feels stretched across his face. Not quite happy, not quite not, but it feels good all the same. Been a while since he smiled so much, and the muscles on his face still feel unaccustomed to the motion, feel at times like maybe they're stretched the wrong way round.

Jasper digs the trowel deep into the flowerbed, and scoops out another weed, sticky earth still clinging to its roots. Roots long and thin as a woman's hair. As tangled. And it makes him think of her for a moment, her hair all tangled and dirty, matted up in his dirty hands that last time, and the blood darkening her lips, and he drops the weed, surprised, his smile quickly falling. But it's just a dandelion. He sees that again now. The roots, fair and thin and blonde. Her hair was midnight. Darker maybe. Thicker. Darker even than this earth. He shakes his head to clear it. It's the heat, he tells himself, it must be the heat fucking with my mind. And he picks up the trowel, metal handle hot in his hands. Roots another dandelion out.

He can smell the rich musky odour of the earth on his hands. Mud and manure and whatever else Lizzie's piled up beneath the roses to keep them growing so fresh in such a drought. Mama used to crack raw eggs over the rosebush roots. Used to say that gave them life. And she'd wink when she said it, the laugh lines around her eyes winking at him, too. He wonders if Lizzie does that now. The eggs. Wonders if that's her secret. Inside, he used to dream sometimes of digging out. They all did. Would all have paid good money back then for the rusty trowel gripped firmly in his hand. He smiles. Inhales the rich odour of the earth crumbling across his hands. Smells like freedom.

It strikes him as odd how much he's enjoying the feel of the cool earth against his hands. Back when Daddy was alive he couldn't stand it. Couldn't stand the smell. Growing things never came naturally to Jasper, and he can feel inside himself that that has not changed. Weeding, though, that's different. That's something useful he can do. And it feels right somehow, pulling out the dandelions like this – rough as they're pulled from the earth, but somehow a gentleness to the action, too, like he's releasing them. Feels good to end their lives.

When he was a boy, he plucked a whole bouquet of dandelions once. Not when they were pretty yellow flowers, but aged already, white and feathery and ready to spread their seeds. Must have been a dozen clutched in his tiny scabby hand. And he had to be careful for the wind not to blow them and ruin them. Those were Lizzie's wishes. The wind couldn't be let steal them. And he made sure of that.

Her eyes lit up when she saw them. The dandelions. She was so tiny back then. So frail, it had seemed to him, a tiny thing to protect, though she'd always been a tomboy, too, had always been there behind him trying to keep up, begging him to let her tag along. It was after the first time Daddy smacked her, the dandelion bouquet. Jasper can't remember what it was she'd said or done. He's not sure he ever even rightfully knew at the time. But it was the first time Daddy's wrath had fallen down upon her – that was how small she was. And so Jasper went out among the tall prairie grasses and he plucked her that bouquet. Grasses chest high, that was how small he was. And then, inside, he found her under her covers hiding, sobbing into her pillow, cheek all pink and raw. And he gave her that bouquet. And whispered, 'Hush now, I brought you somethin'.' And when she'd wiped her red eyes and finally turned to him, her whole little face glowed gold. That's how he remembers it. Gold. And he gave her each dandelion one by one instead of all together, and told her to make a wish, and blow it out, and there were dandelion seeds scattered all over her quilt, all across her room. That's how he likes to think of Lizzie. That's how, inside, he remembers her. Back before. Back when she still thought wishes came true. Back when he thought they just might, too.

Hands buried deep in the soil, Jasper tugs at another weed, fingers blindly entwining with its roots. The rich smell of the earth around him distracts, and it takes Jasper a while to realize he is being watched. Later, thinking back, he can't quite say what first alerted him. Maybe she moved. Or a twig snapped. Or a breath was slightly louder than the rest or a little out of place, out of pace with the others. Or maybe he just looked up. But when he did see Doe Eyes standing uncertainly by the edge of the porch, half masked by its shade, he was not surprised. Couldn't quite identify the feeling, but it was like a part of him knew she was watching. Felt her watching. Expected it all along.

The girl smiles when their eyes meet. Like that's what she's been waiting for. For him to look up. Simple as that. Too much understanding for a little girl's eyes. Bobby's eyes, as quick to judge, yet so much of Lizzie there too: the brown skin and thin limbs, and dirty blonde hair. For a second, squinting into the sun, Jasper thinks it is Lizzie, standing there, watching him. The Lizzie of his memories. Eyes refocusing, he sits back on his heels. Wipes sweat from his brow with the back of his dirt-streaked hand, leaving a small trail of soil where his knuckles rubbed.

'I want to show you something.' She turns and hurries around further into the shady side of the house.

Slowly, Jasper rises. Knees stiff. Back stiff from bending over the flowerbeds so long. He glances at the house, tall and silent and weathered beside him. Lace curtains drawn, like no one's home, but windows opened wide. He drops the trowel onto the flowerbed, where it lands with a soft thud, and, without thinking, wipes the earth from his hands onto his jeans. Realizes the stains caused only as his hands come up clean. But it's too late by then.

Doe Eyes' head peeks back around the corner of the house. 'Come on!' Then disappears again.

He follows.

It's not far. Just out behind the house and round the other side of the chicken coop. He stops when she does. Not sure what he's supposed to be looking at, he waits for her to speak. Her eyes are glowing. So blue. So bright in the shade of the coop, and her dark blonde hair seems like prairie grass, burned some cross of caramel and brown, glowing golden toffee as it blows in the breeze. But she doesn't speak, just stands there, smiling. Then, impatient, 'Don't you see it?'

He glances across the prairie again. Across the gold. Looks back to the house. At the coop, red paint peeling. At the girl. 'See what?'

She stamps her foot. A childish gesture. Impatient and rash. And he feels better seeing it, seeing the child in her so clear. Still, it's been years since he was around a child. Or a woman. Still seems strange to keep their company. To keep anyone's company outside wrought-iron bars and tall electric fences.

'There! Don't you see it?' Voice nearing a whine, Doe Eyes points to the back of the coop.

Once-red paint weathered nearly brown now peels off it in long, thick strips. Flakes off in tiny chips. Shady this side, the far side from the house, the house shadow stretched long and thin across the back lawn, like a finger reaching towards them. He can hear the hens inside the coop, clucking. The soft ruffle of their feathers. Can smell their shit. Their soiled straw. His eyes glint, pupils dilate, as they adjust to the shadows of the light behind the shed. And then he sees it. There, attached to the back of the coop, rests the paper thin exoskeleton of a cicada, shed and discarded in its final moult. Now hollow and empty. Ghostly in its frame.

He squats down next to the July fly so that it is eye level. Brown and flaky as an autumn leaf. As frail. He can see right through where its eye once was. 'Well, I'll be . . .' His breath releases in a soft whistle as he bends closer.

'Cool, isn't it?' Her eyes are glowing.

'I reckon that's one word for it.'

They stare in silence at the discarded husk before them. She kneels on the grass beside him. A tiny crack along the spine where the July fly shed its skin and climbed free. He imagines the creature, all slimy and new. Wonders where it went. Where it is now. At length, Jasper turns to the girl beside him. 'Do you want it?' he asks. But he does not wait for her answer. Rises quickly, crosses the lawn and snaps a small branch off of a shrub. Returns and kneels at Doe Eyes' side again, twig in hand. The girl watches his every movement. He can feel her eyes on him, prying into him, but he doesn't turn to meet her gaze. Ignores it. Bends over the July fly's shell instead. Intent.

The shade from the chicken coop across his face feels good, cool. Studying the task before him, Jasper whispers, 'We've got to be real careful now,' and gently pries at the creature's legs with his tiny twig. Inside the coop, a chicken clucks as feathers rustle feathers, sound muted through the weathered boards.

'You know,' Jasper continues softly, 'it's a rare thing to find a July fly's husk like this. Takes thirteen years for 'em to shed their skins. Did you know that? Yep, thirteen years.' Gently he shakes one leg loose from its grip on the coop. Moves on to the next. Hand steady. 'That's longer than you've been livin', ain't it?'

She giggles.

The second leg comes free. 'I got to be real careful now, you see, so as I don't crack the shell. It's a frail thing, a July fly's skin. Like china.' He smiles. 'See how you can nearly see right through it? Yep,' he murmurs, more to himself now than to the girl. 'It sure is just 'bout paper thin.'

He can feel the girl's breath across his fingers, warm and sticky, as he slowly works the July fly free. He likes the feel of it. The catches in it as sometimes she holds a breath or skips one, afraid he'll crack the shell. He wants to be careful for her. Wants his hands to be steady enough, tender enough, not to ruin it. For her. But it's been a long time since he felt another's breath upon him.

'Careful!' she gasps on her inhale, and he likes the breathless feel of it across his hands. *Yes, careful, Jasper, careful.* And he struggles to focus on the bug before him. Third leg pried free. Fourth. The husk rattles slightly in the breeze, barely holding the shed now. The hollow eye sockets stare out bleakly. Blindly. He thinks back to his first night back home, and wonders why Lizzie mentioned it then. That memory. Wonders why she brought up the July fly from all those years back that, when he was a boy, shed its skin on him. All those years back. 'Mistook him for a tree.' That's what Mama'd said. *Mistook him for a tree . . .*

'Must feel good to hold onto someone and shed your skin like that.' That's what he'd told Lizzie that first night home. He repeats the words to himself now, as he struggles with the July fly's final legs.

Doe Eyes leans closer, watching him, breath trapped inside her as she holds it, suspends it, waiting. His hand falters. The final leg snaps. A sound softer than a twig broken underfoot, more the sound a leaf makes, falling. But crisper.

Jasper does not see the leg break off. He does not see where the limb lands. Though he hears its snap amplified, ringing in his skull. The exoskeleton falls free into his palm. Dry as a corn husk. Pebble smooth. And he has to struggle to control his hand not to fist around it. He stops himself just in time. Uncurls his fingers to reveal the shell cradled in his palm. Five-legged. Deformed. A face not even a mother could love. Grotesque and beautiful. Transfixed, he stares.

Doe Eyes' breath releases in a sudden gush, and she claps her hands and laughs. 'You did it, Uncle Jasper! You got it!'

In his palm, it seems mummified. Shrunken. He looks up into her blue eyes. Child eyes. Woman eyes. Extends his hands out to her. 'Do you want to touch it?'

She grins. Nods. A little girl's nod, filled with excitement. She reaches out her index finger and gently runs it along the side of the shell. Wrinkles her nose. 'It feels funny.'

He smiles. 'I collected these when I was a boy. Had a whole row of July flies up on my windowsill.'

'Really?' Big blue eyes pop up to meet his, then fall again. 'What happened to 'em?'

He shrugs, but does not incline his head. His smile feels forced, like it's bent the wrong way round. 'Maybe they came back to life 'n' flew off somewhere. Maybe they shed new skins.'

She giggles. 'Don't be silly.'

'Well, then,' his smile broadens, 'maybe they're just hidin' somewheres.'

'Can I have it?'

He looks down into his palm. At the broken form within it. 'Yeah, you can have it.' A pause. 'Hold out your hands.' He picks the July fly up and places it in the girl's cupped palms. 'Careful now, or you'll break him.'

She giggles, gazing down with a mixture of delight and disgust. 'How do you know it's a him?' Blue eyes up to his.

He pauses.

She pops right up off the grass, all brown and gold and taller than him. Doesn't wait for an answer. Long legs and long arms not quite yet grown into. Seems odd to look up at her. She hesitates a moment, once standing, glances down at Jasper, and he thinks for a moment that she's gonna speak to him, gonna say something, but she doesn't. Just smiles instead. This goofy kid smile that doesn't mix so good with the woman she's becoming. And the smile makes him feel funny inside. Warm. A feeling he's not used to. Then, still grinning, Doe Eyes calls, 'I'm gonna go show Mom!' and she runs off, July fly cupped in her palms before her. 'Mom! . . . Mom! . . . Mom!' getting fainter and fainter as she nears the house.

Jasper stays on the grass a while, listening to her voice and footsteps fade. Leans his back against the coop. His head. Feels good sitting in the shade like that. A respite from the brutal sun. I could get used to this, he thinks. *Yes, sir, I sure could get used to this.*

Yet another slow night at the diner. Wasn't too bad at the start. A few truckers from up north en route to Waco had passed through and stopped in for their suppers. A rowdy bunch, but decent tippers. Katie always likes it when the diner has a bit of a buzz inside it – makes the nights pass faster. But after that first haul of truckers had gobbled up their feed and pulled off in their eighteen-wheelers, not another single hungry soul had called round for supper, and Katie found herself looking and looking again at the Elvis clock hanging by the door.

It is late now, though, and the diner nearly echoes, it's so quiet. Radio's been shut off already, and the ketchup bottles have been filled, as have the salt and pepper shakers. Cutlery's been rolled and laid out for the morning. Tables, only just washed down, glisten as though new, muted lamplight hiding the chips and scuffs that in daylight mar them. The lights in the pie case and the glass Coca-Cola fridge have been shut off, and now both stand dark and solemn and cool.

From the kitchen, final pots and pans can be heard banging as Tom hangs them up for the night. Above the kitchen's clatter, his whistle drifts in and out of hearing. A Bing Crosby tune that had played on the radio earlier that evening. Katie smiles, hearing it. Hums along with him in her head, though she can't remember the words exactly. Something about a lover saying what's in his heart. Or not saying it. She searches her memory. The only words she can recall are the chorus. 'So take the sweetest phrases the world has ever known, And make believe I've said them all to you.' She smiles and shakes her head. Why is it Tom only ever hums sad songs when they're locking up?

The lights on the highway sign were shut off nearing half an hour ago, and the diner strikes Katie as gloomy without the familiar warm glow of the pink neon lettering reflected in the windows to wash across the floor. Usually the mirror image of the *ny's* in 'Penny's Diner' reflects inside and spreads out across the tiles, staining them light pink. Bubble-gum pink. Except translucent. Katie likes that. The transparent shine of it. But now the only light comes from the overhead lamp, and there is nothing warm about its glow.

Katie is mopping the floor. Her final task. Once that's done, all she needs to do is let Tom know the front is clear so he can come out and lock up behind her. Katie usually hurried the mopping. Couldn't wait to get out of there and home. But things are different now. Home is different now. And Katie takes her time as she dips the mop in and out of the soapy water, as she wrings it and lifts it, and watches the tiles start to shine. Fact is, she doesn't like Joanne not knowing. Doesn't like her sister's pestering questions. The answers she does not have to tell her. The others she cannot share. Katie doesn't like the thought of coming home to that. She knows how Joanne's mind works. She knows Joanne will start to hunt for answers. And that scares Katie. That's what keeps her eyes, seeing and unseeing, glued upon the tiles. For once, she doesn't mind one bit – she could mop all night.

But then there's Josh, too.

She glances at the clock. Quarter to two. He should be here any minute to pick her up. She hasn't seen him since he stopped in the other night, and her usual butterflies at the thought of him fly low with apprehension in her gut. The argument never was quite resolved.

He pulls up as she's dumping the dirty mop water outside. *Just my luck that he'd see me now.* But she smiles into his headlights anyway and waves, heart skipping its accustomed beat just at the thought of him. She hopes she doesn't look too sweaty. Hopes she doesn't smell too much like fried food once she sits beside him.

She winks and waves before turning to go inside and finish up. Hopes she looks cute. Hopes he's not still mad. But glancing back out at the parking lot all she can see is his high beams, and she's fairly certain her attempt at a sexy wink was more like a startled, blinded blink.

She dumps the bucket quickly in the pantry, hangs up her apron, and quickly pokes her head into the kitchen, shouting, 'Tom, I'm off!'

He does not look up. Just pauses mid whistle and calls what he always says, every night, 'OK, baby girl, I'll lock up behind ya.'

But she's gone before he's even stopped speaking. Doesn't have to wait for the words to know what he'll say. She slams the door behind her and hurries into the pickup where Josh is waiting.

They don't speak at first. Road dark around them, before them. Even darker as they turn off the feeder by the interstate and roll onto unlit country roads. Prairie blacker than sky. A deer-crossing sign catches their high beams, glowing bright-sun yellow as they speed past. A moonless night. And Katie does not look for stars.

It's Josh who finally breaks the silence. 'How you been?'

The space between them in the pickup seems vast. A whole canyon there in the seat between them. Katie wants to slide up next to him on the front seat. Wants to wrap her arms around his. Wants to lean her head right there on his shoulder, crown nestled into his neck. Their familiar way. But she does not move. Does not try to breach the space between them. 'All right.' Only his profile meets her searching eyes. ''N' you?'

He shrugs. 'All right too, I reckon.'

Silence for a beat. Then, 'You mad at me, Josh?'

'No.'

'You mad 'bout somethin' else?'

'No.'

'Well, what is it, then?'

'It ain't nothin'.'

Purr of the engine the only sound.

She turns to him. Voice soft. 'Don't lie to me.'

The tyres screech and squeak their halt, the sudden force of the pickup stopping tossing Katie forward slightly, her hands catching the dashboard just barely in time to brace herself.

'Fucking hell, Katie.' He's facing her now, and there's fire in his eyes, and Katie feels her heart skip a beat, but not in the good kind of way like it usually does. 'What the fuck do you want from me? You want me to sit here 'n'

97

pretend like everything's just perfect? You want me to act like I don't care what's goin' on with you? Well, that's bullshit. I ain't gonna sit by and smile and just wait for somethin' bad to happen.'

'Who says somethin' bad's gonna happen?'

'Who's to say it ain't?'

She says nothing. Stares out of the window at the utter dark nothingness of the road ahead. Angry, but not fully sure she understands why. She can feel his eyes on her. *Who's to say it ain't?* Bites her lower lip to keep her nerves steady. Silence stretches long between them. The air in the pickup thick, too thick, hard to breathe. She wishes she was home already. No, not home. Just anywhere but here.

He turns, back straight in his seat, no longer facing her, looking out into the darkness before them. Impenetrable. Slams his hand against the steering-wheel and the horn goes off. The sound startles her, and Katie jumps. Josh's breath releases in one low, long gush. 'Fucking hell . . .' Tone discouraged. Fire spent.

She doesn't look at him. Speaks to the small patch of light illuminated by the high beams on the road before them. 'I don't wanna fight.'

'Me neither.'

She turns to him then, his face still too shadowed to see, the cab itself too dark to show his features.

He reaches out an arm. 'Come here, baby.'

And somehow the space between is suddenly not so far, and she slides across the seat until his arms are around her. And they kiss. And everything's right again. Everything's gonna be OK again. She can feel it. The anger boils down and cools.

They stay like that a moment. Or an hour. Time no longer in existence. No cars or traffic on these back roads. The engine idling. Neither speaks. Neither moves. Time passes or does not pass. His arm around her feels like safety, and she closes her eyes. Imagines for a moment that the moment might last. It's a nice thought. A thought on lonely nights she will climb back to, seeking refuge.

It is Katie who breaks their silence. 'The Saunders' truck drove by the house yesterday.' She feels his body stiffen. Regrets her words already.

'What happened?'

'I dunno. I wasn't home. Joanne told me 'bout it. Said it just drove by.'

'Eddie's truck?'

She shrugs. 'Who else's?'

Josh is silent, but Katie can feel the tension coursing through him, steady as a second pulse. As full of life, as dangerous and as deadly. She raises her chin to search his face. 'Do you think there'll be trouble? Have you heard anythin'?'

He pauses before answering. 'I ain't the only one that dislikes him back. You know that, Katie.'

'We don't want no trouble, Josh.' Voice a soft, soft whisper.

He smooths down her hair to soothe her. 'I know that.'

''N' other folks?'

He pauses. 'They know that, too.'

'If you heard someone was fixin' to do something, you'd tell me, wouldn't you?'

His hand is on repeat, smoothing down her hair,

petting her, stroking her calm. 'Course I would.' But his pause before his answer catches her heart and squeezes and makes it hard to breathe.

She lifts her chin again, struggling to see his face. Only shadows there. 'Do you think he's gonna do somethin'?'

'I would, if I's her brother.'

Out across the prairie an owl calls.

'Don't say that.'

'I told you, Katie. I know he's your kin 'n' all, but it's just a matter of time till he's set off again 'n' folks get hurt, 'n' I ain't the only one that ain't just willin' to set back waitin' for it.'

'Don't say that.'

No stars. No streetlights. Only the dark blanket of night around them, and suddenly the darkness seems too thick, too hot, despite the open pickup window. Josh kisses her forehead. 'Best get you home.'

Long hours have passed since the evening primroses peeled open. Closer to their closing now than to their bloom. When she was a girl, Lizzie used to marvel at how, just past sunset, they would open. Petal by petal, like tiny yellow mouths. She used to sit right there on the front porch, waiting till the last golden rays turned pink and deepened purple. Used to go down in the flowerbeds right at that final moment of sunset. Careful not to step on the low-lying marigolds. The gentle lilies and daisies bedded there. Used to hold her breath as each night she watched the miracle of the primroses blooming and re-blooming. Like some sort of magic forever on repeat and unexplained. She never could understand what made them close up so tight again. Why their flowers did not stay bloomed.

Fireflies dart across the dark lawn, zigzagging as they chase each other, their glowing bulbs the only lights on this dark night. Tag, you're it! as they collide. No stars above. Moon new or else just hidden. A cloudy night, but not cool, day's heat still a thick blanket spread out across the land. *Maybe it will rain tomorrow.* Crickets call out their usual summer symphony. From somewhere a July fly briefly joins their song only to fall silent and not be heard again.

Lizzie's been sitting there since before the sun set. In Mama's old rocker. Back and forth, back and forth, unaware of time's passing even as she's watched the night slowly fall; the hours stretch longer as the shadows begin to shorten. Joanne came out some time back and kissed her goodnight and went up to bed. Katie's at the diner still. Her girls. Her heartbeats.

He was one once, too. Bobby. Her heart's greatest beat. Now a still void of memories sugar-sweetened by time and retrospect.

The screen door creaks open, snapping her thoughts back to here. To now.

'May I join you?'

She nods.

He sits in the rocker beside her. Gazes out across the lawn into the utter blackness beyond. 'Dark night tonight, ain't it?'

Their rockers creak as both slide back and forth, back and forth. Different rhythms. Same sound. She listens to the crickets. Finds comfort in their call.

'I still miss him,' she says at last. 'Somethin' awful.'

He does not answer her at first. His rocker slows though not quite still before its rhythm picks back up again. She surprises herself with the words. Hadn't known she meant to speak them.

'Can't say as I feel the same.' Voice thick as syrup, but burned rough round the edges, not sticky smooth.

Her turn to pause her rocker. 'That don't surprise me none.'

She can feel Jasper's eyes on her.

Voice raw, unpractised, he replies, 'Sometimes I miss the him before. Not the him of when I . . . left. Like they was different people.'

She nods. Can understand that. At least partially.

'How long's it been?' A bit too loud despite his hushed tone.

'Eight years.'

'Them girls of yours remember 'im?'

She pauses. 'Reckon Katie must. Don't know 'bout Joanne. Reckon she remembers somethin'.'

He nods. Lets the silence between them gain weight before he breaks it. 'You divorce 'im?'

A single chuckle escapes her. Not a happy sound. 'Things ain't ever so clean cut round here. I'd have thought you'd remember that much.' Teasing in her tone, though no real laughter.

He snorts. Waits for her this time to break their silence.

'You know,' she says at length, 'I think a part of me always thought he might come back. Even after all that happened.'

'Not any more?'

'Why would he?'

Neither speaks. Neither breaks that silence. A star fades in and out of sight as dark clouds shift.

'Liz?' Voice so uncertain.

'Ummmm?'

'Do you blame me?'

She weighs the question. Holds her pause. She did once. Blame him. When Bobby first left. Couldn't help but think back then, *This wouldn't have happened if . . . But what's the point now in speculating? In second guessing?* Aloud, she says, 'He was never the same after all that happened.'

Jasper lets out a long, low breath. 'I'm sorry for that.'

'Well . . .' She looks out across the vast blackness of the prairie. At the few shadows visible there. The fireflies scattered in between. 'Good luck finding many folks round here that'd believe it.'

That snort again. No amusement in it. Prairie grasses rustle in the breeze. Crickets sing and fall silent and sing again.

'Reckon he left 'cause of me?' Not one star shining in that clouded sky.

'In part,' she lies.

Silence, as both are lost in memory. In thought. After a while, he says, voice scarcely above a whisper, 'Sometimes I wonder if people ever really heal.'

The creak of their rockers, back and forth, back and forth. Time passes. Crickets sing. To the darkness, at length, she says, 'I don't think they do.'

And he does not reply.

*

She holds the cicada shell carefully. Lifts it to her face and inhales deeply. Breathes in the earthy smell of it. Foreign to her nose. Sour almost. And musty. A bit like old people. Or potatoes dug fresh from the garden, the dirt still clinging to their skins. Or Grandma's closet back when Grandma was alive, before Mom moved into Grandma's room and cleared out all Grandma's clothes. Joanne used to hide in there, back when she was little. In Grandma's closet. Back when Katie still played hide and seek with her. When they were really small, Mom even joined in, too, sometimes, and Joanne would always shriek with laughter when she was finally found. That's what the cicada smells like – those long minutes in the closet waiting for that laughter.

Once, Katie did not come to find her. Joanne heard Katie counting on the stairs ... *fifty-five, fifty-four, fifty-three* ... all the way backwards from one hundred. Like they always did, in that same loud voice so the other could be sure to hear them counting. Giggling, Joanne had tiptoed down the hall. Careful not to creak the floorboards with each careful step. She opened up the door to Grandma's room. Winced when the hinges squeaked. The floral curtains were pulled open so that sunlight spilled across the floor in a thick golden rectangle, wooden crossbeams on the window neatly dividing it into four. The shadowed outline of a cross. She remembers that. Remembers, somehow, that sunlight so clearly, how it was there divided. Careful still, Joanne crossed the room on tiptoe. Opened the door to Grandma's closet. The hinges squeaked as it pulled open towards her. She had to stand on tiptoe just a little to open it. That's how small she was. The door clicked shut behind her.

Still giggling, still trying not to, she slipped into Grandma's closet behind the shoe rack, Grandma's long skirts and dresses spilling down over her as they dangled off their hangers. Dark greys and blacks and coloured calicos. Long and dark and musty above her. The smell of old person, of shoes and mothballs thick around her. Katie's voice still a steady count muffled and drifting from the stairs below.

Then, 'Ready or not, here I come!'

And Joanne waited.

And waited.

And it seemed so very long. She watched a spider cross the floor and slip into a crack at the base of the boards. Had to try real hard not to scream or run and go get Mom. But she knew it was OK: Katie would find her soon. At first, it was hard not to giggle. She was proud she had hidden so well. That it took Katie so long to find her. Then Joanne heard Katie's voice outside. Couldn't hear the words. Just the call of it. The rise and fall of her older sister's tone. And a car door slam. And an engine start. And then she didn't hear Katie any more.

The realization slapped her, knocked the laughter right out of her. Joanne put her head down between her knees. Breaths short and shallow. She didn't cry at first. Stared down at her toes. The floor beyond. At the line of light that filtered in through the crack in the door and cut across her ankle. *Katie was not going to come and find her.* She wondered why her sister'd bothered counting. Why no one else came looking. How no one else realized she was missing. Then she did cry, softly, each sob a tiny hiccup that shook her chest, rocked her body and made it hard to breathe. Mom would find her soon, though. Or Grandma. Surely, she told herself, someone would find her soon. But there were no footsteps on the stairs and no one came.

That was the last time Joanne played hide and seek.

Joanne lowers the cicada from her nose and studies it. The off-brown colour of it. A bit like dried bark. Or peanut butter left out too long, and now solidified. Its legs feel prickly in her palm. All five of them. Rough against her skin, though the rest of the July fly is smooth. Carefully, she places it on Katie's vanity. Positions the bug so its hollow eyes blindly stare out at her. Adjusts it so that it stands between Katie's perfume and hairbrush. Likes the look of it there. Alien and ugly among the pretty girlie items that scatter her sister's vanity. Nail polish. And magazine cut-outs. And mascara. And creams. And photographs of Katie and her friends. Joanne wonders where that sixth leg went. Wishes Uncle Jasper hadn't broken it off, even though she knows he didn't mean to. She wonders, if she'd looked, if she might have found it. If it might be there still.

'There,' she says out loud. 'You can stay right there.' And she places the July fly on top of last month's *Seventeen*.

No one there to hear. To answer. Just her and the exoskeleton perched before her. Dark and silent in its hollow frame. She imagines Katie's face, finding it. The way she might shriek. And jump up. And knock the little stool right over. Magazines and nail polish and photographs all knocked over and scattered across the floor. Joanne smiles. But picks the July fly up once again. *No, the vanity's not the spot for it, that won't do.*

She crosses the room and stands by the window, July fly still cradled in her palm. Looks out into the pitch dark of night. The clouded, starless sky. The flickering porch light at the Greys' is the only light for miles. She misses the stars. Wishes she could look up and map the constellations. Scarcely any air blows through the slightly cracked window, so Joanne pushes against it till it swings open all the way. Sticks her head out and closes her eyes. Feels the warm air slide up against her skin. Sticky. Even without the sun's heat. She stays like that a moment. Thinking. Imagining a million what-ifs that take her far away. And bring Daddy home. And make Katie her friend again. And solve all the mysteries of Uncle Jasper's crime. And keep summers year-long, no such thing as school.

Far off, across the prairie, a pack of coyotes calls, voices shrill and wild as they howl. Joanne's eyes pop open. Not 'cause she's scared. Just as reflex to the sound. She's lived nearly her whole life in this house. Was only just walking, really, when they left town and moved in with Grandma. She is used to the creaks and groans and moans of the house and to the calls of the prairie that surrounds it. She finds comfort in the sounds.

Katie should be home before too long. It's late, and Joanne knows she's supposed to be in bed, but she likes having the room to herself while Katie's out. Likes looking at Katie's things when Katie's not there. Likes how she can push open the window all the way and stick her head right out without her sister complaining that she's letting moths and June bugs in. Without complaining that she's moving, touching, Katie's stuff.

Reluctantly, Joanne closes the window till it's once more only cracked. She's thirsty. Looks around the room for a glass of water. There is none. *Mom didn't bring one up tonight.* She lets her breath out long and slow. Mom always brings up water when she says goodnight. Has as long as Joanne can remember. Leaves it by the bedside table. To drown witches. And end nightmares. And give the sleep fairy a swimming-pool to leave good dreams in. But Mom didn't come up earlier to say goodnight. It had been Joanne who eventually went downstairs. She'd been scared Mom might tell her off for skipping bedtime if she didn't. But Mom hadn't even seemed to notice that Joanne had come down late. 'Night, hon.' Didn't even remind her to brush her teeth. Just sat in Grandma's old rocker staring out across the open acres as further darkness fell upon them.

Joanne crosses the room and opens the door. Thirsty. No light escapes from under the other doors, and the hall before her feels ghostly quiet, even though the grand-father clock downstairs ticks loudly as it counts down the hours. She hesitates there in the doorway, throat dry, lips dry. Glances back into Katie's room, their room, not sure what makes her pause. She faces the darkened hall again. Licks her dry lips, then turns the door knob slow as she is able so it won't click too loudly into place as she shuts the door. Carefully, she tiptoes along the hall. Down the stairs, wincing as the floorboards squeak. She doesn't want to wake Mom or Uncle Jasper. Doesn't want to have to explain why she hasn't yet gone to bed. Why she didn't brush her teeth.

Halfway down the stairs, she realizes the July fly's still clutched in her hand. She pauses. Looks up the stairs, and thinks of going back and putting him somewhere safe, maybe on Katie's vanity, for now anyways, but she doesn't. Tiptoe, tiptoe, tiptoe down the remaining stairs. House unfamiliar in its darkness. The wood of the stairs surprisingly cool on her bare feet.

At the bottom of the stairs, Joanne stops. Hears something. Strains to listen. Voices drift in from outside, their deep honey tones just scarcely above whispers. Whole house around her dark and silent, except those drifting whispers. Before her, the front door is unlocked and open, just the screen door shut. She pauses a moment, uncertain. Thinks about that glass of water, throat still cracked and dried. Thinks about the kitchen, just around the corner, so close now. How cross Mom'd be to find her so long awake and out of bed. She looks back to the screen door. Strains to hear the voices, but they're too hushed to hear clearly, and all she can make out is the murmur of them. Like thunder rumbling softly far away. She sucks in a deep breath, the air cool in her lungs. Slowly, step by careful step, Joanne creeps forward. *Almost there now, almost there . . .*

She crouches next to the screen door, just below the window-ledge. The curtains blow open around her, and she can see through the screen door out onto the porch just a little. Just enough. The porch light casts long patch-worked shadows across the terrace and out into the lawn, and it takes Joanne a moment to adjust to the lamp's soft glow, to decipher the shadows before her.

Mom and Uncle Jasper sit side by side in separate

rockers. Their shadows overlap on alternating rocks, forward and back, blurring as they cross. She can see only their profiles. Solemn and stern and lined heavy, deepened by dark shadows. They do not speak at first. Silent, solemn shadows. Like twin scarecrows of themselves. Or an old black-and-white photograph come alive. Joanne feels like she's dreaming, and her heart beats faster as she watches them, like it's flying in her chest. She knows she shouldn't listen in. Doesn't care. Holds her breath as she waits for them to speak. Prays she won't be seen.

It doesn't take long for them to talk. Their rockers creak and squeak on the floor as both rock back and forth, back and forth, steady as cricket song.

'Eddie Saunders' truck drove by yesterday.' Mom's voice calm and hard. Not quite angry. Not quite not.

His rocker stops. 'That so . . .' Then it resumes its rocking.

Joanne catches her breath, afraid to release it, afraid she'll be found. Peering out of the screen door, she wishes she could see them better. Could see their faces. Read their eyes.

'I'm gonna be frank with you, Jasper. I won't have no trouble round here. 'N' I sure as hell won't have my girls mixed up in any kind of trouble. We got troubles enough of our own, you hear?'

His voice is soft but weathered when he answers. Like the words pain him. 'You want me gone?'

She does not reply at first and, for a moment, Joanne thinks her mother might not answer. Neither does Mom's rocker pause or slow. Nor does she turn to face him when she finally speaks. 'Reckon there ain't much point in that.'

Uncle Jasper nods slowly, like he's chewing something over, his head's shadow rocking separate from the slow back and forth of his rocker's shadow. 'I appreciate all you doin' for me.'

Silence between them as both rockers rock. Squeak and creak and groan, the floorboards. Crickets out of tune.

'There ain't no trouble comin'.' He adds, 'Not on my account.'

'You sure of that?'

'Ain't no need for trouble.'

'That don't stop it comin'.'

Joanne's knees ache where her weight falls on them, pressing them into the wooden floor. She wants to move. To stand up. But she dares not. Carefully she lets out her held breath. Draws another. Rattling in her lungs.

'I saw it, too,' he says.

'Saw what?'

'What I'm guessin' musta been Eddie's pickup. Down the country road, comin' up from town.'

Mom turns to look at him, the movement one quick snap that startles Joanne and nearly makes her jump, but she catches her scream before it sounds, forces it back down inside her and holds her body still.

'You coulda told me sooner.'

'Weren't no need to mention it.' He pauses. 'Nothin' happened.'

'You sure it was him?'

'Reckon it musta been. Thought it at the time.'

Mom nods. Turns back out to face the darkness of the prairie. 'It ain't easy,' she says, 'havin' you back. Reminds me of Bobby more than I'd have guessed. Makes me think.'

Uncle Jasper rocks in silence, profile unreadable, shadows further deepening the contours of his face.

'You know,' Mom says, 'I never thought he'd leave me. I never once saw that comin'. Does that mark me a fool?'

A hiccup in the cricket song that softens the darkness of the night.

'Why'd he go?'

Mom snorts. No humour in the sound. Not even a trace of laughter. 'Folks never looked at him the same after. Don't take no genius to figure that one out.'

'They thought he . . . ?'

'Him leavin' didn't help none either. I'd say most folks still think he played his part. Run away from the shame of it. But he weren't shamed. Never had no reason.'

'Just why did he leave, then?' Voice barely a whisper.

'Couldn't take it no more. The whispers. The glances. Shit, Jasper, if I'd been him I'da up 'n' left, too. Can't find it in me to hold that bit against him.'

Cricket song the only sound. Joanne forgets to breathe. She's never heard Mom talk about Daddy like this. Wonders if Katie has. If Katie knows all this.

'I shouldn't have gone back to the garage like that.'

'You were a fool to.'

'I never thought they –'

'Exactly.' She cuts him off. 'You never thought.' Then, more softly, 'Why'd you do it, Jasper?' Words shaky and thin as prayer.

His rocker stops.

Joanne can't breathe. Her stomach feels all tight and knotted. A pause that seems to last for ever. At length, he says, 'Don't ask me that. Don't ever ask me to talk 'bout her.' Words barely a whisper. Cracked and strained.

'You owe me that much. You owe me some sort of explanation.' Tension thick in Mom's voice. Tone taut and strained.

'We've gone a long way now past sorry.' A coldness to his voice. Rocker held still.

'Sorry ain't got fuck to do with it. You can't just pretend like you done nothin' wrong.' Mom's voice rising, angry.

'You think that's what I'm doin'? You reckon I don't think back on that day and pray to God for what I done?'

'Damned if I know. But sure as hell it ain't God's forgiveness you should be seekin'.'

'Whose forgiveness do you want me askin'?' he says, '*Yours? Hers? Eddie's?* What God done to you that He ain't done to all of us? When did you lose your faith?' His voice rising now too, creeping close to angry. Fire in his tone.

'It ain't lost. It's gone. It was gone when they found her like that. Gone when they locked you up. Gone when they called Bobby in 'n' asked him all those questions. It left when I saw them pictures 'n' all that blood, and damn you to hell, Jasper Curtis, if you ever speak to me of faith.' A pause that seems to last for hours. Air suddenly too thick to breathe. The fire of Mom's words still burns in the air. 'Rose always deserved better than you.' Mom's voice a cold snarl. Hard and sharp and cutting.

A sound escapes him she has never heard before. Not quite a growl. Not quite a moan. The rocker skids as he stands up, knocking back so that it hits the wall with a loud, solid thud. 'That bitch got what she deserved,' he snarls, voice completely changed. Wild and fierce. And it scares Joanne, and her fists clench and she feels a tiny snap right in her palm. Looks down. The July fly. She'd forgotten she still held it. Had forgotten to cradle rather than clutch it. Scarcely breathing, she unclenches her hand, uncurling each finger back till it stretches into an open palm. The exoskeleton's fragile husk has shattered in her palm. Crushed into a million tiny fragments impossible to mend. Only the head remains intact, face distorted and partially caved in. For a moment she forgets she's hiding, and a tiny moan escapes her. The sound a weeping willow might make before bending down beneath the weight of the wind's harsh breath.

Uncle Jasper turns to the door. 'You hear that?' Still fire in his tone. His footsteps come closer as he crosses the porch. The sound of Mom's breath catches and releases again, and the gentle scrape of Mom's rocker pushes back as Mom rises.

Joanne does not wait. Jumps right up and turns and runs fast as she can up the stairs and up the hall again. Slams Katie's door shut behind her, and it shakes the frame. She shuts off the light and jumps under the quilt real fast, and closes her eyes real tight, like maybe she's been up there, sleeping, all this time. Heart racing. Beating. Slamming in her chest. Breaths short and shallow. Like her heart might break a rib. Reminds her of waiting all those years back in that closet to be found. Except this time she prays it is Katie who comes and finds her huddled there, frightened and alone. Still thirsty.

Her ears strain, but only silence meets them. Not even the call of a coyote. Or the ringing of the hour on the grandfather clock. No footsteps on the stairs.

In her clenched fist, Joanne still clutches the shattered exoskeleton of the July fly. One million pieces crushed as sand. When sleep eventually finds her, her hand does not release it, rather grips it more tightly, crushing the already ruined husk into tiny chipped bits of shell and dust.

Ear pressed to the wood of her daughters' bedroom door, Lizzie can't quite say why she didn't run after Joanne straight away. She wanted to, but somehow her feet stayed stuck. Right there, useless, at the ends of her legs. And then there'd been Jasper too, his rage, to deal with. Too many buried wounds newly bruised. When she eventually did climb the stairs, they felt too steep, the hallway too narrow. Too dark. Like everything was closing in on her, the whole house caving in, too warm, trying to suffocate her. She could feel Bobby's absence from the photos on the wall in a way that she normally did not. Newly raw and burning. She did not need light to see he was not there. And even now, ear pressed to the door of her girls' room, Lizzie can feel the lack of him, an ache inside her loneliness, drawn tight around her. Only silence meets her prying ear. *Joanne must be asleep by now.* Carefully, she twists the knob. Opens the door slowly, just a crack, before the point where the hinges squeak.

This was her room once.

Waning moonlight casts deep shadows through the

room. Teddy bears and dolls and photographs transformed at this hour. Strange, silent witnesses. One of Joanne's feet has fought free of the sheet and hangs off the side of the bed. From her shallow breathing, Lizzie can see her daughter sleeps. She watches her a moment. Joanne's eyelids flutter, as though seeing in a dream. Slowly, Lizzie pulls the door shut. Holds the latch so it won't click.

Still careful to be quiet, she opens her own door and slips into her room. Changes quickly in the darkness and slips into her empty bed, the sheets cool against the uncovered bits of her skin. It is a long while till she falls asleep. Eyes trying to make sense of the shadows on the ceiling. She counts sheep for a while to numb her mind. Recounts them to be certain. Switches to stars for a while. She wonders where he is, and if he's sleeping too. Wonders, not for the first time that night, if he ever misses her. Their girls.

She knows inside her, Bobby's never coming home. She knew it that morning so long ago when she drank that coffee alone, his lips gone from hers already, never to return.

When sleep finds her, Lizzie dreams Joanne is a baby again. A little delicate thing. That, no matter what, won't cry.

She wakes before the rooster's called, dream still fresh in her mind. She lies in bed in the half-light till the sun's fully risen and day forces her out of bed.

The drive into town is silent. Sun fully risen and already burning hot despite the early hour. Lizzie and the girls squeeze into the pickup's cab, Lizzie's brow furrowing as she concentrates behind the wheel, squinting in the too-bright sunlight. Katie sits leaning out of the open window, hair tied back, fallen golden strands tickling her forehead, nose, lips. Sandwiched between her mother and sister, restless and squirming and sweaty, Doe Eyes' face is blank as she stares out of the window. Emotionless. Twisting round to look at her through the cab's back window, Jasper cannot read her thoughts. Her mood. Nor does he try or care to. Not then. He does not regret frightening her. Does not really care how much she may have overheard. He is not watching his family on this drive.

He sits in the pickup's truck bed, back against the cab, legs stretched out long before him as the sun and wind chap his lips, dry his tanning skin. Feels good to feel the day like that. The fresh air and sun upon him. Lizzie took the back roads when she'd picked him up from Texaco the other morning, bypassing town. It feels good to watch his boyhood homeland now flash by. Most of the drive looks as he remembers. *Maybe not so much changed, really, after all.* Whitewashed homesteads, few and far between, dot the open prairie. Long drives twist up from the road to curve before each doorstep. Rusted-out pickups and old sedans clog people's driveways, car hoods often left popped open, oil spills staining the ground. Occasional Mexican hats and Indian blankets, now both grown past their peak, still bloom wild in the open fields. Little specks of colour among a sea of dried-out brown. Like he remembers from springs and summers long past. *Must be nice,* Jasper thinks, *to just grow free like that.*

There are longhorns grazing in some fields they pass;

in others, horses. Corn grows dried out and shoulder high as they turn off the country road onto the busier freeway that cuts through town. Just like it had ten years ago. Even the elementary he attended hasn't changed at all since the day he left it, save for a few trailers set up on cinder blocks serving as extensions out the back. But closer to town there are more stop lights than he recalls, and Jasper notices the Taylors' tyre swing no longer hangs from that oak halfway up their drive, and some mailboxes seem freshly painted brighter colours, not the greys and blacks and deep reds of his childhood. Pastel colours, rather, pretty and bright. And closer still to town there are houses he does not recall, a small apartment complex just off Main Street that was not there before. Brown bricks, grey doors, two storeys. Flimsy tin awning covering single-occupancy parking spots. Dark windows with plastic blinds, not curtains. Reminds him of a prison with its doors all in a row, reminds him of her place all those years back, and he is forced to look away. Just for a moment. To look down. At the rusty bed of the truck on which he sits. He does not look up again until he feels the pickup's engine idle and halt. He does not see the stares he gets as they cross Elm and First. The old lady pointing to her friend. He does not know the wind has blown his uncut hair in a way only describable as 'wild'. He has yet to put much thought into the idea of familiar faces.

Lizzie slams the door as she gets out of the truck. Pauses to find and hold his gaze, her hand still on the door handle. 'You ready for this?' No smile on her lips.

He forces a grin as he swings down onto the pavement. 'Ready as I'll ever be.'

And then she smiles. He didn't expect that. It warms him up inside. Catches him off guard. Makes his smile creep towards genuine. And he likes that feeling on his lips, thrilling and strange and nice. He likes how his face melts there before her. There was seldom occasion to smile in prison.

The night before, Jasper had sat for a long time looking at the stars. Out on the front porch, in the rocker, though, he'd sat still, unmoving. The sound of his rocker creaking on the weather-worn floorboards at that hour had been too great for him. He needed silence. He needed a great dark void of nothingness to sit still inside. Not to hide in. Not really. Just a place no thoughts could enter. He hadn't meant to scare the girl. Hadn't even known she was there. It had surprised him when Lizzie didn't run after her daughter straight off, though. *Nosy little bitch*. He had thought that maybe Lizzie was the kind of mother who would do that. The kind who might have held her daughter and rocked her back and forth. But there had been no comfort in Lizzie's eyes as, cold, they'd turned upon him. 'What do you want?' she'd asked him. Voice scarcely above a whisper. 'What the hell do you want from us?'

He could have stayed angry with her if she'd gone after the girl straight away. His rage could have fed and grown. Festered inside him. He knows that feeling well. But she'd stripped him of that when she'd whispered. Like the whole world stilled and calmed. He hadn't even realized he'd been halfway through the door till then. Didn't even know full well his intentions. The hall dark before him. The door upstairs already slammed, and footsteps fallen silent. *What the hell do you want from us?* she'd asked. He had walked slowly back to the rocking chair upon which he'd sat before. Perched on the edge to hold it solid. Looked out beyond the shadowed garden to the deeper darkness of the open prairie. 'I didn't mean to scare her none.' His voice too loud.

'That damage is done.'

'You reckon she was there long?'

A sigh as if her soul slipped out. Tone hard but not completely unforgiving. 'Long enough, no doubt.'

He had nodded. Had looked down to his hands, clasped in his lap before him. The unevenness of his nails visible even in the darkness. Skin not as calloused as it once was. Softly, 'What does she know about me?' He had not raised his eyes.

'She knows that you're her uncle.'

'That it?'

'You really want her knowing more?'

He had looked up then. Had paused. 'They know why their daddy left them?'

Lizzie's turn to look away. The fire drained from both of them. 'How do you tell a child?' she said softly, so softly. 'How do you ever tell a child . . . that?' He had barely been able to hear her. Pleading in her voice as her words hung between them. A hiccup in the cricket song around them. He had felt her deep breath in more than he had seen it. As if she'd sucked all the air right out of the night and gathered it up inside her. 'Sometimes,' she'd said, voice weak and cracking, 'I tell myself maybe you're sick. Maybe that's all this has ever been. Sickness. And maybe for a while there it spread a bit.' She paused. Hand on the door frame. 'I tell myself that sickness passes. I tell myself that, these days, every sickness has a cure. But then other times I don't think you're sick after all. This ain't no cancer we're dealin' with. Sometimes I don't think that sickness is the problem one bit.'

'What's my problem then?' Snarled more than he'd meant to, but no true malice in his words. Just anger. Just hurt.

Their eyes had met, faces barely visible through the shadowed darkness. Expressions lost. That pleading was in her voice again. No doubt, he thought, it must also be in her eyes.

'How the hell do I know, Jasper? And how do I tell a child when I don't know myself?' She had turned then, disappearing into the darkness of the house, the screen door shutting behind her.

He hadn't moved for quite a while after that, staring at the dark horizon till pink and deep purple streaked the pre-dawn sky. Katie came home just short of sunrise, the smell of the diner still thick and stale upon her as she passed him. He nodded to her but did not say hello. There was something timid in her smile as she hurried through the door. As she pulled it tightly shut behind her.

He sat there and watched in silence as the sun rose. It had been ten years since he'd seen that. And when the pinks turned black to gentle blue, his face had relaxed as though some long-drawn-out pain had finally eased. He rose only once, right before dawn broke, and strode down the garden path and opened up the picket-fence gate and stood there. Stared down the road a good while. Out across the open grasses. No cars. Nobody. Then he had turned and shut the gate again. Latched it. Unlatched it. Latched again. Slowly, he walked back up to the porch. He opened the screen door and peered inside the still sleeping darkness within. Listened to the silence. Shut the screen. Because he could. Sat down again. Because he could. To watch the sun rise.

The thrift store Lizzie guides him into is not a shop Jasper remembers. It was a café before. The C-A-F-É block-letter outline still just barely visible as it arches from one side of the picture window up across the other. A frosted-glass ghost of what used to be. A bell chimes as they enter and rattles silent. No a/c, just a ceiling fan half caked in dust that spins in slow rotation, barely moving the stuffy air. The shop smells mildly of cat piss and mothballs, a smell that slaps the nostrils and jerks back the head, but passes as the senses adapt to the musty odour of the old café and the second-hand merchandise that now fills it. Water-stains peel browning wallpaper at the top corner of the back wall, little flowers on the print faded paler than pastel. Jasper can remember when those flowers still had colour. When the now threadbare carpet once lightened the once different room.

The shop seems dark after the brightly lit truck drive, and Jasper has to pause a moment to let his eyes adjust. Dust fills his lungs. Chest. *It used to smell like coffee beans and baking pecan pie* . . .

Three mannequins stand in the window. All female. And Jasper can't help but let his eyes wash over them, their porcelain curves. His eyes unstitch the seams of their blouses, slowly unzip their skirts. Their long legs go up and up . . . flesh too white, too perfect, unmarred.

'Jasper.'

He turns. It's Lizzie. A searching in her eyes he doesn't quite recognize.

'Pick out what you need.' She gestures to a rack of men's clothing, that funny look still clouding her eyes. 'Just the basics, mind you, I ain't made of money.' She turns and walks briskly across the shop to where her girls, Katie giggling, browse through summer dresses.

Jasper blinks again, adjusting. Shakes his head to clear it of the mannequins. Their long, slender legs. The store is mostly women's clothes. Some children's hung on racks against the walls. Undergarments and T-shirts lie half folded on tables below the racks. Second-hand books are scattered across a table in the centre of the room, piled in uneven stacks, disorderly, mostly paperbacks, covers bent and stained. A cookbook is visibly ripped. An old *Webster's Dictionary*'s pages are tarnished dark with watermark. Jasper runs his fingers up a weathered romance novel's spine. Lets the pages fall open. He raises the open book up to his face, buries his nose deep in it. Inhales. Holds the scent in his lungs. Exhales. He can feel Lizzie's eyes upon him, watching. Reluctantly, he shuts the book. Returns it to its pile.

Some ladies' undergarments lie on a small round table, spread out on top of a stained white tablecloth. Silky. Lacy. Flirty stuff. Eyes never leaving Lizzie, Jasper steps closer and lets his fingers run over the soft fabrics. It's been a long while since he's seen a woman's underthings. Even longer since he's touched them. There's this silky lavender panty laid out on top of the other sexy drawers, and his fingers pause on it. Separate to smooth out its wrinkles. He wants to pick it up and hold it to his face. Wants to breathe that scent deep again. He wonders if the panty smells of woman. The sweet juice between a woman's thighs. He likes that colour, that shade. Lavender. Different. Hearing a whisper, he glances up to see Lizzie lean down to speak softly to Doe Eyes. Doe Eyes nods slowly, scratching behind her ear. A hanger clicks as it fits back onto a rack. He turns. Disgust sours Katie's usual smile, judgement thick in her eyes as they bore into him. Startled, Jasper's hand jerks up off the panty. He looks down at the silky lavender fabric, hand, palm flat, suspended above it. But he's not embarrassed. Not really. His cheeks have never been fast to colour and he does not feel himself blush now. His fingers curl in slowly, palm closing. He looks back up to Katie in time to catch her gaze before she turns away. Something about her beauty bothers him more than her disgust. Hard to believe she's the same baby he once bounced on his knee. The world has been kind to her. He can see that now. More than a few men in prison would have sold their souls to look upon her pretty face. He wonders how she'd react to a hand laid rough upon her.

Behind the cash register, at the back of the room, a large woman sits perched, her fat spilling off her stool to float around her in unnatural orbit. Long hot-pink nails stick off stubby fingers, matching hot-pink lipstick that's smeared across pursed lips. Hair short and curly, dyed blonde with the grey roots growing through. Blue eye-shadow. Almost electric. Almost the colour of the sky on this clear day. Too much rouge on her cheeks stains them several shades darker than 'blush'. A part of Jasper wants to walk right up to that woman and poke her. Right there in that fat. Wants to see if his touch pushes her off the stool or if his finger merely would get lost in all those rolls of fat. He wonders what it would feel like to touch them.

She glances up as Jasper steps to cross the room. Does not glance down. A smile breaks and parts her hot-pink lips, front teeth lightly smudged the same hue. Eyes wide. Too wide. Unnatural. Smile, clearly forced. 'Well, I'll be . . .' Let out in one single breath. Like a prayer might be. Or a curse.

'Morning, Esther.' Lizzie's voice calm, even. In control.

'Morning, Lizzie. Girls.' Voice forced, sugar-coated.

'Mornin', Esther,' the girls chime.

Her beady eyes never leave Jasper. 'Anything I can do to help y'all today?'

It is Lizzie still who answers her. 'Well, Esther,' she glances at Jasper, 'I reckon my brother here could use a few things. Nothin' too fancy, mind you, but a few things all the same. You got much in for men?'

Jasper already stands by the shop's single rack of men's clothing. A few flannel shirts, faded T-shirts, a long tweed jacket, a shorter denim one. A few well-worn suits hang in a row, all dark save one that's ruffled down the lapels and dyed light blue. A few folded-up jeans lie on a shelf nearby. 'Not much to choose from, really.' His words surprise him. He had not meant to speak. Lizzie and Esther both start. He can feel their eyes on him. Without meaning to, Jasper looks up across the room and into the electric smears that overshadow Esther's stare. And he knows her. He can't believe he knows her. But it's Esther, *Esther Reynolds*. He kissed her once when they were small. Just children, really. He kissed her on the lips back before a kiss had meaning. A church picnic. Hiding under the table, the chequered red and white cloth falling all around them, colouring the filtered light that fell upon them. Faces sticky from eating watermelon. Fingers sticky, too.

Time had not been kind to her. He can't help but wonder how he must look to her.

'Esther?' A smile cracks his face. Softens it. Involuntarily, smile spreading, growing, he steps forward. 'How you been? This shop here yours? Is Roy still round?' But he stops mid-stride, as her forced smile fades. His extended hand falls down to his side before he's even fully reached for hers. *They giggled all those years ago, sticky noses brushing as they'd kissed . . .*

She is not smiling any more. Her already too-bright cheeks are now coloured an even brighter rosy hue. She reaches for a paper fan laid on the counter. 'Roy's still here all righ'. Works the oil rig just south of town.'

Roy. Roy Reynolds. His childhood best friend. 'It'd be awfully good to see him,' Jasper muses aloud.

Her fat face hardens. All the sugar sweet flushed from it. 'My brother's a busy man, these days. Ain't got much time for reminiscin'.' She flashes a smile that does not stick. That does not reach her eyes. Or return her face from shadow.

'He doin' well?'

'He married Sarah Parker a few years back.' Lizzie smiles at Esther. 'They have a fine baby boy now, ain't that right?'

Esther falters, plasters her smile back on, unfurls her fan. Leans back. 'That's right.'

'Well . . .' Jasper folds his arms across his chest, not sure what to do with them. They suddenly feel too long. Awkward in the stuffy room. There was a time when he'd have been at that wedding. Was a time when he would already have held that baby boy. He doesn't want to meet Esther's eyes again. She's not the same girl he kissed. Innocent and teasing. Full of wonder. He can see that now. He can see fear cloud her eyes when she looks at him, and a part of him wants to squeeze her hand and tell her not to worry, wants to hold her still till the fear leaves her eyes. A different part of him wants to terrify.

Esther keeps her smile unnaturally bright. She fans herself. Hot-pink lipstick stretches to the contours of her grin. 'I got some nice new dresses in the other day now, Lizzie. You see that red one with the white flowers? Thought that might look lovely on Miss Katie there,' she says. Katie smiles, nose wrinkling as she glances across the room to where the dress is hung. Esther continues, smile still there but fading slightly, 'Ain't sure we have much that would suit you, though.' Her voice goes cold as she meets Jasper's stare. 'Chances are you'd do better shopping elsewhere.' There is ice to her tone beneath the sweet. An unwelcome in her smile not quite there before. Jasper feels rage swell inside him, filling him with hate. A familiar feeling, seldom truly gone.

Jasper grabs a collared shirt, two T-shirts and a pair of jeans and flops them onto the counter. He glances that the sizes are near enough right. Doesn't really mind the style, cut or colour. Fashion was something Jasper'd seldom given thought to. He turns to Lizzie. Hates doing so. Hates asking her permission. Like he's less of a man in front of Esther, with Lizzie buying his things. In his gut, the anger boils, bubbles. 'This all righ'?'

'Course it is.' Lizzie reaches into her handbag and pulls out a handful of crumpled notes. Fives. A ten. A few singles. He feels like a little boy again whose mama's buying him his trousers, and a part of him thinks back on school shops of years long gone when sometimes Mama used to bring him here to this very café back when it was that, and they'd share pecan pie while she drank coffee. Except that was different then. Back before the anger.

Esther fingers the clothes he'd laid down uncertainly. She glances up and out across the shop, through the window beyond. As though judging something. As though gauging. Then that phoney smile plasters back across her lips, and even before she's spoken, Jasper wants to wipe it from her. 'I'm sorry,' she says, 'these items ain't for sale.'

'What do you mean they ain't for sale?' A quietness to Lizzie's voice. A sound kin to danger.

Across the room, Doe Eyes glances at her mother uncertainly. Katie places a shirt back on the rack and takes her sister's hand. 'Come on, Lady,' she whispers softly. 'Let's go wait outside.'

Lizzie's voice again, even more dangerously quiet: 'What do you mean these ain't for sale?'

Esther swallows. Glances out towards the shop front, past the frosted C-A-F-É silhouette letters. She shuts her paper fan and lays it down. 'I'm sorry, Lizzie, these items just ain't for sale.' A pause as her hot-pink nails fidget with one of the shirt collars. Electric blue lids flick down to lift back up. 'I meant to take them off the shelf myself.'

'Bullshit you did,' Lizzie says.

A moment passes as the women's eyes meet.

'Now, Lizzie.' Esther glances at Jasper, the fear in her eyes slightly rising. He likes the way her jaw trembles when she looks at him. 'There ain't no need for trouble. I told y'all you might do better shopping elsewhere.' She picks the fan up again, closed tightly in her fist. Unfurls it. The nervousness in her eyes appeals to Jasper. Just a little. It stirs something long lain dormant inside him. A bead of sweat runs down her plump chest to disappear in folds of fat and cleavage. Jasper's eyes follow it. He studies the moisture on her skin, her brow. The anger in him turning in his gut.

'You won't take my money?' Cold, cold, hardened voice.

Until just days ago Jasper would have never guessed that his sister could use that tone. He never would have pictured her grown up to be so hardened.

The whir of the ceiling fan is the only sound in the muggy shop. As if all breath is held. Katie's whispered voice cuts through the silence: 'Come *on*, let's *go*.'

Doe Eyes hesitates. Katie steps back, tugging her sister's hand.

Esther locks her eyes on Lizzie. Glances to where the two girls mutely struggle. Katie pulls her sister towards the door while Doe Eyes' feet stubbornly trail behind her. Quietly, as though talking to a child, Esther's voice softens. She reaches across the counter and gently places her hand on Lizzie's wrist. 'It ain't you I'm refusing, hon.'

'Course it ain't,' Jasper sneers, words a snarled whisper.

The colour leaves Lizzie's face. She nods, as though understanding is just now dawning. Repeats, 'It ain't me.' No question in her words.

Esther retracts her hand. Looks at the floor. 'That's what I said.' Then, braver, she looks back up, jaw quivering, her voice held newly loud and strong. 'We got no men's things for sale today, I'm afraid.'

Jasper feels the rage inside him sour to laughter, boiling in his insides, ready to explode. Holding down the anger, the laughter, he cuts in, 'Now look here, Esther,' tone forced civil, forced what he thinks might sound sweet, 'I ain't here for no trouble. I ain't back for no trouble neither. I just need a few things is all. Now your brother and I, you know we go way back. Roy was always good to me 'n' I got no hard feelin's towards your lot.' He watches as another bead of sweat escapes the sweaty folds of her neck to run down her bosom. Watches as the drop disappears into the dark crease of her cleavage.

She forces her eyes to meet his. Holds his gaze with a determination that surprises him. That almost turns him on. Her words snarl now, the sugar all gone: 'We don' serve your kind here.'

'My kind?' He leans forward slightly, the anger in him swelling like poison under his skin, mixing with his bloodstream, turning his insides black.

Her lip quivers, but her eyes and voice stay strong: 'You know what you are.'

There is silence, the only sound the whir of the ceiling fan. Then Jasper's laughter explodes. He can't help it. The deep dark laugh that boiled up in his insides forces its way out. An evil sound. Even he recognizes that. 'You stupid cunt,' he laughs, 'you stupid, stupid cunt.'

Lizzie throws a handful of crumpled notes onto the counter. More than is owed. She swoops up the clothes in one swift motion, leaving the counter clear. 'If you don't want my money,' she says, 'I reckon you know where you can return it. Come on, girls. Jasper.' She turns, quickly crossing the room in four large strides. The bell chimes as the door swings open. Lizzie freezes in its frame. Face drained of all emotion. Jaw hardened. Katie and Doe Eyes are quickly at their mother's heels. The three of them pause there all looking back at Jasper, like they're waiting for him, and they are, Jasper supposes, but he can't control the laughter in him, can't stop it spilling out.

Jasper does not watch them leave, still doubled over, laughing. He does not hear the bell chime again as the door reopens. Nor does he know how long he's been in the shop alone, bent double, laughing in Esther Reynolds's face. It's a small hand in his that snaps him out of it. Tanned browner than prairie grass. The shock of the touch silences him completely. It's been a long time since a hand held his with any care. Calluses round the first knuckle of her palm. And yet, somehow, her skin feels smooth, too. One finger, the index, is sticky. Big blue eyes meet his. For a moment he thinks it's Lizzie. But that can't be: the age is all wrong. And then there's that doe look he's growing used to. Bobby round the eyes.

Joanne smiles. Nothing uncertain, nothing afraid in how she regards him. Just a curling of her lips that's not quite happy, but comforts all the same. 'You OK, Uncle Jasper?'

He looks back across the counter to where Esther cowers. The silence left by his laughter hollows the room, like a newly forged canyon. Fan spread open but unwaving, Esther watches him, face like a blow-up doll, expression locked with permanent horror and surprise, mouth gaping open. He wonders how that girl with sticky watermelon lips grew into the whale before him. Wonders briefly what her lips would taste like now.

He leans forward across the counter and takes Esther by the chin. Roughly, but not quite rough enough to bruise. He holds her face still as her eyes try to elude him. Eyes gone dark with fear. Been a long time since he saw that in a woman's eyes. Her cheek beneath his squeezing fingers feels baby soft. Tears well in her eyes, but do not fall. He leans in closer, an inch from her lips. He can smell her hairspray he's so close. Can smell the cakey chemicals of her lipstick. The sourness of her breath. He turns her face from one side to the other. 'You used to be such a pretty girl . . .' Esther recoils and he releases her, pushing her face back, disgusted she exists, disgusted at himself for caring that she judges him, for caring he falls short. His hand lowers back to his side.

Joanne's hand slips into his once again and squeezes. Her face looks up to his as though searching for his answer, but he can't recall the question now, or even if there was one. His halted laughter hangs heavy in the silence of the shop, suspended in the heat. The ceiling fan clicks as it rotates. There's a slight wheeze to Esther's breathing. And that odour of cat piss somehow smells fresh again. He wonders who the cat belongs to. Where the cat is. Or if maybe the smell stems from Esther, not the carpet.

Joanne's gaze holds fear inside it. And something else, too, he can't quite name, but that he knows he hasn't seen for quite a while.

'I'm sorry,' he says, voice shattering the stagnant calm. He looks up and around as though just woken and still dazed. 'Yes, yes, I'm fine.' He smiles down at the girl beside him, turns to Esther. She's trembling. Shaking on the stool so that her fat jiggles. Her eyes are wide upon him, electric blue lids barely visible. 'Esther.' He releases Joanne's hand and shoves both of his deep into his pockets, shoulders hunching with the motion. He looks down at the stained carpet beneath his feet. Looks back up and finds Esther's eyes with his own. Fear still lives in her gaze. He smiles. 'It was awful good seein' ya, Esther. Been a long time. I'd be obliged if you'd tell Roy I was askin' for 'im.'

He nods once, then turns. Doe Eyes is waiting for him, one arm outstretched to take his hand again. Joanne. Joanne is waiting for him. There's this funny smile on her lips – seems unnatural with the fear still in her eyes, her face cast in shadow, the light of the shop window behind her. Tanned and lean and wiry. Brown and gold and blue. More and more traces of woman quickly creeping in every day, taking over. She looks almost like an angel standing there. No wings, but dark blonde hair as a halo shining. He thinks of his mama. Her deep faith. Thinks again of Melvin Douglas and his fondness for little girls. For the first time, he thinks he might just understand what about them got Melvin ticking. Almost. He takes Joanne's hand and follows her.

Jasper glances back just once, through the glass of the door as it shuts behind them, bell chiming. Esther still sits motionless, paper fan closed, clutched tight to her chest. She does not call after them. Does not rise. Or try to stop them. Fat still floating in orbit around her as she spills off her stool. Her hot-pink lips lie in a thin, straight line. Tears silently roll down her cheeks, leaving trails through her rouge. To Jasper's surprise, Esther raises her hand. It does not wave, just hangs in the air between them, suspended.

Lizzie swings the cab door open and throws Jasper's new second-hand clothes onto the seat. A tangled pile of blues and blacks and greys. A bit of off-white. She slams the door and leans her forehead against the hot glass. Closes her eyes. Can feel the metal of the door handle still burning hot in her hand. She tries to let her mind go blank. Tries to focus on the heat against her head. The heat in her hand. But she can't clear her mind. Can't calm it.

'Mom? You OK?'

Lizzie stands up quickly, head pulled off the glass. 'I'm fine,' she snaps, smoothing the front of her blouse as she straightens.

Katie nods. Looks down the street. Arms crossed before her. 'You want me to drive home?'

Lizzie stares down the road, eyes following the same path as her daughter's. Sun so bright it's hard to see. Concrete cooking in the heat. Mirages down the way. Small shops line the street, some open, most closed years, now rusted shut. Butcher, baker, both long boarded up. Grocer only open half days most of the week ever since the Piggly Wiggly opened up off I-10. The barber's red and white post still spins, door left open to let whatever breeze might wander in. The elementary just up the way is shut for summer. City Hall lies back down the road behind them. Courthouse, jail, what used to be a fire station, all rolled into one. The garage where Bobby once worked looks more like a scrapyard than a repair shop, rusted bits of cars and bicycles piled high, like raked leaves gathered up and discarded together. Each window in town seems dark in contrast to the brilliance of the day. Not a cloud in sight. She looks back to her daughter. 'I reckon I can drive still.'

'All right.'

Flags still hang from nearly every lamppost left over from the Fourth of July. Lizzie turns to lean her back against the hot metal of the pickup's body. She runs a hand through her tangled hair. Windblown. Feels the sun upon her. A small white Ford sedan drives past, old Mrs Anderson behind the wheel. Seeing her, Lizzie waves without thinking. Even feels a smile spread automatic on her lips, though she would not have thought herself capable of smiling in that moment. Mrs Anderson was one of Mama's schoolgirl friends. Married to a lawyer. No family of their own. When they were children, Mrs Anderson used to bring them a plate of fresh-baked chocolate-chip cookies still hot from the oven every Saturday afternoon when she'd call round to visit. And Mama would always pause whatever chore was at hand. And Lizzie and Jasper would take the plate of Mrs Anderson's cookies out round the back, and they'd hide in the sheets hung out on the clothesline and giggle and stuff their faces till their stomachs hurt.

Once Lizzie got chocolate on the sheets. Mama's nice clean sheets hung up to dry. New sheets, too. Little sticky fingerprints, all dark and brown and chocolaty. Lizzie had caught her breath. She'd be in for a spanking for sure. Big tears had welled in her eyes. But Jasper had just smiled. 'Don't fuss,' he'd said, and winked. Tears choked her throat, making it hard to breathe. Chocolate still coated her lips, her tongue. Her fingertips. 'Now watch,' said Jasper, and he'd smiled. He took another cookie off the plate. Broke it open to its gooey centre. Lizzie's throat had relaxed a little. Mouth watered. She sat up straighter, watching. Jasper took the broken open cookie and ran it over where Lizzie's fingerprints had stained. He pushed the chocolate in hard to the fabric, gooey centre right on the cloth. Ran it in circles, wider, bigger. A big brown stain beside them. Sheet still cool and wet from Mama's wash. 'It's just mud now,' Jasper'd said, and they'd laughed. They'd laughed till their sides hurt. Till tears stung their eyes and they could open them no longer. And later that night when Mama'd pulled the washing in, Daddy's belt had come down hard and swift, but Jasper had not cried out. Not even once. Lizzie had wanted to tell Daddy it was her fingerprints. That Jasper'd only been helping. But she was too scared. Tears ran down her cheeks as she'd seen Daddy's belt unfasten. 'You think you're smart, boy? Well, this will smarten you up . . .' and then she'd run from the room before her brother's spanking.

Years later Lizzie'd called round their house to ask Mr

Anderson to represent Jasper at trial. He was the best lawyer in the county. Everyone knew that. Mrs Anderson had answered the door. Silver hair tied up. But still a smile on her lips. Always a smile there waiting, warm as chocolate and just as rich. 'Elizabeth! What a surprise!'

'I'm sorry to bother you, ma'am.' Lizzie had shuffled her feet. She could remember that. Had shuffled her feet on their welcome mat. Joanne just a baby there on her hip. Moths buzzing and thudding as they beat their fragile bodies against the porch bulb. Light a muted yellow gold, night dark with heavy rain. 'Is Mr Anderson here? There's somethin' awfully important I got to speak with him 'bout.'

The smile had left Mrs Anderson's face. Lizzie would never forget that. The smiling woman stripped of her smile. Skin suddenly older, sallower, a different shade of pale. 'Of course.' Mrs Anderson had stepped aside, letting Lizzie enter.

Their house was beautiful. Hardwood floors, a deep dark oak. Walls crisp and white and filled with nicely framed family photos. Mostly black-and-white. Some coloured. An oil painting of the sea hung above their marble mantel, waves violent and frothy, foaming as they beat a lone sailboat ashore. She'd stood uncertain for a moment in the door to their sitting room, just taking it all in. The deep mahogany bookshelves that ran floor to ceiling. The leather couches lined with tiny brass buttons. The red and gold carpet. The deep gold curtains that reached all the way down to that dark floor.

'Come in, Elizabeth.' Mr Anderson was seated in an armchair by the darkened fireplace. Wrong season for a fire.

But it'd been raining out that night. She could remember that. A chill to the late March air. A freshness kin to cold.

Mr Anderson already knew why she was there. She could tell that much from the sad knowledge in his eyes as he regarded her. She'd never known Mr Anderson well. Had only really made his acquaintance through formal handshakes at church gatherings. He was semi-retired. Overweight, but not fat. A puzzle lay scattered on the coffee-table before him, less than a quarter complete. A watercolour of a museum piece she did not know or recognize. He smiled at her, that same sadness still lingering in his eyes. 'Come in, sit down.'

'Thank you, sir.' Lizzie sat on the couch across from him, shifting Joanne to balance her on her knee.

'Coffee, dear?'

A gentle hand on Lizzie's shoulder. A soft squeeze. She looked into the weathered blue eyes of Mrs Anderson, and felt warmth there. Shook her head, 'No, no, I'm fine.'

'Nonsense.' That lovely warm smile. 'I'll brew a fresh pot.' And Mrs Anderson slipped from the room. The smell of cinnamon lingered behind her.

'Do you like puzzles?'

'Excuse me?'

'Puzzles.' He gestured to the table before them. 'Do you like them?'

'I . . . I wouldn't know, sir. I haven't played too many.'

'No?'

'No.'

'Why's that?'

She hesitated. 'Seems I always end up missin' pieces.'

He reached down and took a border piece into his hand.

Turned it to study it. 'They're good for the mind. Puzzles.'
A smile tickled the corner of his mouth. An ornate Victorian clock ticked the passing minutes. Raindrops beat against the windowpane, racing down the glass.

'Sir, I ain't here to learn 'bout puzzles.'

'Aren't you?' A bemused smile now broke his features, deepening his wrinkles. No malice in it, but Lizzie felt uncomfortable all the same. She felt herself go hot and red.

'I find,' he said, more gently, 'that puzzles relax my mind.'

'It's my brother, sir.' Her voice faltered. 'It seems he's in a bit of trouble.'

'Yes.' Mr Anderson fit the puzzle piece into place. Sat back to admire its placing. 'I'd heard.'

'We need a lawyer, sir.' Her turn to pause. 'I was hoping you might be him.'

A long silence stretched between them. He leaned back in his chair, elbows on the armrests, fingers entwined before him.

Regarded her.

Somewhere, far off, thunder rumbled. The call of a barn owl caused them both to turn towards the window. Glass streaked with raindrops. Raindrops caught the room's light, tiny rainbows reflected in each tiny drop before its downward race. Odd to hear an owl call like that in such a heavy storm.

His voice, deep and calm, like thunder, he said, 'I'm not sure you can ask that of me.'

'Why's that?' She turned quickly with the words, eyes defiant, jaw tight with stress. And hope.

The wind howled as it cut round the house. A high, whiny sound, slow to fade. Fingers still entwined before him, he shifted in his chair. 'I have a conscience.'

The words slapped her. She stiffened. In her arms, Joanne gurgled and found her thumb with her mouth and sucked. Lizzie bounced her slightly on her knee. A mother's instinct. 'You think I don't?' Words harder than intended. Joanne squirmed.

Mr Anderson shook his head. 'That's not what I said, Elizabeth.' A throat-clearing pause as he looked down to his hands, then up again. 'Do you think your brother's innocent?'

'He wouldn't hurt no one.' She knew her words untrue even as she spoke them. Anger in her tone, her heart. She looked back to the window. Past the raindrops out to the darkness beyond. Then softer, scarcely a whisper, 'I don't know what to believe any more.'

Mr Anderson leaned forward, resting his elbows on his knees, hands newly clasped together. He had an earnest face. One deep-set wrinkle that creased his forehead. Crow's feet round his eyes, his mouth. 'That girl still in hospital?'

'Yessir.' Voice barely a whisper. Throat too tight to swallow.

'She doing OK?'

'She'll live.' A hollowness to her words.

He nodded. 'It may not seem it now but, trust me, that's a blessing.'

Lizzie leaned back, the leather of the couch smooth and cool against her back. Held Joanne tight to her. 'They called Bobby in, too. You hear that? Called 'im in to question.' Her voice rising, spiralling.

His still calm. 'They have reason to?'

'Bobby didn't do nothin'.' Words spat more than spoken.

'They charge him?'

'No.' She shook her head. 'They didn't keep 'im long.' A pause that felt like hours. She broke it. 'Jasper turned up at his shop, that's why. Turned up there all covered in blood.'

Silence between them a moment. He was the one finally to break it. 'I don't like being the one to tell you this now, Elizabeth, but I feel it's best you know what rumour's spreading.' He paused. 'They're sayin' Jasper couldn't have acted alone. Not on this one now, but the others. Folks are sayin' he had help. Seems most fingers are pointing at Bobby.'

Lizzie snorted. 'That's ridiculous. Bobby never hurt a fly.'

'I know, I know.' Both hands up as if to stop her. Something soothing in his tone. 'But don't you worry, that Saunders girl will clear Bobby. You've nothing to worry about there. She'll say who put her in that state.'

Lizzie let out a long breath. 'She ain't sayin' nothing, though. That's what I heard. She ain't said even one word yet.'

'An' Jasper?'

'He ain't said much neither.'

Mr Anderson leaned back in his armchair again, crossing his legs as he reclined. A flash of lightning lit the room an eerie blue, and Joanne let out a tiny cry as thunder shook the house. Lizzie rocked and shushed her, rocked and shushed her, holding her close to her chest. Raindrops still beat with fury against the windowpane.

'You'll be hard pressed to find a jury that will let him walk.'

She let his words hang between them. Knew them inside her as true. Shook her head. 'He ain't done all they sayin'. He ain't capable of it.' Defensive. Petulant. Like a child.

Mr Anderson's voice softened. 'Elizabeth . . .'

She raised her eyes to find his.

'I can't defend a man I think is guilty.'

The door swung open. Mrs Anderson's warm smile brightened the room as she entered. 'Now, here we are, dears, fresh hot coffee! Do you take milk and sugar, Elizabeth?' Kindness and something close to sadness hidden in those blue eyes. Bright and clear as crystals. She set the tray down on the edge of the coffee table, shaking her head as she brushed puzzle pieces aside.

Mr Anderson let out one dissatisfied breath and tossed his hands up in mock frustration. 'The problem with puzzles,' he said, smiling, turning to Lizzie, 'is having the space to sort them!' And then he winked. Lizzie had long thought back on that wink. Had wondered if maybe there'd been some meaning in it. Some code or double message she'd been meant to take away. She'd tried to take heart from, to find strength within, that wink, but as the years had passed, and Lizzie'd thought back on that moment further, that smile further, she'd thought more and more that maybe he was just a kind old man, only offering her reassurance, no deeper coded meanings. No secrets. Just a smile. Just a playful wink. And nothing more.

Desperation rose in Lizzie's throat. Somehow she found the words, 'No, ma'am, black is fine.' Her cup was poured. Set before her. Dark as the night outside.

She left soon after, too proud to beg for his aid. Too soul-weary for chit-chat. Coffee barely touched. Throat too tight with worry to let her drink. In the hallway as she was leaving, right before she'd reached the door, Mrs Anderson had caught Lizzie's arm. Her grip firm, fingers digging into Lizzie's skin, their eyes had met. 'Sometimes,' she'd said, 'when there's evil in this world, all we can do is pray.' The older woman's eyes searched Lizzie's another moment. 'Be careful, hon.' And she released her arm.

Lizzie squints slightly as she follows Mrs Anderson's sedan with her gaze. Right into the sunlight. She blinks and the car's already turned, crossing the railroad tracks heading west, back out into the open stretch of the prairie. Early mornings, the tracks are scattered with migrants, Mexicans mostly, looking for work for hire. The sun is high in the sky now, though, and even the last stragglers not to find a day's work have cleared out and moved on, leaving the tracks empty. Tyre-tread marks lead from the paved road to crisscross each other in the sand beside the tracks. The only remaining testimony that the ranchers and oil men driven in from the bigger towns looking to hire had in fact been there. Lizzie'd known it wouldn't be easy, Jasper being home. She'd known that trouble might raise its head again. But she hadn't expected Esther to refuse them like that. She'd hoped maybe life could go on again. Could resemble something close to normal. To how life's meant to be.

A bell chimes and Lizzie turns. Jasper and Joanne walk up the sidewalk towards them, shop door swinging shut behind them. Hand in hand. Like father and daughter might. Lizzie feels her throat go dry. Jasper meets her gaze. Holds it a moment. Looks down to where his hand holds Joanne's. Releases it. Joanne looks up at her uncle, opens her mouth to speak.

'Girls, get in the car.' Lizzie's voice low, level.

'But, Mom . . .' Joanne starts.

'I said *now*.' No messing in Lizzie's tone. She can still hear her brother's laughter ringing in her ears. *What was I thinking, letting this man into our home?*

Jasper looks back at his sister. Face blank. Hand fallen by his side, palm still up and open as though waiting to be held again. 'Go on,' he says softly, and Joanne closes her mouth into a pout. Leaves his side. Climbs up after her sister into the pickup's cab, door not quite slammed but still shut hard enough to make the truck shudder.

The laughter's left Jasper's face, though that doesn't soften it, his eyes clouded with a darkness Lizzie doesn't understand, nor is sure she wants to. They gaze at each other for a moment in silence, Jasper standing on the sidewalk, hands by his sides, head somehow still held tall. Not proud. Not exactly. But tall all the same. Lizzie leans her back against the side of the pickup again. Can feel the metal hot through her shirt. Hot against the back of her legs. The sun still hot upon them. *Must be nearing noon, from how high the sun now sits.* It is Lizzie who breaks their silence. 'Don't know what was funny 'bout that to you.'

He raises his eyes from the pavement to meet hers. 'You wanna have this conversation here?' Voice infuriatingly calm. As though everything is normal. As if they are just a normal family come to town to do their shopping. His voice deep and low.

She bites her lower lip, peers down the traffic-less street. Stop lights more for show than regulating traffic: whatever cars not local that do pass through town rarely ever stop. From somewhere music drifts. A country song, singer's voice low and sad, words too muffled to make out. 'All right,' she says, and walks round to the driver's side. Starts up the engine on the third try, motor coughing and sputtering before catching.

A knock on the back window. She meets his gaze in the rear-view mirror. Eyes so familiar yet so unknown.

'I can look at that for you,' he calls, gesturing towards the hood, and he nods before turning.

Lizzie shifts her foot onto the gas. Reverses out back onto Main Street. Says nothing. Trains her eyes away as they drive past Bobby's old garage, now 'Frank's', bought out long ago.

Joanne sits in the dark shade of the porch, bare feet on the first step, hands on the floor behind her for support, shoulders hunched high by her ears. Her sister sits a ways behind her in one of the rockers, feet drawn up onto the seat before her, painting her toenails. Red. Strands of golden hair drop across Katie's face, fallen loose from her ponytail. She holds her lower lip between her teeth, twisting her lips with concentration. In the driveway, not far before them, Uncle Jasper leans under the open hood of the pickup, but Joanne can't see him from where she sits, only the pickup bed, cab, its open hood, Uncle Jasper's hand and arm from time to time as he reaches up and holds the hood or grabs another tool. Even from where Joanne sits, his hands are black with grease.

'Katie?'

'Ummm?' Her sister does not look up.

'Daddy used to fix cars, right?' Joanne can feel her sister's eyes upon her, but she does not turn. Stares at the pickup instead. Eyes locked on it.

'That's right.'

'And Uncle Jasper used to work with 'im?'

'You know that already.' Tone not quite annoyed.

She twists around to face her sister. 'You ever see Daddy do it?'

'Do what?' Katie's focus is back on her toes again, brush held steady.

'Fix somethin'.'

Katie laughs. 'I seen 'im fix loads of things, Lady.' She smiles at her little sister. 'He used to come home each night and toss us in the air, and his nails were black like an oil man's.' She winks.

Joanne smiles. Looks back out across the garden and over to the drive where the pickup sits parked. She wishes she could remember those dirty hands, or the prickles on his chin Katie's told her he used to tease them with. 'And Uncle Jasper?' she asks. 'You ever seen him fix anythin' before?'

Voice gone quiet. 'I guess at some point I musta.'

Joanne scratches a mosquito bite by her ankle. Twists her leg to study it. 'Katie?'

'Yeah?'

'Why don't you talk much to Uncle Jasper?'

For a moment Joanne does not think her sister is going to answer her. The sun has lowered in the sky just enough to start to cool. Deep shadows stretch from the house out across the lawn, past the garden, reaching for the road.

'I talk to him fine.'

Joanne swings her legs round to face her sister full on. Crosses her legs before her like an Indian. 'Nuh-uh. You never say nothin' to 'im. Don't you like 'im?'

'I don't have to like 'im none.' Her voice gone whisper soft.

'But . . .'

'He ain't our daddy, Joanne. He ain't no replacement for 'im neither. Don't you confuse that.'

Anger in her sister's tone she had not expected. Joanne lets her mouth fall shut. Looks down at the floorboards, cracked and lined with age and wear. 'I know that.' Her turn to whisper now. Cross.

'Joanne?'

She raises her eyes.

'Uncle Jasper ain't what you think he is, OK? He ain't our friend. He ain't here to be our friend. He's been away a long time for a reason. You understand?'

'Then what's he supposed to be?' Joanne shifts her weight quickly, pulling her feet beneath her so she can sit up on her knees. Her words are more defiant than she'd meant them to be. She looks at her own unpolished nails, cuticles overgrown, bits of mud where none should be. She wishes she had her sister's pretty nails. She wonders if maybe Katie will paint hers for her. Doubts it. She picks at a loose flake of paint on the railing beside her. 'Everybody needs a friend,' she says quietly, voice barely a whisper.

'Not everyone.' The firmness of her sister's tone makes her glance over. Katie's eyes are hard, her jaw too. She looks a bit like Mom.

A cloud blocks the lowering sun and casts the whole prairie momentarily into shadow. Chickadees chirp themselves silent. Crickets sound. The wind shifts, and the clouds pass. The sun burns down again, still hot, even as the evening cools. Pink stains the horizon. Uncle Jasper's hand appears on the pickup's hood, fingers black with oil and grease. The engine sputters and starts. His hand disappears again.

'Katie, who's Rose?'

She feels rather than sees her sister freeze. 'Who told you that name?'

'I overheard Mom and Uncle Jasper talking last night.'

A pause. Then, 'What'd they say?'

Joanne likes knowing something her sister doesn't. She sits up straighter, taller. It feels good to be the one with knowledge. To hold her sister's attention. 'Mom told Uncle Jasper he'd never deserved Rose. Or something like that. And then he got real angry.'

Katie is quiet a moment. 'Don't you ever ask Uncle Jasper about that name. You hear me, Lady?' Worry in her tone.

Joanne turns to face her. Their eyes lock and hold. A

148

crow calls and falls silent. From further afield another answers, cry carried by the wind. There is fear in Katie's eyes. Wild and open and raw. And Joanne doesn't know what to say. Her tongue won't work any more. It scares her a little to see Katie afraid.

'Promise me.'

Katie's voice is still taut with strain, but Joanne's tongue won't work. She struggles to find the words. The wrong ones slip out. 'Who is she?' Voice barely a whisper it's so soft.

Katie pauses. 'Eddie Saunders' baby sister.'

The click of metal hitting gravel startles them both and makes them jump. Joanne giggles nervously. Down the driveway, Uncle Jasper curses loudly as he stoops to pick up a fallen wrench. Joanne turns back to Katie and holds her sister's gaze. No longer afraid, though she can't name what's caused the change, she asks, 'What happened to her?'

Katie puts a finger to her lips. Joanne wants to object, but the look on Katie's face keeps her silent. Katie jerks her head down the drive, indicating Uncle Jasper. She places her finger over her lips again. Squirming to hold her questions in, Joanne looks out past the garden across the prairie to where the horizon touches the gold of earth with sky. The evening primroses have just begun to bloom. Soon Mom will turn the porch light on.

'Katie?'

'Yeah?'

Her heart pounds in her chest. She feels she's so close to knowing now . . . 'Did Uncle Jasper make Daddy leave?'

'Nobody *made* Daddy leave. He chose to.' Katie's voice is hard, the same end-of-conversation tone Mom some-times uses. Joanne wonders if when she's older she'll be able to speak like that too, if she'll learn to stop questions with just her tone. Or a look. She pulls her knees into her chest and hugs them. Shifts so that her back leans against the porch railing. Katie dips the brush into the polish. Wipes the sides of it on the nozzle of the bottle as she pulls it free. Brush to nails again. Delicate strokes. The chemical smell of the paint sticks to the still warm breeze.

Joanne's mind is racing. She can't believe Katie actu-ally told her who Rose was! She never imagined her sister might actually answer her. Excited, she leans forward slightly, voice a strained whisper. 'He scared Esther Rey-nolds earlier. In the shop.'

'With that laugh of his? Yeah, I know, gives me the creeps too.'

Joanne shakes her head, happy to be in control of the conversation again, happy to know something her sister doesn't. 'No, after you and Mom left, when I went back in to get him. He grabbed Esther by the face so that her cheeks pushed together and her lips popped out like this.'

Katie looks sharply up. 'No way.'

Joanne nods. 'I swear it's true! He pushed her cheeks together 'n' I thought for sure she was gonna cry, but she didn', and then he released her 'n' I took 'is hand and he spoke real nice to her, like nothin' ever happened.'

'Did he hurt her?'

Joanne tilts her head, thinking. 'Ummm, dunno. Don't think so.' Her brow creases. 'But she looked real scared.'

'Did you tell Mom?'

'No.'

'You gonna?'

Pause. 'I don't know. I hadn't thought.'

'There's a lot of folks round here don't want Uncle Jasper back. You know that, right?'

'That why she wouldn't sell to 'im in the shop?'

Katie's turn to pause. 'Yeah, that's why.'

'Will every shop be like that? Why don't they want 'im back?'

Katie smiles. 'You ask too many questions.'

Joanne lets out her breath, frustrated. 'Are you *ever* gonna tell me what he did? I know you know, don't you? Katie, *please* tell me! I have to know!' Excited now, her voice spirals almost shrill.

'Sssssh!' Katie puts her finger to her lips and glances down the drive towards Uncle Jasper. 'Keep your voice down, idiot!'

Joanne crosses her arms over her chest, brow furrowed in a pout. 'Are – you – ever – gonna – tell – me?' she mouths, exaggerating each word to the extreme.

Katie's face breaks into a smile, and it's as if the sun sits high in the sky again. She looks out over the prairie, and for a second Joanne doesn't think her sister will answer her. She just sits there, smiling. When she finally speaks, her voice is calm, all fear washed from it, musical and sweet. Joanne wishes she sounded like that, pretty. 'One day I'll tell you, kiddo, OK? I promise that. You deserve to know.' A seriousness beneath her sister's smile. Katie dips the brush back into the polish and screws the lid tight. 'There!' She holds out her feet before her, hovering in the air. 'What do you think?' Red toes flash and wiggle in the fading sunlight. The colour of Mom's roses that line the drive. No, deeper, darker, more like blood.

'You'll really tell me one day?'

Their eyes meet. Katie smiles. 'Course I will, Lady. Just don't hold your breath.' And she winks.

And Joanne can't help but smile.

He knows the girls are talking about him. It wouldn't take a genius to put two and two together either, what with how they keep their voices real low and how every time he glances up one or the other is glancing over at him. It makes his blood boil, just a little, seeing them judge him like that. *Who made them jury?* But at the same time Jasper can't blame them either. When he first came to Huntsville, there were rumours, too, whispers and glances. Men who had to be defied. Others, respects paid to. He had had his fair share of scrapes, in the beginning that is, when his pride had still held power over him. He had beaten one man till all his teeth came out, face an unrecognizable fleshy blood pool, mouth a bowl of blood with bits of bone stewing in it. Must have been teeth at one time, those bits of bone, but they sure weren't when he saw them swimming there before him, the boy coughing so that the blood in his mouth seemed to boil. He couldn't remember the kid's name now. That's all he'd been, a kid, really. Jasper himself barely much older. It had won him respect, though. It had stopped the others talking. Yes, of course there'd been solitary confinement to survive, the odd smack off the guards for misbehaving thereafter. But he'd come out of solitary a changed man. Head on his shoulders again, rage safely bottled down deep inside. Guards couldn't fault him once for bad behaviour. Not after that. He cannot recall that boy's name now, and he feels a bit guilty for that. Feels like he should somehow remember. Like maybe he owes the boy that much wherever he may be. Truth is, though, Jasper realizes, as he bends over the pickup's greasy engine, he can't even remember the boy's face. Before the fight, that is. He remembers the bloody mask too well. The crunch of the jaw as the teeth splintered beneath his fist. As they crumbled and splintered again.

It was 1969 the last time he worked on an engine like this. Feels good to work with his hands again. He could almost be back in the shop with Bobby, working side by side, except Bobby would have had the radio cranked up loud, and there would have been no setting sun warm upon his neck. Feels good to feel the day again. He'd missed that. More than he'd realized. Being kept inside all that time.

He hadn't expected that off Esther earlier. It makes him wonder how Roy sees him, these days. How the rest of folks see him. 'I am what I am,' he mumbles to himself. It felt good touching Esther like that. Even though it was just her face. Even though she'd grown so fat. Felt good to touch a woman's face. Felt good to see her start to respect him again as they were leaving. He would never hurt her, he tells himself, not really. He'd never disrespect Roy like that for one thing. There was a time they'd been joined at the hip, he and Roy. Another lifetime ago. Before the trouble started.

His hand slips and Jasper drops the wrench he holds. It clatters itself silent on the pavement of the drive. Too loud in the still evening. The girls silence and glance over. He can feel their eyes upon him. He doesn't like feeling watched. Especially now that he's free. *How*, Jasper wonders, *do I win the respect of two young girls?* He surprises himself with the thought. Is surprised to find he cares what they think of him. Especially the younger one. He'd like her not to judge him. Inside, something tells him fighting isn't the way to stop the girls talking. Not this time. Not ever. Not in this free-man's prison known as life.

He stoops and picks up the wrench. Cusses. Walks back to the pickup and buries his head under the hood. Elbow deep in grease, he tries to focus on the task at hand. Inhales the grease and oil. The gasoline. He pictures himself living again those years that he wasted, imagines an existence where life is as simple as a hard day's work. He could have had a good life, he reckons. Those could have been a great ten years. Yes, if things had just been different.

He doesn't know how long she's been standing there. He hadn't noticed when the hum of the girls' voices fell silent. But the crickets are fully singing now, and purple chases the streaks of pink that spread across the darkening sky. Behind her, he can see her older sister still sitting up on the front porch, leaning back in one rocker while her feet rest on the arm of the other, legs out long. Waiting for her toes to dry. Unknowingly sexy. Teasingly so. Or maybe she does know, he thinks, maybe women always know just how much they tempt. He takes a rag and tries to wipe the oil off his hands, though it doesn't seem to do much good. Fingers still stained dark, dark beneath his nails, dark in the contoured lines that cross his palms.

She watches him. One bare foot wraps around her other leg to scratch behind her calf. No polish on her nails. He likes that. The rawness of it. The immaturity. Her eyes question his. A slight hesitation, then she steps forward to look under the hood beside him. 'Did you fix it?'

'Just 'bout.'

'What was wrong with it?'

'Fan weren't turnin' right.'

'Was it hard to fix?'

'Not if that's it fixed now. If it acts up again, well, that's another story.'

'How do you know if it's fixed?'

He hesitates. 'Have to turn the engine on. Let it run a while. Listen to how the motor sounds. Watch how that belt there turns.'

'Oh.' She leans away from the engine so that her weight rests on her heels. Arms out long before her, hips pulling back. Fingers still clutching the frame of the hood as she leans away.

It's nearly too dark now to see the nuts and bolts of the engine clearly. He finishes wiping his hands. Sets the cloth down. Falters. Uncertain. Out of practice how to speak to little girls. How to speak to any girls, really. But then again, he never was that practised. His voice catches in his throat, deepening his tone. 'I'm sorry if I frightened you. Last night. Or there earlier. In town. That wasn't my intention.'

Her head turns faster than a blink. Eyes wide upon

him, taking him in. 'That's OK. I wasn't scared. Not really. Or . . . well, last night I was, but not earlier.'

He nods, staring into the dark engine. 'Why'd you come in after me?'

Doe Eyes straightens, twisting side to side as she thinks. At length she shrugs. 'Everyone needs a friend.'

His turn to straighten, silent. Wary. 'You think I'm your friend?'

'Aren't you?'

He looks back down into the now dark engine before them. He'll need a flashlight soon if he's to work on. It's been a long while since he had someone he'd call a friend. There had been Roy, of course, all those years ago, back when they were boys, and even Bobby for a time. They had been friends. And Pascal Ramirez, whom he'd spent that summer laying tarmac with on that job just west of Waco. But there were no friends in prison. Not really. Brothers, maybe, of a sort, forged by blood and bond, but no, no friends. Not really. He's never been friends with a girl before that he can recall. Especially not a child.

He gestures towards the pickup. 'You wanna see if she's fixed?' His voice sounds husky, even to his ears.

Joanne's eyes sparkle as she turns to him. She nods.

'You stay there 'n' I'll start 'er up. Watch that fan there to see if the belt moves. Holler at me if it doesn'.' He drops the dirty rag onto the pavement, hands still stained. Glances up to the house, lights just now flicking on inside. In the shadows of the porch, Katie still reclines, and he can feel her eyes even when they're not upon him, watching him, watching them. He sits behind the wheel. Turns the key in the ignition. First try, the engine purrs.

There are butterflies in Katie's stomach even before Josh's pickup pulls up. She watches its lights from a great distance moving across the prairie towards her, as though racing to catch her before the fall of night. All she wants is his arms around her.

She rises before he reaches the drive, steps inside and runs up the stairs real fast, two at a time, like when she was a kid. Like Joanne still sometimes does. Her room is dark, silent. Messier than she'd like. But it doesn't matter. Not now. She crosses the room quickly, stepping over discarded clothes. Glances in the mirror. Pulls her hair down and brushes it out. Long blonde strands reach to her waist, tangle and catch in her comb. She can hear his truck now on the road. He'll be pulling up any minute . . .

She hurriedly applies some more mascara. Blinks at herself in the mirror to let it set. Sprays a bit of that perfume Josh gave her. Her neck, her breasts, each wrist. It smells a bit sweet, like bubble gum, but she likes it. She likes that he likes it. She likes that he bought it for her, and she likes the shape of the pretty pink bottle. She feels pretty when she wears it. Sure beats sweat or the smell of fried food from the diner. Katie grabs some lipstick, a light pink shade called 'Petal Rose', and tucks the tube into her front pocket, then runs back down the stairs, across the landing. Calls out, 'Josh is here, Mama. I'm goin'!' She opens the door right as Josh cuts his engine.

And somehow the whole evening goes quiet.

She pauses in the doorway, uncertain, not sure what feels wrong. The evening is humid still, and the day sticks to her. Sweaty strands of hair cling to her, wrap around her waist and limbs. Uncle Jasper slowly rises from where he's bent over the toolbox, wiping the grease off the tools as he sets them back. Her grandfather's tools. His father's. Joanne sits cross-legged there on the gravel beside the tool box. She's holding a wrench in her hand, tightening and loosening its grip on thin air. She looks up when Katie comes out. Smiles. Then looks to Josh's pickup as he cuts his engine and grins that big goofy-kid grin of hers. 'Hey, Josh!' Joanne calls, waving excitedly, and she jumps up real fast and starts running to his pickup. Katie'd like to run to him, too. For a moment, she envies her sister that she can. That she can run without looking stupid. That being cool doesn't matter yet. Shit, Joanne wouldn't even know what playing cool meant. But inside Katie's running. She's across the garden already, leaping the picket fence, weather-worn, paint peeling, she's falling into his arms already, and he's holding her. Inside she's calling out his name, she's screaming it on repeat. Katie raises a hand as Josh steps out of the truck. She leans against the porch railing and smiles. Finds his eyes with hers across the garden, still bright blue even in the growing shadows. But his eyes aren't soft and teasing. Not tonight. He glances to her, and their eyes catch but don't hold. There is no smile for her, and she feels her own fade.

Joanne runs to Josh and hugs him, and he swoops her up and spins her around and sets her down real fast, and

Katie wishes that were her. She's jealous of her sister's giggle. It doesn't matter that Joanne is just eleven: Katie wants Josh's touch only for her. 'Hey, li'l missus,' Josh says, as he ruffles Joanne's hair, and she squirms away, giggling, but there isn't the usual laughter in his tone. His eyes are stormy, his smile clouded.

Joanne is tugging on his arm, pulling him down the drive. 'Did you meet Uncle Jasper yet? You gotta meet him! He just fixed Mom's truck!'

'That right?' Josh's voice is slow and strong. Guarded. 'No, I ain't met 'im yet.'

Oh, please, God, no, Katie thinks. *Don't be like that.*

Jasper stands cleaning the last of the grease from his hands. He regards the boy without emotion. With a coolness that chills Katie, despite the evening's humidity. The primroses have fully opened now, last streaks of pink deepening to purple in the sky. The moon, a thin sliver, has just risen, and a few stars can be seen, their light still dim. Crickets call, fall silent and call again. A few birds sing as they nest down for the night. Their songs somehow both interrupt and complement each other. Katie likes the sound, the song of another day's end on the prairie.

'Hey, Josh,' she says, quickly crossing the garden to walk to him. Her voice sounds weak to her, shaky. She tries to will it strong. She forces a grin as she's close to him, hoping it doesn't look contrived. 'Come on.' She jerks her head towards his pickup. 'Let's get out of here.'

'Hey, baby.' Something's off in his voice too. She can hear it. Feel it. She tries hard not to look at Uncle Jasper. Can feel his eyes upon her as she reaches up to peck Josh's lips hello with hers. She closes her eyes a moment, then pulls her mouth away from his, still tasting hello on her lips. She finds his eyes with hers.

'Let's go.' This time whispered only for his ears.

He looks down at her and his face softens. 'OK . . .'

She slips her hand into his, his palm warm and strong around hers.

'You her boyfriend, I take it?' His voice too loud in the still evening. Overpowering the birdsong. The crickets' song. A harshness to his words, as though judgement's just been passed.

Josh's hand releases hers. She pulls the other back from where it rested on his chest while she kissed him. She can sense his body tense. 'Yes, sir, that's right. I'm her fella.'

Jasper nods as though expecting that answer. He tosses the greasy towel from one hand to the other as he grinds dirt only soap and hot water can lift further into his hands. He leans back against the still-open hood of the truck, one leg casually crossed before the other. 'What's your name, boy?'

Josh hesitates. 'Joshua Ryan.'

'You Chuck's boy?'

'That's right.'

Jasper tosses the towel aside and raises his eyes to the boy's. 'I never much liked your father.'

She can feel Josh stiffen. 'He don't much care for you neither.'

Jasper smiles. 'I'da guessed as much.'

She can feel her uncle's eyes move to her. Not undressing her. Not exactly. More the opposite, really, as though desperately trying to dress her with his eyes, to add and add more clothing. She can feel him appraise her, and doesn't like it.

'What's it like?' Josh's words surprise her. 'Being free?'

'You tell me.'

Josh snorts.

There is a coldness to her uncle's voice that makes her spine crawl. She takes Josh's hand again, whispers, 'Come on, let's go.'

He stands solid. Eyes locked on her uncle. Jasper holds his hands out, inspects the stains still black upon them. Folds his arms across his chest. 'Your daddy still knockin' about with Eddie Saunders 'n' that crew?'

Katie forgets to breathe. She looks quickly for Joanne. Joanne's eyes widen as she skips through the garden, pretending not to listen.

'A bit.'

'A bit?' Jasper grunts.

'That's right. I said they're friends.'

'Yeah, well . . . You tell your daddy 'n' his fine friends I ain't back for trouble.' His eyes go dark and cold. 'You pass that on, you hear? Eddie ain't got no business how I see it drivin' his truck by here.'

Josh spits on the ground and takes his time answering the older man. 'Way most folks round here see it, you ain't got no business being back.' Defiance in his words, his tone.

'Josh, please, don't.' Words a soft whisper. Hands to his elbow, softly urging, pulling, *Let's go.*

Jasper nods real slow. 'You ever been in a fight, boy? A real fight? Now, I ain't talkin' 'bout some schoolyard scrape or a smack among friends. I ain't talkin' 'bout no whoopin' off your daddy neither. You ever known real pain? No, I doubt you ever known a man's pain, boy. With that pretty baby face of yours. So you'll show some respect, you hear? And if you ever so much as make that pretty girl of yours shed one single tear, I swear to Jesus I'll make you better than sorry.'

Josh's mouth hangs open, then snaps shut real sharp. It takes him a second to draw himself up tall again. 'I ain't afraid of you.' He spits a big white wad of mucus onto the grass. For a moment it glistens silver-white against the dark of the lawn before it evaporates into nothing there before them.

Jasper ignores the spit as if it never happened. Stands up real casual, uncrossing his legs as he steps forward. As if Josh never spoke. He glances back down into the dark hood of the pickup. Bits of engine catch and reflect what little light remains. Other nuts and bolts, the fuel pump, the carbonator lie cloaked enough in shadow to have disappeared from view. Jasper waves his hand dismissively as he turns to glance down at the engine. 'Now, like I said, I ain't here for trouble. You spread that word.' He shuts the hood and turns to walk away.

For a second, Katie thinks Josh isn't going to answer him. Inside she prays he won't. She tightens her fingers on his arm, her nails digging into his flesh. 'Josh, it isn't worth it,' she whispers hoarsely. *Too late.*

'Don't you worry!' Josh calls after her uncle. 'I'll be sure to tell my pops 'n' Eddie you was askin' for 'em! Eddie'll be real pleased to hear he ain't allowed to drive down this road no more.' He laughs then, this short hyper-laugh, almost panicky, almost hysterical in sound, high-pitched, the way he and the boys might laugh when bullying Naveen Simons or one of the other nerds at school. Except that laugh always seemed more normal then, more harmless. Just jocks being jocks. And taunting a smaller kid at school was one thing.

Jasper was another.

Her uncle turns slowly. He'd reached the first step of the front porch and his foot has to come back down off the step before he turns. The greasy towel is still clutched in one hand. 'Don't be a fool, boy.' Disdain thick on every word. 'Go diggin' up what don' concern you 'n' all you'll find is pain.'

Josh shrugs his arm, shaking Katie's hand free. That laugh again. More panicky this time, it lasts only a second, but that second's long enough. 'Go diggin'? Fine choice of words. We go diggin' 'n' I reckon we could uncover you a whole 'nother sentence in Huntsville.'

'Josh! Stop it!'

Something clouds her uncle's face. A look she's never seen before, more animal than man. His face twists, contorts into a snarled smile, no humour in his eyes, no humour there at all. A look that will haunt her. 'I served my time, son.' His words hiss round every *s*. 'Who do you think you are, judgin' me? Go diggin' if you're so sure. Heck, hold on, I'll lend you my shovel.' Something deadly in his eyes. This cold, hard darkness. And something wild in him, like a cornered animal about to pounce.

Josh falters.

The door opens and the porch light pops on. 'Evening, Josh.' Lizzie's voice is winter cold.

'E-evening, ma'am,' he sputters. Shading his eyes from the sudden light, looking around, uncertain, as though someone else hidden might spring out.

'Why don't you take Katie out now, like you'd planned?' Lizzie's voice is civil but lacks its usual warmth. 'I ain't sayin' you're not welcome here, Josh,' she continues, 'I know Katie's awful fond of you, and I want my daughter to be happy, but I think it's time you left tonight. There's no need for this. There's no bad blood between our families, boys. Let's keep it that way.' Lizzie leans against the door frame, face half in shadow. Her voice is even, not one word out of control. The sight of her mother comforts Katie. Takes the chill from her spine.

Jasper stands silhouetted by the light cast from the porch, his face completely lost in shadow.

Katie takes Josh's arm again. Carefully, not certain he won't pull away. 'Come on,' she whispers. 'Mom's right. Let's get out of here.'

Josh falters again, his eyes still on her mother. 'Ma'am.' He dips his head, the way a man with a ten-gallon might, except his head is bare. 'I'm sorry. I –'

Lizzie cuts him off: 'I know, Josh. No harm done. And no need for none of that anger, neither, you hear?' Her eyes shift to Katie. 'You two best be off, I think . . . Joanne!' Joanne looks up, wide-eyed, from the corner of the garden where she'd stood still. 'Them potatoes in the kitchen sink won't peel themselves. Get to it.'

'But, Mom . . .' Her whine sounds shrill in the stillness of the just fallen night.

'I said *now*!'

Katie feels almost sorry for her sister as she watches her

go inside. Joanne hangs her head and solemnly pushes past their uncle up the steps. She pauses for a moment, standing before their mother. Opens her mouth to speak. Says nothing. Steps inside. *Smart kid*, Katie thinks, and can't help but almost smile.

'Now, you have her home before twelve,' Lizzie calls, voice firm. 'And you kids have fun, you hear?'

'Yes, ma'am,' Josh says, and without even looking at Katie, he turns back towards where his truck is parked. Up at the top of their drive, just barely pulled in off the country road. 'Come on.' His words are angry, spat at her, sharp. He doesn't look back to see if she follows him.

But she does. She always does. All she wants is his arms around her, telling her everything's all right. 'Josh!' she calls after him. 'Please. Don't be like that!' She has to struggle to catch up to him.

Josh opens the door on the driver's side, cussing under his breath, and slams it hard behind him. Katie wishes he'd thought to open the door for her on her side like he usually does. She would have liked Mom and Uncle Jasper to see him do that for her, but she knows Josh's mind is far from his manners right now. She opens the door herself. Pauses to look back at the house. Her mother and Uncle Jasper stand like two dark scarecrows silhouetted by the porch light, the garden a tangle of shadows before them. A firefly flicks on and off as it floats across the lawn. 'I don't want no trouble,' she hears her uncle call out softly behind them, voice barely above a whisper, really. Had the wind blown a different way she would not have made out his words. 'You spread that word,' he calls. 'I'm done with trouble.'

She slides onto the seat beside Josh and shuts the door.

They sit in silence for a second. He doesn't look at her. Says, 'I hope to hell that same poison ain't runnin' in your veins,' then turns the key in the ignition and pulls off.

He pauses in the kitchen door, uncertain what has stopped him. Maybe it's the warmth of the light spilling from the room. Maybe it's the tune she's humming. Her back is to him. She stands on a small wooden stool so that her hip bones are even with the sink. Head bowed over the work she's doing, the peels fall one by one into a mountain in the washing-up bowl as she places each potato in a pot, ready to be boiled. He didn't think he made a sound, but he must have because she turns. No smile, not at first, and he wonders what she sees in him, what scars of anger must still line his face. She'd said they were friends. He wonders if she meant it.

'I didn't mean to startle you.' His voice rough, husky, still too long out of practice at trying to sound 'nice'.

'You didn't.' She turns back to the sink.

He stays in the doorway, uncertain if he should enter.

She looks back again. 'You can help, if you want.'

'Help?' Even to him his voice sounds broken.

Her focus is back on the task at hand. 'You ever peeled a potato before?'

He takes a cautious step forward. Cocks his head. 'It's been a while.'

Joanne places a now nude potato in the pot with the others. 'It's real easy. You can't mess it up. Here, I'll show you.' And she bounces down off the stool, crosses the kitchen, opens a drawer and pulls out a peeler. 'You'll need this.' Still no smile on her lips. Tiny drops of water drip from her wet hands onto the floor. Seems strange not to see her smile. She crosses the kitchen again. Steps back up on that stool. Somehow he finds himself beside her.

For the second time that night, Jasper is aware of just how much he's come to enjoy working with his hands. He likes the feel of the earth still clinging to the potato skins before he washes it off. Likes the rhythmic pattern of the peeling, the simple satisfaction at seeing the peel pile grow, the pot fill. Carrots are next, mud thick upon them, colouring the water as it pools down the drain. His mind drifts there for a while, as they work in silence side by side. He thinks about helping his mama in that same kitchen all those years ago, when he was even younger than the girl now standing beside him. He thinks about these Russian dolls Roy's mother used to have where one lady fit inside the other, over and over, smaller and smaller. Lizzie and Esther used to play with them sometimes when Mrs Reynolds wasn't looking. He remembers a story he'd overheard in prison told by some spick he never himself knew, about a donkey down in Mexico in the boy's native village that got into the corn and nearly ate itself to death. He wonders what got him there – from potatoes to dolls to corn. He wonders what happened to that donkey. He feels at peace. Listens to her humming.

It's only when she speaks that he realizes it's now he who hums.

'Uncle Jasper?'

He glances at her. Keeps on peeling.

'Why didn't you like Josh?'

'I got no problem with the boy.'

They peel again in silence. 'Uncle Jasper?'

'Yeah?' Voice gravelly.

'What'd Josh mean when he said that thing about diggin'?'

The carrot feels cool in his palm, its outside so rough still but the inside polished smooth. Like a different vegetable altogether. He turns to her, unsurprised to find her eyes wide upon him. He'd known they would be. He can feel when her eyes are on him; he has grown to know her at least that well. He hadn't expected the openness of her face, though, as she looks trustingly up at him. That childish innocence clouded by all the mystery of woman that's slowly seeping in. No, that he hadn't quite expected, and it stuns him, the innocence of her, the beauty she will one day grow to be, despite her awkwardness now. He doesn't want to tarnish that. Sometimes it seems that everything he touches stops shining.

'Why was he thinking of diggin'?' Joanne asks, big eyes searching his. 'What was he lookin' for?'

Jasper swallows. Forces a smile. 'He ain't thinkin' of diggin'. That was talk is all.'

'You offered him a shovel.'

'I did.' A peel falls loose and hits the bowl barely making a sound. He can feel her eyes still on him.

'What's buried?'

He pauses. 'A treasure of sorts, I guess.'

'Buried treasure?' Voice shrill with excitement.

He glances at her, frowning, then away. 'You could call it that.'

'Like a pirate?'

He peels a long strip of orange skin. Watches as it falls into the bowl. 'Different kind of treasure.'

'Oh.' Her brow furrows in thought as she falls silent again, and they switch to snapping the ends off a pile of green beans. He likes the crisp snap of the beans, the gentle thud as the discarded ends hit the sink. A sound that's barely sound. The clock ticks. Somewhere in the house a floorboard creaks and falls silent. She turns back to him, brow still deeply furrowed. 'Is it valuable?'

'What?'

'The treasure.'

He tosses the green bean he holds into the pot and reaches for another. Rinses it beneath the running tap. 'It ain't worth money if that's the answer you're after.'

'Did you bury it?'

He snaps the end off the green bean, pulling its stringy green spine. Tosses it aside and reaches for another. 'A lot of folks round here seem to think I did.'

'Did you?'

He looks at her a long moment. Forces a tired smile that even his own lips don't trust. 'What do you think?'

She shakes her head. So much innocence in those eyes. Wider even, maybe, than a doe's. 'I dunno what to think.'

He nods. 'That's a good way to be, Doe Eyes. You stick with that.'

His breath catches, afraid to make a sound. He hadn't meant to call her that. Not out loud. For a moment she freezes, brow deeply creased, then her face glows as she beams up at him.

*

It's a long time before they speak. Josh is driving too fast, and she wants to tell him to slow down, but Katie's afraid that if she breaks their silence he'll just start yelling at her, so she holds her tongue. Bites it for a while, but then they hit a pothole, and the whole pickup lurches, bouncing up off the road. When it comes down again, loose gravel spins out from under the wheels, hitting the pickup's body with tiny hollow thuds. Another pothole throws Katie forward. She catches herself against the dashboard, using the heels of her hands to brace herself. Bites her lip as she's thrown forward, her teeth lightly nipping her skin. A single tear runs down her cheek. Hot, sticky, she wipes it away. Josh doesn't notice, eyes glued to the road before them, or if he does, he doesn't show it. There aren't streetlights on these back-country roads, so the road before them is visible only in tiny bursts illuminated by Josh's high beams as they hurtle forward. Looking out of her side window, Katie can see nothing but the dark stretch of prairie around them. They pass no other cars.

They almost miss their turn. A small dirt road that leads down to the creek. One of those roads you have to know about to find, and even then at night it's hard to spot. A road too small to have been mapped or named. Their tyres squeak and burn as Josh cuts the turn too sharp. The kind of turn that leaves black skid marks on the pavement. Katie has to brace herself not to fall into Josh as they turn. She wants to fall into him. She usually would. She wants this whole stupid thing behind them. But it's not that simple. Nothing seems simple any more. So she holds onto the door handle, the leather of it smooth, cool in her palm. Josh grips the steering-wheel tight enough to turn his knuckles white. The radio is off.

The road is narrow now, scarcely wider than the pickup, and Josh is forced to slow a bit as they ease downhill. The only incline for miles. The only thick growth of trees for miles, too, as branches reach out, scratch at the sides of the truck, and attempt to reach through the open windows as the truck rolls past. The creek is different than the prairie. It's a bit of a drive north, but worth it all the same, their hidden oasis tucked into the beginnings of hill country. Trees grow thick along the creek bank, tangled roots twisting around each other in their quest for water. Vines hang down from some of the taller trees, and long thick beards of white moss from some branches – kids often use the vines to swing across the creek or to swing out and drop down into the water when the creek is swollen high enough. It's been a good few weeks since the last rainstorm, though, and the creek is low, tangled roots along its bed even more exposed than usual. There are more rocks around it than sand. In the day, the foliage is thick enough that the shade stays nice and cool. At night, nearly all the stars are blocked by overlapping leaves.

There are a couple of other trucks already parked along the creek bed. Light from a fire flickers where it dances further up the bank. The murmur of voices and laughter drifts to them, carried on the wind. Josh pulls up off the dirt road and cuts the engine. Turns to open his door. She catches his wrist before he can, his hand that's still on the steering-wheel. 'Josh?'

He says nothing.

'You OK?'

He turns to her then, but she can't see his face. It's too dark in the pickup. 'I don't want you livin' with that creep.'

She lets out a breath too long held. Collapses back against her seat, hand coming up to press her palm against her forehead. 'God, Josh!' She can't keep the annoyance from her voice. 'We've been over this!'

'You want me to just pretend I'm OK with it?'

'No . . .' She presses the heel of her hand further into her forehead. Can feel a headache starting.

'It ain't right, what he's doin'.'

'Oh, yeah? What's he doin' that's so wrong?'

'Men like that should die in prison.'

She takes her hand down and looks at Josh's profile. A tiny bit of moonlight illuminates his features enough for her to see the anger chiselled there. 'He ain't *that* bad, Josh. Yeah, he gives me the creeps, and he's got this weird laugh, and he's a bit odd and all, but I mean . . .' Her voice trails off. She thinks of Uncle Jasper earlier in Esther's shop, touching those women's panties. Of the look on his face when he touched them. The look on his face when he noticed her watching him. She thinks about how his eyes ran up and down her legs while she sat on the porch waiting for her toes to dry. Thinks back to photographs in newspapers long ago. 'I don't know,' she whispers finally. 'I don't know what to think. I'm scared sometimes, Josh.' Her voice cracks then, falters, and she can feel the tears burning behind her eyes, and suddenly his arms are around her, and she knows it's going to be OK, surely everything is going to be OK. He holds her like that for some time, saying nothing, stroking her long blonde hair.

She can still feel the anger in him, tense in his arms around her, but at least his arms *are* around her. She feels safe.

At length she whispers into his chest, 'Did you hear 'bout Esther Reynolds?'

His hand pauses on her head. 'No.' His words cautious, guarded. 'Tell me.'

'He grabbed her by the face. Scared her real bad, I think.' She sniffs back a sob. 'Joanne saw it.'

'In town?'

'Yeah, in her shop.'

'Did he hurt her?' His voice has gone real quiet.

'I don't think so. Not bad anyway.' Her voice chokes up again. 'I don't know . . .'

'It's OK . . .' He presses her tighter to him. 'It's OK.' He strokes her hair again. Pulls her from him gently to sit her up so he can see her. Takes his index finger to lift her chin so their eyes are even. 'He ever hurt you, baby?'

She chokes back another sob. 'No.'

He searches her eyes. 'You sure abou' that?' The intensity in his gaze frightens her a little.

'Yeah, I'm sure.'

'He ever touch you none?'

'No, he never touched me! What you gettin' at?'

'Nothin'.' He pulls her to him again. 'Just worryin' 'bout you is all.' He kisses her on her forehead, real soft, his hand behind her neck, now resting where skull and spine meet. There's something reassuring about just feeling his hand there. Someone hollers from by the campfire, the sound of their call and the laughter that follows carried upstream on the breeze. Josh and Katie instinctively look over. 'You wanna go join the others? Ray's meant to

173

have beers.' He smiles at her, his voice gone back soft again.

She feels her own smile break and spread. 'Oh, he's got beers, does he?' She playfully pulls at the collar of Josh's shirt.

He's grinning now, full on, teeth white in the moonlight. 'Yeah,' he nods, 'that's right.'

'Well, then, I guess we'd best go over.' And she leans across the cab to lightly kiss his lips. She can feel the anger easing from him as his body starts to relax.

There's nine of them round the campfire. Hank Trident lit the thing right in the centre of a large boulder to stop any chance of the fire spreading. That's how dry things are. One spark and the whole prairie could go up. Or that's what Hank's told them anyway, and his daddy volunteers at the fire station so he ought to know. The boulder sits right at the edge of the creek bank. Usually, when the water's at normal levels, the stream comes right up high on the boulder so that you can sit on it and let your feet dangle down deep into the cool creek water, but everything's gone so dry lately that there's a good couple feet between the top of the boulder and where the water starts. Dark lines on the rock hint where the water should be. It's too late now for fireflies, but the mosquitoes are out, and every now and then someone stands up swatting and cussing before moving closer to the fire to seek refuge in its smoke.

Ray Credinski brought beer, just like he'd promised, and somehow or another Kristen Maylor got her hands on a bottle of tequila her folks had brought back from somewhere across the border, the other side of

Brownsville. There's a worm in the bottom of the bottle that makes the girls shriek. The boys act like they aren't bothered, when truth is there's few among them that truly want to drink that worm.

When Katie and Josh stroll up hand in hand, the whole campfire goes quiet. That awkward silence, like a conversation's just fallen short. Katie can guess what the topic must have been. News travels fast in a small town. And a convict released, anywhere, is pretty big news. A chill finds its way down her spine and she shudders even though the night is warm.

'Hey, Katie. Josh.' Ray slaps him on the back. ''Bout time y'all showed up!' He hands them both beers, and Josh pops the tops off them with his teeth, and everyone whoops and hollers. An owl calls from further down the creek bed, its voice echoing off the rocks as it travels away from them, their noise and their fire, bad for its midnight hunting. Emma Golepi gives Katie a swig from the tequila bottle. For a moment she thinks she can see the worm's eyes looking at her through the glass as she drinks, its twisted golden brown body floating there in the liquid before her. Katie wonders what it tastes like, who will end up eating it. The tequila burns her mouth, her throat, and she coughs after the bottle leaves her lips, and everyone laughs. *There is something nice*, Katie thinks, *about laughter shared between friends. Nothing nasty in the sound. Not like Uncle Jasper's.* Katie coughs again as the tequila goes down, her face screwing up at the sour aftertaste. She can feel the trail the liquor's left inside her, raw and burning from lip to gut. She takes another swig and feels it follow the same path. Josh grabs the bottle from her and takes a long swig, then lets out a big whoop, shakes his head, pulls her in and kisses her, and everything tastes like tequila, and everything burns. That good burn. She likes the taste of alcohol on her boyfriend's tongue. The burn of both inside her. Her head is spinning, but she's not drunk, not yet. Voices swirl around her, mixing with the flames of the campfire. For a moment, everything seems good again. Seems normal. She closes her eyes. Feels the heat of the fire on her face. The burn of the tequila still raw inside her. The creek just barely gurgles, it's so low, and she has to strain to hear it. Crickets sound, then silence on its banks. Far off a coyote howls, and she can feel the call inside her, reaching up to that sliver of moon.

'So what's it like, anyway, living with a madman?'

Katie's eyes pop back open.

'Ray!' Emma smacks his arm and everyone giggles nervously.

'Hell, no! I'm serious!' He stands up. Firelight dances across his face. He's not a bad-looking boy. If it weren't for his acne he might even have been handsome. Katie can see why Emma likes him. He takes a long swig from his beer. 'Ain't nobody I known lived with a madman before 'n' I wanna know what it's like!'

'Shut up, Ray!' Emma smacks him again. Looks across the fire to Katie, 'Sorry' etched in her eyes.

'Yeah, what's it like? What's he like?' Kristen leans forward, dark hair spilling over her shoulder. 'I bet he's a total creep.'

Josh snorts and stands up too. 'You can say that again.'

'No, he isn't!' Katie playfully throws an empty can up at Josh, who towers over her. He dodges it and laughter ripples through the group, subtle as far-off thunder. Katie's not quite sure why she defended her uncle so quickly there. Like it came automatic. Maybe because of what he said to Josh about if he ever made her shed one single tear . . . She's not sure. Seems wrong, anyway, how everyone's against him. Seems wrong, yet inside she knows it's justified. She shies away herself.

'I met 'im the other day in the station when he first got off the bus. Seemed damn creepy to me.' Eric Hayden takes a small swig from his beer. Lets it rest in his hands before him. He absentmindedly pushes his ten-gallon hat up on his head a little to scratch at his forehead. Lets the hat fall back down again, low over his eyes.

'You actually met him?' Kristen's dark eyes shift to Eric as she swigs the tequila and passes the bottle further on round the circle.

'Well . . . sort of. He bought a Coke is all. Asked after a job 'n' I told 'im there was none goin'.'

'Ewwww, can you imagine just seeing him workin' in a shop somewhere? I'd die!'

'What's he like, Katie, for real?' Hank this time. Usually the quiet one of the group. His folks farm longhorns west of town. A scar runs down from his nose and across both lips, mauled by a bull back in the fourth grade. He's second cousins with the Reynolds. Everyone's gone quiet, looking at her now, and Katie doesn't like the feeling. She doesn't want to be the centre of attention. Not tonight. Not for this.

She looks down at her red toenails shining in the firelight. Her flip-flops are in Josh's truck. The boulder feels smooth and solid beneath her bare feet. She focuses on her toes as she speaks. 'He gives me the creeps a bit, but he's all right, I guess.'

'Does he talk about prison?' Beth Miller, sitting next to Kristen, leans forward, eager, hungry for gossip.

'No, he ain't really said one word 'bout it that I heard.'

'That's a bit weird, isn't it?' Ray takes another sip of beer.

'He's a hell of a lot more than weird, if you ask me.' Josh swigs the tequila. Passes the bottle on.

'Does he ever talk 'bout –'

Katie cuts Kristen off: 'No. None of us talk 'bout it. We can't really. Joanne don't know.'

Silence round the campfire as they all take that in. The wind shifts, rustling the leaves above them.

'Now that's fucked up.' All eyes turn to Hank. The firelight deepens the dark shadows of his scar. He shrugs. 'That's how I see it is all.'

'How can she not know?'

'Yeah, that's real messed up.'

'Are you gonna tell her?'

'What about when school starts?'

Katie's head is spinning. The fire feels too hot. Somehow the tequila's wound up back in her hands, that worm, floating in it, staring up at her. The way it moves inside the liquid, she can't quite make up her mind if it's alive or dead. *It must be dead*, she thinks.

'Someone needs to go and teach him a lesson, if you ask me. Make sure he ain't gettin' back to his old tricks.' Josh spits a big wad of chewing tobacco, back braced, tall, like he means business. His fists automatically coil and release by his sides.

'Josh!' Katie tries to say, but he's not listening, and her

throat locks, and all she can manage is a whisper that doesn't even sound like his name. She feels tiny sitting there by the fire. Helpless. She watches as the worm floats across the ripples on the top of the tequila, bottle held loosely in her hand. Firelight turns the liquid gold. She wonders if that's how tiny she'd look, cast upon some ocean. Or if she'd be tinier, some little speck in a world impossibly large.

'Been years now since anyone went missing.' Ray flicks ash from his cigarette into the fire.

Eric takes a long swig of his beer. Locks eyes with Katie for a moment across the rising flames. Looks away. His ten-gallon hat rests on his knee now. Absently his fingers trace its brim.

'Yeah, well, that's 'cause he was locked up, ain't it?'

She wishes Josh would just stop speaking.

'What about Rose?' It's Eric who's asked. His hat rests on his head again and his eyes look up from under the ten-gallon's low brim to hold hers.

Silence round the campfire.

'What about her?' Her throat's so dry she can barely squeeze the words out. She doesn't want to be here. Doesn't want to have this conversation.

'Anybody told her he's back?' Katie's eyes hold Eric's. She says nothing. Doesn't know how to answer him.

'Eddie knows.' Josh snorts. 'And he's gonna know a whole lot more too once I tell him 'n' my pops what Jasper said tonight.'

She tears her eyes from Eric, looks up to Josh, eyes pleading. 'Don't stir shit up, Josh, don' make it worse for us.'

'Ssssh, baby, I ain't stirrin' nothin'.' He comes round the back of the campfire and sits down on the boulder beside her. Puts his arm round her and pulls her close to him. 'I'm just lookin' out for you is all,' he whispers, and she can feel his breath on her cheek, in her ear. She lets her head lean into him, her eyes close. He takes the tequila bottle from her. Chugs a long swig, his head tilted back, the worm creeping closer, closer, to his parted lips. But he doesn't drink it. Pulls the bottle down right before it touches his lips. Passes it on. Worm still floating there, unnatural in the liquid. *Dead or alive doesn't really matter,* she reckons, watching as the bottle's passed and drunk and passed again, worm seeming to swim and dive in the golden liquid as the bottle's tilted and righted again and again. *One way or another,* she thinks, watching, *its own life has passed, and if it is living, surely this ain't the life it chose.*

It's late when the knock comes, but Lizzie is not sleeping. She's in bed, sheets pulled across her, pillows fluffed up behind her back, just sitting there, staring at the shadows. The moon is just a tiny sliver in the sky, and it casts no light into her room. The knock doesn't scare her – her heart doesn't even pass up one beat – but she hadn't expected it either. She knows already who will be on the other side of that door when it opens. Her daughters do not knock like that. She pauses before she whispers, 'Come in,' her voice unpractised at this late hour, throat tight and dry.

The knob jiggles as it is turned, hinges groaning. 'Did I wake you?' His voice husky, grainy, in the darkness. She cannot see his face, just the dark outline of him in the doorway, the even darker hallway looming behind him. She thinks of nights they spent whispering as children, telling secrets. Remembers that night before her wedding day, how he'd knocked on her bedroom door all those years back, pissed drunk, straight home from Bobby and the boys, the smell of drink oozing off his skin, out of his pores. Stale on his breath. He had come into her room that night smiling ear to ear, same way he had on prom night his junior year when he'd first told Lizzie he was in love. And, of course, the next day she'd told everyone who'd listen just how smitten Jasper was. He and Rose would never have been right for each other, though. Even if so much had been different. And her and Bobby? Well, that night before their wedding day, Jasper'd told her, pissed drunk, stumbling into her room, 'I envy you, sis. He makes you real happy. You hold on to that happiness,' he'd said, swaying as he spoke, words slurring. 'You ride that happiness straight out of here.' And she'd thought back then she could.

'It all right if I come in?'

She pulls the sheets tighter round her, even though the room is warm. Window's open, but still the air hangs heavy. 'Yeah, you can come in.'

He leaves the doorway and crosses the room and sits down at the foot of her bed. His eyes go over her for what feels like too long, and she doesn't like it. She pulls the sheets right up to her chin, the moisture on her skin sticking to and catching the fabric. 'You all right?' she says, her voice unsteady.

Jasper sits hunched, looking down into his hands, clasped on his lap before him. 'I couldn't sleep.'

'Oh.' *What does he want her to do? Read him a bedtime story?* 'I wasn't sleepin' yet neither.'

His face turns to her. Her eyes have adjusted enough to the shadows of the room that she can just make out his features. 'What was keepin' you up?'

She sighs. 'Hard to quiet the mind sometimes.'

He nods. 'I know that feeling.'

'Is it . . .' she hesitates over the words, searching for the right ones '. . . hard being back?'

For a moment Lizzie thinks he might not answer. He looks back down to his clasped hands. 'Sometimes it's hard just being.' Voice a husky whisper.

She's felt that these past years herself. 'I'm sorry, Jasper,' she says at length.

Confusion creases his brow. 'What for?'

Her turn to look down. 'For everything. I'm sorry if we ever done wrong by you. If we made you how you are.'

His body tenses, then relaxes as he slowly shakes his head. 'It ain't you, Lizzie, who done wrong.' His face is pinched, twisted with emotions she can't even begin to identify.

'You know what they still say about you, don't you?' She raises her eyes to his.

'I can guess.'

She nods. Wants to say more. Leaves it at that.

'Lizzie?' he asks at length, voice rough in the silence of the room, the deeper, darker silence of the prairie around them.

'Yeah?'

'You believe me, right, when I say I'm done with trouble?'

She is silent a moment. Lets out a long breath. 'Yeah, I believe you, Jasper, it ain't that.'

'What then?' His voice surprisingly soft.

'I got this gut feelin' trouble ain't even close to done with you.'

He laughs then softly. That brother laugh she's missed. 'Shit,' he says, grinning in the darkness. 'Guess I'm screwed then, ain't I?'

She moves over on the bed so he can lean back against the headboard with her. Seems strange sitting there like that, so little space between them. She keeps the sheets wrapped tight around her. It's been a long time since a man sat on her bed. Even if he is her brother. Feels strange somehow. Wrong. Like that ice cube all those years ago that he'd run up her leg.

His voice startles her, breaks her thoughts up. 'Lizzie . . .' his whisper soft '. . . have you ever tried to find him?'

She can see their dark outlines just barely reflected in Mama's old vanity, two dark shadows sitting side by side, not touching, but close, her feet out long before her, his still rooted to the floor, body slightly twisted to one side. She doesn't have to ask him who he means. 'No, I ain't never tried to find 'im, Jasper. I thought on it a time or two, but I just don't have the heart.'

'How come?'

She snorts. 'He'da come on home by now if he'd wanted to. He ain't comin' back, Jasper. No sane man would come back here.'

He laughs, and she realizes what she's said. 'I'm sorry. I didn't mean it like that.'

His voice, still soft in the darkness, plays with her. 'Yes, you did.'

The buzz of insects outside merges to form a single low hum. 'You heard from him since he left?' Something comforting about the deep gravel tones in Jasper's voice at this late hour.

She closes her eyes. 'I ain't heard one word.'

'And the girls?'

'What 'bout 'em?'

'Ain't right him not bein' a father to them.'

'Right got nothin' to do with it.'

'Why'd he go, Lizzie? Really.'

She sighs. 'He just couldn't cut it no more, Jasper. Folks round here weren't too kind to us after what you done. He had it worst too, I guess, what with you 'n' him grown so close back then.' She pauses. 'He didn't love us enough to stay. Not me, not them girls of ours neither. That's what it all boils down to. And how do I tell them that? I've asked myself a million times on a million sleepless nights why we wasn't enough for him, but I still ain't got no answer. That's the million-dollar question, ain't it? Why couldn't he have loved us enough to stay? But wishin' don't change the truth none. And there was a lot of rumours back then goin' round after you was locked up. A lot of rumours.'

She can feel his frown more than see it. Can feel the heat of his body still uncomfortably close beside her on the bed.

'What kind of rumours?'

His voice so low that even next to him she can barely hear it.

'Surely you know.'

His head shakes, face lost in shadow.

She sighs. 'Folks thought maybe he'd had somethin' to

do with what you done. They seemed to think maybe Bobby'd . . .' Her voice falters. Steadies. 'Didn't help none neither, you going back to the garage like that, all covered in blood. Shit, Jasper, what the hell were you thinkin' going there?'

His voice harder than before. 'I didn't know where else to go.'

'There was nowhere you could go, Jasper. Nowhere you'da been welcome. I know that.' She snorts. 'Shit, there ain't nowhere to go when you done what you did. You could have had the decency to leave us out of it, though. Ain't a day that goes past I don't wish you'd picked a different door to knock on that night.' It's been years since Lizzie's talked about why Bobby left. About what happened to him all that time ago. Her mother had been the only one she'd ever told, and the rage is in Lizzie still, deep inside, locked tightly to her heart as it has been these past long years. She had thought that when she finally spoke about it again all those years of rage would release, but as she talks she just feels numb inside. Chilled, despite the humid night.

Aloud, she says, 'Seems like just yesterday sometimes, the police coming in the garage like that and finding the two of you. Is it strange that I've pictured it? I see it like I was there, even though I wasn't.' She tastes salt. A tear runs down her cheek and seeps into the valley of her mouth. She wipes its track with the back of her hand, drying her face. Feels the numbness spreading inside her, thinning into pain.

'Eddie Saunders 'n' his crew didn't make it easy for Bobby neither after you was locked up. They was convinced he must have helped you with what you done.' Her voice cracks. 'They went down to the garage one night when he was just 'bout closin' up. Roughed him up real bad thinkin' they could get him to confess. But Bobby, he didn't have nothin' to confess to.'

She sees again his battered face when finally she'd found him. One of his canine teeth had been crushed, broken shards of tooth stuck in his gums and lips. His left eye was so swollen black it would neither open nor shut. It just sat there disfigured on his face, not quite seeing, not fully not. She'd never seen skin that purple before. Like the skin itself was angry and about to tear off and combust itself to explode. They had tied him to the wheel of a Chevy he'd been fixing. That was what he'd told her. There were cigarette burns on his hands. His stomach. His neck. 'I begged him to go to the police after,' she says. 'Or the hospital at least, but Bobby wouldn't have it.' Her voice catches in her throat and she has to draw a deep breath to clear it. 'It weren't too long after that night that he left. Still had the bruises on him to prove their wrongdoing, but he left anyway. Bobby wasn't cut out for the world you left us in. He couldn't handle the sideways looks, the whispers behind hands. Sometimes I think you got off easy, goin' to Huntsville like that. We was the ones left here in your mess.'

Jasper's voice is low. 'I never meant to bring no trouble on you 'n' Bobby.' He's looking away from her, across the room and out of the open window into the pre-dawn darkness beyond.

'See, that's the problem, Jasper,' she says softly. 'You

never mean to cause the trouble, but trouble always finds you.'

'You blame me for him leaving.' A statement, not a question. Not the first time he's said it.

'Yeah, that's right.' Her voice is rough in the darkness, unpolished. 'I blame you. I blame your stupidity. I blame your stupid lust. And your pride and that goddamned ego of yours. You ain't right in the head, Jasper Curtis. I'm sorry to say it all blunt like that, but if that's not the God honest truth, it's the only excuse I can make for you.'

His voice is harder than before. She'd expected him to bristle. 'I don't need your sympathy.' Words almost a snarl.

'Good, 'cause you ain't gettin' it.' She keeps her tone level. Draws the sheet tighter still around her. No stars can be seen through the window. A barn owl breaks the stillness of the night, calling as it hunts.

'What if I told you Bobby *had* helped me?' His voice, ice on this warm night, chills the room around her.

'You'd be crueller than I'd counted on.'

He chuckles, weighing her words. They sit in silence for a long while, shoulders not quite touching, but still close enough to feel the heat radiate off each other's skin. She wonders how long he'll stay there. Wonders what he's thinking. Wants to ask him, but finds her voice has left her. She keeps seeing Bobby's face all those years back after Eddie Saunders and his lot had finished with him. Another tear rolls down her cheek and she does not raise her hand to wipe it. Tastes the salt instead.

At length Jasper rises. Stretches by the bed beside her,

and he seems so tall there standing above her as he leans from side to side. He rolls his shoulders back. Looks up to the ceiling, then back down to her. 'I'd best let you get some sleep.'

She nods. He crosses the room in four short strides. Opens the door. Reminds her somehow of that morning when Bobby left, the way he, too, paused with his hand on that door knob. 'Jasper!' The sound of her voice surprises her. She had not known she meant to speak, but the words spill out before she can stop them. 'He didn't help you, though, did he?'

He freezes in the open doorway, hand still on the knob. He fidgets with the knob looking down at his feet. Raises his eyes to hers. 'No, Lizzie, he didn't help me. What I done I done alone.' He nods then to her. Just the once. Starts to leave, then pauses once again. Turns back to her. 'I been cravin' chocolate ice cream somethin' awful,' he says. 'I don't suppose there'd be a chance of getting some one day real soon?' Like a child there, asking.

She forces a smile, not sure how to take his request. 'I'll see what I can do.'

'And, Lizzie?'

'Yeah?'

'Will you drive me to church tomorrow?'

She pauses. 'Your mind made up on goin'?'

'It's set.'

She studies his frame there in the shadows. The muscles that stretch his T-shirt tight across his arms and chest. Not a young frame any more, but a fit one nonetheless. He doesn't stand quite as straight as he used to, shoulders a bit more slouched. Deep-set lines crease his features even in shadow. She pictures him in church alone. The whole town there around him. Shudders. 'Reckon I might as well go on in with you, then.'

He nods. 'I'd be obliged.' And shuts the door behind him.

The church looks just like how Jasper remembers it. Prairie stretching flat around it, like a big open sea. Prairie grass blows to and fro like crashing golden-brown waves. Pickup trucks and a few sedans are parked haphazardly on the fields, scattered in front of the church, like boats newly docked in harbour before a coming storm. No real parking lot. Just the open field. Even that hasn't changed. In fact, it seems to Jasper that nothing about the church has changed one bit in all the years since his childhood. Same perfect whitewashed exterior. Same big oak doors left open wide. Same reverend in those doors smiling, shaking hands. Same people mostly, older, more tired maybe, still filing in through that still-open door. He likes the familiarity of it. Dandelions and daisies and tiny yellow buttercups dot the field that serves as parking lot, grass uncut but kept short by the steady flow of Sunday traffic. A few Texas bluebells dot the open prairie, tiny stains of blue among the dried-grass brown.

Lizzie stalls the engine still pulled up on the main road. She doesn't drive down the well-worn dirt path that leads onto the field in front of the church. She waits instead. Her brow is deeply furrowed, ageing her. *In a different world, in a life less hard*, Jasper thinks, *she would look pretty*. This is not that world. Not that life. He is sorry for

189

the depth of that wrinkle. Can't help but feel he partly put it there. And he is sorry, too, about Bobby, about what Eddie Saunders and his crew must have put him through. He notices a bit of grey just off Lizzie's temple he hadn't seen before. He looks back out across the field. To the small cemetery half hidden behind the chapel. Says, 'Is that where Mama's buried?' eyes never leaving that hallowed ground.

'Yeah, she's there.' Lizzie's foot finds the gas and the pickup lurches forward onto the dirt path. She parks at the end of the field, close to the road as she can. For a moment he wonders if she's changed her mind. If she'll just leave him here after all. He hadn't expected her to come to church. Not after Reverend Gordon's last visit. Not after her callous words about God. But she'd woken up that morning with a fire in her, cooking pancakes like they absolved all sin, fussing at him and Joanne to wash their faces. She'd snapped at Katie to wear a longer skirt. Had braided Joanne's hair so tight Joanne had started crying, saying it hurt her scalp. Jasper knew his sister was staying busy to keep herself calm. He could see the worry in her just barely held at bay.

Now, sitting in the truck, she turns to him. Joanne and Katie sit sandwiched tight between them, Joanne on her sister's lap. Jasper can barely see Lizzie over her two girls, but he can hear her just fine, her tone calloused hard as she looks out of the window, away from him, out to the church beyond. 'Just what exactly are you hopin' to have happen here?' she says, not even masking the disdain in her tone. 'You expectin' a warm welcome?'

He keeps his voice calm. 'I'd like a word with God is all.'

'God don' talk back.'

Jasper reaches for the door handle. 'He don't need to.'

'Are you lookin' for forgiveness, Jasper?' Her words stop him, door half open, one foot nearly to the ground, hand still on the handle. His eyes meet hers. ''Cause folks round here ain't ready to forgive just yet.'

He hesitates a moment. 'Mama would have liked this. Us all comin' here.'

She closes her eyes. Tilts back her head, hands still on the wheel at nine and three o'clock. 'All right,' she says, 'let's do this,' and she opens her door and climbs down onto the grass outside.

It's a beautiful summer morning. He can't help but notice that. Sun high and hot in the sky. Not a cloud in sight. The heavens that perfect blue July hue so huge above him. He has to squint when he looks up it's so bright, the whole sky that is, not just the sun. Feels good to feel the heat on his skin. He closes his eyes. Lifts his face to the sun. Lets its beams fall down upon him.

There was a chapel in prison. Nothing fancy, but a chapel all the same. One stained-glass window above the altar with a stained-glass Jesus on it, hung and dying on his cross. It was the only splash of colour in the place. Only window in the whole place without bars on it, too. Except it didn't matter, 'cause the window didn't lead anywhere, just to a wall behind it. He'd sat in that chapel long hours. Not praying. Just liked the quiet there. The prison's priest had sat beside him once that first year. Had asked him, 'Do you come here seeking your soul's salvation, son?' and Jasper had answered him, 'Padre, I have no soul to save.'

He was younger than Jasper, that preacher, though not by much. He had a flat, moon face. His pockmarked skin was scarred from what must once have been bad acne, scars like moon craters hollowing out his cheeks. His hair was prematurely greying round the temples. He had squinty eyes. And fat full lips, like a woman's, but dry and cracked, not moist as a woman's should be. Jasper had stared at those fat, dry lips, enthralled, fascinated by the depth of the cracks that chapped them. The bright soft pink of them contrasted with the sallow moon craters on the man's skin. 'Would you like to confess your sins?' the young priest had asked him.

'I ain't Catholic.' He'd been looking at Jesus when he spoke, not at the man beside him.

'I speak in here to men of many faiths.'

Jasper did not bother to turn to the other man. 'Confession don't matter none once you're convicted,' he'd said. 'You still serve the same term.'

The preacher had nodded, pockmarked skin sallower as his smile fell. 'And what of your soul?' he'd said. 'What of its salvation? Of its sentencing on the day of reckoning when you stand before the gates of Heaven?'

Jasper had laughed at that, long and low and soft. 'The day you start worryin' 'bout your sentence up God's way,' he'd said, 'is the day this shit-hole's behind you. When your balls drop, Padre, you'll understand better. You'll wank one out for God one day and realize you're still not satisfied. Then you'll sit in here as I do just to hear the quiet.'

Jasper can't help but think of that now, walking up the path to the church of his boyhood Sundays. Can't help but wonder if maybe that squinty-eyed boy preacher was right and there is another sentence awaiting him in the hereafter. But, truth be told, Jasper's never fully believed in Heaven, and most of his life it's seemed to him that Hell and Earth are one. This is his hereafter. He's come for his reckoning.

Mama had died the first week of January. Six years ago this coming winter. It hadn't been a big funeral: a few of Mama's churchgoing friends, the ladies she played bridge with, what little family there was left. There was no snow that winter, but the ground was still so frozen solid, it took the gravediggers two days to dig her grave deep enough. Like the prairie itself wasn't ready to take her back just yet. That was how it had felt to Lizzie when Reverend Gordon had called round to say the funeral would need to be delayed a day. It had felt like God teasing her, letting her keep her mama there in that coffin like that for one more day, mocking her prayers, for what is the value of that wished-for one more day with the one you've lost, when that one is dead already? The gravediggers poured boiling water on the ground while they were digging. Or that was what Lizzie had been told anyway, that one kept stepping into the church to boil the water while the other dug out the newly defrosted ground. They'd sprinkled clumps of mud on Mama's coffin, not dirt, and when the mud hit the casket it made a hollow thudding sound, like the gate on the cast-iron fence by Daddy's old shed slammed shut.

When they'd found that the cancer in Mama's left breast had spread, Dr Fieldsmen had given her six months to live and, compliant as ever, six months to the day from his visit, Lizzie had come upstairs to find her mother tucked up in bed, quilt pulled up to her chin, peaceful as though just resting, but cold and dead and lifeless. Lizzie could not untangle the sheets from her mother's death grip. Fingers stronger in death than Mama's arthritic hands had ever been in life. Delicately, Lizzie had leaned across the bed to try to shut Mama's eyes, but rigor mortis had set in there too, and Mama's eyes refused to close. She stared up and into Lizzie, unseeing. It was then that Lizzie had cried. The girls were home from school by the time she'd stopped, the sun just setting.

Now, walking across the churchyard, Lizzie can't help but think back to that cold January morning, grass iced over so that every footstep had crunched. That was the last time she'd come to church. Six years ago this coming winter. She brings the girls to their grandparents' graves, of course, from time to time, but never on Sundays, and never round a service when the whole town might be gathered. Since Mama'd died, Lizzie'd avoided the townsfolk as much as possible. She couldn't handle the pity smiles. The whispers only barely masked behind raised hands. She'd grown to dislike crowds. *Funny*, she thinks now, tearing her eyes from the church's graveyard, *how life speeds up just so we can stand still for all eternity.*

The church bell is ringing, calling all inside. Its clatter drifts loud to soft on constant repeat as wind carries the sound above the graveyard and out across the prairie beyond. A few mockingbirds sing with the bell, imitating it with their harsh cackle. Most folks have made it inside already. Before, Lizzie hadn't wanted them to be too early, but now, seeing how full the lot is, she doesn't want them to be the last ones in, either. She glances quickly around the nearly full space, searching for stragglers. A few pickup doors still slam as churchgoers hurry not to be late. Ahead of them, the tiny church glistens white, reflecting the sun's heat. Reverend Gordon smiles ear to ear in the door before them as he greets and shakes hands with all who enter.

Picking up her pace, Lizzie glances back at her family. Jasper walks just one step behind her. His eyes down, hands hidden deep inside his pockets. Shoulders hunched a little. Katie is a couple of steps behind her uncle, arms crossed over her chest. A frown, deep-set on her brow, mars the perfect sunshine that usually lights her face. Lizzie doesn't see Joanne at first. She stops walking, turns and surveys the field they've just come across. She raises her hand to block the sun from her eyes. Looks out across the field. Sunlight reflects off car windows and mirrors, making it hard to see. Joanne is halfway back to the truck, squatted on the grass, the hem of her dress trailing in the dirt as she leans over, prodding a crayfish burrow with a stick. 'Joanne!' Lizzie snaps. 'You get over here now, you hear?' Her voice nearly echoes as it carries.

Joanne looks up, startled, and drops the stick. 'Yes, Mama,' she calls, and starts running.

Lizzie watches her daughter till she's reached them, her hand still up to block the sun. Eyes squinting. She grabs Joanne roughly by the arm, and pulls the girl to her. 'Let me see your dress,' she scolds, dusting it with one hand as she holds her squirming daughter with the other. 'Now, mind you keep up,' Lizzie says, and releases her. She hadn't meant to be quite so rough, to grab her daughter quite so hard.

Joanne says nothing. She steps away from her mother and smooths her dress with both hands. A funny smile plays at Jasper's lips, and Lizzie doesn't like it. She can't quite say why she doesn't like it, but to her it's like that smile is the other Jasper, the one trouble finds. She shivers even though the sun's heat bakes down upon them, tanning, burning all it touches. A flock of blackbirds rises from some distant shrubs, spreading up and out over the prairie, like a dark cloud. Lizzie turns, hearing the birds' calls as they rise in flight. She watches as they move as one, sweeping over the prairie as they dive and rise and dive again.

'Morning, Elizabeth! Girls!' The cheer in the reverend's voice sounds more surprised than joyful. Then, softer, more reserved, his tone changes, 'Morning, Jasper,' and he smiles, but his eyes do not, and Lizzie can't help but wonder why she's doing this, why she's agreed to be here. Then she thinks again of Jasper, imagines him all alone inside the church, the congregation around him, like a hungry mob, and she remembers her place again: she knows why she is here. The thought of Jasper alone with the townsfolk chills her insides, tightens her throat. She can't help but feel that, with her there, she can look over him, can protect him in some small manner. Though from what or whom exactly, she cannot say.

Lizzie smiles. 'Morning, Reverend.'

He matches her forced bright tone. 'Lord's blessed us with a fine, fine morning.'

She glances up at the cloudless blue of the sky above them. 'Sure is fine all righ'.'

'Reverend.' Jasper nods to the other man and extends his hand. He's smiling.

She sees the reverend hesitate. Hates him for it. Jasper's hand hangs there between them. Extended. Waiting. Reverend Gordon takes it slowly, with great care, as though he touches something that might stain. The two men's eyes meet. She can see Jasper's grip tighten slightly. 'What's wrong, Reverend?' Jasper whispers. 'You afraid my sins rub off?'

The reverend releases Jasper's hand quickly and forces a laugh, no merriment in the sound. He directs his words to Lizzie again, even though Jasper still stands sneering before him. 'It's great to see you, Elizabeth. Makes my heart smile to see you ladies come on back to church.' He nods towards the girls, then turns to Lizzie again. 'Your mother'd be mighty pleased to see y'all back in God's house. No doubt her spirit's smiling down on y'all this fine, fine mornin'.'

Lizzie pictures her mother laid out in bed as she'd found her all those years back. Cold, dead eyes open wide. She wonders where her mother was then, if she'd bothered looking down or if she'd merely been delighted at the escape that cancer had granted her. 'Thank you, Reverend,' is all Lizzie says, and she nods to him once more.

He turns back to Jasper, opens his mouth to speak. 'Well, son . . .' he begins only to fall short.

Mrs Gordon hurries out of the church door and rushes across the short landing to her husband's side. 'Darling,' she coos, cutting him off. 'You 'bout ready to come in and start the sermon? Mrs Hillcrest says she's in a real hurry this Sunday 'cause little baby Sue got a fever 'n' she knows Caroline didn't get one wink of sleep last night, what with the baby cryin' 'n' all –' The reverend's wife stops abruptly. 'Oh,' she says, and stops speaking altogether then, mouth hanging open slightly, eyes wide and dazed as she surveys the family before her. She's a good few years younger than her husband, but not unseemingly so. While his plump form has passed middle age and sunk into the further declines of maturity, Regina Gordon still has the sharp features of a much younger woman. They'd met in Dallas, over twenty years ago, back when the reverend had first studied ministry. She'd grown up in the city, her daddy'd sold used cars, and it had taken her a while at first to adjust to small-town life, but then, once she did, it suited her completely. She fed off gossip. Lived to tell one neighbour on the next. Small-town life suited Regina Gordon to a tee, and she holds herself now with the confidence of a woman who has power. *And she does*, Lizzie thinks. *The preacher's wife's always been respected round here.*

'Darlin'.' Reverend Gordon flashes another smile and puts his arm around his wife's slender shoulders. 'You remember Elizabeth? The late Mrs Curtis's daughter? And her two girls?'

'Oh! Yes!' Mrs Gordon smiles. 'Your mother was such a fine woman, Elizabeth. You know, I still remember her in my prayers.'

Lizzie feels her insides bristle. She's never liked this woman. The hurtful gossip that she spreads hidden behind that saintly smile. 'That's mighty kind of you, Regina, but I'd appreciate it if you'd let my mother rest in peace awhile. She must be awfully tired receiving all those prayers of yours. The way I see it, there's more livin' need our help than dead 'n' prayers just waste our breath.'

The smile falls from the other woman's face. 'That's a rather unholy perspective, Elizabeth.' Regina tries to force a laugh, but her smile's failing. Falling.

'I ain't had much time for faith.'

Regina's eyes narrow above her pointy nose, as though looking down at Lizzie even though Lizzie is the taller woman. Her mouth opens then closes as though in search of words, then her eyes shift slowly to Jasper, who's been standing silently, patiently waiting to be recognized. He grins. 'Hi, Regina. I reckon you ain't aged one day since I seen you last.' His eyes search her up and down.

'Oh.' Mrs Gordon almost laughs, then stops herself, a nervous sort of giggle escaping her lips before she seals them shut. She smooths down the front of her dress self-consciously. 'Hello, Jasper.' She nods. 'I see you're . . . Welcome back.' She does not take the hand he's outstretched to greet her. It hangs there a moment, suspended, before he lowers it to his side.

Lizzie clears her throat. 'Thank you, Reverend, Regina. We don't wanna hold y'all up no more.'

A few other stragglers have crossed the field and nearly made it to the church doors. Lizzie can hear their footsteps slow as they come closer. Glancing over, she is surprised to find she does not recognize the family that approaches. Regina has found her smile again. Fake as her husband's but with a coldness to it that his most times warms. 'Will you be stayin' for Sunday school, girls?' she purrs, beaming at Katie and Joanne.

'We hadn't planned on it,' Lizzie answers for them.

'Oh, but you must! It'll be such a nice treat for the girls to see their friends a bit, don' you think, Elizabeth?' She turns to Katie, smile warm and welcoming. 'I teach the youth group Sunday school for high-schoolers myself, you know, and we just have a blast! I just can't get over how pretty you've grown, Katie! You were only this high last I saw you. We'd just love it if you'd join us after church for Sunday school. It ain't *all* Bible reading.' Regina laughs. 'We do have fun, you know!'

Katie smiles, looks to her mom. 'Well, maybe –'

Lizzie cuts her off, 'Thank you, Regina, Reverend,' places her palms on her daughters' backs and gently pushes them through the open doors before them.

'Reverend.' Jasper nods to the other man, his hands buried deep in his pockets. 'I must say I sure am lookin' forward to this sermon. God knows it's been too long since I been to church.' He flashes that brilliant grin of his. Playful, teasing. The same grin that in boyhood meant some mischief was to follow. He nods to Regina, 'Ma'am,' then turns and follows his family inside.

Lizzie had hoped they might enter unnoticed. Walking through the wide oak doors past the reverend and his wife, she now realizes that that wish would have taken a miracle. All it takes is Lionel Davies's little boy whispering into his mother's ear, too loudly, 'Who's that?' and it seems like the whole congregation rotates as one and notices them. Lizzie wants to turn around right then and there and go back through those big oak doors, across the lawn and into her truck and all the way back up the road, back home again. Far from here as her truck will take her. Instead, she steels herself inside, though bracing for what exactly, she cannot say. She takes her daughters by their hands. Starts to lead them down one of the back pews. Jasper's hand on her shoulder stops her. She can feel the roughness of his palm through the thin fabric of her dress. The dryness of his skin.

'There's seats closer to the front,' he whispers.

Her eyes search his. 'What's wrong with this? What you tryin' to prove?'

'I'd like to see is all,' he whispers, then walks with conviction down the centre aisle, his head held high.

He walks the same path she walked all those years ago, back on her wedding day, when Bobby had been at the altar, smiling as he waited for her. That was the last time, the only time, Lizzie had walked through a nearly full church and down the aisle. Her wedding day. And on that day, the faces looking back at her had been all smiles.

The whispers explode as Jasper begins his procession forward. A sound like wind building, growing, gaining momentum, as it swirls round the church. The girls look to her, and Lizzie nods, and they follow their uncle down the aisle. Lizzie trails last behind them. Like some strange wedding procession, she thinks, at a wedding where the bride is hated. Most faces are turned to Jasper and do not even look at her. Most eyes watch his entrance with a sort of silent fury. But then the focus shifts to her as well, to her girls as they follow him, and Lizzie can't help but wonder if this is what it feels like to be Jasper, to walk among such hatred.

Jasper nods to familiar faces as he passes them. Finds an empty pew three-quarters of the way towards the front. They sit down, the whispers still growing, growing all around them, howling like wind. It is not a happy sound, not a peaceful sound at all, and Lizzie wonders briefly if their mama *is* looking down and if she's howling too. Not everyone remembers to whisper any more, and voices rise, getting louder, angrier all around them.

The hinges squeak and groan as the church's heavy oak doors are pulled shut. For a moment, Lizzie feels her heart quicken, panic rising in her chest, tightening her throat. The reverend walks quickly to his pulpit and holds out both his hands, palms up, to his congregation. 'People, people, please,' he calls. 'Let us not forget, this is God's house.'

'He shouldn't be here!' someone calls out. She turns but cannot see who spoke. A young man's voice. There's a murmur of agreement from the rest of the congregation, like a restless, uneasy wave swelling around them.

'Children, children, please!' Reverend Gordon calls, palms still out and open. 'Let us calm ourselves. We are all God's children. He turns his back on no one. Even sinners are granted salvation when they repent.'

'Amen,' Jasper murmurs, and Lizzie wonders if she is the only one to hear him. Around them, whispers crackle, bodies shift as people strain to look over, or as people avert their eyes and fidget. A few boys and men stand up near the back of the church trying to see better. Esther Reynolds's chubby cheeks have flushed bright red, and halfway across the room Lizzie sees her whisper to the woman beside her. Esther's small beady eyes never leave Jasper. It takes Lizzie a moment to realize that it is Sarah Reynolds beside Esther. The other side of Sarah sits her husband, Roy. Lizzie wonders if Jasper has seen him yet. She turns to her brother, uncertain if she should point out his old friend. Jasper's face is mural calm as he sits in his pew, eyes focused on the preacher and the altar before them, as though there is no sea of commotion surging around and behind him. He sits with his eyes crystal clear, like a man who's seen God and has come for his salvation. Lizzie turns back to Roy. His eyes meet hers, cold as stone, before he looks away. Esther leans across Sarah to say something to him. Roy listens, then nods. Eyes cold and hard. They used to play tag when they were little. All five of them together. Right out the back of this very church. And they'd giggle when their fingers brushed one another's skin, calling out, 'You're it!'

Lizzie turns away.

The pew beneath her feels hard, unforgiving. The fabric of her dress itches round the collar. Lizzie closes her eyes and imagines the open stretch of prairie outside these wooden walls. She imagines the sun warm upon their faces, air fresh and hot as it blows against their skin. She imagines the only sounds are birds singing, the wind blowing, the rustle of dried grass. She imagines it's just the four of them, her girls and her brother and her, and no one else on this earth, just the wide open space spread all around them.

She opens her eyes.

Across the aisle, Mrs Anderson meets Lizzie's gaze and smiles. No trace of happy crosses her face. Though pity is etched in the lines around her mouth. Pity is cradled in the unfallen tears that well in her eyes. Mr Anderson beside her does not look over, and Lizzie does not return her sad smile. Just stares till Mrs Anderson finally looks away.

Where are they? she wonders then. *They have to be here.* Dread fills her. She turns to scan the room, dread twisting her guts like sickness. She can feel them there. The hostile anger that surrounds them. The anger she can't blame them for yet that she will always hold against them. She struggles to see between prying faces. Tries not to scan the room too obviously. Doesn't want the whole town to see her searching for them, though she knows it must be obvious. Then her breath stops. And she sees.

The Saunders sit across the aisle, midway back in the church, whole family to the one pew the way most folks in these parts sit, except their family's grown big enough that now they nearly fill two pews, Eddie and his wife and their brood sitting behind the rest of their family. Old Mrs Saunders' skin, loose and hung with wrinkles, deepens her already deep-set frown into an even darker scowl. Her grey hair has been gathered up and pinned into a loose bun at the nape of her neck. Her cold blue eyes stare at the back of Jasper's head as though trying to see inside him. Her lips a thin, straight line. Beside her, her husband sits straight-backed, face expressionless, eyes hollowed out and sad. He holds a hymnal in his hands, resting on the back of the pew before him, veins bulging he grasps it so tightly. His cheeks flush red. Next to them, their children, oldest to youngest, sit in a row. All grown now, most with their own children beside them. All there, except, of course, Rose.

Built like a quarterback, Eddie Saunders leans forward from the pew behind his family to whisper in his father's ear. He sits at the end of the row, right by the aisle, elbows on his knees, one fist clenched in his opposite hand so tight his knuckles are starting to go pale. He's looking at the floor, head shaking slightly from one side to the other. He looks up to his father again, and his lips move, but Lizzie cannot read what words lie hidden there. Eddie was always a beast. He'd been the high-school football star for the whole county back when they were all in school, had even gone to A&M on a football scholarship for a while. Unfortunately for Eddie, his mind had always been his weakest muscle, and it hadn't taken long for his grades to get him off that scholarship. He was still a local hero of sorts, though, for having gotten his team all the way to state his senior year. No one even seemed to mind that they'd lost that game. Just getting to state had been enough, and Eddie'd been a hero ever since. There had been the feeling at the time that maybe the whole town had value. That year they went to state. It was a feeling most folks round there weren't used to. And then, when Eddie came back home to help his father round the farm after all the trouble happened, folks looked up to him even more. Him coming home like that. Rumour had it, he'd left a good construction job in College Station to come on back. Lizzie'd never told anyone about what had happened to Bobby the night before he left. Most folks, she knows, still see Eddie as the football star he once was, the good son come on back home. Eddie was a few years ahead of Jasper in school, so though Lizzie'd known who he was she had never really known him personally. It was Rose who had been nearer to her age. It was Rose she had known.

The years have not weakened Eddie, though some of his muscle has turned to fat. A beer belly now spills onto his lap. She thinks of Bobby all those years back, come home from the garage that last night, of how the other men must have overpowered him, those cigarette burns on him, his face a purple mask. She feels sick to her stomach.

She can feel Jasper's eyes on her. Boring into her. Her head hurts. The hissing of whispers so loud now around them.

'People! PLEASE!' Reverend Gordon shouts again. 'Please! Respect God's house!'

The swell eases slightly. Calms a moment. Everyone still on the edge of their pews. Unsettled. The reverend looks uncomfortable. Sweat rolls from his brow down his chubby cheeks to pool in the hollow of his neck. His mouth hangs open a moment, as though even he's surprised to have quieted the congregation for a second. 'Folks,' he says, regaining a bit of his usual robust tone, 'this is church now, please! This is a house of peace! A house of God!' The whispers die down even more, everyone still edgy, angry, as they shift on their seats. 'I am ashamed!' Reverend Gordon shouts over the dying whispers. 'Do we now yell in God's house? Do we take His name in vain under His own roof?' The reverend's fist, risen and shaken with the words, now slowly falls. The congregation hushes before him.

'Now, I had planned,' he says, 'to talk to y'all 'bout forgiveness today.' An angry murmur rolls through the congregation once more. He holds his hands up and waits for silence. 'I had thought I'd speak to y'all today 'bout what's wrong 'n' right. 'Bout good 'n' evil 'n' 'bout how through our faith in God's great glory our souls will prevail 'n' triumph above the evils in this world!' A few 'Amens' ripple through the congregation. 'I had thought,' Reverend Gordon continues, his voice growing louder with each word, 'that I would stand here today before you 'n' quote God's good book to you 'n' that those among you who have sinned would fall down on your knees 'n' repent 'n' beg God in all His glory for forgiveness. I had thought,' he continues, finger pointing up to the sky, 'that when the Bible tells us to forgive, that is God's will, we must forgive. Brothers and sisters, I had thought forgiveness was our only option as good Christians, for to walk in Jesus's footsteps, we must forgive those whose sins He's died for. Or so I thought.'

The whole congregation sits hushed and still before him. Their silence nearly eerie in the wake of their previous uproar.

'It seems to me, though,' his voice softens, drawing them in, 'that nothing in this world is ever black and white. Is one person ever truly all good or all bad? Now,' he laughs a little, 'it'd be real easy, real tempting, yes, to call a fellow a rotten apple. Or to assume just because the apple's rotten that maybe the whole tree needs to be chopped down.' Lizzie doesn't dare to look at the congregation around them. 'But we do not pay for the sins of our fathers.' His voice rises again. 'Or our sisters or our brothers. We do not pay for the sins of our children. See, I've thought on forgiveness a lot this past week, folks. I spent many sleepless nights prayin' to the Good Lord himself to guide me so I might best guide my flock.' A murmur of respect and appreciation ripples through the congregation, like cricket song carried on an evening breeze. 'I asked the Lord to show me the path into God's light. I prayed down on my knees for the Lord to forgive *me* my imperfections. And this is what He told me: He told me, "Son, I gave man free will." Uh-huh. That's right. Free. Will. And because God gave us this great choice, this independence that as Americans we so prize, He gave us the choice, no, the power, to decide for ourselves just how rotten an apple is.' A stillness settles over the congregation. Almost eerie in its calm. 'Now I don't know 'bout you, folks,' Reverend Gordon chuckles, 'but if I bite into an apple and a worm crawls out, I sure as hell ain't gonna forgive the apple for that bad taste there lingering in my mouth. And I ain't gonna take another bite just to ensure that apple ain't gonna surprise me with another worm. No, sir, I'm gonna find me an apple that's to my taste the whole way through.'

He surveys the congregation before him. His eyes skim over Lizzie to rest on Jasper for a moment as he waits for his words to sink in. He paces before the pulpit now, hands clasped behind his back as he begins to speak. 'Forgiveness,' he says, 'is a beautiful thing. A fine, powerful thing. And is God forgiving? you might ask. Well, yes, He in all His great glory 'n' kindness, He is the Ultimate

Forgiver. He can see into a man's soul 'n' see the good from evil. But we, God's mere children, we do not have this gift, now, do we?' He pauses and looks out over his congregation, hands reaching out down low as though looking for support.

Murmurs of 'Nuh-huh,' and 'No, sir,' ripple through the room as bodies shift and heads shake.

'We cannot look into a man's soul 'n' see the good from the evil,' he continues. 'We see a man's actions. A man's morals. We see the decisions he makes that show his knowledge of wrong from right. And when a man transgresses, when the evil inside him boils up 'n' the devil himself whispers temptations in his ear, well, folks, I'm afraid to say, there are some unforgivable deeds in this good, kind world God created for us. The Bible teaches us to forgive those who have wronged us. To turn the other cheek.' Lizzie can feel his eyes stop over her. She does not raise her gaze to meet his. 'But some acts of evil,' the reverend continues, 'are too great to repent. Has God himself ever forgiven Lucifer his betrayal? Are we to forgive the devil himself or his demons and their dark deeds? And when the devil so controls a man that that man acts as his servant, are we then supposed to forgive that man?' He pauses. 'I say, "No."' A murmur breaks the silence of the church, quickly growing louder. He holds out his hands to quiet them, his voice gaining strength again as he speaks. 'I say, God gave us *free will*. He gave us the *choice* to forgive. To choose whom we forgive. He gave us the moral compass by which to gauge a man's transgressions. By which to gauge the level of his repentance. So this, my children, is what I say to you: walk into God's light. Follow His path of righteousness. And when you come face to face with the devil, don't stop 'n' ask him how he's been doing. Don't forgive the devil for introducing evil into the world. You stick on God's path, y'all hear? Make your own mind up on what's unforgivable. And you find an apple, folks, you don't like the taste of, no need to eat it up. Y'all just go on and hand them rotten apples straight back to the devil himself.'

A few 'Amens', then all fall silent. Jasper sits like stone beside Lizzie on the pew. She turns back to the reverend. He's smiling that fake smile, holding up the hymnal, telling everyone to turn to page 123. As one, the congregation rises. And Lizzie pops up, delayed a second behind them. Her legs feel weak. It's too warm in the church. No a/c. No fan. Just windows open along each wall, and barely a breeze blowing in through the screens.

Around her, music erupts, voices spiralling higher as they praise the Lord. She feels dizzy. Like the whole church, not merely the music, swirls around her. Like she's caught up in a twister, spinning across the prairie, too fast for even God's control. Her girls beside her look like angels, the way the light spills in and dances through their golden hair. Katie holds the hymnal open for Joanne, pointing on the page to where they sing. She tears her eyes from them, her babies, her beauties. Looks to her other side where Jasper stands beside her. He is not singing. Not quite. Jasper never was much of a singer. But his lips are moving, and it takes Lizzie a moment to decipher if he's mouthing the lyrics or his own silent prayer.

*

Joanne doesn't remember ever going to church. Not really. She has a fuzzy memory of Grandma's funeral, but she was only five back then, and she recalls the cold graveyard more than the church service. She remembers vaguely the reception after. How cold the old farmhouse felt. How much Mom had cried. How strange the house felt without Grandma in it. They go to Grandma and Grandpa's graves out round the back of the church a time or two each year, and they lay down wild flowers if the season's right, and Mom wipes down the headstones, keeps the graves tidy. But for Joanne actually sitting in church seems a completely new experience.

When Mom had finished braiding her hair that morning, she'd stopped in the kitchen doorway before going upstairs to change and had looked at Joanne a long moment. Joanne, rubbing her sore scalp, had had tears in her eyes, the braids were so tight and neat. 'You all righ'?' Mom had asked her.

She'd looked up, surprised. 'Yes-um.'

Her mother had hesitated. 'Now I don' want you takin' all this God talk too much to heart, you hear? This Sunday thing ain't gonna become a habit.'

'Yes, ma'am.' And Joanne had looked down again, scalp pulled so tight by the braids that she felt her forehead might be stretched tight like that for good.

Now the braids have loosened slightly, not enough to be messy but enough at least that her head no longer aches so bad. She likes the church. The quiet hush of it when the reverend's not speaking. She even likes the way the whispers seem to swirl and whirl around the room, though she doesn't like the fact that the whispers are about them; she simply likes the sound they make. Like wind through the trees down at the creek where Katie sometimes takes her swimming. That sort of sound. And Joanne likes the smooth, polished feel of the pew beneath her. She likes it when they sing, and she likes that Katie helps her find each song in the hymnal. She wishes that she was closer to Uncle Jasper, though. She looked at his face once while the reverend was talking, and something in Joanne told her to reach out, but Uncle Jasper was too far, Mom and Katie between them, so Joanne didn't try to touch him, though she would have liked to hold his hand. She wonders if her daddy came to church when he was a boy. What pew he might have sat in.

It feels like all eyes are on them. An uncomfortable sort of feeling, like when you think a ghost might be in the closet, or a spider might have crawled right into your pillowcase. It's the feeling Joanne gets when Mom's cross with her, and she knows she's in for a spanking, except this time Joanne isn't really sure what they've done wrong. 'Why's everyone so angry?' she'd asked Katie, when they'd first arrived and the angry whispers had swirled up all around them.

'Hush, Lady, not now,' was all Katie'd hissed in reply.

Joanne is getting very tired of being told 'not now'.

She twists round in the pew slightly to see who sits behind them. Katie elbows her hard in the ribs, and Joanne has to bite her lip to keep from squealing. She looks over to her uncle and finds his eyes upon her. She smiles. He stares at her as if not seeing her. As though looking through her and off into the distance at something or someone far away. After a while, he looks back up to the front of the church, and Joanne follows his gaze, past the reverend to the large white cross stood up at the end of the church as altar. The church itself is very bare. Wooden walls whitewashed on the inside and the out. Pews old oak, just like the door. Two steps elevate the front of the church where the reverend stands, and behind him towers the huge white cross, two potted lilies with some candles at its base. To the right, the choir stands, wearing long silky purple robes that reach all the way down to their ankles. Joanne can't help but think they must be hot standing there like that, wearing those pretty robes. She's too hot and all she has on is the dress Mom forced her to wear, one of Katie's hand-me-downs, white mostly with tiny blue flowers on it. The stitching where the waist comes in itches against her ribs. Joanne doesn't like dresses. She never has.

When the sermon's ended, and the last hymn has fallen silent, Mom stands up quickly, turning to Katie and Joanne. 'Let's get out of here,' she hisses, whisper almost too loud, even though others now have started to stand and talk as well. Around them, neighbours shake hands, families hug, friends exchange stories and laughter, but there's a subdued atmosphere in the church. An uneasiness in the way glances flick over but do not rest on them.

'What about Sunday school?' Katie asks, smiling and waving to Kristen Maylor across the church. 'Aren't we stayin'?'

'Not if I can help it,' Mom mutters. 'I think it's best we head on home.'

Uncle Jasper rises slowly. Stretches as he rises. Yawns.

Mom turns to him. 'You got what you wanted here?'

He meets her gaze. 'Not quite.'

They stand, eyes locked, unmoving.

'I don't reckon it's wise to stay long.' Her eyes dart around the church then search his. She folds her arms across her like she's cold, but Joanne can see small beads of sweat running down the nape of her mother's neck, leaving trails of moisture in their wake as they race beneath the collar of her dress.

He smiles. 'We're in God's house now, Liz. I don't aim to live free like I'm still locked in prison.'

'I ain't controlling you, Jasper. I ain't your guard. But if you don't want to walk home, I suggest you listen when I try to steer you clear of trouble.'

He looks at her a long moment. 'There's unfinished business here.'

'There's unfinished business everywhere, Jasper.'

He smiles then. Nods once. 'Ain't that the understatement of the day.' Then he turns from them and starts up the aisle, heading towards the door, the congregation parting like a sea around him, opening to let him pass.

When he's honest with himself, Jasper knows full well there are three reasons why he'd wanted to go to church. First off was the routine of it. It seems to him that coming home and going to church go hand in hand. It would feel wrong somehow not to go. He associates church with his mother. And he'd like to see her grave. Where she lies next to Daddy. He'd like to see his parents, and just sit by their graves awhile. He'd like to belong somewhere, like Mama and Daddy always belonged here. He'd thought, maybe, that God would have him, that the church might have opened its arms to him, but sitting on the hard pew, Jasper could not block out the whispers. Most of his life, Jasper has felt unwelcome. Like he doesn't quite fit wherever he is. He had hoped that that could change.

Jasper had wanted to go to church for the freedom of it. He wanted to go because he could. Because no one could stop him. Because it was his choice freely made and because it was something as a free man that he could say he'd done. Something normal to do. He never would have guessed he'd spend so many hours in prison thinking on freedom like he had. Defining and redefining for himself all its contexts and possible meanings. Ten years is a long time to study a word's definition. He would like to feel free again. It is hard sometimes to remember just what it means exactly. To be free.

The third reason Jasper wanted to go to church was to see her. He realizes that now. Not that he'd expected her to be there. Not really. But a part of him had hoped. And now, walking back up the aisle through the church towards its exit, he feels the anger boiling up inside him, rotting his insides. But he does not want to go home just yet. He does not want to run away, to give them reason to whisper louder. He aims to live and to live a normal life, God willing.

He's nearly to the church door before he stops. Roy stands with a few other men just to the left of the exit. The church doors are open wide again, and the reverend and Regina both shake hands with all who pass, saying goodbye to those few not staying for Sunday school. He can't remember the last time he saw so many women. So many bare ankles, slender calves going up, bare knees . . .

It makes it hard to focus. Hard not to think of lifting up a woman's skirt and ramming himself inside her. *When was the last time he parted a woman's thighs?* He thinks of her again. That mole just below her pelvic bone. He shakes his head to clear it. Looks again to Roy.

There'd been a time, as boys, when they did not part company. Sat beside each other at elementary. Shared their lunches. Would walk out across the prairie that separated their homes and meet there in those wild fields to play cowboys and Indians or to throw a baseball back and forth. When they were older, they would walk across the prairie late at night, his daddy's old Hungerford held tight in Jasper's hands, like a torch before him, rabbit hunting, except there was no light coming from it, and most times there were no rabbits.

Roy's mother was Polish. An escapee of some war or other, she'd grown up Texan, though had never fully lost her homeland's accent, her voice an odd singsong combination of Warsaw mixed with country, her *r*s rolled in all the wrong places. That was how Roy had got his name. Named after his mother's dead grandfather – some Polish farmer, last name Roychezki, he'd never met and whose image he had always been expected to uphold. 'Roy!' his mother had used to scold. 'What is wrong with you? Your grandfather was Polish man, strong as bull. He lift car one hand, no problem. What is wrong with you? You weak like American. At least have strong Polish name.' And she'd pinch his cheeks, and Roy, always a slender child, would try to puff his chest out and sit up a bit taller. Jasper had always liked Mrs Reynolds. She'd been good to him. He'd never had a reason to think on her unkindly.

Roy is no longer the boy Jasper remembers. He is not the young man he used to pal around with. Jasper can see that even from a distance. Roy has the same slender build he's had his whole life; the years have not changed that. His shoulders curve up and in slightly, concaving his chest. He's grown a beard that is trimmed short and tidy. A few bits of grey streak it, but there's none on his head as yet. Jasper wonders how he must look to Roy. How much changed. He clears his throat. Approaches the other man.

'I was startin' to think you might not say hello.'

Roy turns slowly to him. No friendly spark of recognition lights his face. 'I wasn't plannin' on it.'

Jasper nods. Looks down at his feet a moment before raising his eyes to the other man again. 'I would have said hello to you, you know. If things was different 'n' I was in your shoes 'n' you in mine. I'd still say hello to you.'

Silence hangs between them. The type of pause where a man might spit tobacco, had they not been in church. Roy holds Jasper's gaze, expressionless. 'That's where you're wrong,' he says, ''cause I'd nevera done what you done.' Roy takes a box of cigarettes out of his shirt pocket. Taps the bottom of the pack against the palm of his hand. Takes a cigarette out and puts the box back in his pocket. 'I heard you was out all righ'.' He twirls the cigarette between his fingers. 'Didn' expect to see you in a place like this, though.'

'I'm as free a man as any.'

'Yeah . . . well . . .'

Behind Roy, Sarah bounces a baby on her hip. She glances over at them, and Jasper just manages to catch her gaze. Her forehead creases as she looks away. He never would have pictured them together, but he can see why Roy married Sarah. Not that she's beautiful. In fact, far from it in Jasper's eyes, but there's a sort of maternal grace to her that appeals to him. Her breasts beneath her cotton dress are swollen plump with milk. The baby weight that still clings to her hips broadens her petite frame. He wonders if he sucked her tits he'd taste her milk. Wonders what it would be like. Imagines himself there sucking. 'I'd heard you got married,' he says at length, tilting his head towards Sarah.

'That's right.'

Jasper nods. 'And that's your boy?'

'That's right.'

Jasper nods again, surveying the church around them. The hushed voices kept low enough just to whisper past him. Makes him angry, all those whispers. Like he's the main attraction and they're all just waiting for him to start the show. 'I saw Esther the other day,' he says. 'In town. I asked her after you.'

'She told me.'

There'd never been awkwardness between him and Roy before. Not like this. Never anything like this. Jasper studies the scuff marks on his shoes. He'd hoped maybe they could be friends still. Even after Esther refusing him in the shop like that. He had imagined them out rabbit hunting just like they had so long ago. Jasper runs a hand through his hair, searches inside himself for the words he's after. There's so much he'd like to say. 'I'd thought maybe I'd hear from you.' His words hang between them, rawer than he'd meant.

'We ain't friends no more.'

Jasper nods. Real slow. 'We ain't friends?'

'You heard me.' Roy's voice is firm, hard. Cold.

Jasper smiles. No joy on his lips. 'Right.' He nods. 'You know,' he says, 'your mama, she must be real proud hearing you talk in your man voice like that, layin' down the law for me right there. Asserting yourself like that. Being a man in front of your woman here.' His smile slips into a smirk. 'Looks like you're all grown-up, huh, Roy? Fuckin' the girl next door, spreadin' your seed. Well, I say, bullshit.' His voice grows louder. 'Bull. Shit. I see right through you. You're still the same skinny brat that pisses his bed. The same coward you always been.'

'Wanna test me?' A coldness in Roy's eyes Jasper does not recognize.

It stops him short, then Jasper laughs. 'I'd test you anytime anywhere, no problem. But I ain't here for that.'

'Why are you here?' The woman's voice surprises him. He turns. It's Sarah, baby still bouncing on her hip as she rocks him side to side.

'Sarah, you stay out of this.' Roy's voice is low.

She looks at Jasper defiantly, no fear in her eyes. It's been a great long while since a woman did not fear him. Since one looked at him with such fire. Her eyes make him uncomfortable. Make his heart beat twice as fast. Somewhere out on the prairie, chickadees call and fall silent, their voices overpowered as a mockingbird speaks crow. 'Why are you here?' she says again, voice unwavering.

Jasper's face twists, more animal than human, then shifts back. 'This is my home,' he answers.

She shrugs Roy's hand from her shoulder. 'Well, this is our home, too, you bastard, 'n' we don' want you in it.'

Anger flushes her cheeks bright red in the heat of the room. It makes his blood quicken. He can just barely smell the soap off her skin. The milky scent of baby sick stuck to her. Lust burns at his groin, growing, and he wants to take her and taste her and suck on her swollen tits. He wants to feel if her flushed skin is hot. Not that she's pretty. Not that he's attracted to her. Just that it's been so long since he touched a woman, and the cloth of her cotton dress against her moist skin stirs longings in him.

He'd forgotten Sarah and Rose had been friends. *No wonder*, he thinks, *Roy hates me*.

'I think you'd best go.' Roy's voice is low and even. No messing in his tone. No room for messing either.

Jasper looks from Sarah back to Roy. He can tell the other man has seen his lust. The chatter of the church has died down some, a pool of quiet all around them as those close enough to hear have fallen silent. Most of the congregation have filed out of the church by now, some folks piling into their cars and pulling away, but most walk round the back of the church to where a handful of trailers propped up on cinder blocks house the Sunday school. The laughter of children drifts indoors as they chase each other across the lawn. Jasper used to run like that, not so long, so very long ago. Seems another life to him standing there now, facing the hostility in his once best friend's eyes.

'You're not welcome here.' Roy's voice is firm.

'Last I heard, this is God's house. Not yours.'

'I'm just sayin' what everyone here's thinkin'.'

'Well, bravo.' Jasper claps his hands together twice. 'Looks like you grew a spine in the last ten years.'

'Yeah, well.' Roy looks down to his feet, then up again. Face like stone.

'I'll be outside.' Sarah touches Roy's arm, then passes behind him to walk across the church. There is a grace to her movements Jasper had not noticed before. He wonders if it's new or if in their youth he had merely failed to recognize it. She and Esther stop by the doorway, looking back. But not at him, at Roy.

Jasper envies him that.

He tears his eyes from Sarah, and looks back to Roy. The other man is watching him. He shakes his head with a sort of disgust, and Jasper can't help but wonder what it is Roy sees in him that he so dislikes.

'We're done here,' Roy says. 'You hear? And you stay away from my family.'

'I ain't here to hurt nobody.'

'Damned if I care why you're here, Jasper, so long as you stay clear of me and mine.' Roy does not wait for an answer. He crosses the church quickly without looking back. Jasper watches as Roy puts his arm around Sarah. As she and he and Esther shake hands with the reverend and disappear into the brightness of the day beyond. There's a pain in Jasper's chest he has not felt for some time. He shakes his head to clear it, but the hurt's still there the same.

A hand slides onto his forearm and squeezes lightly. He had not heard her approach. He is not sure how much, if any, of his conversation with Roy she overheard. 'Let's go on home now,' Lizzie whispers, and he closes his eyes, seeking comfort in her voice.

When he opens them, she's looking up at him, waiting. He nods once, stiffly. 'All right,' he says. 'Let's go.'

She releases his arm, says nothing. Starts towards the door. Mutely, he follows.

The sun outside is scorching hot. Mirages down the road glisten invitingly, like cool pools of water. Katie tilts her head back to feel the sun more fully on her face. The heat of it relaxes her closed eyelids. Feels good to be outside where what little wind there is can cool. Her lips are dry and she can feel the heat from the sun start to crack them. She lowers her face. Opens her eyes. Most folks have left the church by now, but she still doesn't see Mom or Uncle Jasper. Katie hears her name from somewhere and shades her eyes to look around. A bunch of her friends stand round the back of Josh's pickup. It's Josh who called her. She smiles, waves and crosses the field, hurrying to join him.

Josh leans against the back of his truck, one foot crossed in front of the other. 'Hey, Princess,' he calls, and she can't help but smile. He puts his arm round her shoulders and keeps it there. She likes the warmth of his arm around her even though the day is hot. Something about just knowing it's there reassures her. She reaches up to her shoulder to hold his hand in hers.

'I can't believe your mom brought him here.' Ray Credinski leans against his own truck, parked next to Josh's.

'I can't believe *you* came to church!' Emma Golepi laughs. 'We *never* see you in church!'

Katie half smiles. 'Yeah, I know.' She leans into Josh to feel the comfort of him.

'He ain't gonna last long,' Josh whispers, 'if he carries on like this. You know that, don't you?'

'Don't say that, Josh.'

'Just seeing him gives me the creeps.' Kristen brushes her hair out of her face. 'Do you feel weird changing with him in the house? I'd never have a shower!' She shudders.

Katie looks down at her sandals. Her red toes peep out at her. She thinks of the tender way he speaks to her sister. 'He ain't all bad,' she says quietly.

Josh snorts, his arm heavy round her shoulders. She follows his gaze across the field. Then forgets to breathe.

Eddie Saunders is crossing the lawn towards them. Three men walk beside him. Two, Katie does not know or recognize. The third is Josh's father. Her saliva catches, newly sticky in her throat, and she finds it hard to swallow. Instinctively, she clutches Josh's hand more tightly. He shakes her grip free and steps forward, all smiles. Extends his hand to his father first, then solemnly shakes Eddie's. 'Sir.' He nods to the older man and to the men behind him.

'All right, son, all right.' Mr Ryan chuckles and smacks his son on the back. He's dressed nicer than most folks. His snakeskin cowboy boots look like they've never seen stirrups. His collar stands stiff with starch, an antique bola tightening his top button with a turquoise stone set in pure silver. He has the polished look of a big city doctor or lawyer. Only the dark stains round his short-kept nails hint that he's an oil man. Katie's never quite liked Mr Ryan. Or, rather, it's not so much that she's ever disliked him, she simply knows when she's been judged and found not up to standard.

'Dad, you remember Katie?'

Mr Ryan turns to her. His smile is delayed. 'Of course I do.'

She can feel Eddie's eyes boring into her. She extends her hand to Mr Ryan. 'It's nice to see you again, sir.'

He takes her hand. Nods to her. Something in his eyes she has not seen before. 'Josh's been tellin' me so much about you lately.' He flashes a smile that does not soften the dark contours of his face. 'Seems your family is the talk of the town once again!'

She can still feel Eddie's eyes locked on her. She's never met him before. She's never met any of the Saunders. Till Uncle Jasper came back home, the Saunders had never seemed important to her. Had never seemed real. They were just a family she'd been told young to keep far away from.

'You're his niece, aren't you?' The words more spat at her than said.

She turns very slowly to face him. Her reply clumps in her throat and stays there. Mutely, she nods.

Eddie Saunders steps forward towards her. He reaches out one calloused hand and gently lifts her chin so that her eyes meet his. His voice is rough. 'You're a pretty thing to keep so close to him.' He turns her face slowly from side to side. His gentleness surprises her. She doesn't know what to say. Just looks at him, uncertain. He smiles then, slowly, releasing her chin. She can still feel the roughness of his calluses even after he's moved his hand. 'Tell me,' he says softly, 'are you close with your uncle?'

She hesitates. 'Well, no, sir, not particularly.'

'I'd thought as much from what young Josh here's told me.' He leans his back against the tail of Josh's pickup. 'He's mighty soft on you, that boy.' She feels herself blush. Glances shyly at Josh in time to see his cheeks, too, go red. 'He's worried 'bout you, you know,' Eddie continues, ''n' frankly I can see why. Ten years ago you'd just 'bout been your uncle's favourite type.'

Her heartbeat quickens. 'I appreciate your concerns, sir,' she says uncertainly, 'but I don' think my uncle would harm us none. Mom trusts him.'

He laughs then, lightly, not for long, then falls silent. 'I heard he threatened Esther. That true?'

She doesn't want to answer him, but she knows she has to. 'Yes . . .'

'Good,' Eddie says, 'I'm glad you told the truth there 'cause I already heard the story off Esther. I had to see, is all, if you could be trusted.' He folds his arms across his chest. She'd never expected him to be so tall. 'See,' he continues, 'Josh there he's mighty sweet on you 'n' he said we could trust you. He said you're a decent girl. Ain't your fault, I guess, the family you're born into.' Eddie pauses. 'You strike me as an honest girl. Is that right, Katie?'

'Yes, sir.'

'Then tell me,' he says, voice lowering, 'honestly now, do you feel safe round your uncle?'

'Now remember,' Mr Ryan chimes in, 'be honest.'

Josh beside her squeezes her hand.

'No,' she whispers.

'Excellent.' Eddie grins. 'I'm glad to hear that now, I really am. You've got yourself a smart girl there, Josh, not just a looker.' He slaps Josh hard across the back, and Mr Ryan and the other two men chuckle. 'Now, Katie,' Eddie says, 'I need you to be honest with me again, OK?'

She nods.

He smiles. 'Do you think your uncle would hurt anyone again?'

She thinks about Uncle Jasper that first night punching the wall. About the way he grabbed Esther Reynolds's face. About the tender way he holds her sister's hand. She shakes her head. 'I don't know, sir,' she whispers. 'I really don't know my uncle very well at all.'

'He gives you the creeps, though, don't he, baby?' Josh's hand feels warm against her back, comforting, pressing.

'Yeah.' She looks past the men to where Kristen and Emma stand beside Ray, all three silently watching. 'He gives me the creeps all righ'.'

Mr Ryan steps forward. 'We want to keep you safe, Katie.' He's smiling.

Josh turns to her excitedly. 'I told you I'd tell my daddy 'n' Eddie how he was talkin'. I told you we'd set him straight. I'm done worryin' 'bout you, baby. You don' got to worry no more.'

'Wait.' She pulls nearly free of Josh's arms. 'What do you mean you'd "set him straight"?'

It is Eddie who answers her. 'Don' you worry none no more. That boy there's vouched you ain't like your blood. We won't let no harm come to you.'

Her voice falters. 'I don't think he means us no harm.'

Her eyes search the men around her almost desperate, almost pleading. 'He's family.'

'Now, Katie,' Mr Ryan smiles, 'doesn't the Bible itself teach us the devil charms in many disguises?'

'We need your help, Katie,' Eddie says softly, in a voice like he's confiding in her, like he and she are the only two people on earth. 'Don' be scared now,' he says. 'I'm gonna be keepin' a close watch over you. Your fella's daddy here 'n' I go way back, 'n' I'm happy to do his boy a good turn. Especially when I know first hand what your uncle is capable of. You understand me?' He searches her face and, slowly, she nods. 'Good,' he says. 'I wouldn't wish what happened to my sister on even my enemy's seed.'

She looks at Josh. His father. The other two men standing tall and silent. She looks across the lawn, past the scattered pickups back towards the church beyond. Joanne is playing tag with some other kids her age. Their laughter carries on the humid breeze. She does not see her mother or uncle. Reckons they must still be inside. She looks back to Eddie. 'What do you want me to do?'

Clouds rolled in low on the horizon just before supper. Heavy dark rain clouds that layered the sky in overlapping shades of grey and stone and slate. The parched earth has started to crack open in angry gashes between the tufts of tall, dried prairie grass. *It really is a miracle,* Lizzie thinks, *how well this garden's lasted.* Of course, she does water it, but only from time to time when all the other chores are either done or can wait. It's late enough, now the primroses are in full bloom. There's a smell of moisture in the air even though the rain has yet to fall. The wind has picked up a bit, and there's an unseasonable chill to the breeze, like a storm close by is brewing. Moths beat against the porch bulb, their fluttering wings flickering the light. Far off, thunder rolls, and the dark slate clouds move past more quickly. Nearly dark now, but no stars shine through the heavy layers of cloud.

It is her voice that breaks their silence. 'What do you want in life, Jasper?' This time no harshness to her tone.

He takes his time responding, his voice husky and low when he finally does answer. 'What do you mean?'

She looks out across the dark stretch of prairie before them. Another far-off crack of thunder rumbles around them, shaking the beams of the porch. 'I mean,' she says, 'what did you imagine when you was locked up? Your life is far from over. Did you see yourself with a wife one day? Kids?'

'My life was over the day they locked me up.'

She shakes her head. 'No, Jasper, that ain't what I mean 'n' you know it.'

'You want to know if I want a wife 'n' kids?'

She smiles. 'Yeah.'

He looks out across the darkness of the prairie. 'I never saw myself the marrying kind.'

'I guess I never seen you that way neither.' Silence stretches between them. 'You're good with kids, though,' she says at length. 'I hadn't expected that. Joanne's quite fond of you.'

He is silent a long moment. 'She's a good kid.'

No crickets or cicadas call out into the twilight, the approaching storm warning all to seek shelter. Lightning flashes, illuminating the open prairie. Wind bends the stems on rose bushes down the drive.

'We sure could use the rain,' she says.

He rises from his rocking chair and walks to stand at the top of the porch steps, holding on to the beam of railing that connects porch with awning. He leans forward out into the darkness, craning his neck to look up into the blackness of the newly fallen night. 'I can't remember the last time I felt a raindrop.'

She doesn't know what to say to that.

Thunder crashes far out to the west and rolls across the prairie, but no lightning strikes to light the sky. They wait in silence, but still no raindrops fall. And then their soft patter on the roof, light enough to have to strain to hear. A grin breaks across Jasper's face. A look kin to joy. Jasper extends his hand out beyond the awning of the porch into the darkness beyond. Palm open and stretched out flat. It hangs there a moment, suspended as the tiny raindrops catch in his palm and drip off his fingers, down his wrist. Slowly he curls each finger into a tight fist, tiny misty raindrops sticking to his knuckles, running down his arm. His profile is to her, half in shadow, half lit yellow by the porch light. 'In prison,' he says, still grinning, 'I always liked to listen to the rain.' He turns to look at her square on, face lit newly with a boy's delight.

A smile plays at the corner of Lizzie's lips. 'We sure could use this rain,' she says again, and she rises and goes to stand beside her brother, looking out to her garden and to the prairie beyond. It's too dark to make out most of the flowers, but she imagines them all the same, stretching up on their stems to embrace the falling rain.

She imagines the cracked dry earth ripped open, the rain healing its scars. She closes her eyes, listens to the gentle thudding of the falling rain. She can feel the light misty spray blowing against her face. She opens her eyes again. Jasper moves beside her. Carefully, as if with great reverence, he walks down the porch steps to stand before the house, his arms outstretched, his face up to the sky. His back is to her, his frame barely lit now by the porch light's muted glow. She watches as the raindrops mark the back of his T-shirt, like whip lashes, the light grey fabric stained dark by every drop. She wonders how it must feel to him, standing there in the rain for the first time in ten years. He turns to her, a manic glow in his eyes, or maybe, she thinks, it's just the way the porch light reflects in his irises. He's grinning. He's laughing. The normal laugh that is her brother. He runs both his hands through his wet hair, smoothing it all back. Closes his eyes, his face lifted up to the sky.

She feels like she's intruding on a private moment there, watching him.

The rain doesn't last long. The drops, quick to fall at first in small, delicate, dewdrop-sized splashes, stop nearly as unexpectedly as they started. Jasper lowers his head and opens his eyes. His outstretched arms fall limply by his sides. Thunder rumbles again, but further away this time, as if it's running off. 'That was nice,' he says, still smiling. He nods slowly, looking around him almost as if dazed. His eyes meet hers. She thinks she sees his cheeks colour slightly, though Jasper never was a man to blush. 'That felt real good,' he says, still smiling. 'Yessir, that felt just like I remembered.'

There is sadness in her smile. She can feel it on her face. She traces a raindrop's trail as it slides down the porch railing. She hadn't realized her fingertips were so dry until she felt the moisture on them. She had never pondered what it would be like for him in there, not even feeling the rain. She had always been more of the school of thought that he had earned his cell and all the restrictions that had come with it. She straightens. 'We've got an early start tomorrow,' she says briskly. 'I suggest you get some rest.'

'Sis?'

She's halfway through the door already, but his word stops her. *When was the last time he called her that?* She does not turn, simply stands frozen in the doorway. Waits.

'This is what I want in life,' he says at last.

She half turns then. Her mouth opens to answer him, but she can't quite pick what words to say. Confusion furrows her brow. 'What is?'

'I want to feel human again. I want to feel close enough to normal.'

'Ain't one of us normal round here, Jasper.'

A smile tickles his lips, but does not quite reach his eyes. 'Wouldn't that be funny, then, if I could be the first?'

Three gentle scrapes at his door. More like scratching than knocking, really. For a second it reminds him of the way Rico Martinez across the cell block used to claw at the bars on his cell, scraping paint off with his nails, nails screeching as they slid down the bars, but then Jasper's eyes pop open and, blinking, he recalls where he is. The scratching pauses, then sounds again. Nails on wood much kinder, softer than metal. He sits up. Listens for another moment. Then slips on his jeans and rises.

Outside, no crickets call; sky dark and clouded. The wooden floorboards feel cool beneath his bare feet. He leans his ear against the door. Closes his eyes. All sound the other side stops and Jasper listens to the silence. His own breaths the loudest sound. Slowly, he cracks the door.

Doe eyes peer at him, wide and dark in the dim light. A part of him had known it must be her. He opens his mouth to speak. Joanne puts a finger to her lips, then turns and tiptoes down the hall. He glances at Lizzie's closed door. Halfway down the hall already, Doe Eyes looks back at him and beckons. Wondering if he's dreaming, Jasper mutely follows.

She tiptoes down the stairs featherlight before him. The oversized white T-shirt she wears as nightgown gracefully bobs and floats around her. There was a time when he, too, could have descended those stairs without creaking a single step, but those days are long behind him. He winces as a stair groans under his weight, then freezes, a reflex left over from all those Christmas mornings years back when he would sneak down before Lizzie to see the tree. A part of him, he realizes, still expects his parents to wake and come scold him for being out of bed. A smile cracks his stern exterior. It's been a long, long while since he smiled like that. Longer still since he cared to tiptoe.

Downstairs, a tiny crack of light spills from the sitting room. Buttercup yellow, like the flowers outside. Joanne opens the door slowly so the hinges won't squeak, just like he used to all those years ago. 'Come on,' she whispers, and steps inside.

He follows.

Two sheets stretch between the sofa and Daddy's old easy chair, held in place by books and clothespins. Though the rest of the room is dark, a lamp inside the makeshift tent glows yellow gold, lightly illuminating the room.

'Do you like it?' Joanne whispers, face glowing. 'Come on!' In one swift motion she drops down and crawls inside.

Jasper hesitates. Watches her shadow cross its legs and settle down inside the tent. It's been years since he had a reason to crawl. *When was the last time a little girl pulled him out of bed? Or a woman, for that matter?* There has not been much light or laughter for him these last long years, no time for play. When he was a boy, he used to build forts in that very same spot between those very two chairs. Used to play cowboys and Indians and use the fort for shelter. Joanne's dark shadow within the tent leans forward, elongated by the light. The sheet pulls back and her head pokes out. 'Come on,' she whispers, smiling brightly, then disappears again.

Still wondering if he's dreaming, Jasper lowers to his knees. She pulls the tent flap back, and he crawls forward. Pillows lie scattered around and underneath them. Two glasses of milk sit off to one side next to a plate with two peanut-butter and jelly sandwiches. A teddy bear slouches down the back. One of Mama's old lamps covered with a yellow dish towel gives off the tent's golden glow.

'Do you like it?' she whispers, all gold herself, tangled hair a fiery halo catching the lamp's gentle light.

He can't help but smile. 'It's been a long while,' he says quietly, 'since I sat in a fort like this.'

She beams. 'Katie used to build forts with me. She builds *the* best forts. And sometimes she used to wake me up and we'd come down here and do puzzles and play cards and tell secrets and stuff, except Katie never really told me that many secrets, I just told her all of mine, but still . . .' Her hands fidget in her lap, pick at a scab on her knee.

'How'd you know I wasn't sleeping?' His voice sounds rougher than intended.

She shrugs. 'I couldn't sleep.'

It feels strange sitting in a child's fort. Feels wrong somehow being so close to a little girl, in her nightgown, at this late hour, yet it feels so comfortable too, so right. He feels calm around her.

'I'm sorry,' she says quietly, 'that they weren't nicer to you.'

Thoughts scattered, he bristles slightly. 'Who?'

Doe eyes meet his. 'Everybody.' She pauses. 'I liked church. Do you think we can go back? They might be nicer next time.'

Wood creaks against wood as the house shifts. The buzz of a beetle falls silent. He chooses his words with care. 'There ain't too many people left, Doe Eyes,' he whispers, 'that might be kind to me.'

A smile flutters her lips up, then she's pulling at a hangnail with her teeth. 'I don't think you seem so bad.' It's like an egg cracks inside him, yolk melting warm through his gut. A funny feeling, to which he is unaccustomed.

Wide eyes search his. 'Are you going back?'

It takes him a moment. 'To church?'

She nods.

A sad smile softens his jaw. 'I ain't plannin' too far ahead just yet.' Wind blows in from the cracked window, rustling the sheet around them, the cotton cool as it brushes against his arm. He clings to her words. Silently replays them. It feels good to be seen as someone not so bad. Especially by her. He wishes the whole world could see him, just for a moment, through her wide eyes.

Her smile still flutters on her lips. A shyness to her that was not there before. 'Uncle Jasper,' she whispers, 'how come you call me that name sometimes?'

Her question snaps him from his reverie. Automatically, he bristles. 'What name?'

'You know . . .' She giggles. 'What you called me there right before I asked about church.' Her eyelashes flutter as she glances down and looks back up again.

'You don't like it?'

That shyness still about her. 'No, I like it.' She lifts her eyes to his. 'Daddy called Katie "Lady" when she was young.'

'Oh.' He is not sure what to say to that. Not sure just what she wants of him.

She cocks her head, regarding him, brow deeply furrowed. 'Do I look like a deer to you?'

He laughs. Can't help but laugh. 'Somethin' like that, Doe Eyes.' He winks. 'A deer too fine for huntin'.'

Her smile casts a light all its own, warmer than the rays

off a midday sun, and for the first time Jasper can remember since many long years ago, it seems he can't stop smiling. Even had he wanted to.

'Here.' She tosses him a pillow and leans back herself, snuggling up to the teddy bear. With a finger she traces a crease on the sheet above her. 'Did you 'n' my daddy ever build forts? Were you friends when you was small?'

The question surprises him. 'Naw, but your mama 'n' I built a good few.' It's been over ten years since he felt so comfortable in such a tiny space. He leans against the pillow she threw him. Stretches his legs out long so his feet stick out through the side of the sheet.

'Katie says Daddy used to build the best forts. Even better than hers. She says Daddy used to build us forts like this at night too, so when he left she kept buildin' 'em, 'cause I couldn't remember.' She pauses. 'I never seen Mom build a fort.'

'Do you remember your daddy much?' He hadn't intended to ask that.

The words hang heavy between them. Down the hall the grandfather clock stops chiming. Her brow creases. He prays she is not re-evaluating, judging him all bad.

She shakes her head. 'All I know are stories.'

Silence stretches as he ponders that, neither knowing what to say.

'Are you hungry?' she asks, her whisper to him oddly musical in the silence left by the grandfather clock.

Mutely he takes the sandwich she offers. He was a boy the last time he ate a peanut-butter and jelly sandwich. With grape jelly. Reminds him of how his mama used to make them, back when he was small. Except the crusts have been cut off. He savours the creaminess of the peanut-butter, smooth and thick against his tongue. He wishes for a moment he was a boy again, clean slate for life ahead. 'Thank you,' he says quietly.

She's chugging milk from her glass. 'For what?' She wipes her lips with the back of her hand.

He smiles. Can't help but smile. 'For this,' he whispers, 'for being my friend.'

He would not have thought it possible, but somehow her face glows brighter. She looks so like her mother in that moment, he muses, and yet so different too, a creature all her own. Awkward and breathtaking, somehow, all at once.

She grins. 'Do you wanna play Go Fish?' Long shadows flicker and shift.

The warmth in his gut spreads. 'You'll have to remind me how. It's been a long time since I played.'

Katie cuts the engine as she pulls to the top of their drive. Muted light flickers from behind drawn curtains. Usually at this late hour the house looms dark and silent. She pauses on the front porch, key in the door, and again in the hallway she freezes, staring at the light that spills from the crack under the living-room door. For a moment she wonders if maybe Mom is sitting up, or maybe a lamp was accidentally left on. She stops with her hand on the door knob, not sure if she wants to enter. *What if it's him in there?* Laughter on the other side. Carefully, Katie opens the door.

Two silhouettes sit hunched, dark shadows within a glowing yellow makeshift tent. The kind of tent that she and Joanne used to build together. The kind her daddy made for her when she was very small. It takes Katie back to those nights spent alone with her father before Joanne was born, to the card games and board games they'd stay up late and play. For a second she is confused, not sure what she is looking at, not sure how this cherished memory could be so brought to life. Then from under the sheet Uncle Jasper's voice asks, 'You got any Jacks?' and Joanne's shadow sits up taller as she smugly giggles, 'Go fish.'

Katie's heart tightens and twists. Anger gnaws at her gut, twisting her insides sour. How dare Joanne recreate this memory with *him*?

'What the hell are y'all doin'?' Katie's voice cracks the stillness of the night.

Inside the tent both shadows freeze. Then, giggling, Joanne pops her head out of the flap. 'Katie! You're home! Come play with us!'

Katie switches on the overhead, flooding the room with light.

Stiffly, slowly, Jasper crawls from the tent to stand blinking with his head slightly bowed. No shirt on. His hair a slept-in mess. Joanne scrambles to her feet all smiles, her T-shirt nightgown hanging down just above her knees. 'Mom'll kill you when I tell her you stayed up this late.'

The smile drops from Joanne's lips. 'Katie, no, please don't . . .'

'Get upstairs. Now.'

Joanne's lip pouts. 'You're not my mom, you can't tell me what to do.'

'I swear to God,' Katie whispers hoarsely, 'you get upstairs to bed or I'll make you more than sorry.'

Joanne opens her mouth to protest again, but it is Jasper who speaks. 'Listen to your sister, Doe Eyes,' he says gently. 'We can play some other time.'

Joanne's mouth closes, then opens again only to close once more. She turns to their uncle. 'You promise?'

Jasper nods.

Joanne hugs him round the waist, real tight. His eyes close as her arms slip around him, then open as, hesitantly, he lowers his arms to hug her back. Over Joanne's head Katie and Jasper's eyes meet. She does not like to hold his gaze. Nor does she like the tenderness with which he regards her sister. It makes her uncomfortable. As does his nickname for her: *Doe Eyes*. Another stab in Katie's gut she does not quite understand. She never should have shared those memories of their father with her sister. They were not Joanne's to take.

Joanne releases their uncle, murmuring, 'Goodnight.'

'Goodnight.' His eyes follow her out of the room.

Katie does not feel comfortable alone with their uncle. Though half a room away, he feels too close. She doesn't understand how her sister can hug him. How she can act like he's her dad. Katie folds her arms across her chest more for comfort than against a chill. She struggles to find the words she wants to say. 'Joanne's just a kid,' she spits out finally.

Jasper says nothing. Just stands there staring at her, fort still aglow behind him. For a moment Katie wonders if she should stay another moment, should say something else. She thinks about how Joanne accused her of never speaking to their uncle. She opens her mouth to speak, to tell him to leave her sister alone. No words come out, just air. She thinks of Eddie at church that morning. Of his kind smile when he asked for her help. Angry, hurt still, Katie runs out of the room and up the stairs after her sister.

It is some time till Jasper stirs. He can still feel her arms tight around him. The pressure of her face against his stomach. Her small hands around his back. It's been a long while since anyone hugged him. A long, long while indeed. And he wants to savour the feeling. To replay it in his head. A part of him fears that once he moves the moment will be over, lost and gone for ever, distant as a dream. He had always shied away from hugs, even before prison, but standing in the too-bright sitting room in the dead of night reliving the innocence of her embrace, it seems to Jasper there is no purer feeling, no greater peace on earth.

He hadn't expected the parole office to be in a strip mall. Not that Jasper had spent much time pondering just where the office would be. In fact, he'd scarcely thought on it at all in the days since his release, but sandwiched between a nail salon and a Tex Mex restaurant was the last location he would have imagined.

It seemed to Jasper as they raced along the freeway that the whole country was newly dotted with strip malls and fast-food joints. He didn't remember it being like that before. Or cars driving so fast. Or there being so many cars on the road for that matter. They must have gone that fast before, he knows, the cars that is, but prison had had its own pace, and he nearly felt dizzy among the speeding chaos of I-10. He was glad when Lizzie had exited the highway. He felt he could breathe better somehow on the feeder with open fields around them once again.

Now, seated in the stuffy room across from his assigned parole officer, Jasper wishes intensely that someone somewhere in the office would open a window to let a bit of air in. 'The goddamned a/c is broke,' were the first words his parole officer had said to him. And the man hadn't been kidding. Sweat runs thick down Jasper's forehead, stinging as it reaches his eyes. He can feel his shirt dampening at the armpits and around the collar. He can feel that dampness spreading. Lizzie'd insisted he look 'presentable' that morning. She had even ironed one of his new shirts for him, but now his hair is damp with sweat, and Jasper feels about as far from presentable as he reckons he can get.

The receptionist out the front, when he first entered the building, looked like an ex-con herself. She had her hair done up all big and curly in a style he was unfamiliar with. Her blouse hugged her every curve. It seemed a bit too tight for that sort of job. A bit too low-cut. But she wasn't particularly pretty, and Jasper reckoned it was the averageness of her face that let her get away with dressing like that. She had a bit of a snaggletooth that further stole her beauty when she smiled, but even when her mouth was shut she looked nothing short of common. He liked her hair, though, all big and frizzy. He liked the shape of her under that blouse. Even if her tits didn't seem extra firm or perky.

She'd barely glanced at him when he'd come in. 'You Yancey's ten thirty?' she'd asked, not bothering to look up from the fashion magazine she was gazing at.

'Yes, ma'am.' He had glanced at the scrap of paper clutched in his hand. 'I'm here for Yancey James Sutton.'

She had looked up then. Had held his gaze, head cocked to the side, regarding him the way a cocker spaniel might. 'How many years you do?' she'd asked. Her eyes had weighed him up but somehow had lacked true judgement. Like maybe she didn't already know his story, didn't know just who he was.

He had tried to smile, but it felt unnatural, like his skin somehow had gone too tight. 'Long enough, I reckon.' His eyes had drifted down again to the fabric stretched across her breasts.

She had flashed her snaggletooth. 'I'll take you right on back, then.' And he'd followed her down the hall.

Now, sweating, his parole officer, Yancey Sutton, across the desk studying him, Jasper wonders what her name might be. That receptionist's. He ponders asking her on his way out. Just her name, that is. He wonders if he could maybe one day have a woman — one not too pretty — like that. One used to scarred men who might not care about his history. But inside he knows that certain things in this life are not to be.

Yancey sits quietly behind his desk, regarding Jasper. His hands clasp together just under his chin. His elbows rest on his swivel chair's arms. He leans back, shifts his weight and crosses his arms over his chest as he reclines. 'Sorry 'bout the heat,' he says. 'Goddamned window won' even open.' He gestures towards the tiny rectangular box of light that serves as the room's only window. More a skylight, really, than anything. A clock on the desk ticks to keep time. Back out in Reception, the phone rings. 'I'll do us both a favour and cut the bullshit,' Yancey says, leaning forward. 'Even without this file, I know who you are, you hear? And I know jus' what you done.' His fingers tap a closed file there on the desk before him.

Down the hall, the phone rings a second time. A third. Jasper holds his tongue. He lets his eyes wander to the calendar on the back wall. Some photograph of a long-horn waist high in a field of Indian paintbrushes, the Texas flag blowing in the background.

Yancey's eyes narrow, as though he's summing up the man before him. 'I'm gonna level with you,' he says. 'You 'n' I can sit here week after week disliking each other all you want, but fact is if you want to keep your freedom you'll keep me buttered up.' He smiles. His teeth are stained yellow from years of chewing tobacco. His lips have the purple swell of a man who's long liked his drink. 'You understand me, son?'

'I understand you.' Jasper's voice is low but firm. He can hear the sweet call of the receptionist's voice as she answers the phone way off down that hall. He turns his focus back to Yancey. It's been a long while since anyone not a clergyman referred to him as 'son'.

Yancey is nodding. 'Good,' he says, and nods again. He's an older man, not too far off retirement, silver-haired with a gut that stretches and pulls the fabric round the buttons on his shirt. His cowboy boots are snakeskin with a bit more of a heel than is common for most men. He is not a tall man, though he does not quite seem short

243

enough to warrant the extra heel. Perhaps because of the confidence with which he holds himself. Sweat runs down his brow, his cheeks, the side of his double chin. 'So here's the deal,' Yancey says, smiling once again. 'We can work together 'n' keep things real sweet between us, or if you act up, I can make a phone call real easy, any time I want, and that's you gone. You hear?'

Sweat runs from Jasper's chin down the front of his neck. He wipes it with the back of his hand, then wipes his hand on his jeans. 'I hear you.'

'Good,' Yancey says, and nods again. He takes out a folder from a drawer and lets it fall onto the desk before him. Right on top of the other, thicker, folder already there. 'I'm familiar with your case, Mr Curtis. Been lookin' over it all mornin'. But, shit!' He grins. 'There's few folks this side of the Rio Grande that ain't familiar with your case, now, are there?' Yancey chuckles to himself real soft and low, as though letting Jasper in on some private joke. Automatically, Jasper bristles. 'Now I ain't gonna be your new buddy,' Yancey continues. 'I got enough friends of my own. And I ain't here to hold your hand as you get used to the big bad world once again. If you don' assimilate back into society, that's on you.' He fidgets with a pencil before he lets it fall onto the folder before him. 'Half the boys I see go straight back into the penitentiary.' He pauses, as though to let his words have impact. Lets out a long breath and shakes his head slightly. Then his expression changes and he leans forward with a playfulness he had lacked before. 'There's just one thing, in your case,' Yancey smiles, malice playing at the corner of his lips, 'that don' add up to me.' He leans back in his chair, and slowly places one foot and then the other up on the desk before them.

Jasper regards him without expression, watching the sweat patches on the other man's shirt spread.

'See, it just don' make sense to me,' Yancey continues, 'why the hell they let you out.' He laughs then, long and loud, pleased with his own wit.

Jasper smiles. Unamused. A cold, hard smile that does not soften his features. 'Are you my parole officer, sir,' he says quietly, 'or my next jury?'

A slow grin breaks across Yancey's face. 'All right, son, all right.' He nods. Real. Slow. 'You want to play your hand all close to your chest like that, you go on right ahead. I won't stop ya.' The men regard each other in silence. Yancey's desk is covered with discarded scraps of paper. Bills, official court documents, police reports, all mixed together. Piles of folders stand like tiny columns around the room. Papers stacked high. Yancey flicks open the folder before him and lifts out a stack of papers. He taps it against his desktop to even the pages out, then sets it down before him. He reaches into his drawer again and pulls out a pair of reading glasses. He pauses a moment, holding Jasper's gaze, then puts the glasses on and picks up the stack of papers. 'Let's see now . . .' he says, scanning the sheet. 'Where are we? . . . Yes. All right. You livin' back home, that right?'

Jasper watches the man before him coolly. 'That's right.'

'Your folks' place, is it?' Yancey marks notes on the paper held before him. Jasper cannot see what words he writes.

'My sister's now.'

Yancey glances over the stack of papers. He flips through a couple of documents and lets the pages fall into a pile. 'Where're your folks at?'

'Dead.'

'All right . . .' He makes a mark on a page. 'You plan on stayin' there awhile?'

'I got nowhere else to go.'

'You payin' rent there?'

Jasper hesitates. 'At the moment, no.' Then, louder, 'That land's half mine.' More defensive than he'd intended.

Yancey looks over his glasses at him. The lenses on them have fogged up from the heat. He takes them off carefully and wipes them on his shirt to dry them, but it's so hot his shirt is moist with sweat, and the fabric only streaks the glasses, does not fully dry them. He looks to the files and papers before him. 'You finish high school?'

'Yes, sir.'

'State requires you to work. With the conditions of your parole. And you're not to leave the state, and not to leave the country neither.' He pauses. 'You lazy, boy?'

Jasper shakes his head. 'I never had any problem with workin'.'

Yancey snorts, as though what Jasper's just said amuses him. Jasper feels his blood go cold, despite the muggy heat that fills the room. He'd like to show Yancey just what he's capable of, just what he can do. He'd like to work the other man's face into a nice dark shade of purple. It's been a long while since anyone laughed at Jasper.

Been even longer since anyone got away with it. Jasper cracks his knuckles. Reminds himself that he's all done with trouble.

'Before prison, you were –' Yancey flicks back another page.

'I was a mechanic, sir,' Jasper cuts him off. Can't quite keep the sneer from his tone.

Yancey leans back in his chair. He's not laughing now. But he's not quite respectful neither. Slowly he nods. 'A mechanic,' he murmurs. He glances down to the stack of papers before him. 'Are you aware,' he says, 'of the where-abouts of Ms Saunders?'

Jasper recoils from the surprise of her name. Anger fills him and he has to shove it down to keep himself from leaning over that desk and grabbing the man behind it. He swallows, struggling to keep control. 'I reckon I could find her, if I was so inclined.'

Yancey slowly removes his glasses and sits up straight. '*Do* you intend to find her, Mr Curtis?'

'Can I ask you a question . . . sir?' The words spill out of Jasper before he can stop them. His lips curl as the words leave them, the disdain in his voice unmissable.

Yancey nods, slowly placing his glasses on his desk. 'Shoot.'

'Are you trying to be my friend here, or my next girl-friend? 'Cause it seems to me for jus' meetin' we're gettin' awful cosy.'

A slow grin spreads across Yancey's face. 'Damn, boy!' He claps his hands together. Once. Twice. 'That just made my day. Got ourselves a firecracker!' he calls down the hall. Then his tone shifts. Eyes narrow. 'Now, you listen here and you listen good, you smart alecky mother-fucker. I control your life. You wanna piss? I tell you where to do it. You understand me, boy? You ain't free till you're free of me.'

Jasper bites the inside of his lip till he tastes blood. Something about the feel of his teeth locked into his flesh calms him just a little. The clock ticks. Out in Reception the phone rings and is answered, and her voice sounds sweet again.

'Now,' Yancey says, reclining once more, 'you need a job, don' you? Conditions of your parole ... Let's see what I've got here for a fine convict like yourself, shall we?' He grins. The playful, malicious glint returns to his eyes. 'Yes, sir,' he says, 'we've got a bright future for you right here. Must be your lucky day. There's a chicken factory a bit short on staff. It's halfway to San Antonio, but I'm sure you won' mind the drive.' Yancey looks down, marking quickly on a form.

'A chicken farm?' Jasper cannot mask his surprise.

'That's what I said.'

'What kind of work is it?'

Yancey looks up and holds his gaze. 'Honest work. That's what kind.'

Jasper bites back the words he wants to say. He can feel them boil up inside him. He swallows his anger. Says instead, 'I never done dishonest work.'

Yancey snorts but does not answer him. He's ticking boxes on some form Jasper cannot read.

Jasper clears his throat. 'What will I be doing there?'

'Does it matter?'

He hesitates. 'Yes.'

A smile plays on Yancey's lips. 'Why? What does it matter what scum like you do?'

Jasper looks to the tiny window that teases him with light. It's hard to breathe in the room it's so stuffy. So hot. 'It's my life,' he says, his words hanging vulnerably between them. He waits for an answer that never comes, then asks, 'Ain't there any other jobs goin' I might be better suited for?'

Yancey doesn't even bother looking back to the list he had previously referred to. 'See, that's the problem, son,' he says. 'You ain't suited for a good life.'

Jasper can't bite his lip any more. The rage inside him boils up and spills out. 'You must not get any action,' he snarls, 'when you're not fuckin' people over.'

Yancey smiles. A look on his face as if he's enjoying this. 'I sure as hell get a whole lot more than you do, son,' he says, and chuckles lightly.

Jasper's fingers dig into the armrests of his chair. He can feel his nails cut into the cracked dry leather. It's like he's in prison all over again, no air, no room to breathe, some guard up in his face telling him he's unworthy to live. And maybe I am, Jasper thinks, maybe that's why death has always come more easily.

Yancey Sutton tears off a corner of the piece of paper he'd been writing on. His eyes mock Jasper, and Jasper wishes this were prison after all and not the office he sits in now. In prison there were ways to deal with enemies, even if they were guards. Outside, it seems to Jasper, it's too hard to tell just who's right and wrong. Seems the whole world, these days, is made up out of enemies. Of wrongs he's done he'll never be able to put right. He takes the paper the other man's handed him. A phone number and an address are scribbled there.

'You call that number 'n' they'll give you your work details. Pay ain't great, but you weren't an easy sell.' Yancey chuckles. 'Now get on outta here.'

Jasper rises slowly, paper still clutched in his hands, eyes still lowered to it. He is in the doorway already before he stops. 'I ain't gonna be one of the ones like you mentioned earlier,' he says. 'One of them ones that goes on back. I'm done with trouble. I just thought I'd tell you that.'

Yancey shakes his head. 'Boy,' he says, 'you got trouble stamped all over you,' and returns to the papers on his desk.

The sun bakes the concrete, reflecting, blinding, off everything it touches. Uneasiness has crept over Lizzie, and she cannot quite place what's newly unsettled her. Watching Jasper walk into the parole office for a moment had felt like he was gone again. And there'd been a part of her that breathed easy when she saw him walk away. There was another part of her afraid to let him go. Afraid he might not come back. She sits out in the parking lot waiting for Jasper to return from his parole meeting, parked in the shade cast by the buildings. Sunlight reflects off car doors and mirrors. She's got the window rolled down; her elbow rests in its open frame. The engine and the radio are both off. A small part of her thought of just driving away. Of leaving him there. But where would he go? The townsfolk had certainly made Jasper's unwelcome clear in church the day before, scorn etched deep on every face. What would she tell her girls if she came on home alone? The question she does not ask herself, is 'Would you miss him?' She's not sure she has an answer to that. She's not sure she's ready to know it. Joanne would miss him. She had never thought her daughter would grow so fond of him. *What was I thinking letting a man like that get so near her?* And yet Lizzie feels it's OK somehow. She trusts her brother not to hurt her child. Or so she tells herself again and again. It's good for Joanne to have a man to look up to; Lizzie simply can't help but shudder at the choice of man. *And yet*, she thinks, *whose fault is it but mine?*

She's still thinking about her daughters when the door to the parole office finally swings open, and Jasper steps blinking from the dark shadows of its doorway. He shields the sun from his eyes, though he still stands in the building's shade. Like some pale creature out of a dream, newly released from some long-forgotten nightmare. She does not honk her horn. He knows where she is parked.

He stands there, letting his eyes adjust to the brightness of the day. What little rain fell the night before has long since dried up, the whole world around them still parched and cracked and dry. *We need a proper rainstorm*, she thinks, and wishes for a breeze to cool, but when the wind finally does gust, the air still feels hot, and there's dust that blows along with it, sticking to her sweaty arms and neck as grime. He starts to cross the parking lot to her. His hands deep down in his pockets, shoulders hunched. Had she just seen him now for the first time in all those years, would she have known him as her brother? A part of her thinks not.

Then her heart locks and she wants to scream. She can

see what is about to happen before it does. Her mouth opens, but there is no sound, and she is not certain what she meant to scream. A warning? But, no, there are no words for this, and her mouth falls closed again, silent.

Lizzie watches recognition dawn on Jasper's face. The woman stops short, maybe twenty feet from him. She's wearing a green dress with a floral pattern that reaches down just below her knees. White sandals. Her dark hair is long and loose and blows behind her. *Oh, God, no,* thinks Lizzie, *please, God, no.*

Jasper opens his mouth to speak. He says something Lizzie cannot hear; nor can she read his lips. He stands motionless. His arms rise slowly, outstretched, palms open as though pleading. The woman spooks like a rabbit. Zero to full speed in a blink. Runs inside the nail salon, door swinging after her. Jasper stares after her, but does not follow. He stands a moment and runs his hand through his sweat-soaked hair. Then he turns back towards Lizzie, and slowly starts walking to her.

He opens the door and slides onto the seat and closes the door after himself. Hard enough that it shuts tight. Just short of a slam. Lizzie can't control her breathing. Her mouth's gone all dry. He does not look at her. Says, 'I hadn't counted on that.'

Both hands on the steering-wheel, but the engine still off, Lizzie stares straight ahead, afraid to turn to her brother, afraid of what she might see etched in his face beside her. 'What'd you say to her?' Lizzie's voice scarcely a whisper it's so soft.

For a moment she is not sure he plans to answer her. 'I

told her she looked beautiful.' He turns to her, his eyes unfocused as though seeing another face than hers.

A trucker from Illinois spilled his coffee on her near the start of her shift, and now, as she sweats, Katie can smell the overwhelming richness of the brew as its odour clings to her. It smells to her like she's sweating coffee, and that, mixed with the deep-fried scent that always clings to her after even the slightest moment in the kitchen, is enough to make her stomach turn. She wonders sometimes just how Tom does it, stuck in that sweltering kitchen all the time, bent over the cooker and hot tubs of grease, deep frying. But then again, she thinks, Tom doesn't also have the coffee smell to deal with.

She's nearly certain that trucker spilled the coffee on her on purpose, too. Right across her breasts when she'd leaned over to take his plate away. The coffee hadn't been hot, he'd been there nursing it for the last couple hours, but the shock of the liquid against her flesh had still made her cry out. She hadn't liked the gleam in his eyes as he apologized either, his eyes glued to the stain as it spread across her chest. It's dried now, the stain that is, but the dark colour of it against her white blouse still draws unwanted attention to her cleavage, and Katie feels self-conscious with every customer she serves.

The dinner rush, if you could call it that, is long over now, the diner mostly empty. Tom's sitting on his stool in the kitchen, smoking a cigarette and flicking through yesterday's paper, the usual sizzle of the kitchen quiet all around him. A trucker sits at the counter finishing off his chicken fried steak, his jeans low on his hips so that his crack hangs out as he leans forward, his pants too tight to accommodate the large expanse of his gut. A family sits in a booth by the window, a mom and dad and their little tot, up now long past her bedtime. She's a cute kid, and Katie's enjoyed watching her while she worked. Katie brought the tot crayons earlier while her parents were waiting on their food, and the little girl drew stick figures and a house. The parents had chatted to Katie for a while, and they had seemed real nice. They were from Dallas on their way down to South Padre Island. When Katie said she'd never been to Dallas, they had laughed and said they didn't believe her. After that, she didn't have the heart to tell them she'd never seen the ocean. 'That's why we're taking Molly,' the woman had told her, smiling. 'This'll be her first time to the beach.' They seem to Katie a happy family. The kind of family she hopes herself to have one day. The kind that eats together and takes vacations. And laughs at the nonsense their little girl coos. The kind she would have liked to grow up in. She wonders if maybe, one day, she and Josh will have that together. A family like that. She wonders if he'll send for her next year when he's off at college. If he'll remember to drive back home to see her. It seems to her that maybe, if he could just take her with him, she could truly leave all this behind. They could start their own family and find some new place to call home. They could just pass through towns like this.

Katie wipes sweat from her forehead with the back of her hand. Above her, the ceiling fan struggles to move the stagnant air, shaking as it rotates. She's topping up the Heinz bottles with extra ketchup. Not Heinz, but

Penny reckons no one will taste the difference, and so far she's been right. 'Penny sure does know how to save those dimes!' Tom had said to Katie one evening, when they were closing up, and Katie had laughed real hard when he'd said that to her. Tom had chuckled, too, though Katie's fairly certain Penny would not have found it as amusing, her staff laughing at her expense like that.

A bell chimes as the diner door swings open. Katie turns. 'Josh!'

He grins. 'Hey, baby.' But there's something off in his smile, in the way he says his name for her. He crosses the room to the counter in front of where Katie's filling up the ketchup bottles. The trucker, three stools down from him, glances up as Josh sits down, but when he sees Katie lean across the counter to peck Josh a quick hello, he mumbles something under his breath, and turns back to his food.

There's something off in Josh's kiss, too, but still Katie forces a smile. *Maybe I'm imagining things.* Out loud, she says, 'I didn' know you were comin' in to see me tonight.' She smiles her cutest smile. The one she knows he likes.

'I hadn't planned on it, baby. Something's . . .' he hesitates '. . . come up.'

She feels the smile fall from her face. 'What is it?'

His eyes drop to the stain on her top. A smile briefly plays at the corners of his mouth as he nods towards it. 'That's a new look.'

'Oh, shut it.' She crumples up and throws a paper napkin at him. It bounces off his shoulder onto the counter before them.

He smiles at her, and for a split second it seems

everything's going to be OK. Then his smile falters and he leans forward across the counter. 'We're fixin' to ride on up to your house,' he whispers. 'I wanted to swing by here first, see that you was here.'

Her throat goes dry. Her chest feels cold. 'Why?' she whispers. Her eyes search his.

He takes her hand and holds it on the counter before them. 'I wanted to make sure you were safe.'

She feels her hand go clammy in his. 'Why wouldn't I be safe, Josh? Why are you going to my house?' Confusion wrinkles her brow.

'We have to do something, Katie.' His voice is hushed but urgent. 'We can't just let him go round scaring folks.'

She pulls her hand from his and straightens. 'No, Josh.' Her words pierce the stuffy room, too loud against the muted backdrop of the radio. The trucker looks over, then grunts and turns his attention back to his dinner. In the booth by the window, the father is still drinking his coffee while the mother holds the tot and rocks her gently back and forth. Behind Josh, parked out front, is his pickup, another older model of truck parked up beside it. Katie can see shadowy silhouettes moving in both vehicles. 'Just how many of y'all,' she whispers hoarsely, 'are fixin' on goin' on up to mine?'

He follows her gaze out of the window. 'There's a good few.'

She can barely speak, her throat's so tight. 'What are ya'll fixin' on doin'?'

He reaches out and runs the back of his fingers down the side of her cheek. 'We have to put the fear in him is all, baby,' he coos. 'We can't have him going round the way he is.'

'Did something happen?'

He hesitates.

'Please,' she whispers, 'what happened?'

'He saw Rose,' Josh says quietly, 'and Eddie ain't havin' that.'

The Elvis clock on the back wall chimes the hour, and Elvis's hips swivel and jiggle the time. Katie's whole body goes cold. Like all the sweat on her brow has seeped back into her head. 'What about Mom? And Joanne?' Her heartbeat quickens to panic.

'Don't worry 'bout them none, baby,' he murmurs. 'Nobody got beef with them.'

'Then why were you checkin' if I was here, if it's gonna be so safe?'

He hesitates. 'Just in case,' he says eventually. 'You know I don't like you near him.'

Her turn to pause. 'Be careful.'

Outside, one of the pickups honks its horn, calling him. He grins. 'I'm always careful, baby.' And he turns to go. He's halfway out of the door before she stops him.

'Josh?'

He turns.

'Don't hurt him, OK?'

The trucker looks up from his meal again. The father up from his coffee. The mother looks to the father, and the tot, oblivious, sticks a crayon in her mouth and gurgles rather loudly. Josh nods to Katie and shuts the door behind him. The headlights on both pickups switch on, momentarily flooding the diner with light. She watches as Josh climbs into his and as both trucks pull out. Her hands are shaking when she picks up the Heinz and she has to set the bottle down so she doesn't spill its refill. A small bit of tomato ketchup slips down her fingers to the outside of her right hand just under her pinkie. She stares at the drop of ketchup transfixed, her mind miles up the road, back home already. *The colour of fresh blood.*

There is no moon, but the sky still glows blue-black, alit with stars. Jasper lies in his boyhood room, his feet hanging off the end of his bed. His hands are behind his head, and he gazes up at the white of the ceiling sky above him. Carefully, one by one, he relocks the doors inside his mind that hold back his memories. There are places he does not let his mind wander. Things better forgotten. There are parts of him so filled with hate, so coloured by hatred, that he has grown to loathe them. To loathe what lies inside himself.

He hadn't thought he'd see her. Not like that. Not so soon. He doesn't want to think about her. The way she was. Before. Or the way she looked today, her face newly flushed with surprise. And fear, he reckons, yes, that was fear in her eyes. He doesn't want to think about how that might make him feel.

They didn't speak the whole drive home and dinner had been no different, Joanne pestering them with questions that fell on deaf ears till eventually even she'd fallen silent, moving the peas around her plate, piling them in tiny stacks held together with mashed potato. He had been glad when his own plate was clean. Was glad that Katie was at the diner and her judgemental eyes were off him. He did not go out on the front porch with Lizzie after dinner. Did not watch the sunset. Went straight up to bed instead. The girls' bedroom door had clicked shut long ago, and Lizzie's footsteps followed down the hall shortly after. The house is silent.

It takes him a moment to notice the headlights that reflect off the road to dance across his white, starless ceiling sky. Circling like searchlights. *Odd*, he thinks, *cars drivin' out this way at this late hour.* Then he hears the engines purr and spit and rev. Horns honk and tyres squeak. Engines are fed more juice and revved more loudly. He hears the shouts of men; the crickets go all quiet. Though the room is warm, Jasper feels a chill pass over him, and the tiny hairs at the back of his neck stand on end with warning.

He sits up slowly, swinging his feet to one side, placing them lightly on the floor. The wooden boards feel smooth and cool beneath his bare feet. He sits, body tensed, ears straining. He does not go to the window to look out. He can guess what lies below. Since church, a part of him has known this must be coming. A part of him has been waiting. Slowly he rises from the bed and pulls on his jeans and the old Coca-Cola T-shirt he wore straight out of prison. He does not look in the mirror. Does not pause to put shoes on. He opens the door slowly so it won't squeak, though why he's being so quiet he cannot say – the racket outside is more than enough to wake the whole house.

He steps out into the hall, the floorboards creaking under his weight. The voices outside call louder now, jeering, taunting. He can almost make out their words, but cannot recognize the tones or tell how many men are out there. A click behind him makes him turn sharply. Joanne peeks from her bedroom door, dirty blonde hair tangled around her, shorts and top barely covering the woman she's becoming. *Don't ever change*, he thinks. *Don't ever age.*

She rubs the sleep from her eyes. 'What's going on?' She yawns, too tired still to know that she should be afraid.

'Get back in your room,' he growls.

Her big eyes widen and blink. Awake. She steps back inside the darkness of her room, closing the door. He waits to hear the latch click shut, then turns and goes downstairs.

He can hear the voices now, louder, growing in confidence.

'Coward!'

'Bastard!'

'Cunt!'

Louder with every step he takes.

'You come down here, you son of a bitch!'

The stairs squeak as he passes over them. He pauses a moment to let the old house settle around him. Something about the cool wood of the steps against the soles of his feet calms him just a little. Downstairs is flooded with light. They've parked up around the house in a semi-circle, high beams still on, filling the house with light. He walks forward, blind, knowing this house, trusting where his feet must lead him. It's like he's a teenager again, sneaking out in the dark, except this time the world is all light. Too light. He does not belong in such a world of light. And yet he walks forward, hand up to try to shield his eyes. He fumbles a moment with the screen, then again trying to find the door knob. He opens the door. He knows that, if they were so inclined, they could shoot him, right there, spotlight nearly upon him, framed by the open door, illuminated by their high beams. A nearly perfect target, he reckons, yet he still walks forward. He stops in the centre of the porch, hand still up to shield him, eyes still blinking, fighting to adjust.

There are four pickups surrounding the house in a rough semi-circle. One, he recognizes as the truck Katie climbed into beside her boyfriend just a few nights before. Another, he sees, is the same deep blue truck he'd spotted when he was first home and walking the back roads. Eddie Saunders' truck. He does not recognize the other two vehicles, a rusted-out old Chevy it's hard to guess the colour of, and an old green Ford that's best days clearly are behind it. He cannot tell how many men there are: the high beams off the trucks are too bright to see much else beyond them, but he'd guess, from the shadows he can decipher, maybe fifteen. Maybe more. Eddie's truck is parked up right in front of the house, dead centre in Mama's garden. Three of Mama's rose bushes lie uprooted, tyre tracks pressing them into the dry earth. Jasper does not take the time to assess what other damage may have been done, but inside he feels a sadness settle, unlike those in his life that he has known before. He feels a new affinity with the garden, looking at it destroyed, the beds he only just weeded with his own bare hands.

That garden was his mother's pride and joy.

The jibes and jeers fall silent as Jasper emerges from

the house, the silence he steps into almost more frightening, more deadly, than the shouted angry sounds that lured him out. Some of the men are holding shotguns. Others rifles. Some just baseball bats. Eddie Saunders stands front and centre, his Winchester semi-automatic casually slung over one shoulder. 'Well, well, well,' he says. 'Look what scum we've found here.'

Jasper slowly reaches above and pulls the cord on the porch light, hoping to illuminate the faces in the darkness before him. Light spills onto the lawn, brightening the deep shadows of the closest men's faces. One hand still shades his eyes from the intensity of their high beams. 'You mind turnin' those lights down, boys?' His voice is even. 'There's a woman 'n' child sleepin' inside.'

Eddie's laugh cuts through the darkness. Others follow suit and chuckle, but it's his laugh that sticks in Jasper's ears, repeating, burning. 'Since when do you give a fuck,' Eddie snarls, 'about anybody but you?'

Jasper scans the men before him, looking for familiar faces, but most stand in front of the glow of the high beams, their faces blacked out and lost in shadow. 'This here's my property,' he says firmly. 'Y'all weren't invited. I suggest you find your own ways home.'

Eddie laughs again, but it is far from a happy sound, and Jasper cannot make out his expression. The high beams off the trucks turn all the men into silhouettes, shadows of themselves. 'Speaking of invitations,' Eddie laughs, 'I don' myself remember us all invitin' you on back.'

'This is my home. I don't want trouble. I ain't back for that.'

'What are you back for? A bit of free pussy? Back to finish off what you started, you sick fuck?'

Jasper closes his eyes and lets the words absorb into him. Become him. *You sick fuck. Yes*, he thinks, *I am*. He smiles. 'What's wrong, Eddie? You didn' miss me all these years?'

Eddie looks down to his feet, slowly shaking his head. He clicks his tongue. 'Jasper, Jasper, Jasper,' he says. 'What are we gonna do with you, huh? See, I was of half a mind to shoot you when you just came out there, but that's too messy, ain't it? That's not really my style. No, I got a life to live 'n' you ain't worth givin' it up for.' Eddie spits a big wad of tobacco onto the ground beside him. It lands on an evening primrose, tightly closed for the night, stepped on and trodden down into its bed. 'The problem is,' Eddie continues, 'I just can't let her see you. I thought at first, maybe, when I heard you was gettin' out you'd be wise enough not to come on back here. Thought you'd be smart enough to know when you're not welcome. But, shit,' he spits another large wad of tobacco, 'you ain't even smart enough for that. I thought then maybe the paper had it wrong a bit, maybe you'd come out of Huntsville all reformed 'n' shit, so I gave you the chance. Didn't I give him the chance, boys?'

Around him the other men murmur and mumble their agreement. 'Damn right, you did,' a voice shouts. A young man's voice. Familiar to Jasper but hard to place.

Eddie nods, as though listening to, as though taking in, the men's reassurances all around him. 'It's a real shame,' he says, 'they couldn't fix you while you was locked up in there 'cause, frankly, I don' see the point in keepin' somethin' alive that only causes misery.' A murmur of agreement spreads from the other men. 'You don' keep a dog that bit someone alive, now, do you, boys?' he says more loudly, his voice risen to carry.

Jasper stands with his hands shoved deep in his pockets. His shoulders hunch slightly. His face is a blank mask, cold, without emotion.

'Now I don' know about the rest of you,' Eddie says, 'but it sure ain't right by me, this scum standin' here, going to our church, shoppin' in our town. You gave Esther Reynolds there quite the fright the other day, you know.' He raises his voice again so it will carry. 'Ain't that right, Roy?'

'Yeah, that's right,' a shadowy figure by Eddie's side responds. Jasper would know that voice anywhere. Roy's voice. He closes his eyes against the sting of that betrayal. Opens them.

'See, we can't have that.' Eddie spits again, his tobacco juice disappearing into the blackness of the lawn. 'We can't have you goin' round touchin' folks, threatenin' them like that. And I certainly can't have you bumpin' into my little sister.' He pauses. The men around him hush. Like the whole night's gone quiet. 'It ain't right, her goin' through that.' A murmur of agreement ripples across the lawn. 'It ain't right at all.'

Somewhere far off on the prairie an owl calls. No moon, but endless layers of stars light its hunt. Jasper wishes he could just lie down there in that ruined garden and gaze up at those stars. He wishes he was that owl off hunting. His familiar rage is rising in him, slowly coming to a boil in his gut. He knows he will explode soon. Can feel the anger building. Like before prison. Like before he learned to dumb it down. 'What do you want of me?' he snarls, stepping forward. One step at a time. Down onto the dew-soaked grass.

'I thought we'd made that clear.' Eddie half chuckles. 'We want you gone, boy! Consider this here your goodbye party.' He swings the Winchester off his shoulder and holds it ready before him. To his left, a shadowy figure taps the baseball bat against his open palm on repeat, filling the stillness of the night with a kind of eerie applause.

Jasper never sees the rifle butt that hits him. He feels his jaw disconnect and push to the far side of his face. A splitting pain straight after. He falls forward onto his knees. Tufts of grass beneath his palms feel wet with dew. There are shining stars before him, constellations on the lawn. He blinks. It's been a long while since he took a hit like that. Even longer since he'd dealt one back.

The next blow comes before he has the chance to right himself. A rifle barrel to his temple that almost brings his dinner up. The stars on the lawn spin faster. He does not raise his hands to fight back. A small part of him thinks it is fitting if this is how he goes. Jasper never was a fighter. Even with the rage inside him. He had always preferred to inflict pain. It wasn't the fighting part that thrilled him, it never had been. It was how another body could recoil from his that had always driven him forward. He stops counting the blows. Stops differentiating between baseball bats and rifle barrels. The occasional fist or open palm, he does take note of, their blows slightly softer. His own pulse echoes in his ears, muffling his hearing. Like the whole world makes the sound of a heartbeat speeding up.

A shot reverberates, breaking through the pulse. *So this is how I go*, he thinks, and shuts his eyes. Another blow, a rifle barrel, to the nape of his neck. Another gunshot that booms through the pulse beat of his hearing. But he does not feel the bullet. Nor was there a bullet before. He opens his eyes. Or tries to. Blood cakes his eyelashes, sticking top and bottom lids together. His vision is blurry. The blows have stopped, though. There is space to breathe again around him. He inhales. A sharp pain cuts through his ribs and his eyes close once again as he falls forward.

'Get the hell off my property!' Lizzie's voice. A tone he's never heard her use. Don't-fuck-with-me conviction heavy on every word.

Jasper blinks. The blood on his face feels warm. Sticky. The blood in his mouth tastes acidic, like stomach bile, but thicker.

'Don' get involved in what don' concern you!' Eddie's rifle is aimed at where Lizzie stands on the front porch, their daddy's old Hungerford semi-automatic held before her, barrel still smoking.

'You gonna shoot me, Eddie?' she says. 'You go on right ahead.' Her own rifle barrel is fixed on Eddie, though she scans all the men with her eyes. 'I hope y'all are real proud of yourselves,' she calls, 'a whole gang of you beatin' one man like that. *What big men you are.*'

Jasper tries to speak, but his mouth is too full of blood to get his words out right. Blood catches in and fills his throat and he is forced to swallow it. He struggles not to vomit.

'You stay out of this, Lizzie. This here don' need to concern you none.' Roy's voice. *Which hand*, Jasper wonders, *was Roy's? Which baseball bat or rifle barrel was held in that hand?* He spits blood onto the grass before him. A pain in his side colours the world white. He closes his eyes. Struggles to reopen them.

'I'd heed his advice if I was you.' Eddie's voice is cool and calm, a dangerous sound.

'This here's my property, boys,' Lizzie says, her voice as hard as stone, 'my home. You've vandalized my garden, trespassed on my land, and threatened my family. I'm well within my legal rights to pick you all off right now, one by one, if I so choose.' She pauses a moment to let her words sink in. 'And to tell you the truth, boys, right now I'm mighty inclined to choose just that.'

'Now, Elizabeth, really.' Chuck Ryan, Josh's father, steps forward into the light, his son just visible behind him. 'Why don't you just step on back inside 'n' let us men finish our business here?'

Lizzie cocks the rifle barrel, ready to take another shot. 'Next time I fire this gun,' she says, 'I ain't shootin' up in the air. Now get the fuck off my land.'

'You threatenin' us, bitch?' Eddie takes a step forward towards the porch.

She looks down the barrel at him, finger on the trigger. 'Give me one excuse,' she says, 'I beg you.' She takes a step forward, slowly descending the stairs, rifle still held high and focused on him.

Slowly Eddie lowers the aim of his own rifle. 'All righ',' he says, nodding slowly, looking at the shadowed faces of the men around him. 'All righ', Lizzie.' He chuckles lightly, an empty, hollow sound that further stains the darkness of the night. 'You win this round. We'll be on our way. But this sure as hell is far from over 'n' you'd best be careful whose side you take.' He spits a wad of tobacco onto the ground. It lands in the grass beside Jasper. Foamy. Frothy.

Jasper watches as tiny rainbows catch the light to form and reflect within the bubbles of the other man's saliva. He reaches slowly out and lays his hand there on the grass. Right on top of Eddie's spit. Feels wet, like dew, but warmer. Feels like everything has a pulse. His heart beats in his head so loudly. The grass has a pulse, the dew, even Eddie's spit. He lifts his hand and brings it up to his chest, arching his head back, looking up to the sky with closed eyes. He rubs his fingers together till they dry. Then, slowly, a smile spreads across his broken face, trails of blood dripping from his nose and mouth. A cut on his forehead drips blood too, and he can feel it warm and sticky as it runs the length of his face.

Lizzie stands beside him now, rifle still raised and levelled on the men before them. 'There ain't never been a choice,' she says.

June bugs beat against the porch light, their tiny bodies gently thudding as they bang against the bulb. Around them the prairie is silent, as though waiting for some unknown cue. There is no cricket song. No hum of July flies. It is Jasper's laughter that finally shatters the stillness of the night. A sound more wild than had a coyote called. 'You stupid, stupid cunts.' He laughs, blood boiling up out of his mouth like foam. 'You should have ended it. You should have killed me when you had the chance.'

The kitchen light spills warm and golden out across the floor, stretching towards the sitting room. She stands just in shadow, hidden in the hall. He sits in the middle of the room, his head tilted back to stop his nose bleeding. His profile is to her but even that looks newly grotesque, deformed around his jaw. 'How'd you know they wouldn't shoot you?' he asks her mother. His voice cracks as though too long unused.

Her mother dips the cloth she holds back into the basin beside them, staining the water pink. She wrings it out before she wipes his face. 'They all got families of their own,' she says. 'Life they'd miss too much locked up. Much as they hate you, they ain't prepared to massacre our whole family.'

His bloody lips part in a broken smile. 'You sure 'bout that?'

She cannot see her mother's face.

A floorboard creaks beneath her feet and they both turn to her. For a moment Joanne wants to run. A scream catches in her throat, releasing as a tiny squeak. His face, full on, looks like a monster's to her. His lips discoloured and swollen. His jaw, out of its socket, twists round too far on his face. Both eyes are narrow, swollen slits. Her lip trembles, looking at him. She wants to cry.

'Come here, sweetheart.' Her mother's arms open, and she rushes into them, sobbing. Shaking. 'It's OK now,' Lizzie coos. 'It's OK now, darling.' With her hands she smooths down the tangles in her daughter's hair.

When Joanne finally lifts her face from her mother's arms, her eyes are still puffy, her breath shallow and jagged. She wipes snot running from her nose with the back of her hand, then wipes the back of her hand across her stomach, smearing the snot across her T-shirt. Her lower lip quivers. Slowly, Lizzie lifts her daughter's chin to look her in the eye. 'You're OK now,' she says quietly. A statement not a question.

Mutely Joanne nods. Tears swell in her eyes but do not yet fall. She turns to her uncle. He sits on the kitchen chair beside them, looking up towards the ceiling light. Her eyes widen as she takes in his injuries. The cuts on his lips, the cut by his brow, the angry swollen colour of his flesh. She'd never seen a fight before. Not like that. She'd seen the bullies at school picking on the smaller kids, and she'd seen the boys in the schoolyard have their scrapes as well, but usually the teachers pulled them off each other before anyone was truly hurt. James Tucker had a shiner back in fourth grade once from a baseball accidentally hitting him in the eye, and he'd let Joanne touch it while it was still bruised. It hadn't felt like much. Just warm, and like puffy flesh. But James Tucker's black eye was nothing compared to the swollen purple mask now covering her uncle's face. Looking at it makes her want to cry.

When she'd first woken up, she'd been scared. Straight away when the truck doors had slammed and woken her. She'd gone out into the hall. Had hid under the covers after Uncle Jasper told her to get back in her room. The voices scared her. The shouts. She didn't understand what was happening. That was why she got up eventually and snuck to their bedroom window. She wanted to hear what the men were saying. She wanted to see who was there. She heard her mother rush down the hallway, footsteps heavy on the stairs. Shortly after, the gunshots sounded. One. And then the other. And then the trucks all pulled away.

It was still some time after that, though, before Joanne regained the use of her legs. Folded and bent beneath her where she crouched below her sister's window. She couldn't see much from there. Just the porch roof and a bit of the lawn before it. She'd seen the trucks all parked up in her granny's garden, though. She'd seen the intensity of the light spilling from them. Crushed flowers all around them. She'd seen the hunched-over, crumpled figure of her uncle on the ground, a swarm of men upon him.

Now her lip trembles as she looks at him. 'Are you OK?' Her voice, choked with tears, is whisper soft.

He looks at her. Or, at least, she thinks he looks at her, but his eyes are so puffy, nearly swollen shut, that it's hard for her to see his pupils. His lips try to curve up into what she knows must be intended as a smile. But with his jaw so twisted on his face, his skin so swollen dark and angry, there is nothing friendly about his face, nothing reassuring. 'Don't I look it?' One swollen eyelid struggles to wink at her. It half closes slow motion and opens as though with great pain.

'Can you see OK?'

He snorts. 'Never seen better.'

Uncertainly, she perches on the edge of the kitchen chair beside him. 'Does it hurt?'

'Joanne. You stop pestering your uncle, you hear?' Her mother's tone is firm, but not cross.

His lips attempt their broken smile once again. 'I've been worse off, Doe Eyes, don't worry.'

She tries out an uncertain smile of her own. Looks above her uncle to the kitchen clock. It's late. Her sister should be home soon. 'Mom,' she asks, 'do you think Katie's all right?'

Her mother is folding a bandage to wrap on Jasper's head. 'I'm sure that girl's just fine wherever she is,' she says, under her breath.

'That was her fella out there, weren't it?' His voice is harsh, though hushed.

She sees her mother glance to her uncle, then quickly away. 'In part,' she says softly.

He nods as though this answers something.

'Uncle Jasper?' she whispers.

'Yeah?'

'Why were those men here? What did they want?'

'They want me gone.'

'Oh.' She looks down to her feet, then up again. 'Are you gonna leave?'

He looks to her mother, then to her again. 'No,' he says, his voice deep in his chest. 'I ain't ever been one to be run off.'

She tries to smile then, but it doesn't feel right on her face somehow. Like maybe she's outgrown it. 'Uncle Jasper . . .' she says uncertainly '. . . why don't anybody like you here?'

'I promised your mother I wouldn't tell you.'

Joanne glances to her mother's back, bent over the sink, rinsing the blood-soaked cloth. 'That's a stupid promise,' she whispers, still watching her mother.

His broken lips struggle to smile again, but his jaw is still twisted the wrong way. 'I'm startin' to think that myself,' he murmurs, a sadness deep set behind his puffy eyes.

'Joanne, you stop pestering your uncle, now, you hear?' Mom's tone sounds more stressed than truly cross. She leans over Jasper, tilts his head back towards her and wipes his bloodied, swollen brow with the damp cloth. 'You need stitches.' Her hand is shaking slightly as she pulls the cloth away to rinse it out again.

'I'll live.'

A truck engine pulls up the drive and cuts off. Mom crosses the room in two quick paces and pulls the curtain back to glance out the window. Her Hungerford semi-automatic stands upright beside her, propped against the sink. Joanne stares at it, as though seeing it for the first time, though she has known of this gun's existence since long before Grandma died. It is kept behind the grandfather clock. She has known her whole life not to go near it, not to touch it, that 'guns are not toys'. A single tear runs down her cheek and she wipes it away with the back of her hand. 'Mom,' she whispers hoarsely, 'are they back?'

Her mother lets the curtain fall into place. 'No, sweet,' her voice softens, 'it's just your sister home.'

The front door opens and closes. Footsteps carefully come up the hall, one foot after the other as though testing if it's safe. 'Mom? Joanne?' Katie softly calls. 'You there?'

'In here!' Joanne's voice shakes.

Her mother crosses to the icebox, pulls out a bag of frozen peas and hands it to her uncle. 'Hold this to your face,' she says. 'It'll bring the swelling down a bit, though I reckon your jaw's dislocated.'

He spits blood into the basin beside him. It floats a second on top of the water before swirling down and staining the liquid red. Katie stands still in the kitchen doorway, her mouth hanging open, just like in a cartoon, Joanne thinks. When Bugs Bunny sees something unexpected his jaw drops right down to the floor. 'Hi, Katie,' she whispers.

Her sister says nothing. She stands in the doorway staring at Uncle Jasper. The smell of grease and coffee spills off her to fill the room, overpowering the sweet stench of Uncle Jasper's sweat, the muskier smell of his drying blood. He turns to her slowly, lowering the bag of peas from his deformed, swollen face. Joanne watches as her sister's eyes widen.

'Take a good look, sweetheart,' he says, 'I'm finally as ugly on the outside as the in.' And he laughs then. Or tries to laugh. Blood gets caught in his throat and he has to spit it out again. He holds his ribs with his arm, as though it's sore to breathe.

'Go upstairs, girls, both of you.' Mom's tone is firm. 'There ain't no more to see here.'

It is a long time before Lizzie's hands stop shaking. She tried her best to control them in front of Joanne while she tended Jasper's wounds. She tried her best to keep them still after, as she tidied the kitchen, washed her brother's blood off the counters, dumped it down the drain. But her hands shook the whole way through. They shook as she wrung his blood from the damp cloths. They shook as they rubbed disinfectant on his cuts. They even shook when she'd opened up the icebox and pulled out the peas. A part of her had wondered if maybe she was meant to shake. If shaking was her way from here on out. But a part of her knew as well that when she'd aimed her rifle barrel at Eddie Saunders' head her hands had not once trembled.

She had guessed that trouble might come knocking, though had not expected it to call so soon. Nor had she anticipated the gang that accompanied Eddie Saunders. She had hoped most folks would just leave what happened in the past behind them. She realizes now that she was wrong to think people might have forgotten, to think that he might ever be forgiven. Not here. She's not even fully sure she's forgiven him herself. Or if she even wants to.

She does not turn her light on when eventually she goes upstairs to her room to rest. Though exhaustion sends aches through her limbs, she feels anything but sleepy. She does not bother changing nightshirts. Is unaware that his blood stains the one she wears. She crosses the room in darkness, holding her daddy's rifle tight enough that she can feel the blood draining from her knuckles. She sits down on her bed. The same bed she and Bobby shared for a while. *Before Eddie done what he done to him and Bobby run off* . . . She lets hate fill her. Pictures Bobby's swollen face all those years back. The cigarette burns still hot on his flesh. She pictures her brother's twisted jaw, the angry purple flesh swelling around his cuts. His eyes barely able to open. And her whole body starts shaking. Convulsing. Not just her hands any more, but everything. Her legs quiver and tremble where she sits. Her spine shudders as though chilled. Her jaw is shaking. Her hands . . . her hands. She looks down at her hands and so much hate spills into her. So much anger and malice and rage. Like all the emotion from the last

275

ten years locked up and held dormant inside her has suddenly gushed out. 'I should have shot him dead,' she says, out loud, to the empty room around her, and suddenly her hands go still. She holds them out before her, just able to decipher their outlines in the darkness of the room. Still. Not a single tremor runs through them. Not a single tremble passes over her. Slowly, she lowers her hands to her sides. She pulls the sheets back and slips into bed under them, grabbing the Hungerford as she does so, slipping it into the bed beside her. Slowly her body curls around it, entwining with the rifle as if it were some long-lost lover. Sobs shake her body till even her anger has left her, and she lies immobile, unfeeling, waiting for sleep to find her, the Hungerford held close to her, cradled like an infant in her arms.

The knock on his door is so light he almost does not hear it. It is the second knock, louder this time, though still softened by uncertainty, that wakes him from his reverie. He had been thinking about prison when the first knock came. He had been remembering the naked women drawn above his bunk. Thinking back on them, on their seduction and allure, calms him just a little from time to time. The same way for some that thinking back on a summer sweetheart might soften their heart. They were with him a long while, those girls, after all. His perfect ceiling sky. And he misses them. He misses gazing upon them. He wonders who now sleeps in his old bunk. Who jerks off to those beauties that for a time were his and only his. He is not turned on, remembering their beauty.

That surprises him. *In a different life I may never have met them*, he thinks. And then he hears the knock.

'Come in.' His voice sounds rough in the darkness, even to his ears. His jaw feels stiff to move. Like his mouth is full when it isn't.

Slowly, the door creaks open, and she steps inside.

He doesn't know what to say to her. At first. Her big eyes fix on him. It seems to him inappropriate somehow for a little girl to be in his room at this late hour, yet somehow he finds he doesn't mind so much, a part of him glad to see her standing there. It would be nice not to be alone, he thinks. On this night he could use the company. It's been a long while since a girl entered his room at night, though, a long, long while indeed. Longer still since a woman has.

'What do you want?' His voice is rougher than he meant it. He can't quite control his jaw the way he'd like to. It hurts when he opens his mouth too wide. His ribs hurt when he breathes. Even the shallow breaths.

She hesitates in the doorway, as though surveying the room. As though waiting for some further invitation. One toe on one foot scratches the shin on her opposite leg. Her hair surrounds her head in slept-in tangles. 'Can I come in?' she whispers, rubbing one eye with a fist.

He grunts as answer, so she closes the door behind her and crosses the room quickly to sit at the foot of his bed. She pulls her knees into her, and her big eyes peer over them at him. *She's got skinny legs, even for a kid*, he thinks. Tiny goosebumps mark her flesh, though to him the night feels warm. He sits up. The wall behind him feels cool against his bare back. He feels self-conscious suddenly of the fact he wears no shirt. For a moment he hates her for making him feel that way, but he lets the moment pass. He lets that anger leave him.

'Are you OK?' she whispers.

He doesn't try to smile. He doesn't want to scare her. He saw his reflection earlier on his way up the stairs, and he knows he's far from pretty. 'I'll be fine,' he says.

'Does it hurt real bad?'

He pauses. 'A bit.'

'I'm sorry.'

'It ain't your fault.'

She reaches down and picks at one of her toes. Looks back up at him with those big doe eyes. 'Uncle Jasper?'

'Yeah?'

'Why did those men beat you up?'

Out on the prairie a screech owl calls and falls silent, and he wonders what it is hunting, rabbit or mouse or even a possum maybe. Her eyes stay fixed on him. She looks so like her mother. He fidgets with the corner of the sheet, smoothing the cotton between his fingers. then lets it fall back onto the bed beside him. 'It's like I told you before, they want me gone.'

'Why?'

'I did some things a long time ago. Things you ain't supposed to do. Things that have made me unwelcome.'

'Is that why you went to prison? Because of those things?'

He is silent a long moment. 'Yes.'

She folds her legs beneath her and sits up a little straighter. 'What did you do?' Her eyes so wide upon him. So innocent. It seems to him sometimes that all he does is take the beauty from the world. He does not want to take that wonder from her, to be the one to take her trust away.

He shakes his head. 'Your mama don't want me to tell you. I think you know that much.'

'I'm not a baby,' she says crossly, 'I'll be twelve soon.'

He hates to see her pout. He hadn't realized till just then how fond of the child he's grown. 'I ain't sayin' you're a baby,' he whispers hoarsely to the darkness, her face just barely visible to him. 'I see the woman you're becoming. I see her every day. But I don't want to be the one to force you into her.'

Her brow furrows, pulling darkness to her. 'It's not fair. Everyone knows what you did but me.' She looks down, cross, pouting. 'I thought we were friends,' she says, so soft he nearly has to guess the words she speaks.

He lets her words hang between them a long while. The screech owl calls again, closer, and then only silence sounds. He thinks of the men who beat him that night. Of Eddie with all his vengeful rage. Of Roy and his betrayal. He thinks of Katie's young fella, and wonders if he would have acted differently when he was that age, had a gang gotten him all riled up. He reckons he, too, would have come along for the beating in a different world, where things had been different, and he hadn't been the one set to be beaten. 'All right,' he says. 'I'll tell you.' His words surprise him, but it's too late now, he reckons, and he doesn't try to take them back.

'Are you really gonna tell me?' She forgets to whisper she's so excited.

He puts a finger to his lips and smiles then. Or tries to, his swollen face contorting with the effort. 'I reckon you got a right to know. Don't make me change my mind.'

She leans forward, long legs crossed there at the foot of his bed. 'What'd you do?' she whispers, wide eyes locked upon him.

He hesitates. 'Not now, kiddo.' He watches even in the darkness as her face falls. 'I promise I will tell you. But I need to rest this swollen jaw. You come to me real soon 'n' I'll tell you what I done.'

The sky has started to lighten, but is not bright yet. Only the first birds are stirring, calling their morning songs.

Her doe eyes search his. 'You promise?'

'Ain't that what I said?'

'Pinkie promise?' She holds out her little finger.

He looks at it as though it is an object foreign to any he has seen before. Slowly he raises his own hand. What little light there is catches and reflects off her dirty gold mane and the tiny blonde hairs that line her arms and legs. *That's all she is really*, he thinks, *arms and legs, and tiny golden hairs*, and to him, in that moment, she is perfect. He does not want her to grow up. For a moment he wishes she could for ever stay caught in this divine limbo, not a woman yet, not quite a little girl, as innocent as now. But he knows that is not possible. He can feel time's passing, can see the woman she'll grow into even now as she beholds his wounds. Even now, as she extends her little finger towards him. He could see it earlier, too, behind her fear. The woman taking over. Little girls don't see violence and keep their innocence, he thinks. Little girls don't have murderous gangs wake them up at night and stay little very long.

Slowly, he takes her pinkie in his. 'I promise.'

She smiles then, springs up, leans over him and kisses him on his forehead, right where his mother used to when she'd tuck him in. All those years ago. He's not sure he's ever been kissed by a little girl like that before. At least, not since he's been grown. Her lips feel soft and cool against his angry swollen flesh. And then she's gone, just like that, so fast he's nearly left wondering if he dreamed her. If he dreamed that a little girl could care for him. Could ask him if he's OK. He never would have thought something so good could show care for him. Not after the choices he's made, not after all he's done. He shakes his head to clear it. It doesn't matter, though, he tells himself, not really. When he tells her what he did, she'll look at him just like her sister does, just like everyone he passes seems to as of late. That he does feel sad for. 'What's fair is fair,' he says out loud, and he pulls the sheet up to his chin and lies with his back to the window, willing his tired soul to sleep.

It is strange, Lizzie thinks, how long it takes to grow life, and yet how quickly it can be destroyed. She kneels in her mother's garden, hands caked with earth, salvaging what plants she can. Most of the primroses down by the front gate are still intact but the bushes closer to the porch are completely destroyed, as are all the daffodils that lined the path. Large tyre tracks criss-cross the garden, their treads cutting deep into the flowerbeds. The rose bushes that lined the drive, the ones the reverend had only just praised her for, her mother's pride and joy, now lie in ruins, roses and rose petals spread like confetti across the drive and lawn. Lizzie is glad her mother did not live to see her garden so destroyed. 'I'm sorry, Mama,' she whispers to the earth, as she uproots the crushed marigolds and tries to restore the tiny patch of tiger lilies now bent parallel to and pressed into the earth.

There was blood on the grass by the porch steps. Lizzie had stared at it a long while when she'd come down that morning. She'd dumped a pail of water over it, but it hadn't seemed to make a difference. She didn't want her girls to come down and see the blood there on the ground outside their home. Jasper's blood. She didn't want them to have that memory. If she could have, she would have erased the memory of last night altogether. She tore the blades of grass up with her hands instead till a patch of bare earth spread before her. The grass roots had cut into her palms. Now the bald patch of ground between garden and porch stands out more even than the blood had. But she can't remove its memory. She can't get the blood out of her mind.

The first time Jasper ever hurt anybody, he couldn't have been much older than ten. Daddy'd given him the old Hungerford to learn how to hunt, and Lizzie'd tagged along one day with him and Roy, following them far out past her daddy's land and into the open prairie that stretched on beyond. Of course she'd known they were going hunting. She was young, not dumb. She'd seen her daddy come home with piles of rabbits tied up by their feet, ready to be skinned for Mama's stew pot. She'd been raised on a farm her whole life – Lizzie had never been overly sentimental towards animals, even as a child. That was the way on a farm. That was the way she'd learned. But there was something about the way Jasper had killed that rabbit the day she'd tagged along that had stayed with her for many years after, had haunted her for a while, and then, when he was in jail, she had found that her mind often wandered back to that crisp autumn day when they were children still. The first day he'd ever truly scared her.

'You wanna see how a rabbit takes his clothes off?' he'd said to her, teasing.

'Rabbits don't wear clothes, Jasper,' she had said, sure her older brother was somehow tricking her.

'Yes, they do,' he'd said, grinning. 'I'll show you.' And he'd shot the next rabbit they saw. Except he didn't shoot to kill. She understood that now, looking back, but then she'd thought he'd missed by accident.

'Jasper, Jasper! He's hurt!' she'd cried.

Roy had been real agitated. Like maybe he'd known already. 'Don't, Jasper,' he'd said. But she had not known yet what was coming. She was too little still back then and had not understood.

Jasper went over to where the hurt rabbit had fallen. He'd shot it in its haunches, and it was bleeding too bad to hop away. He picked it up and held it real tender to his chest and called her over to him. Its blood ran onto him, down his shirt and leg. She was scared. 'Come look, Lizzie,' he'd said, and he'd bent down real low so she could see it better. She reached out and touched its soft fur. It trembled under her touch. Its eyes so filled with fear. 'Now watch,' he'd said, 'and I'll take his coat off for you.'

He held it in his arms the whole while. Even as he got his knife out. Even as he carved into it, skinning it alive. She screamed when she saw what he was doing. And there were tears on Roy's cheeks as he begged Jasper to stop. It was that memory that came back to Lizzie when she had first heard what, years later, he had done. It was that memory more than anything that had assured her of his guilt. She loved her brother, he had always been good to her, but that day out on the prairie, she had seen the darkness in his soul, and she knew him capable of relishing the pain caused to another.

She has tried and tried over the years since to remember what might have happened earlier on that day. Had Daddy maybe beaten him? Had Jasper been bullied in the schoolyard? But, no, to her recollection, it had been a normal day. Till poor Mr Rabbit had shed his coat. She couldn't stop crying after that. The whole way home, walking through the tall prairie grasses. And Jasper had promised her he'd never do that again. Had picked her a bouquet of wild flowers. 'I'm sorry, sis,' he'd said. 'I thought you'd find it funny.'

She had sat through one day of Jasper's trial. All those years later and now so many years ago. Mama had refused to go. Had said she didn't want to see her son in 'that light'. But it had seemed to Lizzie that one of them ought to be there, so she had gone. Alone. Reporters had swarmed around her on the courthouse steps, the flashes of their cameras still exploding in her eyes even once she'd stepped inside. Experts had been brought in that day to discuss Jasper's mental health and a lot of big words had been thrown around that Lizzie had not heard before. Then they'd called him a psychopath. And that word she did know. And she understood then what Mama had meant about not wanting to see Jasper in 'that light'.

It is those memories that come back to her now, her hands caked in earth, as she tries to repair the lifeless plants crushed all around her. A single tear rolls down her cheek, and Lizzie quickly raises her hand to brush it aside, dirt smearing across her face as she does so.

'Mama must be rollin' over in her grave.'

She looks up. Jasper leans against the porch railing. The swelling on his face has gone down a bit, but the purple bruises have turned black, the skin between them a discoloured yellow-green. 'Jesus, Jasper,' she shakes her head, 'I never seen you look more handsome.'

He snorts, the corners of his lips nearly quivering up into a crooked smile.

She sits back, her feet tucked beneath her, and shades the sun from her eyes. 'What you gonna do?' she asks him.

''Bout what?'

''Bout last night.'

He shrugs. 'Ain't much I can do, I reckon.'

'They'll be back, you know,' she says quietly, her voice like stone.

He looks out beyond the garden to the open prairie. 'Yeah,' he says, 'I know.'

'And what do we do then?'

'I didn't want no trouble, Lizzie.'

'It's a bit late for that now.'

He nods. Says nothing.

She lets out a long breath she hadn't realized she'd held. Her eyes search his. 'I don't know what to do, Jasper. I don't know where to go from here that don't end up back in trouble.'

He walks down the porch steps and across the lawn to kneel beside her in what's left of their mother's ruined garden. Carefully he takes the rose bush held in Lizzie's hands and coaxes its bent stems back as upright as he can. Thorns cut his bare hands, but he ignores them. 'I spent my whole life crushing beauty,' he says softly, so softly she has to strain to hear him. 'It'd be nice to watch things grow awhile.'

'I wish they'd let us,' she says softly.

He looks back at the house a long moment. 'So do I.'

Sunlight filters through the trees to chequer the earth with shadow, dark opposing light, leaves overlapping, creating deeper, darker shadows. No grass grows beneath the trees, just smooth, dry earth littered slightly with fallen leaves and pine cones and the odd beer can left behind to rust. A thin layer of fallen pine needles carpets the rough rocks along the creek bank. The creek is just a trickle, really, not deep enough in this drought for swimming, but Joanne wades out into its shallows anyway, giggling as the cool water flows over her bare feet. He smiles, watching her face relax as she giggles and splashes. Her sister sits on a rock along the bank, feet dangling down so that her toes just skim the water. When he was a boy, he remembers that boulder at nearly water level. They used to lie on their bellies on that same rock, used to watch dragonflies as they hovered above the water, dipping and rising, eating all the mosquitoes. There used to be rainbows caught in their iridescent wings when the light fell down just right. There must have been more rain, he thinks, those summers. They used to climb into the trees and drop down into the water when it was deep enough.

He is surprised in a way that he is here. Just his two nieces and him. No one else, far as the eye can see. No homesteads or newly built houses. Not even a car to hear passing up on the country road. He likes the still of it, this place, likes the sound of the wind whispering through the large grove of pines, talking softly through the leaves of the tall oak trees. The only trees for miles, really, lie along this creek. He likes the gurgle of the water as it flows past them, even if the water is so low. For the first time since his release he feels a different sort of freedom, like now, finally, he is truly unwatched. Well, he almost feels that way. He doesn't take kindly to Katie's wariness around him. The way she's always watching him, as bad as a prison guard. He can feel her eyes boring into him even when he looks away. It makes his skin itch.

It had been Lizzie's idea, him going with the girls. Katie had come downstairs late morning, her hair and face all done up already, a bounce in her step he didn't see the occasion for. 'Mom, I'm takin' Jo swimmin',' she'd said.

Her mother had regarded her a long moment. 'All righ',' she'd said. 'You go on 'n' take her, then. But your uncle's comin' with you.'

He had looked over from his coffee. Face still a

deformed swollen mask, coloured the colour of 'bruise'. Katie's eyes had darkened as they'd passed over him.

'Mom –' she'd hissed.

'You wanna go out?' Her mother cut her off. 'Your uncle's goin' with you.'

'What'd I do,' he'd asked quietly, as they were leaving, 'to deserve this great honour?'

'Keep them safe,' was all his sister had whispered, and there'd been fear deep within her eyes.

Now he sits upon the earth close to the creek bank. Slowly, he takes one shoe off and then the other. He places them to his side, lined up beside each other, as though waiting to be stepped into. He rolls one sock off, then the other. Wipes the fluff from between his toes, then places each sock crumpled up inside each shoe. His feet are pale. His toenails are a bit too long and jagged. He dips each foot into the fresh creek water and lets each settle there, right down on the bottom. The last bits of sock fluff separate from his skin and float up to the surface. The water's a little deeper than it at first seemed – it comes just under his knees and soaks the bottom of his jeans, which won't roll up any higher. The rocks beneath his feet feel mossy and slimy. He closes his eyes and feels the filtered sunlight fall upon his face. He wiggles his toes, the water cool around them. It feels like freedom to him, and his bruised and broken face twists into its own version of a smile.

'Uncle Jasper?'

His eyes open. She is beside him somehow. Standing over him. He hadn't heard her approach. *Quiet as a doe too* . . . He squints to better see her face.

'You promised me something last night.' There is a

shyness to her. A nervousness when she looks at him full on.

He nods. 'I must look a monster to you,' he says, his voice like gravel, his jaw still twisted slightly on his face, the cheek around it tight and swollen.

Her eyes take him in and widen doing so. Her nose wrinkles. Then relaxes. 'Kind of,' she whispers, as a smile eases her nervousness away in tiny fractions.

He sets his hands palm down on the earth behind him and leans back a little, letting his shoulders hunch. Letting his crooked grin grow. He studies her.

'You promised me,' she whispers again, softly. Her eyes implore his, search his, and the hardness inside him melts just a little.

'I did,' he says.

Across the creek from them, Katie leans forward, eyes dark with mistrust, her red toenails skimming the water as she swings her long, tanned legs. They distract him, tease him. Any other man just out of Huntsville, he tells himself, would have found a way to touch those legs by now.

'Will you tell me?' Joanne softly asks.

'Tell you what?' Katie raises her voice to let it travel.

Joanne twists one toe down into the soft sand of the creek bank. 'You promised me too, Katie,' she says, turning to her sister. 'You said you'd tell me one day what he done.'

'Yeah, one day, not now!' Katie rises, swinging her legs up from the water to stand tall on the rock, towering above them on the opposite side of the bank. Tiny bits of spray fall from her feet and ankles. 'Don't you tell her,' she says, her focus shifting to him, her index finger pointing at him. She sounds, he thinks, just like her mother. He does not take kindly to her tone.

'Uncle Jasper,' Joanne whispers, 'tell me why you went to prison.'

'Please,' Katie sounds desperate now, almost pleading, 'don't.'

The sisters' eyes meet and hold. He watches them as they stare at each other. Both brown as dried-out prairie grass, browner even, maybe. Both gold as the open fields at sunset, when the sun's gold rays cast down and touch the land. The older – so tall, so beautiful, so tempting to a man. And the younger . . . not grown into her beauty yet, but to him even more captivating. A precious, delicate thing. A thing to protect. It's been a long while since Jasper felt the need to protect anyone save himself. Nearly as long since he had a friend. He'd rather Joanne never knew all the mistakes he's made, but a promise is a promise, Jasper tells himself. And he'd rather he told her than somebody else.

'I hurt a woman,' he says softly. 'I hurt a woman real bad.'

A chickadee flies down from one of the oaks and hops as it pecks at the ground. Both girls turn back to him. Everything gone quiet except the gurgle of the stream. Katie runs a hand through her golden hair, pushing it back from her face. Her lips form a tight, thin line. Her scowl already judges him. But then again, he thinks, she already knows my story.

Curiosity and excitement glow in Joanne's eyes. 'Eddie Saunders' sister?'

His eyes narrow, more against the light behind her

than from the words she's said, though hearing the Saunders name always smarts him just a little. 'You know more than you let on.'

She sits on the earth beside him, cross-legged. Smiles slightly. 'I've just been guessin' mostly.'

A grimace tickles the corners of his swollen lips up before they fall back down. The locked doors in his mind he's guarded so long creak open. The memories spill out. He closes his eyes against the pain. He takes his time, choosing each word with care, knowing what he has to say but not sure just how to phrase it. 'Her name is Rose,' he says at last, voice barely above a murmur. 'She was my sweetheart for a while. Back when we was young.' A tired smile plays with his lips again. 'I bet you didn't know that bit.'

She shakes her head, eyes still wide upon him.

'Please,' Katie whispers, so soft he almost doesn't hear her, 'just leave it at that.'

'I think I might have loved her,' he says gently, ignoring the older girl, 'as much as I was able. I never really been the lovin' kind. Always found it hard to figure out just what love's about.' He can see her still so clearly. Rose. How she was back then. So full of life. Like she was light in a world made up of darkness. He clears his throat. He can almost smell her. Even now. Like she's there hiding behind one of the trees. 'She didn't love me none.' His voice hardens slightly. 'I don't think she loved anybody.'

'What happened?' Joanne whispers.

'She started . . . well, she started seein' other people, I guess you could say. A whole lot of other people, and even though I still liked her plenty, she didn't like me none.'

Tiny tadpoles gather in the water that stills around Jasper's legs. He watches them in silence, not sure what words to say. *How can I soften my sins?* He clears his throat. 'She moved away for a while. After high school. Went down to Corpus Christi for about five years. Nearly six. Came back,' he looks down at his hands pressed into the earth beside him, ''cause her mother was sick or somethin', I can't quite right recall. But anyway, she came on back, and she still didn't want nothin' to do with me.' He snorts. 'She sure didn't mind other fellas, though. Didn't mind datin' them one bit.' He spits a wad of phlegm into the water.

'Jasper, *stop*!' Katie is still standing tall on the opposite bank, hands on her hips as she shouts. 'If you tell her one more word I swear to God I'll –'

'You'll *what*?' he snaps. 'Send that boyfriend of yours back to teach me another lesson?'

Katie's face goes pale. Like the sunshine's been knocked out of her. 'I didn't . . . he didn't mean –' She stops. Fumbles to find her words. Her eyes lower, then rise to battle his. He likes the nervous tremble in her throat before she yells at him. 'I'm telling you, stop! Don't say another word! You can't tell her –'

The rage swells up inside him. Boils and bubbles.

'*Can't I?*' Jasper says. 'Who the fuck are *you* to tell me what *I can't do*?'

For ten long years they had told him when to eat, when to sleep, when he could walk the yard, shower, piss. But Katie is no prison guard. This grove is not a cell. He rises to his feet. 'You think you can control me?' Jasper shouts. 'You think you can tell me what to do? What to say? I'm warning you, bitch,' his tone lowers, 'I'm warning you now.'

Only the water makes sound. Even the wind has gone quiet. He has frightened her. He can see that. He's frightened both of them. The snarl still stuck to his face. Joanne's eyes are so wide upon him. Not a doe any more. Not quite. Like headlights, he thinks, with the high beams left on. He tries to calm himself a little. To push the anger down, but the rage and the memories he's blocked so long are fighting to be free.

Katie turns her head, jaw quivering, braver than he would have guessed. 'Joanne, come on, we're going.' She gestures for her sister to join her the other side of the creek.

Slowly Joanne stands, but does not step forward. She shakes her head. 'I want to know, Katie,' she says softly. 'Please, let him tell me. You promised too.'

'He's a freak!' Katie shouts. 'Don't even talk to him!'

Something inside Jasper snaps. He throws his head back and laughs. Dark sour laughter that cuts short as abruptly as it sounded. His focus is on Katie still when he looks back down. 'I don't need your permission,' he growls. 'You don't want to hear my story? Block your fuckin' ears.'

'You've said enough!'

'I've only just begun, sweetheart.' His words cut through the stillness of the afternoon, the anger in him rising. 'You don't know half of all I've yet to tell.' His fist pounds hard on the earth beside him. 'So where should I start? Huh? What do you wanna hear first? All the good bits? Or should I start at the beginning, save the best for last?'

There is a hiss to his words as he speaks them, fire in his tone.

'You see, once upon a fuckin' time, sweetheart, Rose was workin' at this supermarket. So I slit her tyres that night so she wouldn't be able to drive home. I was waitin' when Rose got off work to offer her a lift. Did you know that? Or do you want me to skip to the best parts now? Like how I pretended I'd just happened to be the last customer in there gettin' some shoppin'. Ain't that somethin'? Except I didn't take her home. No, I bet you know that. I didn't buy no shoppin' neither.' He shakes his head. 'Just a stick of gum.' A smile flirts with his swollen lips but does not linger. 'I had it all planned out, you see.'

That dark night looms again before him. He sees her get in his truck again. Remembers how good it felt when she closed the door and he clicked the locks all down. How good it felt as they pulled away from the lights of the town and down the dark country road. She hadn't been nervous yet. Not at that stage. The smell of her had filled his pickup. Coconut and strawberries. That's what she'd smelt like. And she'd been wearing this mauve colour of lipstick. It had tasted like chalk when he'd finally forced himself on her. Had smelt like the chemicals it was made of.

Katie sinks down till her knees touch the rock she's still perched on. The little trickle of water that fills the stream somehow seems wider than before. Insects hover above the creek's surface, buzzing as they dip and rise. 'Please,' Katie whispers once again, but he can see the fight easing out of her. And it feels good to have won, to have overpowered her even if it feels so odd to talk about it. Odd to tell someone just what he done. He's never just out and said it before. Not like this.

That first night when the police had brought him in to question, Jasper hadn't talked about it as he'd waited in their holding cell. Nor had he spoken of it when Sheriff Adams had cuffed him to the table in the small interrogation room that doubled as the sheriff's office. 'What happened, son?' Adams had asked.

'I hurt my hand,' he'd said. 'See that, Sheriff?' He'd held his cut palm up to be seen. 'I need stitches.' He couldn't remember then when he'd cut it. He didn't remember cutting it. But it was bleeding all the same. 'I need a bandage, Sheriff!' he'd shouted, his voice rising like the anger, so thick and sour in him.

The sheriff had just stared at him as though not comprehending. So he'd shouted it again to get his message through the other man's thick skull. 'Get me a bandage, you cunt!' he'd yelled. And the sheriff had just sat behind his desk and watched him.

'Rose Saunders is gonna need a hell of a lot more than a bandage,' Sheriff Adams had said at last, his voice cold. 'May God have pity on your soul, and may your jury fry you.'

A grey squirrel darts down one of the taller pines and scurries across the grove, disappearing into the tall prairie grasses beyond. The day's humidity sticks to Jasper, like a second skin. He watches as sweat forms on Katie's neck and brow, dampening the tiny hairs that have fallen across her face. Slowly he turns to Joanne, the anger in him still burning. He'd almost forgotten she was there, he'd been so caught up in his telling. Her jaw trembles.

He wants his words to stay inside him now, feels he has frightened her, has said too much already, but somehow he can't stop his story spilling out.

'I drove her out into the prairie to an abandoned oil site. Far out, where no one bothered to go no more. Way out,' he gestures west, 'where the prairie gets so dry it starts to turn more to desert.' He rubs his swollen jaw, once more choosing his words with care. *She is just a child*, he reminds himself. He swallows. 'There was this shack out there. Near where they'd been drilling. Not much to look at, just this little building with some old tools left in it.' Beside them, the creek gurgles as tiny bugs skim across its surface. Leaves and sunlight and his swollen face reflect in the mirror of the water where it stills.

'There's a reason why folks don' like me,' he says softly. 'I ain't a good man, Joanne.'

He can see the fear grow in her eyes, and he'd be lying if he said a part of him didn't like it. He doesn't want to scare her, he doesn't want her to fear or hate him, but old habits die hard, and the fear in her eyes thrills him just a little.

But something about it scares him too. Unsettles him more than he'd like.

'What did you do to her?' He can barely hear her whisper it's so soft.

'No!' Katie is on her feet again, this time crossing the stream to them, water splashing up around her thighs. 'If you tell her this I swear I'll make you sorry!'

'Oh, yeah?' He laughs. '*You*'ll make *me* sorry?' His rage swells up again, colouring his inside black. There is no world beyond his story, beyond this battle of wills. He sees again Rose's naked body bound and helpless before him, lying on that dirty ground. Sees the tools he beat her with. The others he forced inside her. She wouldn't look at him while he fucked her. That had angered him. That's what he'd wanted, really, for her to look at him like she used to, back when they were sweethearts, back when they were young and she'd been his and not everybody else's. So he'd taped her eyelids open. With this black electrical tape he'd found there in the shed. He'd taped them so she had to see him. Had to look at him while he fucked her and fucked her harder again.

Dark sour laughter erupts from him once more. 'You'll make me sorry?' he repeats, the anger in him pumping, throbbing, like a second pulse. 'Then you listen good to what I done: I raped her. I fucked that girl within an inch of her life. Fucked her till the sun come up. I beat her while I fucked her. Must have hit her with every tool in that shed. And let me tell you now, I didn't once feel sorry.'

A tiny chickadee chirps high up in the trees. Breathless, Jasper stops. Pulse still racing.

Katie has stopped mid-stream and is standing in the shallow water. Tear tracks run down her cheeks. A nervous fear clouds her eyes. The fear of a woman that can be overpowered. His favourite kind of fear. She is very beautiful to him in that moment. He likes the way her pulse shows in the tremble of her throat.

A twig snaps.

Joanne.

His heart stops. A tiny moan escapes him. *How could I have said so much? How used those ugly words?* His throat tightens as he turns to her, his face freshly smarting as horror twists his bruises with new pain. She cowers from him, frightened, but it's too late now, the anger's out, and he can't yet reel it in.

'Did you kill her?' Joanne's voice is barely loud enough to sound.

He didn't want to be the one to have to tell her this. He hadn't intended to tell her everything. And yet he feels he's started now. There is no turning back. Her sister drove him to it. Yes, he tells himself, she pushed him across the line. And yet it thrills him to talk about it. To relive what he done. He had not expected to so enjoy the telling. He could talk all day if only they would listen.

'I dug a grave,' he says softly, pushing his anger down, forcing his voice again to what he hopes sounds kind. 'Out behind that shed a bit, near enough where they'd stopped drilling.' He looks from girl to girl as though searching for their understanding. 'I couldn't have taken her back home. Not in the condition she was in.' He looks down at his hands again. A tiny ant crawls over his left thumb, and he watches it a moment before wiping it to its death with his opposite hand.

He looks up and into Joanne's big, scared eyes. Truly like a doe now, he thinks, and no doubt as quick to startle. He struggles to soften his voice so as not to frighten her further. 'I didn't kill her,' he says gently, the rage seeping out of him. 'But I meant to. I had it in my heart to kill her.' Leaves rustle as wind blows. 'These two employees for the oil company called round the site early that morning. Found me 'n' her beside that grave I dug. I managed to get back to my pickup 'n' drove back into town. It weren't long, though, till they had me locked up.'

298

He falls quiet, letting silence fill the spaces between them. A long moment passes without sound. 'Thing is,' he says finally, 'after I dug that grave out there, it raised some suspicions 'bout how that old oil site was bein' used 'n' they found two other bodies out there, buried in shallow graves. Both young girls, both pretty, too, judging by the photographs the papers printed.' He looks down. 'Only charge they had on me was what I did to Rose, but folks round here started sayin' I must have done them other girls, too.' He pauses. 'I reckon most still think I did.'

'Didn't you?' He'd almost forgotten Katie was still there he'd been so focused on Joanne's eyes the last while. The startled look in them. Katie's angry words cut into him, but he does not let her rile him this time. He watches Joanne instead. Watches as she starts to look at him differently. Like he'd known she would. Like in his heart he'd prayed she wouldn't.

Eventually he whispers, 'What do you think?'

The fear in Joanne's eyes muddies them, none of their usual shine. She swallows. 'I don't know what to think.'

His broken face twists into a crooked smile, swollen jaw hurting as it does so. 'Sometimes,' he says softly, 'I don't know what to think myself.'

'Bullshit,' Katie says, stepping onto the bank and pulling her sister up by her arm. 'Come on, Lady, let's go.'

'Go where?' She's frightened and confused, brow furrowed.

'Home.'

Joanne rises, fear still darkening her face. He catches her wrist as she turns to follow her sister, careful not to grip it too tightly. 'Do you hate me now?' he snarls, the anger in him so quick to rise, so quick to turn him man to beast. Instantly he regrets the wild in his tone.

Slowly, she shakes her head. 'I dunno,' she whispers softly. Tears gather in her eyes, but do not fall.

Her words prick him. Pinch him. Catch his breath. He'd been certain she would hate him after knowing what he'd done. He clutches her wrist more tightly. Closes his eyes a long moment, then opens them. 'You don't hate me?' Confusion wrinkles his brow between his bruised temples. 'Aren't you afraid of me?'

'I don't know,' she whispers, and shakes her head again.

Desperation rises in his gut, mixing with hope. A feeling foreign to him. He *needs* her not to hate him. *Needs* her not to grow up just yet, not to look at him with a woman's eyes and a woman's judgement.

'Are we friends still?' His voice sounds husky, too caught up in his throat.

Wide eyes blink back at him, dark with fear. 'I don't know,' she whispers again, her words so soft he can barely hear her.

He tries to smile, to reassure her, but it hurts too bad, and his twisted, swollen face smarts with the effort. 'Ain't we friends still?' he asks again, the desperation boiling up as panic. He grips her wrist tighter.

Her body recoils from him. 'Uncle Jasper?'

'Yeah?'

'You're hurting me.'

He drops her wrist instantly. Grabs her and pulls her to his chest and holds her there against him. 'I'm sorry,' he gasps. 'I'm sorry. I would never hurt you.' He smooths her hair with his calloused hands.

'Let go of her!' Katie screams.

Joanne pulls away from him as her sister wraps her in her arms. Frightened eyes blink up at his. 'You wouldn't still hurt nobody, Uncle Jasper, would you?'

He hesitates. He remembers still how good it felt pushing himself inside Rose, watching the fear in her eyes grow, how good it felt to hit her, and how she'd laughed at his first blow when they'd been driving still. He'd had to hit her a second time, harder, to knock her out so he could drive her to the oil site, could bind her hands and feet. He looks at the little girl before him now, her innocence tarnished. He wishes he could take his words back. Just a few of them. The rougher ones her sister drove him to. Her windblown ponytail glows in the patchworked light. If she isn't an angel, he reckons, he don' know what is. 'No,' he says softly, 'I don't still intend to hurt nobody. I'm all done with trouble.'

They are almost to the truck when he grabs her wrist. Hard. Joanne's walked up ahead of them, and Katie instinctively gasps to scream when she feels his hands upon her. But one of his hands is over her mouth, and even if she were to scream, she realizes, no one but her little sister is around to hear her. There's no one out there for miles.

'Don't scream,' he snarls, 'or I will hurt again.' His breath is hot on her ear, her neck. She can feel his words as he speaks them, his lips are so close to her ear.

Ahead of them, Joanne bends down to prod a crayfish

hole with a stick. Jasper slowly removes his hand from Katie's mouth. She still wants to scream, but she swallows the urge back down. His other hand still grips her wrist tightly. She can feel his short, jagged nails cutting into her. She tries to twist away, but his grip holds strong. 'You're hurting me,' she whispers, still trying to twist away.

'Good,' he growls, his voice still low, his breath still hot upon her. 'You 'n' I need to talk.'

Her heartbeat quickens. ''Bout what?'

''Bout what the fuck happened to my face last night,' he snarls. 'What the fuck else do you think?'

His nails dig deeper into the soft flesh inside her wrist. Her heart pounds inside her chest. She wants to cry out. 'I don't know anythin',' she stammers.

'Bullshit.' His words spit at her. She can feel the heat of the sun warm upon her face.

She turns slightly to look at him. His eyes have gone dark with rage. 'Uncle Jasper, I swear,' she stammers, 'I don't know nothin'.'

'You know who was there. I'd bet good money, too, you knew they was comin'.' His eyes judge her, and she can see he finds her lacking. 'It's a shame,' he hisses, 'something so pretty as you can never be trusted.'

'Are you gonna hurt us?' Her throat feels tight and dry. She has to struggle to get her words out. She looks up ahead to where her sister still bends over the crayfish hole prodding it with a stick. At that moment Joanne glances at them and waves, then looks back down. She must not have seen, Katie thinks, how he's holding my wrist. She wonders where her mama is. Thinks of Josh.

'I would never hurt her,' he says gruffly. 'You keep actin' like we ain't family 'n' I can't make you that same promise. Now,' he says, 'you know who all was there last night, don't you?'

She nods.

''N' you knew they was comin' for me, didn' you?' He twists her arm back behind her, his nails still cutting into her flesh.

'Yes,' she gasps, 'I knew.'

'Good,' he says, 'that's progress.' He twists her arm further behind her back and she gasps again, just a little, at the pain. 'Now,' he whispers, lips so close to her ear that she can feel his breath still, can feel his words upon her, 'you tell that boyfriend of yours 'n' his coward of a father 'n' all their pipsqueak friends, the only one of them got beef with me is Eddie. If he wants me gone, he can come face me like a man. You got that?'

She nods.

'Good.' He releases her arm and she staggers forward, clutching her wrist. 'You pass that on,' he says, ''n' you might want to think twice before you decide whose side you take.' He walks on past her then, up the path towards her sister. 'What'd you find there?' he calls, his tone shifting softer, brighter, like a whole different man.

Joanne looks up and smiles. 'There's a crayfish in there! If you lean down, you can see 'im.'

'Well, I'll be . . .' He takes the stick from her and leans down over the dirt smokestack that leads down into its burrow.

Joanne looks down the path at Katie. 'What's takin' you so long?' she calls, and turns back to her uncle.

Katie's heart smashes against her ribs. The world spins. She wants to sit down. She wants to cry. For a moment, she wants her uncle to look at her with a fraction of the kindness that fills him when he gazes at Joanne. Then her insides sour. Her wrist burns. *It's not fair.* She wants him never to touch her again. She wants to scream. She blinks to stop the world spinning, to stop the tears falling. Somehow she finds the strength to smile at her little sister. 'Come on, Lady,' she calls, walking on past where they crouch beside the crayfish burrow, 'let's get you on home.'

Lizzie hears his pickup on the country road long before she sees it. It stands out a mile anyway, she reckons, what with the bright red colour of it. She does not rise, though, when she first hears it, nor does she after she's turned and seen the truck approach. She didn't expect his visit, but a part of her is not surprised. She wipes her dirty hands on the jeans she wears. Uses the back of her wrist to wipe the sweat from her brow, then the same hand shades her eyes as she watches the truck approach. She doesn't stand till the pickup's pulled up her drive already. She turns then, following it with her gaze and body, lowering her hand that previously had blocked out the sun.

'Afternoon, Reverend,' she says coolly, as the large man opens the door to his cab and squeezes himself out from behind the steering-wheel. A chime goes off with the door held open. Beep, beep. Beep, beep.

'Afternoon, Elizabeth.' He descends from his pickup and slams the door shut behind him. The sudden silence of the beeping makes the day sound newly quiet. He stands a moment, both hands made into fists, fists held to his hips, his elbows pointing out. Softly he clucks his tongue. 'My, my,' he says, 'sure is a shame what happened to this here garden.'

'I take it you already know what happened, then.' She eyes him warily.

He hesitates. 'I confess, yes, I heard.'

'Why are you here, Reverend?'

He looks around at the scattered flowers by their feet, the crushed bushes, the tyre tracks that criss-cross through them. 'May I come in?' he asks.

'I'm afraid I ain't much in the humour today, Reverend, for a social call.'

He nods, still surveying the damaged garden spread before him. 'I'm sorry, Elizabeth, to just drop in like this.' He flashes his brightest smile, and she watches as it falls.

'No, you ain't.'

'I'm sorry?'

'You ain't sorry one bit, Reverend. You called on down here for a reason. I ain't got time to waste today 'n' I don't plan on wastin' your time neither. Why don't you just tell me what it is you want?'

He swallows. His fat face flushes red, though from embarrassment or the heat, she cannot tell. 'All right, Elizabeth,' he says slowly. 'I'll cut right to the chase if that's what you want. Yeah, I know what happened here last night. And, yes, before you ask, I knew that it was comin' too.'

She takes two short strides across the ruined garden to him and slaps him once, hard across the cheek. Hot, angry tears well in her eyes and threaten to fall. 'You bastard,' she hisses. 'Mama thought you were her friend, but I can't name one nice turn you ever done this family.'

A darkness passes over his face, the same way a lingering cloud blocks out the sun. 'I'd be careful, if I were you,' he says softly, 'just how many enemies you make.'

'Are you threatening me, Reverend?'

'No.' He shakes his head. 'Simply offering you some friendly advice. That's why I'm here, Elizabeth. Because I *was* friends with your mother, whatever you might believe. 'Cause she didn't deserve what she was put through. She was a fine good Christian woman, your mother. A fine good Christian indeed, 'n' I don't want to see no harm come to you 'n' your girls. I mean that, Elizabeth.'

Sweat runs down her spine to gather at the small of her back. She can feel it soaking into her blouse. She knows she must stink of body odour and earth. With a dirty hand she wipes her brow. 'Would have been nice,' she says coolly, 'if you'd given us a head's up on what was comin'.'

Pity fills his eyes, and she hates him for it. 'You must have known,' he says. 'Surely you knew some sort of trouble must be comin'.' She does not answer him, and he falls silent. 'Is he here?' he asks at length.

'No.'

'Is he . . .' the reverend hesitates '. . . all right?'

She snorts. 'Depends on your definition of "all right", I guess.' She pauses. 'They beat him pretty bad, but he'll live.' A sparrowhawk flies over them, casting its shadow long over the prairie, and they both turn and watch it for a time. 'I think they would have killed him,' she says quietly, 'had I not come out.'

He nods. 'I think they would have, too.'

Fire rises in her once again, so quick to flare, these days. 'What do you want from me, Reverend? Why are you here?'

'I came to make sure you were all right. You 'n' them girls of yours. It was nice seein' y'all come to church like that. I'm sure your mother was smilin'.'

'Yeah, well.' Lizzie nudges a crushed rose with her foot, then looks out to the open prairie. 'She sure ain't smilin' now.'

The shade from the house stretches its long shadow towards them, but it is not late enough yet for them to be sheltered and the sun feels hot on the top of Lizzie's head, like her whole scalp might catch fire with all the anger that boils up and rests inside her.

'I can't help but feel,' he says quietly, 'you blame me somehow for some part of this.' He holds out his hands to stop her. 'No, don't object. But the truth is, Lizzie, I'm here 'cause I'm worried 'bout you 'n' them girls. I'm afraid there's revenge in Eddie's heart. 'N' revenge don't stop at much.'

She is quiet a long moment. A starling calls out from a nearby shrub before falling silent. A cloud passes by the sun, but is not dense enough to fully mute its light. 'I don't blame you, Reverend,' she says. 'I know we dug our own graves. I know chances are we're diggin' 'em still. Might have helped us some small bit, though, had you urged folks to be a bit more forgivin'. Way I see it, forgiveness is just what we gotta do to try to move on past this. I didn't

307

used to see things like that, I'll admit. There's a lot in my life I been bitter towards. A lot of hurt I clung to. I'm startin' to think lately, though, maybe we all would have been a whole lot better off had we just begun forgivin' a long, long time ago.'

The reverend opens his mouth then closes it. He sighs. 'I don't believe you've forgiven him.'

She smiles. A sad smile that does not reach her eyes. 'That's the problem, Reverend. This town don't know forgiveness. I ain't no grand exception.'

He smiles, too, a sadness of his own darkening its shine. 'None of you deserved what he put you through.'

She shrugs. 'It ain't about deservin'.'

'Tell him to leave, Elizabeth. Tell him to go. Him stayin' won't bring no good to you 'n' to them girls.'

'He got nowhere to go, Reverend. I told you that before. 'N' anyhow, Mama would never have cast him out.'

He surveys the scattered flowers all crushed and spread around them. 'Really is a shame,' he says, 'about this garden. Them roses was the finest I think I ever seen.'

She lets the stillness settle around them. Bees buzz in and around the fallen flowers, gathering what pollen they can, the hum of them composing their own symphony.

He shuffles his feet on the gravel drive, the heels of his boots digging into the ground. 'If there's anything I can do –'

'No, Reverend. There ain't nothin' you can do for us. Not now. I'm not sure there ever was. Facts remain, 'n' not one of us can forgive Jasper, 'n' not one of us can keep trouble from keepin' on comin'.'

'This ain't just about forgiveness, Lizzie.'

She looks at him a long moment. 'No,' she says, 'maybe not. But it got somethin' to do with it, all the same.'

'You trust him?' he asks. 'You trust him round your child?'

She smiles. Sadness shining in her eyes. 'That's the one thing as of late that I got faith in, Reverend. He loves that girl, as much as he is able.'

'And Katie? It ain't right a teenage girl bein' so close to a man like that. Whole town's sayin' it.'

'Why don't you leave my daughters out of this?' No softness in Lizzie's tone, no space for argument.

He opens his mouth to speak, then shuts it. Nods once. Puts his hat back on and dips it slightly to her. He turns to go, then stops, his hand on the pickup door handle. He turns back to her. 'You know,' he says quietly, 'he'll never find welcome here.'

'Yes,' she says, 'I know.'

Katie slows the pickup to a stop in front of their house, up on the country road. She does not pull down their drive. She does not cut the engine. Looking straight ahead, she says, 'Y'all best get on out here. Tell Mom I won' be home too late.'

'Where you goin'?'

'None of your business!' As soon as the words leave her lips, she wishes she'd spoken them less harshly.

Tears well in Joanne's eyes, but do not fall. She turns to slide down the seat and out of the passenger door. Jasper has risen and exited the vehicle already. He stands on the shoulder, feet half on the grass, holding the door open for her.

'Jo?'

Her sister turns.

Katie is suddenly uncertain what to say. Nothing seems quite adequate. Nothing seems enough. 'Be careful, OK?' she says. 'Everything's gonna be OK.' Tears gather in her own eyes.

'Nothing's OK, Katie.' Joanne pushes past their uncle and starts up the path, the garden still in ruins despite what must have been her mom's best efforts to patch it up.

Katie wants to call after her, but she doesn't. She's not quite sure what stops her. Maybe it is because nothing does seem right any more, nothing does seem good. Maybe the kid's right, she thinks, maybe things won't be OK.

Jasper closes the truck door and leans in the open window. It strikes her as almost comical the way the open window frames him, like he's living in a picture frame, his bruised disfigured face the last picture on earth any sane person would frame. She can still feel his fingers around her wrist, jabbing into her flesh. The cuts his nails dug into her skin still smart. But there is nothing, she thinks, comical about this man. Not even bruised there, framed in her car-door window.

He smiles, his twisted jaw further distorting his features. 'You just remember,' he says real quiet, 'that little talk we had.' His fingers drum on the inside of the window, right where the glass rolls up. He nods to her once, then turns to make his own way across their ravaged garden.

She watches him a moment. The slight limp in his left

leg he did not have before last night. Nor that slight laceration at the back of his scalp. Even from behind it is obvious just how badly he was beaten. 'I had no part in that,' she says out loud. No one close enough still to hear her. 'It ain't fair,' she murmurs, 'him layin' that blame on me.' She eases her foot back down onto the gas and the truck pulls forward, back out onto the country road.

Disgust sours Katie's insides. She hates the growing part of her that is jealous of her sister. Jealous of the tender way he looks at her. Almost like a father might. He looks at Katie with dark eyes full of hate and hunger. The hunger that no food can fill, the kind she's seen darken many truckers' faces when she's been working late. It makes her uncomfortable, the way Jasper looks at her. He doesn't like her much, she reckons, and yet, there is a part of him that likes her plenty. She can see that more clearly now than ever, his fingerprints still marking her. In some ways, though, she reckons, she can only blame herself for him not warming to her. She never wanted him to move in with them. She never wanted her friends to look at her funny. She never wanted to be the weird kid living with the rapist. She knows how everyone talks. Knows it will just get worse, too, when school's back.

Katie is not used to not being liked. She doesn't like her uncle – in fact, she thinks she might hate him, just a little, and yet she feels the pressing need deep inside her for *him* to like *her*. It confuses her. Enrages her. *What makes Joanne so special?* I don't need that man's approval, she tells herself, and yet, inside, she feels the sting of him finding her lacking. She *needs* him to like her. She *needs* the whole world to like her. *Will this hurt my chances for Prom Queen next spring?* Katie is not used to a world that looks on her unkindly. She is not used to being second best. Especially not to her little sister. And if having a rapist as an uncle and a freak for a sister costs her that Prom Queen crown, Katie swears to God she'll make them both sorry. *They had better not ruin my senior year . . .*

Josh lives far out the other side of town, but it feels to her like she's there in only minutes, her mind's sped up so fast. She pulls off the main road and down the Ryans' drive. Pecan trees overlap above her, all the way up to the house – Josh's mother's pride and joy. Sunlight filters through their leaves to confetti the road with light. Their driveway is paved, not gravel, the whole half-mile from the country road right up to their door. Katie cuts her engine at the top of the drive, pulling over just to the side. Before her, the Ryans' home looms, two-storey, made of stone mostly, green shutters over the windows. It isn't like any other house in town. Like any other house she's ever seen. Josh's daddy is an oil man. His wealth shows in his home.

Both doors to their four-car garage are open, and music drifts from inside. Some slow-paced country song she's not quite sure she's heard before. She pauses just outside the garage. 'Josh?' she calls.

His head pops out from behind the open hood of his pickup. She smiles. She knew she'd find him here. She's teased him before that that truck is his second girlfriend. 'Hey, baby!' He grins. He grabs a cloth, wipes the grease off his hands and walks out to her, squinting in the sunshine. 'You could have called. I didn' know you was comin'. I would've cleaned up or somethin'.' He puts his arms around her and kisses her lightly, and she settles into his embrace, resting her head on his chest.

She closes her eyes. 'You know Mom never lets me use the phone.' He smells like sweat and oil and his father's aftershave.

'Are you OK, baby?' He lifts her face to his.

She can't hold them in any more. The tears. She buries her face in his chest, clinging to the sweaty, stinky fabric of his T-shirt. She wishes she could stay that way for ever, his arms around her, his smell around her, everything OK. But he pulls her from him, eyes searching her face. 'Did somethin' happen?' Worry creases his brow.

She nods. Her throat's gone tight from crying.

'What happened, baby? Did he hurt you?' Worry quickly turns to anger in Josh's voice.

She holds up her wrist, watches as it takes a moment for her injury to register in his eyes. He takes it in both his hands and gently turns it over.

'That son of a bitch,' he hisses. 'I'll go kill him now.'

'Josh! No!' she gasps through her tears. Hiccups shake her chest.

'What do you mean, no? He hurt you, Katie! Look at that! What did I tell you? What if next time it's worse?'

'There ain't gonna be a next time.'

'Oh, yeah? How you figure that?' She can see the anger pulsing through his veins. Oddly, it makes her feel a little better somehow to see him so upset. Makes her feel cared for. Like she does have value after all.

'He said,' she gasps, still crying, 'I gotta start treatin' him more like family, that's all.'

'He *threatened* you?'

'No! Yeah. I don' know. Maybe.' Tears roll down her cheeks. Warm. Sticky. Drying as they fall, the sun's so hot on her skin.

He pulls her to him again, her face pressed into his smelly T-shirt, tight against his chest. One hand is around her back. The other smooths down her hair. 'It's OK,' he whispers. 'I've got you now. Tell me everything.'

And so she tells him. She tells him about how she came home last night and saw what they'd done to Jasper's face. She tells him about Mama spending all day trying to fix a garden that's beyond repair, about taking Joanne to the creek and Mom sending Jasper along with them. Half her words get muffled in his chest, and some he asks her to repeat. She tells him what Jasper told Joanne. By the time she gets to the part where Jasper grabs her, her tears have nearly stopped, though their salty trails still stain her cheeks sticky. She can feel the stick of them when Josh kisses her and she tries to smile up at him, to assure him she's all right.

'I think he blames me,' she says, 'for what y'all done to him. I think he reckons I could have stopped it.'

From the pecan trees, a bobwhite calls his name and falls silent. Chickadees answer before the harsher cackle of a crow drowns out all other birdsong. The day is hot still, though evening's early shadows have started to stretch across the lawn. A cloud passes over the sun, momentarily muting its heat.

Josh bites his lower lip. 'You know I'm gonna have to tell my father.'

She looks at the bruises now starting to purple around

her wrist. Looks at the tiny curved cuts left from his broken nails. 'What's he gonna do?'

'I don't know.' Josh is silent a moment. 'Eddie'll think of somethin'. Don't you worry, though, baby.' He strokes her hair again, holding her close to him. 'I've got you now 'n' I ain't lettin' go.'

She pulls away from him to look up at his face. 'You promise?'

His eyes search hers. 'I promise.'

Lizzie sits hunched over, mending a pile of washing. She gasps from time to time as her needle goes through the thin fabric of the sheets, pricking her fingertips. Life's hardships weather her face, more worry lines than laugh lines etched within her skin. She smiles when she sees him watching her. A self-conscious sort of smile, that almost brings the youth back to her face, but fails. 'My hands ain't what they used to be.' Her cheeks blush slightly. 'That gardenin' took it right out of me. I usually ain't this careless with the needle.'

He nods. Says nothing. Leans against the door frame like it's all that's left in this world to hold him up. And it is, in some ways, he reckons. The electric lamp on the end table beside Lizzie glows with a muted yellow light. Outside the night is dark. The sky is filled with stars.

'No porch tonight?' he asks quietly. His voice sounds thick and smooth, even to his own ears. It surprises him. It's been a long while since it held those tones. Sounds like honey to him on this warm night.

She smiles. The sad smile again that he is growing used

to. 'I couldn't bear lookin' any longer at what they done to Mama's garden.'

He remembers back when her smile was a happy thing. A long, long time ago.

She glances up from her needlework. 'You can sit in here awhile,' she says, 'if you're so inclined.'

He had been waiting, he realizes now, for an invitation to join her. He sits in the easy chair opposite hers, both positioned close to the fireplace. The air coming down the chimney feels humid, muggy, even at this late hour. Looking at the clean hearth, he reckons it's been a good long while since any fires burned.

'I told her,' he says. 'I told her what I done.'

The needle stops halfway through the fabric. Her voice goes cold. 'Where is she?'

'Upstairs, I reckon.'

'When did you tell her?'

'This afternoon, down at the creek.'

Lizzie lets out a long breath. 'Jesus, Jasper, no wonder she was so quiet all night! Why did you tell her? What were you thinking? She's just a child!' Lizzie's voice rises, climbing up towards shrill.

He ducks his head. 'She got a right to know,' he mumbles meekly. 'She's part of this, too, you know.'

'How the hell is my little girl a part of this?' Her voice echoes off the walls.

'We're all a part of it, Lizzie,' he murmurs. 'There ain't no turnin' back or I'd have turned back long ago. They came here to kill me last night. She got a right to know what I done, what I'm like.' The lamp beside Lizzie lets out a constant low hum. Very softly, he whispers, 'I don't know what I'll do if she starts hatin' me.'

His sister says nothing, her lips a tight line, her brow deeply furrowed. The carpet beneath their feet is threadbare in patches. He remembers when Mama brought that rug home new. It was off-white back then, not grey. And the couches too. He remembers when he was a boy and he'd helped Mama rip the plastic right off them, delivered to the door brand new. She had sat on them with the church ladies. Had served them coffee. Sometimes they had played bridge. And Daddy had sat in this very same chair come home from a hard day out in the fields. He'd take his boots off right there by that hearth, mud falling down to the floor. Mud falling onto Mama's clean carpet. No wonder, Jasper muses, the carpet's now gone grey.

'I been thinkin' a lot lately,' he says, ''bout that July fly all them years back. The one that landed on me.' She looks up from her mending. She's angry with him, he knows, but he can't stop talking. It feels to him he's meant to say this for a while, but it seems only now that he can get the words out right. 'I been thinkin',' he continues, ''bout how they shed their skin. How they sleep for thirteen years. That's a long time,' he says quietly, 'to wait to live a single summer.'

Down the hall, the grandfather clock calls out the half-hour. Outside, wind must be blowing, as the porch chimes sound. He listens for a moment to the music they create, the clock and chimes together. There is something peaceful about that sound. And about the quiet that follows.

*

It's early when Joanne rises. The sun has been up long enough to heat the day already, though the house around her still looms dark and quiet. Katie didn't come home last night. Waking without her sister there beside her leaves Joanne unsettled. *Mom will kill her if she finds out.* She dresses as quietly as she can. Makes the bed neat as she's able. It's not as tidy as Katie makes it, but maybe, if they're lucky, Joanne figures, Mom won't notice the difference with so much else on her mind. Joanne is careful not to squeak the door knob or to click the latch as she slips out of their room. She tiptoes down the hall, passing over the floorboards that she knows will creak. She takes her time opening the front door. Is careful not to let the screen slam shut behind her. She glances back at the house only once, pausing at the top of their drive. All the windows look dark still. The house, garden so torn up before it, looks like it could be abandoned. For the first time Joanne remembers, it doesn't look like home.

She's going to find Katie. That's what's in her head as she starts down the road. She needs somebody to talk to. A million questions twist round inside her, and she needs help to sort them out. She needs someone to make sense of all she's feeling. Joanne doesn't know where her sister is, but she can guess. And she figures if she can make it into town someone will point her to Josh's house. It might be a long walk, but Joanne reckons she's able.

She doesn't think of how Mom might freak finding her not at home. Just puts one foot before the other and keeps on going down the country road.

Not even mid-morning yet, but already the sun is hot on the back of her neck. Hot on the tops of her arms. She'd known Uncle Jasper must have done something real bad for everyone to hate him so. And she knows herself that what he did was wrong, even though she has trouble wrapping her mind around it fully. She still sees him like that hurt dog they couldn't save, the one that'd been run over. It had hurt real bad when that dog died, even though it had never been theirs, even though it hadn't been them who'd run it over. They'd found it lying by the side of this very road. Mom had pulled over and they'd all gotten out. Its fur was wet with blood. Joanne had cried the second she'd seen it. She'd thought maybe they could keep it, if it just survived the night. But in the morning the un-fallen tears in Mom's eyes had told her before she'd even had to ask. Uncle Jasper reminds her of that dog. It seems to her that no one loves him. That he's been left alone to suffer. She can't help but still think of him as in need of a friend. And yet Joanne knows wrong from right. And a part of her thinks her uncle just might have killed those other women.

She doesn't want to think about it, and it's all that fills her mind.

Wind rustles the tall dried prairie grasses that grow tall in the fields all around her. No clouds pass to block the sun. She's so lost in thought she doesn't hear the pickup till it's right behind her. Driving real slow. Too slow. It pulls up beside her.

Eddie Saunders grins through the rolled-down window. 'Where you goin', sweetheart?' The sun reflects off his pearly whites.

Her heartbeat quickens. 'Nowhere.' She walks a little faster.

The truck rolls on slowly, still there right beside her.

'You're goin' awfully fast for a girl that's goin' nowhere.' He chuckles.

She scowls. Says nothing. Keeps on going, one foot, then the other. She wishes he'd just keep on going too.

'You want a lift somewhere?' He's smiling still. Another man sits beside Eddie in the truck. Joanne vaguely recognizes him, but does not know him. He is not smiling, his profile to her, face masked in shadow.

She shakes her head. 'No, thank you.' And keeps walking, eyes focused ahead.

'Awww come on,' Eddie coos, 'it'll take you all day to get to town the pace you're goin'. Let me give you a lift is all. It's the least I can do after causin' that scene up at yours the other night. I just drove by there 'n' had a chat to your mama. Told her I was sorry. It was a miscommunication is all.'

Joanne's brow furrows. She's not sure she believes him. 'Mom told me not to talk to you.'

He laughs. 'That so? Shucks, Ben,' he turns to the man beside him, 'you hear that?'

She wishes he'd just drive away. But he doesn't.

'You know,' Eddie says, leaning out the window, 'I used to know your daddy real well.'

Joanne is curious despite her better judgement. 'You did?'

'Oh, yeah.' Eddie grins. 'He 'n' I got a ton of history.'

She wonders why her mother never told her that. Or Uncle Jasper. Or Katie. She wonders if Katie even knows. She stops walking. Turns to face him. 'Were you friends?'

He smiles. 'Somethin' like that.'

She turns away from him, and walks three more steps,

then turns back, his truck still driving slow beside her. 'Do you know where Josh lives?' she asks. Josh and his daddy took part in Jasper's beating. She's not sure she trusts them any more. But Eddie must know where they live. And she needs Katie. Needs her now.

For a split second, Eddie looks surprised, then a slow grin eases his features friendly once again. 'Course I know!' he says. 'I go way back with the Ryans. That where you're headed?'

She's uncertain if she should trust him. 'Do you know if my sister's there?'

'Well . . .' he says, weighing each word as he says it '. . . I can't be certain, but I'm headed that way myself.' He shrugs as if it's nothing to him. 'I could drop you by there if you wanted.'

She pauses, unsure, the sun so hot upon her. Town seems so very far away. Let alone however much further it might be to Josh's house from there. Her feet are starting to hurt. 'You're *sure* you just spoke to my mom?' she asks.

'Oh, yeah. Course I did. Had to apologize for the other night.'

'And . . .' Joanne hesitates '. . . she forgave you?'

'Why don' you get in the truck 'n' I'll fill you in on the way?'

It seems so nice that he's gonna level with her like that. So different than the adults she's used to. 'OK,' she says, and she smiles cautiously, not really sure if she should smile at the man before her.

'Get on in,' Eddie says, still grinning. He gestures for her to walk round the front of the truck to get in on the pickup's far side.

The other man steps out to open the door for her so she can get in. Ben. That's what Eddie'd called him. She holds out her hand to him, standing in the open doorway of the truck. 'Nice to meet you, Ben.'

There's a smirk to his smile she doesn't quite trust, but he still takes her hand. 'Nice to meet you too, sweetheart.' He spits a big wad of tobacco onto the road. 'Real nice to meet you too.' He releases her hand. Joanne watches as the concrete quickly dries his wad of spit.

'Come on in outta that heat,' Eddie calls, patting the seat beside him. 'I got the a/c on high.'

She smiles shyly, looking forward to the cool air. 'All righ',' she says, and she climbs into Eddie's truck and sits right there beside him.

It is afternoon before the old truck pulls into the drive-way, its engine sharply cutting off. Lizzie is washing the dishes from the lunch she and Jasper just shared. Sand-wiches, nothing too fancy. They used up the last scraps from the brisket she'd cooked the other day. So it's only really the two plates that need washing, and a couple knives, and the roasting tin the rest of the brisket had sat in. It's the tin that she's washing when the truck finally pulls up the drive, her arms elbow deep in greasy, soapy water turned brown from the leftover meat juices. She shuts the tap off. Lets the roasting tin slip under the soapy water till it is submerged. Grabs a dish towel and quickly dries her hands. Her girls know better than to take off without asking. In her mind, all morning, Lizzie's been scolding them. *If they think they're gettin' lunch, they've got another thing comin'* . . .

The door opens, then shuts. 'Mom?' Hesitation in the tone. 'I'm home.'

Lizzie steps from the kitchen out into the hall, still drying her hands on the towel. 'It's about damn time! What are you girls tryin' to do? Give me a heart attack? I wake up 'n' find y'all gone, no note, no nothing. What if I'd needed the truck this morning, huh? No. Not one word out of you, young lady. You're grounded. Both of you.' She looks round. No sign of Joanne. 'You get your sister in here. 'N' remind her, she ain't too old yet for a spankin'.' Lizzie turns to walk back into the kitchen.

'Mom . . .'

She turns sharply. Snaps, 'What?'

Confusion furrows Katie's brow. 'Jo ain't with me, Mom. She ain't been with me, neither.'

Lizzie feels her own brow crease. 'Well, where is she, then?'

'I . . . I don' know. I haven't seen her since yesterday.'

'Since *yesterday*? Where the hell have you been, young lady? I swear to God, if I find out you spent the night at that Ryan boy's –'

Katie cuts her off. 'I did, Mom. I . . .' Her voice cracks. 'I just had to get away for a little while.'

'And you went to *him*? After what he 'n' his father took part in the other night? After the way they beat your uncle to a pulp? An unarmed man to boot. After they *ruined* your grandma's garden, you go runnin' to *him*?'

'Not everyone in this family confides in criminals.'

Lizzie is down the hall in two long strides. She slaps her daughter on the left cheek. Harder than she'd meant.

She can feel the sting in her palm. Can feel it still smart after. 'You dirty little slut,' she hisses, 'off chasing boys when you should have been minding your sister.' She points her finger at her daughter's chest. 'No daughter of mine stays out all night like a no-good tramp.'

Katie's hand automatically goes to her cheek and stays there. Lizzie knows the slap must have hurt the girl, but Katie is careful not to show it. She lowers her hand from her cheek. Her tanned skin glows bright red. 'What kind of mother are you,' she says real quiet, 'that one of your girls stays out all night 'n' the other wanders off missin' 'n' you don't even notice?'

Her words cut Lizzie to the core. More hurtful than any blow. 'Don't you talk back to me,' she stammers. 'Don't you ever talk back to me. I'll ground you the whole summer. Just you watch. Just go ahead 'n' push me to it.'

Silence between them. Neither backing down. The voice from the stairs startles Lizzie. She wonders just how long he's stood there.

'I ain't aimin' to interrupt,' he says coolly, 'but am I right in understandin' neither of you know where Joanne's at?'

Lizzie looks to Katie, then back up to her brother. He leans against the banister with an almost relaxed ease. Long ago, they used to slide down that banister, their laughter enough cushion back then for the hard drop at the stairs' end. 'Yes,' she says, the fire in her suddenly all spent.

Jasper looks from mother to daughter and back again. 'Is it normal,' he asks quietly, 'her goin' off like this?'

'No.' Lizzie sighs. 'She ain't never took off without tellin' me before.'

Silence stretches between them. Around them. Jasper's voice is gravelly when finally he speaks. 'Should we be concerned?'

Lizzie looks to Katie. So beautiful, even when she's mad. *How did I help make something so goddamn pretty?* She regrets slapping her daughter. Wishes she could take that back. But what's done is done, and Lizzie long ago learned that hard truth.

'She's probably just out playing, Mom.' There's anger still in Katie's tone. A glare in her eyes near kin to hate. 'You overreact to everything.'

'Go to your room.' Lizzie manages somehow to keep her voice from shaking.

Katie opens her mouth to object. Shuts it. Anger gleams in her eyes.

'Now,' Lizzie says, and points upstairs.

Jasper steps aside to let Katie pass. She is almost by him when he catches her wrist at the last moment, twisting her round to face him. Katie cries out, startled. 'Are you sure,' he says, real quiet, pulling her closer to him, 'you don't know where your sister's at?' His bruised, swollen face twists, more beast than man.

'Jasper!' Warning in Lizzie's tone.

He looks to his sister.

'Let go of me!' Katie pulls her wrist free and bolts up the stairs. Seconds later her door slams.

There is a darkness to Jasper's eyes Lizzie has grown to recognize, but still she holds his gaze. 'I don't trust that girl,' he says.

She looks at him a long moment. It seems so dark inside on such a brilliant day. Especially in the hall and on the stairs where no windows let direct sunlight in. 'Don't touch my daughter, Jasper,' she says quietly. 'Don't you lay one hand on her. If Joanne's run off awhile, no doubt it's from what you told her. Look in the mirror if you wanna start layin' blame.' She walks into the kitchen to finish washing up. It is a long while till she hears him walk back up the stairs.

Pink streaks the sky, reaching long bright fingers through the quickly falling dark of night. The last orange glow of the sun can just be seen sinking into the horizon, but even that light, too, will soon have vanished. What few evening primroses have not been trampled have opened up full bloom. Birds sing each other lullabies from nearby shrubs, as they tuck into their nests. He's had a bad feeling all day. A restlessness in his soul that tells him things aren't right. Trouble's come calling, and trouble's here to stay. He can feel it in his bones. And it unsettles him. It feels like he's changing inside. He feels wilder than he has these last long years. His blood thick inside him, pumping.

'Should we call the police?' His sister's aged just since afternoon.

He snorts. 'What good the police ever done this family?' His eyes still scan the horizon, half hoping to see a dirty-blonde girl with big round eyes opening the gate. It's been a long, long while since Jasper felt worry. And it sickens him inside.

She doesn't sit in the rocker beside him. Stays in the doorway instead, leaning against the frame. Door open behind her. Moths and June bugs slip past her in their quest for artificial light.

'Do you think she's all righ'?' Lizzie is ghostly white.

He knows he should comfort her. That she is looking to him now for just that. But his own concern won't let him be the brother she is after. A part of him knows what must be coming. A part of him has always been able to guess the worst correctly. 'If she was all righ',' he says roughly, 'I reckon she'd be home by now.'

He turns away from his sister so as not to watch the tears well in her eyes.

Far off across the prairie, high beams break the newly fallen darkness. They watch with bated breath as the lights move closer. Like ghost lights in a swamp, he muses, that he'd long ago heard a Creole in prison talk of. Swamp gases that give off their own glow. That's how the man had described them. Except these lights move with purpose down the country road, coming ever closer.

Silently, Lizzie slips inside. A moment later she is back beside him, Daddy's old Hungerford semi-automatic held before her in both hands. Her stance is wide. Braced for the worst, he reckons.

The pickup parks on the road. The engine cuts off, so that crickets and July flies create the only sound.

'You got a lot of nerve comin' here.' No warmth in Lizzie's tone.

Josh looks nervous as he pauses by their gate. He's come alone. 'Ma'am, I don' mean no disrespect.' He holds up his hands to show that he's unarmed.

Lizzie steps forward from the deep shadows of the porch, rifle still held before her though the barrel not yet levelled or aimed upon him. 'You're not welcome here.' No softness in her tone. 'I'm sorry it's come to this, but

327

actions have consequences 'n' it's 'bout time you learned that. I don' want you callin' round to see my daughter no more.'

He pauses for a second by the gate, uncertain. Then a slow grin spreads across Josh's face. He brings his hands down slowly, unlatches the gate and steps into the ruined garden, scattered, crushed flowers all around his feet.

Lizzie fixes the rifle on him. 'Not another step.'

Jasper leans forward, but does not rise. He could break that boy like a stick if he wanted. He could tie him up and cut him and let him bleed out slowly. But he is just a boy. Just a lemming diving off a cliff. Were I him, Jasper muses, I doubt I would have done much different.

Josh's hands are up again, palms held out and open. 'I ain't here to stir up shit,' he calls. 'I got a message is all.'

Jasper does rise then, and steps from the shadows of the porch. He leans against the porch railing out into the open night. 'Who from?'

'Eddie.'

Jasper spits a large wad of phlegm onto the grass. 'What's he want?'

Josh lowers his hands. He looks real nervous. Scared, even. Like maybe he would have preferred not delivering this particular message. 'He got Joanne.' Pause. 'He says you'll know where.'

A groan escapes Jasper he did not know was in him. A haunted sound.

'You sick son of a bitch!' Lizzie steps forward, rifle focused at Josh's head. Even in the darkness, Jasper can see the boy's face drop all colour. He backs up slowly, hands held high.

'Mama! No!' Her scream pierces the darkness, shattering the still of the just fallen night. The screen door slams behind her as she hurtles through it and down the steps to fling herself in front of Josh. Her mother's rifle still stays fixed upon them. 'Don't hurt him, Mama! Please!'

'Get back inside, Katie. Now.' No messing in Lizzie's tone.

'Mom! No! You can't hurt him! Promise me you won't hurt him!' Katie's voice is shrill, tears streaming down her cheeks.

'He took your sister!' Lizzie screams. 'Those bastards took your sister!'

Feathers ruffle in a nearby shrub as birds wake from their sleep.

'No! Mama!' Katie raises her arm up, palm out, as if to hold her mother off, as if to shield. 'It's OK, Mom! It's ain't Josh's fault! They promised they won' hurt her!'

Silence falls.

The rifle barrel dips but does not lower. 'What?' Confusion deepens the wrinkle across Lizzie's brow. 'You *knew* 'bout this?'

'They said they wouldn't hurt her, Mom,' Katie whines. 'They just wanted to get Jasper out of the house is all.' She's sobbing. 'I swear, Mom, they said they wouldn't hurt her. They promised me!'

Jasper has heard enough. In one swift motion he swings over the porch railing and lands lightly on the ground. Fingers of pain shoot up his leg and knee while others curve around his ribs. He bites his lip, anger pushing him on through his pain. He doesn't run but crosses the garden as quickly as if he had, ignoring his pain with each step. He slaps Katie hard across her face. Hard as he is able. A small cry escapes her as she falls to the ground, holding her cheek. Josh steps back, eyes wide with shock. As he sees Jasper's attention turn to him, he steps forward and swings for the older man. Jasper sidesteps the blow easily, then hits the boy twice, once to break his nose, the next to knock him cold. He turns to where Katie lies crumpled, crushed roses and buttercups and black-eyed susans all around her. It felt good hitting them, letting that anger out. She looks up at him with frightened eyes, and he'd be lying if he said he didn't like it. If it didn't turn him on just a little. His blood pumps through him, wild, thick, like it hasn't in so many long years. 'Because I love your mother,' he hisses, 'I'll let her deal with you.'

The crickets have fallen silent. Dark clouds move quickly across the sky blowing east to west. He turns to his sister. 'I'll need the keys to the truck.'

'I'm going with you.' Rifle now lowered by her side.

'No,' he says quietly, 'it's me they want.'

Her face is ghostly white. Whiter even, if there is such a colour. But when she speaks, her voice is strong. 'Bring her home, Jasper. If you do one good thing on this earth, you bring my girl home safe.'

He holds her gaze a long moment. There is much he would like to say but the words are tangled in him. He nods to her. Just once. And she reaches in her pocket and throws him the keys. Katie lies crumpled on the ground between them, choking on heavy sobs. He steps over her as he moves swiftly to the truck.

'Jasper!'

He stops, hand already reaching for the pickup's door.

'You'll need this more than I.'

Daddy's Hungerford semi-automatic sails through the air. He catches it. There is so much he'd like to say to her, but he finds himself unable. He looks at his sister a long moment.

'Go,' she says quietly. Arms wrapped around herself as if for protection.

Wordlessly he climbs into the truck. Puts the key into the ignition and lets the engine purr.

It's been ten years since he's driven. But it comes back to him like no time has passed. He knows these back-country roads better than the lines that map his palms. He doesn't really need to think about where he is going. There are no streetlights on the country roads, so he turns his high beams on, and with each passing second as he speeds forward, the world unmasks itself for him in flashed snapshots of light. He could drive anywhere. Up to Amarillo. Way out west, El Paso way. He could leave the state. Maybe find a forgotten town where they'd not know his name. But there is a little girl that needs him, and free as speeding down the country roads makes him feel, it is her face he sees round every corner, calling for him, afraid.

Half a mile from the old oil site, Jasper cuts his high beams off and continues on in darkness. He slows so as not to run into the deep ditches that he knows from memory line these country roads. A part of him is aware that he should have a plan. He had a plan last time, ten years ago, on this same road, Rose beside him, uncon-scious as he drove. He'd planned that night out for a long while. There had been a certain kind of peace inside him as he had executed that plan. Had been a nervous excite-ment pumping through his veins. But everything is different now. This is not that feeling. Not that good kind of nervousness, the kind he likes. This is not that drive. He shakes his head to block out thoughts of Rose. Has to remind himself again that this is not that drive.

He slows as he turns off the country road onto the dirt drive that leads to the oil site. No lights for miles, just wide-open dark stretches of prairie that reach out further west into the dark deserts beyond. Little bits of stone catch in his tyres, spin back and hit the bottom of the pickup. Ting ting. Ting ting. As they fall away.

He rounds a bend, and there are lights ahead.

He does not turn his beams on. Drives slowly on through the darkness watching the far-off lights grow closer. He knows that, in this vast isolation, his truck will have already been heard.

There are two pickups parked in the site. Floodlights high up on posts illuminate the disturbed earth, the rusted-out forgotten bits of heavy machinery that were long ago abandoned here, left well and true behind. One of the trucks, Jasper recognizes as Eddie's. The bright blue of its paint stands out in sharp contrast to the dusty drilling site. The other truck is the beaten-up green Ford that helped plough through Mama's garden a couple nights before. Around him, swells of piled earth rise like dunes. The engine hums slightly as it idles. Two shadowy figures stand by the door of the old toolshed. Light spills from its broken windows. Jasper pulls in to his left and cuts his engine. He knows he's been seen. But he had never planned on hiding.

He flips open the magazine on Daddy's old Hungerford, and checks all the rounds are loaded. He didn't think to ask Lizzie for more bullets. A part of him wonders if she had any spare. But it doesn't really matter now, he reckons. What's done is done, and what will be will be.

'It's time now,' he says quietly, and slips from the truck.

The slam of the door behind him echoes across the barren land. Both dark figures are turned to him, but from this distance Jasper cannot make out their features. From what he can tell, both are armed. One, the taller of the two, has a shiny new Winchester laid casually across one arm. The other, shorter, wiry, holds a pistol by his side. It's then that Jasper realizes who it is.

'Evening, Roy.' He lets his voice carry. 'I didn't expect to see you here.'

Roy shifts uncomfortably, his face still in shadow. It is the other, larger, man who speaks. Chuck Ryan. 'Well, I'll be . . .' he says. 'Ain't you lookin' pretty?' He spits a big wad of tobacco down onto the dirt by his boots.

Jasper chooses his words with care. His swollen lips smart as they stretch to form each sound. 'Well . . . I guess I got you boys to thank for that.'

Chuck Ryan's pearly whites flash and disappear.

Jasper kicks the dirt with the toe of one sneaker, and a tiny dust cloud swirls up around his foot. The Hungerford's still clutched before him, finger on the trigger, though the rifle's held at ease. 'Eddie here?'

'Yeah, he's here, all righ'.'

'Can I see him?'

Chuck Ryan laughs. 'You think we're just gonna let you waltz in there?'

'Ain't that why I'm here?'

The floodlights block the stars from view.

'You're gonna have to turn that gun over first.'

Jasper's finger tenses at the trigger. 'Is she here?'

The other man pauses. 'Yeah, she's here.'

Jasper feels the anger boil up in him anew. 'I swear to God, if you hurt her . . .'

Chuck laughs. 'You'll what?'

Jasper wants to shoot him, right then and there. But something stops him raising the rifle. From pulling the bliss of that ready trigger. He needs to know where she is. Needs to know that she is safe. *If you do one good thing on this earth* . . . his sister'd said. He clears his throat. 'Let me see her.'

'We're gonna need that firearm before this goes any further.' Chuck tilts his head towards Jasper, and Roy steps forward. Pistol still held ready by his side.

'If you want the girl,' Roy says quietly, 'you'd best play ball.'

'Where is she?' A desperation to his tone he cannot mask.

Roy hesitates. 'She's inside.'

Light spills from the broken windows of the old toolshed. It looks just like it did ten years ago. Maybe a bit better lit. He thinks he hears a muffled cry, but he can't be certain. It could just be his memory playing tricks on him, recreating the muffled sounds of a different girl on a different night now long ago.

'Go on, Roy,' Chuck calls. 'You bring that antique of his on over here.'

Roy takes another hesitant step forward. 'I'm gonna have to take that.' Jasper can see his face now. The gauntness of his cheeks. The coldness in his eyes.

'How do I know,' Jasper says coarsely, 'that when I hand this rifle over you just won't shoot me dead?'

Roy's face is blank. 'You don'.'

Chuck Ryan laughs real long and low. 'Hurry up now,' he chuckles, 'you don't wanna keep her waitin'.'

''N' if I don't hand the rifle over?' His voice cuts through the darkness.

Chuck's smile falls. 'Then you don't get your prize.'

Roy takes another step forward, his face hard stone. He reaches out a hand, palm up. The other still hangs by his side, fisted round his pistol handle. Jasper can see now that the pistol's cocked. 'Go on, Jasper,' he says, real calm. 'There ain't no other way.' When they were boys, they hunted with that same rifle, wandering hours across the open prairie. They used to bring tin cans to line up and practise shooting. Sometimes glass bottles and milk cartons, too. Roy's hand hovers, outstretched. Jasper watches it. Then he sets Daddy's old Hungerford semi-automatic on the waiting palm.

'Take me to her.'

Roy's eyes hold his gaze, but do not soften. 'You shouldn'ta come back here,' he whispers. 'You never shoulda come on home.' Then, louder, 'All right, Chuck, I got it.' Roy steps round so that he's behind Jasper now, the Hungerford pressed into Jasper's back. Even through his T-shirt, its barrel feels cold. Mutely, Jasper steps

335

forward, prodded by his once best friend. There's a deep hurt there he can't quite confront. Not now, anyway. He thinks of her and only her. Of tanned skin and dark blonde hair and her wide eyes upon him. *Please, God*, he prays, *give me the strength* . . .

'Hold it right there.' He stops before the doorway and lets Chuck pat him down. Reminds him of all those times in prison. All those hands laid rough upon him. Feels like his freedom being taken from him, and it is in a way, he reckons. 'All righ', he's clean.' Chuck straightens before him. The cool rifle barrel still presses into Jasper's back. Not for the first time that evening, Jasper wishes he had a plan, but when he looks up, there aren't even stars to guide him.

The door to the toolshed creaks open and light spills out. Squinting against the sudden brightness, Jasper steps forward. The barrel of his daddy's rifle pushes him on into the light. It takes a moment for his eyes to adjust. For him to see her bound there before him lying in the middle of the shed's dust floor. A moan escapes him, soft and low and wild. A sound he didn't know that man could make. He falls to his knees. The sand floor of the shed feels cool against his jeans. Almost damp. She looks at him, eyes wide and wild with fear. All doe now. All set to startle and flee. Except she can't. Ropes cut into her flesh leaving angry red blisters on her wrists and ankles. 'She don't have to be here,' he snarls. 'She ain't part of this!'

'You made her part of it.' Eddie's voice is smooth and cool as he rises from the far corner to step forward. 'Can't you see that? Can't you see,' Eddie hisses, 'how you're hurting her?'

There are tears in Jasper's eyes he didn't know would be there. Wild, angry tears. And softer ones filled with regret and sorrow. They do not fall, simply well in his eyes till he is able to blink past them. 'It's OK, honey.' He wills his voice calm. 'I'm gonna get you outta here.'

Eddie's laugh is cold.

She never should have gotten in the truck. She didn't know at first. Even as they drove on past town. And they'd talked to her so nice at first, too, had told her she was pretty. Had told her they knew Katie real well, that she was a real nice girl. Eddie had even laughed and said how much he missed her father. It wasn't often that men told her she was pretty. She liked the sound of the word rolling off their tongues. But as time stretched on, they'd gotten quieter. Their smiles had started to fade, to seem forced. 'Will we be there soon?' Joanne had asked. And Eddie had answered, 'Just a little further, now.' But it wasn't. It was *too far*. Joanne could feel it. Town was *too far* behind. And the prairie seemed strange to her, burned golden still, but it stretched out into the deeper scorched browns of desert country, land she did not know.

'My mom's gonna be wondering where I am,' she'd said, nervous, squirming in her seat.

'Don' worry, sweetheart,' Eddie had purred, putting his arm around her. 'They'll know just where you at.'

She hadn't liked that. Hadn't liked the feel of his arm around her. She'd tried to pull away, but he had held her there, pressed against him as he drove, his arm locked tight around her. The a/c blew straight in her face at the angle he held her, and it felt cold on her cheeks. It dried out her eyes and made them sting. Beside them, Ben had chuckled, then looked out the window. She had tried to pull away from Eddie again, but still he had held her close.

When finally he'd cut the engine and he and Ben had opened their doors and slid from their seats, they had stood in their open doorways, their eyes fixed upon her. 'Well,' Eddie'd said, real loud, 'you comin'?'

Her whole body trembling, Joanne had shaken her head. 'This isn't Josh's house,' she'd whispered, looking at her feet. At the double knots that tied her laces. At her scabby knees. At the mosquito bites down by her ankle. She had not wanted to look at the abandoned oil site. Had not wanted this nightmare to be real.

A grin had spread across Eddie's face. 'You know where we're at, don' you?'

He had grabbed her then. By the ankle. And she had screamed. So loud. Louder than she had ever screamed. But there had been no one to hear her. Only Ben. And he was smiling when her frightened eyes found his.

It seemed such a long while till Uncle Jasper came. The other truck had come first. The one with Mr Ryan in it. He'd looked at her a long moment when he'd first opened up the shed door. Roy Reynolds had come in straight behind him and had stopped short and turned right on the spot when he'd seen her. Both men had shut the door, and she'd heard a lot of swearing outside, though she couldn't make out most of the words they said. Eddie had punched her when he'd pulled her from the truck. 'You little bitch!' he'd yelled at her. 'See what you made me do?' His arm was bleeding from where she'd scratched him.

She didn't fight so much after that. Not after he hit her. She let him bind her arms and legs. The gag he stuffed into her mouth soaked all her saliva up the second it touched her tongue. It smelt like old socks mixed with gasoline. Tasted stale. And sour. She tried to turn her face away when first he came at her with it, but she couldn't move much with her arms and legs bound. He smiled as he pressed her cheeks together to pop her mouth wide open. Her face, where his fist had come down, felt swollen and sore. Her ear stung and her hearing sounded like she was under water. She thought of Uncle Jasper and the purple mask he'd been given. Then she had cried till she'd fallen asleep, crumpled and bound on the shed's dust floor.

When she woke, it was dark already. Eddie sat watching her from the corner of the room. Ben paced by the window. Both held guns. She heard a truck pull up outside and then its door slam. Voices called out she could not decipher. Then, clear as day, Uncle Jasper said, 'Is she here?' Joanne's heart skipped a beat, just knowing he was there. She tried to call out, but her gag was too tight. Hot tears spilled down her cheeks. She wondered where her mother was. Where Katie was. *Were they here?* Ben crossed the room and opened the door from the inside. Uncle Jasper stumbled through and said something angry to Eddie. He fell to his knees there before her, a rifle digging into his back. A sound kin to a whimper escaped him, and Joanne wondered what they'd done to him. How badly must they have hurt him for him to make such a sound? 'It's OK, honey,' Jasper says then. 'I'm gonna get you outta here.' And it seems to her in that moment that her hearing clears and those are the first words she's heard for a great long while.

She wants to run to him. To throw her arms around him. She wants to cry and beat him with her fists, wants to scream, 'This is all your fault!' till eventually he will hold her. But her wrists are bound, coarse ropes leaving burns on her arms; her ankles are tied together, and her legs ache with stiffness, unable to change position all these long hours; the gag in her mouth tastes dusty and of oil, and the rope that holds it tightly in place burns against her cheek. So only her eyes implore him, beg him, 'Save me.'

Eddie's laugh is cold. 'Now just how . . .' he chuckles '. . . do you reckon you're gonna do that?'

Uncle Jasper tears his eyes from her to look up at the other man. 'If you lay one hand on her,' he snarls, 'I'll make death your final blessin'.'

Kerosene lamps cast deep shadows through the shed. Empty beer cans and bottles have fallen onto the dirt floor. Others stand discarded between rusty piles of tools. Eddie spits a large wad of tobacco onto the dirt floor. 'You ain't never been no knight in shinin' armour.'

Jasper straightens. 'I wouldn't've pegged you a kidnapper, neither.'

Eddie chuckles and spins his pistol round his index finger to catch it again by its grip. 'You know,' he says quietly, 'I've waited a long time for this.'

'Leave the girl out of it.'

Her heart pounds in her chest. The oil fumes from the rag make her head feel spinny.

Eddie shakes his head. 'I'm afraid I can't do that, Jasper. You see, it's a girl that started all this, ain't it? It's a girl *I* love, my own kin, *my own sister,* that *you* chose to start all this with. So the way I see it, it seems fittin' that it's a girl that ends all this too, now, don' it?' Eddie pauses. 'You see, that's the problem with all you psychotic motherfuckers.' He shakes his pistol at Jasper as he speaks. 'Y'all got no soft spot. No goddamn Achilles' heel.' He spits another large wad of tobacco down onto the earth. A slow grin spreads across his face. 'Except now you got one. I finally found the monster's heart.'

Ben laughs nervously from the broken window where he paces. Eddie rises and walks slowly across the shed to bend down by Joanne. He grabs her roughly by the arm and pulls her up to stand. She tries to cry out, but the gag's too tight, and even to her, her scream sounds more like a whimper. She looks from her uncle to Mr Ryan, to Roy Reynolds, to Ben, and back again. She's too afraid to look up at Eddie. He leans down, his breath hot upon her. Stale and sour with alcohol. She tries to cry out. Tries to break free, but his grip is too strong. Her legs are too weak. His tongue feels hot and sticky against her cheek as he licks the side of her face. The swollen side where he punched her. Inside, every part of her is screaming. She coughs, choking on the oil rag that gags her.

A darkness passes over her uncle's face as he watches.

'It ain't nice, is it,' Eddie purrs, 'watchin' what you care 'bout suffer?'

Jasper's jeans are covered with sandy earth. He kneels still, watching them, his broken face twisted with some form of rage and sorrow. Dirt streaks his swollen cheek from where he wiped his hand. 'What do you want from me?'

Eddie's grip tightens, bruising her arm.

'You want me gone? OK, I'm gone. Just leave her outta it. This ain't no place for little girls.' He runs a dirty hand through his hair and it stands up wild.

Eddie takes his time answering. 'Would you say that it's a place to bring a woman?'

Her uncle opens his mouth, then shuts it. Ben laughs again, that nervous laugh, as he paces by the window. Eddie leans down low once more so that his breath's upon her. 'You wanna grow up, honey?' he whispers right in her ear. 'Want me to make you a woman?'

She shuts her eyes tight, squeezing tears out. *Wake up, wake up, wake up,* she thinks. *I'm ready to wake up now.* Eddie's lips feel warm against her cheek. Less sticky than his tongue.

Jasper feels the rage boil up within him. Like it used to all those long years ago before prison, before he'd learned to push it down. He wants to snap Eddie like two fingers. Wants to grab his tongue and rip it out. He doesn't like the other man's hands on Joanne, let alone his lips, his tongue. She's just a girl, he thinks, but even now, Eddie licking her face, he can see the woman she's so quickly being forced to grow into. Jasper gets Eddie's point. He can see why this is the other man's chosen revenge. Can understand it. A part of Jasper even respects Eddie's choice. Just a little. Respects the depraved cruelty of it. But Eddie never watched what Jasper did to Rose. And Jasper knows himself he'd rather die than watch the child in front of him be forced to grow up like that.

'Wooo-weee!' Eddie hollers, tilting his head back, like a wolf about to howl. 'Tastes like peaches!'

Jasper slowly rises to his feet, one leg, then the next. He

starts forward. The butt of the Winchester hits the base of his skull and for a moment he sees stars before he falls back down. Chuck kicks him hard in the ribs, and Jasper doubles over, coughing. Joanne screams against her gag, barely making a sound. Eddie laughs, sips Bud from a can and twirls his pistol round and round his index finger. The young man Jasper does not recognize kicks a cloud of dirt into Jasper's face as Jasper coughs. Then he grabs another bottle and pops the cap right off. The cap rolls when it hits the earth, drawing a spiral in the cool sand. The Hungerford points down into Jasper's face as Roy stares down the barrel at him.

'Do what you gotta do to me,' Jasper gasps at length. 'Get it over with. I won' even fight back. You just let that girl go free.'

The barrel in his face falters before once again being held steady. Empty beer cans and a few tequila bottles litter the dust floor. Long dark shadows bathe the shed in half-light. Outside the crickets fall silent, then start their song again.

Though Eddie's been drinking, his words do not slur. 'You wanna go home, honey?'

Silent tears stream down her cheeks. She nods. Her throat trembles as she hiccups ragged breaths into her gag.

He draws his index finger down her face, wiping her tears away. 'You know,' he says, real quiet, 'I bet my sister just wanted to go home, too.' There is a coldness to Eddie's gaze that Jasper knows too well. He has seen that look in the eyes of guards before a senseless beating. In the hollowed blank stares of inmates whose crimes make nightmares real. He has seen it in his own reflection. *This is what Eddie's waited for,* he realizes. *Eddie's had ten years to form this plan . . .*

A cold chill runs down Jasper's spine even though the night is warm. He wipes dust from his eyes. Rises up to kneel again, pain stabbing his ribs, then sits back on his heels a bit so that his weight is shared between his toes and knees. His swollen face throbs with its own pulse. He wipes his hands on his thighs and watches even in the half-light as his jeans go from blue to brown. Crickets call in the night. He closes his eyes to listen to their song. To stop the world spinning.

Opens them.

He doesn't see stars any more, and counts that as one tiny blessing. Eddie sits the other side of the shed, on a wooden stool by an old workman's table, Joanne held tight against him, sitting on his knee. His pistol rests beside them on top of an old can of paint. Jasper knows what will happen if he does not act soon. He knows what he did in this very shed so long yet not so very long ago. He knows just what darkness lies in Eddie's heart. Has himself felt that same calling so many times before. It feels to Jasper like time is messing with his sense of now and then. 'I'm sorry, Joanne,' he says at length. His words hang suspended in the humid air between them. 'I really never meant to bring you any trouble.'

Doe Eyes blinks back tears. Her hiccuped sobs further choke the gag into her mouth.

Eddie grins and licks her face again, temple down to chin, and her eyes get wider, wilder, truly a deer about to bolt. 'Ummmm-hum.' Eddie smacks his lips. 'Just like I said, sure does taste like peaches.'

344

'I didn't sign up for this, Eddie!' Roy's face twists, distraught. 'I ain't standin' by watchin' no little girl get hurt.' The cold barrel of the Hungerford lifts out of Jasper's face. Roy thrusts the rifle at Chuck. A moment later, the shed door slams behind him as Roy steps into the darkness, cussing.

The young man laughs and takes a long swig from his beer. Eddie doubles over, laughing so hard he leans into Joanne. His laughter shakes both their bodies. He slaps the knee that Joanne is not perched on. 'I always knew that skinny fucker lacked a spine.'

Chuck Ryan laughs too, but joins in late and seems a bit less certain. Still holding his Winchester, he sets the Hungerford down, propping it by the shed door.

'Hey, Jasper!' Eddie calls, still laughing. 'Watch this.' He reaches a hand up inside Joanne's shirt. Real. Slow. He passes over her flat stomach, his fingertips just visible grazing the dark contour of her belly button. He moves his hand up further over the swell of her ribs. Her chest hammers in and out with short, shallow breaths. Her eyes widen. Eddie's hand stops over her chest just inside her shirt where her tiny breasts have yet to form. He twists her nipple, there beneath her shirt. A slow grin casts light across his face despite the darkness in his eyes. 'Would you look at that?' he says, grinning. 'Ain't nothing there but mosquito bites!'

Jasper's world colours crimson.

He does not care in that moment if he lives or dies.

'Is this your great plan, Eddie? Rape a little girl while I watch?' Jasper spits a wad of blood onto the earth beside him. His saliva catches and reflects the light cast by the kerosene lamps. He allows a smile to twist his battered face. 'Must have taken you a real long time to think this one up.' He scans the shed looking for something, anything, he can use.

Eddie laughs. 'Well,' he says, 'it ain't my fault this girl's your only weakness. I always thought it'd be her sister, but . . .' he shakes his head '. . . guess you're more perverted than we thought.' He chuckles till his laughter's spent and then his voice goes quiet. 'See, I ain't hurtin' her, right now, Jasper. You are. I thought that when we beat you the other night you might finally get the message. Might realize finally where you're not welcome. Might leave well enough alone. But old dogs don' learn new tricks. Ain't that what they say? And you've always been a selfish bastard. You're "all done with trouble". Ain't that what I keep on hearin'? Shit, boy. You don' know trouble. It's time someone taught you just what trouble's like. Your sister ain't here to save you this time.'

Jasper's mouth goes dry. He does not rise to the insult. Eddie looks to his young friend and catches his eye. The young man grunts, nods and takes a long swig before he sets his bottle down. Cracks his knuckles as he rises. The dust stirred up by his boots as he steps forward swirls into Jasper's face and makes him cough again.

'Maybe you don' recognize Ben, here,' Eddie says. 'Ten years can alter the appearance quite a bit when a boy becomes a man.'

The young man looms over him now. Face deeply shadowed, blocking out the light from the kerosene lamp behind him, he is tall and lean and toned. Mid, maybe early twenties. Sandy brown hair cropped short. Jasper closes his eyes, then opens them. The resemblance is there. He knows who this must be.

'I'm not sure we've formally met.' Ben Saunders spits on the ground beside Jasper, just narrowly missing his thigh.

Jasper opens his mouth to speak, but Ben's right hook spins him round instead so that he's on his hands and knees, facing the back of the shed.

'I was just a boy,' Ben says, 'when you done what you done to our sister.'

Jasper spits blood onto the sand before him. 'Well, ain't this sweet,' he growls. 'Y'all should have brought Rose down. Had a whole goddamned family reunion.'

Ben kicks him in the ribs before he can rise and turn and for a moment all Jasper sees is white. Then the pain sets in, splitting his side, and the dark-cast shadows of the dimly lit shed again loom up around him. Another hard boot to his side knocks Jasper over, and he lies clutching his ribs, coughing in spite of his pain. It is a long moment till he is able to rise onto his hands and knees again. Frantically, but still trying not to be noticed, he paws through the sand, hoping for something, anything, he can use.

Ben laughs and grabs his beer and takes a long swig. Eddie pops open another can, Joanne still pressed against him, perched there on his knee. A can of Bud hurtles through the air above them. 'Here, Chuck!' Eddie grins.

Chuck catches the beer in one hand. He leans back against one of the supports holding the shed roof up. The Winchester still points down towards Jasper, but lowers slightly as Chuck pops the can open and swigs. The crisp click of the top popping somehow seems to linger in the air. Almost echo-like. Jasper feels a rusty nail beneath one fingertip, hidden in the sand. *It will have to do.* He glances quickly round the room, checking he is not watched. Masking his movement with another wave of doubled-over coughing that shoots long fingers of pain around his ribcage, Jasper palms the nail, keeping it cupped and hidden inside his hand. From its size, it feels like a roofing or maybe even a masonry nail. He struggles to conceal it in his single hand. Its large flat head presses into the soft flesh below his thumb.

He rises to kneel, the pain of moving again colouring the world momentarily white. 'So what's this all about, Eddie?' he hisses, through his pain. 'Tit for tat? Revenge? Or tryin' to show your little brother that you're a *real* man now?'

The laughter falls from Eddie's face. 'He was twelve when you raped Rose. You sick fuck. You took that boy's innocence. You ruined our family. And now I'm gonna ruin yours.' He turns Joanne's face roughly to him and holds her in place by her jaw. She tries to scream. Tries to struggle. But the ropes that bind her won't let her push him away. Her gag won't let her scream. His tongue plays with her ear. Runs up and down her cheek. Fallen strands of dark blonde hair spill from her ponytail to fall round her face and shoulders. Tiny beads of sweat moisten her skin, run down her throat to pool in the nape of her neck. Eddie lifts her easily and lays her down on the workman's table. She screams against her gag and tries to struggle, but he hits her hard across her temple, and after that she goes all quiet and her limbs are limp.

Jasper struggles to hold his growl in. The rusted nail held in his palm presses into his skin lightly cutting it. There is something strangely comforting about the texture of its rust held against his skin. The length of its shaft. The large round circle of its rusted head. Nothing smooth there. Nothing polished. A feeling kin to pain.

Eddie smirks. 'I must say, I would have enjoyed this more if it was her sister, but she's a fine little thing all the same.' He takes a sip from a bottle of tequila before placing it down on the workman's table, then chugs the last of his Bud and tosses the can aside. His belt buckle jingles as he pulls the leather through its clasp.

Jasper has no time to think. He spins fast as he is able and faces the barrel of the Winchester full on. He shoves the rusted nail up the barrel a fraction of a second before Chuck Ryan pulls the trigger. Jasper rolls quickly and hides his face deep in the protection of the cool sand floor. The Winchester shatters as if made of glass. Its explosion fills the shed with a flash of orange and white light. Chuck falls back, clutching his eyes and throat, tiny fragments of the metal barrel lodged deep within his skin. The Winchester falls onto the floor beside him, its barrel cleanly split.

Ben cusses loudly and drops his beer, jumping back. His eyes widen as he watches Chuck clutch his right hand where his index finger blew off. The finger lies in the dirt beside him, oozing blood. Blood runs down Chuck's throat from where he first clutched it with his bleeding hand as he tried to get the metal fragments from his skin. As the realization of his missing finger sets in, Chuck's screams split through the night with panicked horror, drowning out all cricket song.

Ben fumbles with the Colt he's held by his side, quickly raising it, but it's too late. Jasper springs from the ground, Ben's dropped beer bottle raised high above his head. Sticky, frothy beer spills out of its neck and down Jasper's arm showering the sand with tiny drops of beer spray rain. The bottle comes down over Ben's head just as he manages to pull the trigger. A loud crack echoes through the tiny shed as the bottle breaks over Ben's head and as his skull cracks open. His body falls with a gangly sort of grace to slump down lifeless on the dirt floor. The blood from the crack in his skull slowly colours the sand bright red.

The .22 just fired from Ben's Colt grazes Jasper's neck as he springs forward, leaving an angry gash in the skin between his shoulder and his collarbone.

Eddie turns, his trousers just dropped down, resting on his boot tops between his knees and ankles. One hand fumbles to pull his trousers up, while the other reaches frantically for the pistol he'd discarded. Screaming like a man possessed, Jasper hurtles forward across the tiny shed, broken beer bottle held like a prison shank. He presses the jagged glass into Eddie's jugular to the point where the skin just starts to bleed. The cool barrel of Eddie's pistol presses against Jasper's stomach.

Their eyes meet.

'You don' deserve a happy life. Not after what you done.' Eddie pulls the trigger and the bullet releases into Jasper's gut with a loud crack. He feels where it tears into him. Feels the cool metal of the gun against his gut turn hot. Feels where the bullet again breaks free, ripping through his back.

'Neither do you.' Jasper's eyes hold Eddie's a split second longer. Then the jagged edges of the bottle twist as they sever Eddie's jugular. His eyes pop open wider as the glass goes in, cutting and cutting, and Jasper would be lying if he said he didn't like the surprise on the other man's face as he chokes to death on his own blood.

Crumpled in the corner, Chuck keeps screaming, holding his hand clutched tight to his chest. *He is an oil man*, Jasper muses, *not cut out for blood and violence*. For a moment, Jasper pities him, watching him writhe on the floor. He picks up the Colt .22 that just shot him, fallen from Eddie's dead hand. The grip on it is still warm from the other man's palm. Jasper limps across the shed, bent over as he clutches his bleeding stomach then straightens, forcing himself to stand tall over the screaming, crumpled man. He watches him for what seems like a great while, and yet no time at all.

'You would have watched them hurt her,' he says. And the gun sounds, leaving only silence after.

She looks at Eddie Saunders with fearful eyes. Her heart slams in her chest. The smell of Eddie's breath still lingers thick upon her. The feel of his lips and tongue still burns her cheek. His body lies next to her, slumped over the table; his blood pools under her, around her, and it smells bad and feels real hot and sticky. Uncle Jasper crosses the room to her quickly after the last gunshot fades. The silence after Mr Ryan's screaming stops rings inside her head louder than any sound. She did not see what happened to him. But, inside, she knows. She had closed her eyes when the first loud bang sounded. Had only opened them and looked over once Mr Ryan started screaming, but she couldn't see much, just Uncle Jasper rising up as Ben slumped down. The loud crack of Eddie's gun as he struggled with her uncle echoed through her, as did the gurgles deep in Eddie's throat. She turned her face away as blood sprayed from him. Squeezed her eyes shut even tighter as she heard his body fall. The bubbling noise in his throat had grown louder before it stopped. Then there was that last loud bang that took the screaming with it. And the roar of the silence that followed. Eddie's blood felt warm as it seeped over to touch her skin. It was only then that Joanne had opened her eyes again.

Uncle Jasper sits her up and unties the rope around her gag first. It burns as the ropes peel away. Her cheeks feel dry and raw. He pulls the oil rag from her mouth and she gasps the air in greedy mouthfuls. His hands are already busy untying the ropes that bind her ankles.

She looks at Mr Ryan's lifeless body at the far side of the shed. His face, unrecognizable. His blood, so much blood, staining the dirt floor red. The gash in Ben's head opens like a canyon, and bits of his brains spill out. His eyes are open, wide and blue. The corner of his lip curls up, does not quite smile. She looks at Eddie's bent-over body there on the table beside her. His trousers are still half down. His blood spills from his neck and pools all around her. Frightened, trembling, she asks, 'Are you gonna kill me next?'

Confusion darkens his features as he looks up at her. 'What?' He shakes his head, deep hurt in his eyes. 'No, honey. I'm here to bring you home.'

He's finished untying the rope that bound her wrists. She throws her arms around him and buries her face deep in his chest. Sobs shake her body. Catch and choke in her throat. He rubs her back. 'Ssssh . . .' he says. 'It's all right now. I'm gonna get you home.'

There is blood on Jasper's hands but he does not wipe them clean before scooping up Joanne's trembling form. He cradles her in his arms, like a newborn child. Like a bride brought by her groom across their first threshold together. The girl sobs into his chest as he carries her. He is deeply sorry for what she has seen. Blood stains her hair dark red. Dirt and grime streak her face and body. Her shirt is soiled and torn. As he carries her, his own blood feels warm as it seeps from his gut and dyes his T-shirt red. The wound itself burns where the bullet tore through him. He does not stop to pick up the old Hungerford. Leaves it where it stands, propped up beside all the blood and carnage. Around them, as they emerge from the tiny shed, crickets sing again, calling through the returned stillness of the night.

It is warm still, but not a sticky heat at this late hour. The air on Jasper's cheeks feels like life, feels like living to him. A slow smile spreads across his broken face as he stumbles forward, and he doesn't even mind the pain in his swollen jaw as his face relaxes.

Roy stands by his green pickup, pistol shaking as he holds it up and ready. Jasper stops, not more than three paces from him. Joanne sobs into his chest. Seconds pass that could be hours. Far off a coyote calls and is answered by its pack.

'Go home, Roy,' Jasper says.

Joanne spooks at the sound of his voice. She lifts her head and screams when she sees Roy. Her fingernails dig into Jasper's neck, tearing his flesh. He holds her, trying to calm her struggle. Blood flows from his side, staining her shirt too.

Roy's voice trembles. 'Where the others at?'

Jasper chooses his words with care. 'It's over now.'

Roy takes an uncertain step forward, pistol still ready and aimed. 'What happened in there?'

'Only what had to.' Silence stretches between them. Around them. Far off the coyotes stop calling. Wind rattles the rusted oil pump, causing the metal to groan and creak. At length, Jasper's voice breaks through the eerie stillness of the night around them. 'If I done one good thing in my life, Roy, it's saving this here girl. You know that good as I. Let me bring her home now. What's done here now is done.'

Slowly the pistol lowers. Roy says nothing but steps aside. Jasper strokes his niece's hair, the blood on his hand further streaking her dirty-blonde strands. 'It's OK, sweetie,' he whispers, as he steps forward. 'I'm gonna get you home.'

Lizzie feels sick inside. Like her heart's been taken and left her body ill. Every muscle in her yearns to hold her girl. She sits on the porch staring out across Mama's ruined garden, but she does not see the flowers scattered across the lawn or the dark expanse of prairie that stretches out before her. Nor does she gaze up at the stars. She doesn't dare wish on them. She doesn't even pray. She stares at this flake of white paint that's peeling off the porch railing. Stares at it for hours as if it holds answers for her. But it doesn't. It's just paint. And eventually she tears her eyes from it to gaze out at the night beyond.

She wishes Bobby were there with her, though she knows wishing such things is silly. In a different life, she muses, in a world free of trouble, they'd sit here, side by side, she and Bobby, their girls tucked up safe in bed. But Lizzie has not known that world these eight long years. This is not that life. Her hate for Eddie Saunders boils up inside her. 'You took my husband,' she whispers to the dark. 'Please, God, don't take my baby, too.'

She'd wanted to go with Jasper. Two are surely always better than one. But she knew he was right when he said it was him they were after. This wasn't her battle to fight. *And yet*, she wonders, gazing out at the darkness, *when is my battle if not now?* It was the mother in her, she reckons, that tossed him the gun. That made her stay behind. She has two daughters. Even her tortured soul won't let her forget that love, those bonds. She trusted her brother to bring Joanne home just as she knew herself that Katie would need tending. Yes, reprimanding, but tending also. No matter how angry, deep in her heart Lizzie knows she is not capable of hating her daughter. But now, waiting for him to bring her baby home, Lizzie wishes she had gone with Jasper. She worries he might need her help.

When Jasper had sped out of their drive, the pickup's tyres squealing as he had sharply cut onto the country road, Lizzie had turned to Katie, still crumpled on the grass, holding her smarting cheek. 'I hope you realize,' she'd said, 'just how stupid you've been.'

Katie did not look up to her, nor did she answer back. She crawled to Josh and lifted his head into her lap. Sobbing, she screamed, 'He killed him! He killed him! He killed him!' Her tears fell down onto Josh, onto the parched earth, like rain.

It had taken a pail of water to wake Josh and to silence her daughter's screams. Josh had sat up, dazed, dripping wet, and Katie had flung her arms around him, and started sobbing all over again. Lizzie didn't have the heart to say much to them. Didn't have the energy. 'If they kill Joanne,' she'd said quietly, 'that blood's on both your hands.'

'Mom! They said they ain't gonna hurt her –'

'Believe their lies all you want. If anything happens to her, I've lost two daughters tonight.' And then she had turned and walked back into the house.

A part of her wishes she could hate Katie. But a mother can never truly hate her child. *It's my fault*, she thinks. *I should have left here with their father all those years ago.* An owl calls far out across the prairie, its hoot blown to her on the gentle breeze. She rises and paces, then sits down again. It feels like time has paused and locked her still inside it.

Katie sobs into her pillow, choking on her tears. Mascara runs from her long lashes to smudge the fabric dark. The pillow smells like Joanne. The sticky, sweaty, cut-grass smell that seems to follow wherever her kid sister goes. The whole bed reeks of her. And that only makes it worse. Katie never thought they'd hurt Joanne. Not really. She realizes now, choking on her own sobs, that maybe trusting them was a bit naive. But she'd just wanted Josh to

356

love her, to realize she wasn't tainted by her uncle's sins. She'd wanted finally to win his father's approval, too, so that maybe when Josh went off to college next year he wouldn't replace her with some preppy sorority girl, and Josh and his dad had promised her Eddie'd just take Joanne for a little drive was all. Just to lure her uncle out. That was how they'd described it. 'All you gotta do is lie,' they'd said. 'Just say you don't know where your sister's at.' And it hadn't *really* been a lie. Or so she'd told herself. She didn't know where her sister was at, didn't know just *where* they would take her.

Katie had tried to leave with Josh when he'd finally come to. He'd been angry when he'd woken up, angrier than she'd ever seen him. He'd pushed her off him and gotten to his feet. Even in the darkness she could already make out the bright shiner swelling round his eye from where her uncle'd punched him. A little blood dripped down from Josh's nose and stained his lips bright red.

'Baby, you're hurt,' she'd said, and had reached out to him.

But he'd just pushed her off.

'Josh!' she'd cried, her voice newly shrill as she'd followed him across the ruined garden. 'I'm goin' with you.'

'Like hell you are.' He hadn't even looked back. Trampled flowers all around them further pushed into the earth by their hurried feet.

'Baby, what's wrong? Please don't be like that!'

'Stay here and rot with your kin,' was all he'd said. And he'd kept on walking.

His pride was hurt, she could see that. But his words had hurt her, too. Had cut her deep. 'Don't say that.' Her voice had lowered, whisper soft. 'Josh, I'm scared,' she'd said. 'He hit me too. I don't wanna be here when he gets back.'

The pickup door had slammed in her face. He'd looked out of his open window at her. 'I don't need all this drama,' he'd said. 'For fuck's sake, your mom pulled a gun on me!'

'She wasn't gonna shoot you, Josh, I swear!'

He shook his head. 'When you see your family's true colours, you give me a call.'

She'd stood there a long while till his taillights had faded away. Like far-off stars covered by cloud. But those lights she had known would not blink back into view.

It had been her mother's face that had made Katie realize she'd done wrong. Had been the cold look in her mother's eyes as she'd spoken of losing both daughters. About blood on both their hands. That had spooked Josh too. She could see it in his eyes when her mother said it, but he was a proud young man. He always had been. That was part of what Katie'd always loved about him. His confidence. His pride. And he'd been stripped of that honour when her uncle had knocked him down so easily, when her mother had woken him up with that cool pail of water.

Now, crying into her pillow, the smell of her sister thick upon it, a part of Katie wishes her mother would come to her room to find her. To comfort. She knows her mother's too mad for that, but she can't help listening for footsteps on the stairs all the same. Nothing makes sense any more to Katie. She can't understand why Mr Ryan and Eddie would want to hurt Joanne. Why they would have lied to her. She can't understand why Josh won't just love her. How so much could have changed since last night in his arms. *When Joanne comes back*, Katie tells herself, *I'm gonna paint her nails whatever colour she wants. And if she wants I'll even let her braid my hair.*

She sits next to her uncle in the pickup, the leather of its seats cool against the bare backs of her legs. She watches as the dry, flat desert country they'd crossed into eases back to the familiar stretches of tall prairie grass that extend far as the eye can see. It spreads like an ocean around them, grasses blowing in the breeze, like waves breaking on some dark sea. It seems to her the country road cuts through the prairie like a path of light, lit up by the truck's high beams as they speed forward. Joanne doesn't remember ever going quite so fast. The world seems to spin as it goes by. The sky is light enough that nearly all the stars have faded, but it is still too dark to see much beyond the glow cast by the truck's high beams. A shadow world still full of horrors, but easing slowly light.

They don't speak. She doesn't know what to say to him. A part of her still fears her uncle. A part of her wants nothing but the safety of his strong arms around her. She needs water, and her mouth feels dry. Like all the saliva's been used up. Like how it feels when she's licked a lollipop too long without a sip of water, and her whole mouth's gone dry inside.

Except there's nothing sweet about the taste that lingers on her tongue.

She can feel his eyes upon her from time to time. And she tries to stop shaking when she does. But even though the night's not cold, Joanne can't hold still. Can't keep from trembling. The sweet, sickly stench of blood fills the truck even with the windows rolled down. It makes her want to vomit.

She closes her eyes to block out all the blood, to stop herself staring at the cuts and bruises on her dirty arms and legs. To stop herself getting dizzy as the still dark world speeds by. But when she shuts her eyes, Eddie's dying face comes back to her, his eyes wide, his throat slit, bubbles of blood popping in his open mouth. She turns to the side and vomits. Brown liquid bile. The truck swerves as her uncle asks her if she's all right. When she straightens, she nods once and looks out of the window again. Uncle Jasper is pale beside her, like maybe he might throw up, too.

When she sees her mother's home loom up out of the dark fields, like a doll house all lit up, still far off across the prairie, a small cry escapes Joanne. Not quite a gasp. Not quite a sigh. Her uncle turns to her for a long moment as he speeds forward, down the straight flat country road, the house growing ever bigger, ever closer. She can feel his eyes upon her, though still she does not turn. 'I told you, Doe Eyes,' he says quietly, 'I'd get you home.'

Her voice catches in her throat and silence remains her only sound.

As they pull up the drive, her mother stands on the porch, one hand over her mouth. The light behind her makes her look all shadow. A shadow woman risen up to greet them. Joanne wonders if her mother will be mad at her for taking off like that. For staying gone so long. Uncle Jasper slides from the driver's seat and comes round to Joanne's side. She wants to open the door for him, but her hands won't stop trembling, and she can't get herself to move in time. He opens the door and the sound makes her jump. He lifts her into his arms. As though she weighs nothing. And yet he staggers as he starts to walk, stumbling as he crosses the ruined garden. Her mother screams and falls to her knees, then rights herself and runs to them.

'Get the door!' Uncle Jasper growls, as he staggers another step forward slowly ascending the porch steps one careful step by one careful step. She can feel her own weight in his arms, can feel herself slowly sliding, slipping out of his embrace.

She's never seen her mother so pale before. Can remember seeing her openly cry just once before. The day that Grandma died when they'd come home from school and Mom had sat them down and told them Grandma was upstairs sleeping and would not wake again.

The blood oozing from Uncle Jasper's side feels warm against Joanne. Once through the door he passes her to her mother, slumping against the frame. A shriek comes from upstairs and Katie hurtles towards them, flying down the stairs two at a time, but she stops short halfway down, her eyes widening at the sight of so much blood. Joanne wants to tell her sister that she's OK, it's not her blood, but the words stay stuck inside her. She wants to ask 'Where were you?' Wants to say, 'I needed you.' But her mouth is still too dry.

'What the hell did you do?' Katie asks, and her eyes shift past Joanne to rest on Uncle Jasper.

'Katie, go draw some water.' Mom's voice sounds oddly high-pitched through her falling tears.

Katie hesitates. Her eyes are red from crying.

'Now!' No messing in Mom's tone.

Katie runs back up the stairs and Joanne hears the bathroom door open and the tap in the bath turn on. Joanne wants to tell her mother, too, that it's OK, she's all right, it's not her blood, but the words keep catching in her throat. Like she's forgotten how to speak. *Maybe, if I had some water, I could talk again.*

Halfway up the stairs, now in her mother's arms, half carried, half stumbling along, Joanne looks back over her mother's shoulder to her uncle, slumped in the doorway, barely held upright by its open frame. His T-shirt looks nearly tie-dyed, splattered by so many various shades of red. His swollen, bruised face looks newly raw and angry. His skin is a bit too pale. There are small cuts along his arms, his neck. Shards of tiny metal stuck in his skin. Where his gut was shot, the grey fabric of his Coca-Cola T-shirt has been stained so dark it almost seems he has black blood. Drips fall down from his side onto the floor into a tiny red pool. There is a sadness in his eyes unlike any she has seen before.

In that moment, she is no longer scared of him. Her words catch in her throat, but she finds her voice again. 'Thank you,' she croaks, throat dry and sore.

A broken smile spreads across his broken face. But it does not frighten her. Not like it would have only half a day before. In that moment there is no monster, just a tired, injured man, who saved her, now bleeding on the floor.

'Thank you,' she says again, her voice growing stronger.

His smile spreads as he watches her be carried up the

stairs. He nods to her. A simple incline of his head, the movement so slow it seems to take great effort. But when she's round the corner and through the bathroom door already being lowered fully clothed into the waiting bath, she thinks she hears him call out after her, 'For you, anything,' but the water's loud as it spills from the faucet, and she can't be certain if she wished his words or if he spoke them for her.

He leans against the porch railing, sitting at the top of the steps, his feet resting on the one below, and he watches as streaks of pink stretch like fingers across the pre-dawn sky. It seems to him a miracle that he sat on this same porch just last night and watched that same sun set. He wonders when next he might get to watch the sun rise.

'You need a hospital.'

He hadn't known she stood there. But it doesn't bother him. On this night, of all, he's glad of the company. 'I'd like to sit here, long as I am able.'

She crosses the porch and sits beside him on the step. 'You'll die if that's not treated.'

A slow smile softens his disfigured face. 'They won't let me die, sis. I'll have the best doctors in the county patchin' me back up. Just you wait. Folks round here'll have too much fun fryin' me to let me die like this.'

She turns away from him, hiding her face, and he follows her gaze, scanning the dark prairie that stretches out before them. Last night's crickets and July flies have fallen silent, but it's too early still for birds. 'They'll be comin' for you, then.' More statement than question, really. She doesn't meet his eyes.

He smiles. 'Sooner rather than later, I'd expect.'

She nods. Says nothing. Looks far out down the country road, just barely visible in dawn's half-light. No cars on it yet. 'Mind if I wait with you?'

He smiles again. His head is spinning from the loss of so much blood. His side throbs lightly, with its own irregular pulse. He feels thirstier than he can remember ever being. His lips and skin feel dry and parched. 'I'd like nothing more.'

They are silent a long while as orioles and blue jays and flycatchers awaken to greet day with song. Orange joins the pink and stains the darkness bright. The top of the sun pops up far out over the prairie to the east. It glows more beautiful than he reckons he's ever seen it.

Lizzie's voice breaks his reverie. 'Thank you, Jasper. Whatever you done. Thank you for bringin' her home.'

He turns and studies his sister's face. There are tears welling in her eyes. 'She all righ'?' he asks.

Lizzie looks away from him, far off to the rising sun. 'She won' never be the same,' she whispers, 'but, yeah, she'll be all righ'.'

He nods, weighing her answer. 'And you? Are you all righ'?'

Surprise widens her eyes. A sad smile teases her lips upwards as she speaks. 'Are we ever all righ', Jasper, truly, you and I?'

He chuckles and looks back out across the prairie. The laughter hurts his ribs. More blood spills from his side. It's nearly light enough now to separate fields from sky. Headlights far off down the country road speed towards them. Jasper's smile falls. 'Looks like they're nearly here.'

He's not afraid of prison. He accepted the cold fact of his return the moment Ben's skull cracked open for him. No. Sooner. He knew when he drove out there to save Joanne that his freedom was over. He is not afraid of the electric chair either, which he does not doubt he'll get. It is proving them all right – the warden, his parole officer, Reverend Gordon, everyone in this goddamn town – that makes him sick inside. They all bet against him. All thought he'd fail and wind up back inside. He wishes he could have proved them wrong. That's all. And that he does regret.

'I don't think that is the sheriff after all.' Lizzie squints as she scans the horizon. The truck, closer now, has no flashing lights.

'The girls?' he asks.

She looks at him, confused, alarmed. 'They're upstairs. Asleep, I hope.'

He nods. 'Good. I'd rather she don't see me taken off.'

Lizzie rises, standing to watch the headlights that race towards them. 'I'm serious, Jasper, I don't think it's Sheriff Adams.'

Jasper does not rise. Wants to stay there, home, as long as he is able. 'Course it's 'im, Lizzie,' he whispers, staring east to the just risen sun. 'Who else would come all the way out here this hour?' He turns and watches the headlights' speedy approach. 'I'll be . . .' He falls silent.

The green Ford pickup skids to a stop on the country road just before their home. Its tyres squeak as rubber scars the pavement. Roy's truck. Jasper would know it anywhere after the night just gone. Confusion wrinkles his brow. Desert dust still coats the pickup, muting its bright green. The passenger door opens, and a woman steps out. Dark hair, long and wild, blows into her face. Recognition dawns in Jasper's eyes as he rises. Smiling, he stretches one hand out. She seems to him an angel. He wonders how much blood he's lost to hallucinate like this, to imagine her here and not the law to bind him. Hand still out, smiling, he takes a step forward and softly says her name.

'You killed my brothers, you sick son of a bitch!'

The shot, a single bullet fired from the Hungerford so carelessly discarded back in the oil site's shed, enters Jasper's skull between his eyes before 'Rose' has even fully left his swollen lips. He does not feel the bullet's point of entry. Nor does he feel it settle in his brain. He is smiling still as his body falls. Is smiling still as his body rolls down each step ungracefully. He does not hear Lizzie's scream shatter the peace of dawn. Nor does he hear the birds' feathers rustle in the shrubs or their cries as they startle at the sound of the loud bang. His final thought is of Doe Eyes, blinking bright upon him. Then all he knows is freedom. A world he can find goodness in, where trouble's long forgotten.

August

Lizzie takes a damp towel from the top of the basket and hangs it over the line, pulling two loose clothespins from her mouth to fasten it in place. Once, the towel was white, but years of wear and washing have coloured it some cross of grey and cream. She reaches down, hangs two socks and an undershirt of Joanne's, then shakes out a sheet, rotating it to find the shorter side.

'Afternoon, Elizabeth.'

His voice startles her. She turns, surprised. 'I'm sorry, Reverend, I wasn't expectin' company.'

He smiles. His eyes soften. 'I knocked. When no one answered, I thought I'd look round the back.'

She forces a smile herself. 'Well . . . you found me.'

He chuckles, but not for long. No true merriment in the sound.

The wind picks up a moment, blowing the wash, transforming all the laundry to tiny flags before dying down to let them hang again.

'What can I do for you, Reverend?' She hangs the sheet, secures it, and wipes her damp hands on the front of her shirt to dry them.

'I came . . .' His voice cracks and falters. He looks out across the prairie then back to her, but his gaze does not meet her eyes. 'I came to see how y'all are keepin' out here.' He surveys the line of wash before them. 'Is she . . .'

he hesitates, as though choosing his words with care '. . . here?'

Lizzie looks at him warily. 'She's in her room. She don't answer the front door no more, if that's why you're wondering.'

'Is she . . . all right?'

Lizzie looks out across the back lawn past the old shed and the chicken coop to the prairie beyond. 'School starts up next week. Katie refuses to go. Been workin' in the diner more. I been prayin' lately Joanne'll be ready. For school. That the kids won' be too hard on her. Won' ask too many questions.' A scowl creases Lizzie's brow. 'She don't talk much, Reverend. Not like she used to.'

A smile cracks Lizzie's scowl, but doesn't stick. Tears well in her eyes. 'I bet that's funny to you, ain't it, Reverend, me prayin' when I long ago gave up on God?'

'There is nothing funny about prayer, Elizabeth. God still hears us, even when we doubt.'

'Yeah, well . . .' She doesn't look at him, stays gazing out across the prairie, tears still un-fallen in her eyes. 'I got my doubts all righ'.'

A cloud passes over the sun, momentarily muting its heat.

'I see you replanted the roses. The ones along the drive.'

She turns to him. 'They ain't what they used to be.'

He smiles. 'They'll grow.'

The cloud passes, and the sun high in the sky beats down on them, its rays tanning, burning, all they touch. There were thunderstorms a week ago. Flash floods further south. But still the tall prairie grass is far from green.

The drought may be broken, but its effects still scar the land. Hens cluck in their coop, bothered by the heat.

'Have you ever thought,' he asks, 'of maybe movin', of goin' somewhere you can start fresh?'

She lets his words hang around them. Lets the silence that comes after settle all around them in an eerie sort of suspended peace. She looks to the old farmhouse beside them, boards warped from weather and age. It could use a fresh coat of paint before the fall if she can scrape together the money. From an upstairs window, Jasper's old room, now Joanne's again, she sees her younger daughter peering down at them through the dirty windowpane. Their eyes meet and for a second hold before Joanne's face retreats from the glass. 'This is our home, Reverend,' Lizzie says. 'Where else we gonna go?'

Acknowledgements

Heartfelt thanks to: Marianne Gunn O'Conner and Vicky Satlow, my talented agents who believed in me from the start. Patricia Deevy, my brilliant editor, for shaping my story into its final form. Also, Michael McLoughlin, Cliona Lewis, Patricia McVeigh, Brian Walker, the sales team, and everyone else at Penguin Ireland – thank you all for making my dream come true! Keith Taylor, Sara Granger and Stephenie Naulls at Penguin UK. Also, Gill Heeley for her amazing jacket design, and Alice Chandler for her picture research. Thanks to my copy-editor, Hazel Orme, for her painstaking attention to detail, and to Brian Farell for my author photograph.

Personal thanks to: My family for their love of literature – my mother, who showed me the beauty of books; my father, who always read us the dark tales; my brother, Nick, whose imagination grew mine. All my classmates in Edinburgh who first gave feedback when this began as a short story, and to my teachers, Allyson Stack and Dilys Rose, who encouraged me to dig deeper. Cecelia Ahern, what to you was a small favour changed my life – thank you! Thanks to Erin, who never doubted, and to all my friends and extended family (including my in-laws!) for their constant love and support. I adore you all!

And endless thanks and love to my husband, my calm in every storm without whom I would be lost. X